AMERICAN GOLD

Ernest Seeman

AMERICAN GOLD

The Dial Press
New York

Published by
The Dial Press
1 Dag Hammarskjold Plaza
New York, N.Y. 10017

Manufactured in the United States of America

Third Printing—1978

Design by Francesca Belanger

Library of Congress Cataloging in Publication Data

Seeman, Ernest, 1886–
American gold.

I. Title.
PZ4.S4533Am   [PS3569.E353]   813'.5'4   77-25750
ISBN 0-8037-0349-X

*For Elizabeth
of Tumblin' Creek*

I

An Aerial View of Mink County
(1887)

Perched on her trapeze, flaxen-haired, eight-year-old Anna Pulaski floated high in the hazy blue afternoon air. The broad belt she wore was buckled at the back and under her arms to a silken parachute that was neatly folded in a packet on the swing upon which she sat. Her pale shining hair blew about her cheeks; the ribbons and all the little flags on the trapeze fluttered gaily. Looking down, there was at least a mile drop between the dangling toes of her tightly laced pink satin acrobat's shoes and the John Robinson Circus grounds below. Which distance was increasing every minute, as she was being drawn upward by the *Jacobus* (for that was the balloon's name—proudly painted on its bellyband), which had arisen smooth and steady, as majestic as a star. Little Anna was billed as Mademoiselle Annette— "the Marvelous and Stupendous Child Aeronautical Sensation of Three Continents": who had performed her "Daring and Dazzling Balloon Ascensions before All the Crowned Heads of Europe."

The circus encampment had been set up in the big broomstraw field adjoining Mrs. Roach's boardinghouse on Mink Street, only a little west of the heart of town; and several of the Minktown boys were crowded on top of Todd Jasper's woodshed gawking up at the balloon girl riding farther and farther toward the sky.

"Look at her go, fellers!" Buster Sapp shrilled; while his younger tag-along brother screamed from the ground in back of the shed, "Lemme up, too, Bus! Lemme up!" Danver Boone kept cramming his mouth with popcorn as he stared. Shading his eyes with his hand, little Johnny Anders looked upward longingly. The balloon girl, with her pointed face and long princess-hair, was like a bright bird painted in a picture book.

"Gee whiz! Isn't she pretty, though." Johnny Anders was thinking. "And brave! Looked like she smiled at me once."

Mademoiselle Annette's slant dark eyes were looking intently down to the white circus tents and to the now blurry place from which the *Jacobus* had lately risen out of the fire and ashes of the filling-pit. Where Henry Beer and Papa had filled it up with heavy black smoke from pine knots and straw and old rags and feathers dipped in pitch. Where Joe Needle-Pusher had come to sew up a spark hole. . . .

She always liked to remember the going-up part: where everybody hugged you and told you goodbye and *bon voyage* and not to take any wooden nickels from the Man in the Moon, and you climbed up on the trapeze with the great gray air-horse and Papa requesting the crowd to quit pushing and please stand back . . . and the band playing when you were cut clear and starting up, and you kissed your hands to the crowd in time to the music—the painted ladies, the old pelicans, and all the country thistle-chins gawking at you and your bright red tights like they'd never seen a girl in tights before. (Anna tilted her little nose in the air, her black eyes snapping.) And I know those town girls just loved my Florentine cap and my Scotch vest all paisley-embroidered with scallops, and this white jacket with the big green wooden buttons.

The people were getting more tiny every minute—more like bugs than humans. Pretty soon now would come the cannon-shot signal from her father, who always "gave her the wink"—as Toby Lolo, the clown, called it—when he thought she had gone high enough and it was time to cut loose. A feat that she managed, just before making her bold leap, by means of a ripcord. A tug on this, and a gash several yards long was rent in the balloon, allowing its gas to escape in a few seconds.

For purposes of showmanship, Anna's father used a mortar bomb in his old Civil War ordnance piece—which whizzed and tumbled up to burst at almost a thousand feet. On clear days you could see the smoke from Papa's gun before the sound of its firing or the bomb's explosion came.

The elongated, disjuncted mass of the town lay spread out from east to west somewhat like a long brown tobacco leaf—the railroad track forming the stem down its middle; with here and there the veins of streets paralleling or crossing it.

Along muddy, rutted roads, a traffic of wagons, buggies, and ox carts was flowing townward. It was a Saturday as well as Circus Day, so much of Mink County's citizenry, even bushwhackers from the hills, had come to see the free parade, and maybe a sideshow. But it was mostly the "town tackies" who unclutched their money to enter the Big Tent.

At its edges, the town Anna looked down upon was frayed out and sparse, like an old soft-toned carpet. In the middle it was denser and darker where its chief distinguishments of church steeples and the proud plumes of its tobacco-factory smokestacks were congested. Except for one lone cottonmill stuck away out on the western end.

Also on its western fringe—set in an expanse of grove and bushy, unkempt lawn—some barny, barrackslike structures and a few rambling red brick buildings were strewn about. The struggling little Gilchrist College.

On the southerly side of the town was a height, with large houses and well-groomed lawns, where several of its richest and most righteous rajputs and masters of machinery lived. Officially, it was McLauchlen's Hill. In popular parlance, and often among the sahibs themselves, it was "Swelldoodle Hill." And directly below it, in a poverty-struck and stenchful bottom, sprawled a settlement of factory workers' shacks.

Down from the Hill ran a little nasty creek.

Known to the workers as Sickness Creek.

Out of which their children fished medicine bottles, wine bottles, and some kind of a little newly invented dinkus of red rubber that was like a squeedunk and that children and poor people didn't know the use of. . . .

The little beetle people inhabiting the shanties and hovels of the industrial hive—say down at the end of Ullowee or Success streets, where wind was dancing around among the dry leaves and trash— were mostly black. There to the southeast (and also at all the undesirable and disreputable edges, dumping brinks, and smelly sewage brooklets) lived the black washerwomen who kept their white betters in clean linen. Who nightly, and even now, gathered a mountain of cleansed clothing off miles of clothesline and regarded the sunset with a wry and practical weather-eye. Aeromancers looking for the signs of the "sailor's delight," for the "washerwoman's fright," for the prefiguration of tomorrow.

Running parallel to the railroad track, there was a little mud-colored thread that the tiny doodle-people on the ground walked along and drove their horse vehicles and ox vehicles upon. It was their principal street east and west. One day it would be called Main Street; but it was merely Mink Street that autumn day when Anna Pulaski first beheld it. She had ridden along its up-and-down mudholed length only a few hours ago in the parade. She had been wearing her pale blue satin dress that had pretty ruffles and looked quite royal and she had been seated on a throne on the horse piano. While Tall, Dark, and Handsome George Grotz blasted out "The Pigtown Fling" and "The Girl I Left Behind Me," she had watched the hay rubes, the kids, all the happy suckers, as eagerly as they were watching her and the troupers. The jaspers jamming the curb, the upper windows, the rooftops . . . the noontime crowd swarming out of the factories . . . the look on their faces—ravished with wonder and delight. Especially, when the band struck up. When the pachyderms and the grand spec girls went by. . . . And the sucker-clippers and short-change artists moving among them; and one-eyed Walter Spielvogel, the rubber man, retailing squeedunks and his bobbing red, blue, and white toy balloons that skreeked as they rubbed against each other. The vendors of peanuts and popcorn. Soft-song Sam, the bug man, with his chameleons. . . . And oh yes, she had sniffed then that good tobacco-and-rum smell that seemed to be the main smell of the town. It was a smell that stood out, even above the lion, elephant, and camel smells. A smell that seemed to fuse everything and make you see pictures.

Even away up here, Anna could still get a whiff of Minktown's breath: that strong, sweet aromatized pungence of rum-flavored tobacco. It's sure a good-smelling little town, she thought. But that was before the breeze mixed her up a good full-flavored nosegay—the tobacco smell stirred with the sulphurous and gamy acridness of Sweet and Grimshaw's Red Mink and Big Pelican.

Down below, Anna now saw dimly the slow smoke-streak of a

train creeping out from the little wooden depot. It was a string of toy freight cars pulled by an energetic little bigheaded locomotive that had been the very latest thing, in 1875, in woodburners; and that trailed a long blue smoke-veil and sent up a faint mousy far-away shriek. A horse hitched to a buck wagon was running away, frightened out of its wits by the tooting and fire-spitting apparition. The little man driver was standing up with his foot braced against the dashboard trying to hold the horse in, and his tiny stovepipe hat was hurtling through the air into a mud puddle.

On the boxcars a long canvas sign was tacked on both sides. The letters were two feet tall, but Anna was far too high to read their proud, progressive message:

THIS TRAIN OF 12 CARS OF QUEEN OF THE HAREM SMOKING TOBACCO IS GOING TO KIRBLOCK & CO., SAN FRANCISCO, CALI-FORNIA. FROM J. WARHAM, SONS & CO., MINKTOWN, N.C.

Bisecting the distant plain—the former basin of a primordial sea stretching from New York to North Carolina—ran this track of the Minktown, Richmond & Petersburg Railroad (popularly known as the Malaria, Rickety & Paralyzed; or for contemptful variety's sake, as the Mighty Rattly & Precarious). The giddy prospect was splashed here and there with purple; laced in places with deep blue shadows. There were the faint and sinuous traceries of roads and pikes. And all fitfully flooded, momentarily, by a seething glint of golden afternoon light that sent the shadows running and was a great yellow dog pursuing mountainous and monstrous dark rab-bits—each as swift as a swallow and as big as a town. This bird's-eye view was bounded only by the mist of distance.

Experienced though Anna was, each time she was swept up into the sky was an entirely new and breath-taking event. As she drifted above the outlying woods and fields, she remembered Uncle Toby's telling her how George Washington had ridden over these thousands of ancient acres. And how, before *him*, back in the long ago, General Washington's grandfather had gotten off a ship in Philadelphia and gone horseback riding down to Virginia to some of the King's land to raise tobacco and colored people. Yep, just like Uncle Toby says, everything goes back to some*where* or some*body* else.

Oh from up in the air you couldn't tell much about what was

going on down inside a town. As Fanny Whale, the fat feature, had once chuckled: "You never know what a big woman or a little town is thinking. . . ."

Somewhere beyond the rolling Carolina veld, and far away to the east, was the ocean—that Anna had many times crossed. And Europe, and France, and England (where she had once come down in a lake in her Sunday-best turquoise-blue tights and Turkish tunic and sash, and the red pillbox hat with the feather, and been nearly drowned. But had been revived by a real English lord in a castle whose picture was in her album and who smelled like roses and pipe tobacco; and who had said: "Drrink up, my ducklin', drrink!"—as he poured some of his oldest and hottest whiskey down her throat). England—where she had had tea and crumpets with Queen Victoria—a nice little old lady with a toddy-blossom nose and whiskers on her upper lip. She reminded Anna of a plump, comfortable, clucking old hen. . . . And somewhere to the northeast, under the utmost horizon's fog, lay the city towers of New York. Where she had been last Christmas and had found and become a true *compañera* to her black ragdoll Molly, who was now up here with her, right by her side.

"Don't you be scared," Anna comforted her. "Don't you be scared, Molly honey. I'm just foolish about you, dear. And so glad you decided to come along at the last minute."

But Molly's blue eyes stared before her, unconvinced. She was never one for words. It was really a little vexatious, the glum way she behaved.

Old *Jacobus* was now lifting them through a cold drizzling cloud. Anna clutched the red strap of the pull cord and strained her ears. She wished that awful thick fog would hurry by; and the wind was whistling through the rigging like Old Man Whiskers. She was glad her jacket and tights were heavy warm wool and her cap close-fitting. But she mustn't miss it when Papa gave her the hot bang.

When the scud had blown by and she could see out again, Anna fixed her gaze intently on where, in the blurred and fluent landscape, a number of streams, the Meeno, Cat, and Goose Rivers, Allarbay Creek; wound their ways eastward through maroon and rusty-green smears of woodland and willows. Through the lighter meadows that glistened bright as gold, as the rays of a fiery sun—an hour above the horizon—smote them. She gripped the trapeze lines, contemplating the vast and sun-washed panorama spread out below. An enormous crazy quilt, a titanic brocatel, of aqueous browns and bleary greens that were meadows, woods, wheatfields, cornfields.

"Bee-yoo-tiful! Perfectly scrumdidliumptious, that's what, as Uncle Toby would say. The way those big ones wind around, they look like our big boa constrictors."

Then all of a sudden her bubbling gaiety and courage forsook her. Her child's heart was overclouded as by the racing shadows. There was so much wonder and grandeur—all the loveliness, the frightening uncertainty, the joy-of-living and no one to share it with. Even having Molly along was not enough. She felt herself such a tiny little microbe away up here alone in the airy boundlessness of space.

Ten miles to the north, on the Meeno, was a long range of wooded hills: where the deer and the antiquated thump-keg of the moonshiner still played. Where the Lingles and the Dardens made corn whiskey like their forefathers, and merry-larked-around like their foremothers. Where the feudal antipathies of the Wassons, the Nautrys, and the Cawfields still lived on; and where they still fought fist-and-skull, and to the death. Where they used hog rifles, rocks, barlow knives, or waylaid each other in ambush. . . . And there were still plenty of wild turkeys on those hills; and when they killed a sheep, pretty soon you'd hear a croaking up high and there would come the ravens. And there were still sacred-harp singers, old-timers who had never traveled over fifteen miles from where they were born, natives who had never seen a train nor eaten ice cream.

To the west a dozen or so miles, over in Lemon County, there was another hilly rise and up on the top of *that*, the ancient and venerable village of Temple Hill. North of Minktown—where the Cat and Meeno rivers joined to form the Goose—lay old Colonel Ashley Rutherford's great estate: some thirty thousand acres. And ten miles west of his "Rosemont" nestled the little white-and-green county town of Dillsboro—where Uncle Toby used to live as a boy. Where Daniel Boone, in the fourteenth year of his age, had also passed. Traveling southwest, with his folks, a horse and their dogs, along the old Buffalo Trace. Up the Cat and Meeno rivers. And where, thirty years later, he had set off as guide to a party of land speculators going to the Cherokees' country of the Tenassy to chisel them out of wigwam and home. And where King George's stiff-necked royal governor, in gold lace and the king's "bloody britches," had hanged the first leaders of the Revolution.

Branchtown, three miles north of Minktown, was little more than a sawmill and a saloon. And meadows: in which would be goldenrod, cocklebur, bright red cardinal flowers, the tall and handsome joe-pye weed, the pink mallow, and purple spikes of iron weed.

That little hairline of a road running past it was the old Dillsboro-Walterville Pike—over which had thundered the stagecoaches reeling and rocking north and south. It was the road on which part of Cornwallis's army, under Colonel Calderwood, had strutted to victory at Guilford Courthouse; and, later, retreated pell-mell to Yorktown and surrender. On which Sherman's army of bummers and firebrands had marched back to Washington. Not so many years ago—before the railroad came—drovers from the hill country had driven many a herd of hogs and flock of turkeys as far north as Philadelphia by this route. And after escaping to Washington—where she was destined to become sempstress and companion to one Mrs. Abraham Lincoln, and live at the White House—Lizzie Keckley, the Dillsboro slave, had returned over its ruts and rocks by stage, like a great lady, to visit her people. . . .

When there were no clouds, you could see the faint shimmery outline and the smoke—blue to raspberry—of Walterville: which was a good twenty-five miles away.

The kings and queens of England, Uncle Toby said, had once owned all this land. My, but they had had quite a farm!

It came at last: the zero moment of the bomb's flare and then the report. A cold gust of air came from over on the rosy cloudland and a little shiver passed through her.

"All right, Tar Baby!" commanded Commodore Anna. "Get set to cut the monkeyshine and let's get down from here!"

She buttoned her jacket tighter about her. Then, yanking the ripcord, all ready for the jump, she sang out like a sailor:

"One for the money and two for the show,
Three to make ready and here—we—go!"

But only her heart fell. The pull didn't work! "The dern-darn dickens!" Anna muttered, and crossed herself. "Dammit! What's the matter?"

They were high aplenty and it was getting cold as gee-willikens. She heaved a big sigh of panic and despair. "Looks like we're going right on up to Heaven."

She gave another jerk. Harder. But there was nothing doing—the line was fouled up some way. Then came the idea of climbing aloft and stabbing the canvas with her knife. Mamma had to do it once—someplace over in Italy—and she always took Mamma's knife up with her.

"All right—one more try, and if it don't unkink this time. . . . When you gotta do a thing you gotta." She jiggered the cord, then pulled desperately, though carefully—three quick jerks with a whipping outward motion—setting her teeth and praying hard to Saint Florian.

"Lord a-mercy," Miss Lizzie Crow, at Daskin Proffitt's store, was saying, "ain't it a sight the rash things human beings will do for money now'days?" . . . One-armed Reuben Glass, the miser, sitting on the doorstep of his Peckerwood Street shanty, at the foot of Doom's Hill, looked skyward and wished he had half the money being wasted on this dadblummed newfangled foolishness called a "circus." . . . At 105 East Mink Street, both their gazes bent upward, Mr. W. T. "Sunbeam" Iserman—the many-sided and popular purveyor of Ice, Coal, Insurance, and Real Estate—was saying to the Democratic County Chairman, the Honorable J. D. K. Butler, (who, the republicans said, would steal the Lord's Supper and Him asking the blessing): "Well salt my hide, Honorable, if I ain't glad *my* big feet are on this here good old Minktown mud!" . . . "It's a miracle, sure as hell and God's grace!" said Uncle Pink Lummus out at Priggins Mountain. Although he couldn't read or write, his wife Beulah had read him the Good Book clear through, and his was a brain that took hold like a steel trap. " 'She rideth in excellency on the sky'—Deuteronomy Thirty-three–Twenty-six!" he extemporized. " 'This child is set for fall and rising'—Luke Thirty-four! 'The fowls of heaven have their habits'—Psalms One hundred and four–Twelve! Bless God!" And he jumped up and cracked his heels together devoutly, in the way of the Old Primitive Two-Seed-in-the-Spirit Predestinarian Baptist brethren of those days and those parts. . . .

And down on the circus grounds a large man with huge feet and hands and a walrus mustache—who was standing near the balloon pit—was holding a pistol to his head and praying earnestly, as one beside himself. "O Mother of God!" he was muttering. "Our Lady of Mercy!—please help her. I've shot twice and she hasn't cut loose yet. Something's gone wrong—I know it has. . . . Oh I know I done wrong! I promised you down at Savannah, when I thought she was a goner, that I'd never send her up again . . . but we needed the money so bad. And O sweet Saint Agnes, protector of young maids in trouble, that tiny little speck up there is all I've got—I swear till all is blue if you'll only let her come back to me safe this time I'll never, never let her go aloft again. I promise you, Jesus, and hope you'll rot my right hand if I don't settle down and open a livery stable or something—right here in this town."

Beside him, a stubby little man in clown's makeup picked an insect off the back of his neck. And, from a natural interest in entomology and for the benefit of the bystanders, looked at it crosseyed close to his large red putty nose; made a funny face, and remarked drolly: "Madame Estella will have to put more flea powder on them big pussy cats."

The crowd whooped, diverted a moment from the balloon's perilous situation. Toby Lolo looked about—where could he grab another laugh? A native son of Lemon County, he was a prime favorite with the townspeople. He had risen by sheer dint of flapdoodle and his rough-and-tumble tongue work to the dizzy heights of being star clown of Robinson's Circus, and his illustrious mug was plastered upon barns and fences for miles around.

He doubled back to the big man with the pistol. His painted mouth open, he, too, stared up at the drifting balloon. "Gollywobbles! The wind's taken her!"

The large man with the .38 was now saying: "I'll give you just five more minutes, Lord. If she don't cut loose by then, I'm gonna pull this trigger."

But now to Anna's hand came the boon she prayed for. Came the wonderful blessed feeling of the lace-line ripping smoothly; and that propitious stink of the rank black smoke, so richly compounded of tar and chicken feathers.

For a tense long moment they dropped. With the speed of a falling stone—"like a rock in a hurry," as Mamma used to say—and the sound of the wind shrilling past was terrific. Then the parachute, trailing behind, popped open with a sudden jerk and bellied out with a silken swish. Ah, the brakes were on! and she was changed from a hurtling stone into a smooth-sailing seagull. "Whew!" And Anna heaved a long, fine, huge, deep sigh of relief and wiped the perspiration from her face.

"Bye-bye old Jack!" she shouted back to the great strong brooding horse-bird-dragon that was her balloon. But already it had fallen over on its side like a wounded creature, and was emitting large spurts of its thick black lifeblood and breath.

Anna and Molly went coasting down, down, downward—outstripping the breeze that was abeam and driving them north by east. They were plummeting with steady eagle-wing speed down out of the blue—bound for the lovely green earth-gardens below: where every puddle and mudhole was now decking itself out in royal colors borrowed from the flaming sunset: and where they'd soon be gliding into the haven arms of Papa and Uncle Toby and his wife, Madame Estella de Mittelburger, "The World's Greatest Lady Lion Tamer." Oh now they were bound for the good old solid ground and suppertime!

"Ain't we birds, though, Molly?" she exulted. "I'm a snowbird and you're a blackbird; and the balloon is the mamma bird coming behind with Saint Florian and Saint Agnes riding on it to take care of us!"

A fresh earth-wind seized the parachute and sailed it swift and graceful as a milkweed seed high over rustling brown cornfields. Over the tobacco fields from which the crop had been cut—with only a bright yellow leaf overlooked here and there or a tall stalk being saved for its seed. Past cotton fields it flew—much of their white fluffy produce yet unpicked. In some places Negro hands were picking late, in long bags. Over some country people cutting the bumblebee grass, or broom sedge, for brooms. Everybody stopping work to gaze up and wave. Past crows scattering from the nut-brown stubble fields.

On, on, little Mademoiselle Milkweed Seed was wafted. Miles of woods and meadow inundated by Allarbay Creek; full of the dark wetness of the September rains. The Lowground—that, from the sky had glistened like a prodigious platter of glass—spread almost up to the town limit on the north.

Anna was sailing very low here, and for a while thought surely she was going to be water-dumped. She could see the sanguine glory of autumn leaves—the silver and sugar maples and the waxy, fire-red gums. Festoons of wild grapevines and creepers ran riot. There was a buzzard roost in a knobby dead tree; turtles catching the last warm blessing of their deity, the sun, on stumps and logs. Once a water snake lifted its head way out of water, as if to see what kind of a snake-catching bird of prey this was. A swimming muskrat, carrying an ear of corn in its teeth . . . a swarm of black German bees gone wild . . . the cattail barrens full of scarlet-winged blackbirds piping their vesper *conk-er-reeeeees!*

Anna was getting uneasy. Now she was being swept over a barren ridge of shale and cliff and hoped she wouldn't land *there*. She tried to guide the chute by tugging on its guy ropes. Then she saw that the breeze was pushing it toward the top of a large golden tulip tree that seemed to be holding out its strong arms, like a policeman, to arrest her flight. This far, and no farther, it commanded; and with a scattering of leaves and twigs, she crashed.

A surprised great horned owl flew out of the tree as Anna came tumbling in. There was a ripping of silken canopy. The lines caught and tangled, pitching her forward. She snatched at a branch. Missed it. Caught another; then, agile as a monkey, hung there for a moment, gasping. Then inched herself along the branch to a crotch close to the main trunk.

Then she hauled herself up to a sitting position.

Her Florentine cap was all askew; and "Oh dern-dern!" she breathed, "I've snagged my new red tights."

Her breath was coming fast and she almost felt like crying. "If there's bears or wolves," she told Molly, "we'll be a darn sight safer up here than down on the ground."

Oh it could have been a lot worse. Here she was *almost* in touch again with old Mother Earth and she had one of her very best friends with her. Hadn't she come down before in muddy marshes, in hot deserts, on steep and dangerous rooftops? In a glass greenhouse with Red Velvet roses? Once in a hog lot in the pouring rain. Fierce porkers fighting over her. The old farmer saying: "Miss, you come within the bigness of a mighty fine hair a-gettin' kilt, did you know that?" . . . In Boston the fire department had rescued her down off the roof of a church.

Once over Vancouver hundreds of sulphur-colored butterflies had followed her through the air: swirling, dipping, and balancing, and, she'd had to laugh, they were so like the Gezzalini Sisters' Butterfly Suspension Act. She saw all nature's intricacies more or less through circus eyes. A black-and-brown double-wing stripedy locust, doing its dry rattly standstill dance in the air, was Tilly Joseffy, the shimmy dancer. A tiny measuring worm looked just like her friend Limber Jim, the contortionist. The big "hickory devil" worm that came by sure had a face like a whiteface luey. A black stag beetle was one of the black hammer gang.

As night fell, a few frost bugs started up their monotonous stridulation, and she was startled, too, by a curious choking, pulsating sound, as if a pump were being worked in the mud or a stake being driven into the ground by the strokes of a heavy mallet. It came from here and there back in the swamp among the cattails and rushes. Then something must have flushed it out, for there came from the edge of the woods the bittern's throaty *kok-kok-kok*.

Clutching Molly, she blew hard on the whistle that was to notify the rescue crew where she was and lead them to her. Though the limb she sat on was not exactly as soft as peavine hay, she would be patient and do her part of the job. Which was to keep awake and to keep tootling. She knew that finding her after dark was like hunting for a haystack needle, but they always had located her sooner or later. She could see them in her mind's eye: they would be carrying lanterns, like for possum hunting, and be shouting every little while and then stopping and cocking their heads to listen.

Four spotter parties had gone out early that morning to be on the job. Ready to locate her and bring her back from wherever the gods of the winds and dry leaves should dump her down. The red-clay country roads were something fierce from recent rains, with mud up to the buggy hub in some places. As the wind was holding steady from the west, three of the gangs of "bloodhound boys" went ten miles out to the north, by the Rocktown road, and scattered out in a crescent eastward. She would most likely drift this way; though there was always the possibility of the wind's veering.

Big Bill Kurovitz's boys found her fifteen miles out on the Cat River, in the Rutherford Woods.

As soon as he knew for sure what direction she would be coming in from, Anna's father, Michael Pulaski, went out in a two-horse carryall with Jack Pugotch to meet them at Branchtown—where all roads from the north converged. He took her a jug of hot coffee that Pop Klausner had carefully packed in sawdust, a big pork sandwich, and a whole coconut pie that he knew she loved.

It was close to midnight when they cut through Cackleberry Street. The air smelled sharply of tobacco and rum and everybody was asleep as they passed through, except one of the town's two policemen, who was sipping hard cider in Goff & Johnson's Tiger Saloon (that, theoretically, had been closed up tight as a jug since nine o'clock); and a couple of cottonmill workingmen returning from downtown, where they had attended a secret meeting of the new workers' organization, Knights of Labor, recently started in Chicago. By the dim glow of the buggy lantern, Mike caught a glimpse of their gaunt, pasty faces. And one other man was awake—a lone undertaker in the back room of Mangan & Yarbro's Coffin and Furniture Shop. He was working on a dead man laid out on a table. The man who had been killed in a runaway down by the railroad track.

"They tell me," said Mr. Pugotch, "that this town is now manufacturing around ten million cigarettes a year! And that this Warham's Factory here with the big bell on it employs around three hundred hands. I've got some samples—here, try their Ad Libitum and their Queen of the Harem. The Harem is an all-tobacco cigarette that sells at ten cents for a package of ten. . . ."

Mike Pulaski had been thinking about his vows to Jesus and Saint Mary the Virgin yesterday afternoon. Thinking that this time maybe he'd better keep them. "It might not be such a bad place to settle down," he said aloud.

He was thinking the best thing to do would be to go with the others tomorrow to Walterville and collect what money was due him and his girl Anna. Oh yes, Mr. Robinson would probably be angry and raise hell at their breaking their contract.

*   *   *

A long-legged boy they called Alvie got there first. "Here she be, Mister! Shore as shootin'!" he called to Big Bill. Anna was fluting her whistle at them as shrill as she could blow it—for joy and welcome.

"By Jesus—there she is sure 'nuff—up in that big poplar!" said Big Bill, holding his lantern up. "Say, Honey, why didn'tcha pick a *big* tree?" he joshed.

From his kit bag he took a pair of lineman's spurs, strapped them on his legs and hiked up to fix a rope so she could shinny down. Then, with the help of his "look-all-over-hell experts," he got the bumbersoll untangled and down.

"Look out for that wildcat vine, Miss," one of the country boys warned as she started down, on the last lap of her descent into home-come and happy landing. "Hit's got sharp ketchers."

"Whewie!" exclaimed little Mademoiselle Annette, the Marvelous and Stupendously-cramped Tree-Sitter—jumping up and down to stretch her limbs and then falling down in the deep, fragrant leaves and rolling like a puppy. "It sure is nice to feel the good old ground under you again!"

Big Bill gave her a swig of brandy. "Try this French cream, Skypunkie. It'll warm you up."

Then he threw a well-worn Indian blanket around her shoulders. "Holy hoptoads and bilge water!" he said. "I'm a monkey's uncle if she ain't still a-hangin' on to that little old ragbaggedy whatchama-dad of a Zulu dolly!"

It was the night of October 15, 1887. And though it was never said, written, or trumpeted, this child Anna was the very first human since the human race began to have had an aerial view of Mink County—the very first child of Adam's breed to set eyes upon this place from the topside, though countless pterodactyls, pelicans, hummingbirds, robins, and passenger pigeons had flown over it.

Peace
(1865)

It was April of 1865.

The grass rippled in the breeze in Lorenzo Benson's pasture field beside the red-mud Dillsboro road.

There was a faint odor of flowers hidden in the grass, and the grass whispered: Something is coming.

There was spear grass, bunch grass, and goose grass. Pony and star and marram, wire grass and weeping polly, rough-stalked meadow grass—nodding, whispering. From far aloft in the blue descended the strident screaming of a pair of circling hawks.

Two little girls were playing in a fence corner: Nora McCawley teaching freckled Liza Benson with love grass how to tell when your true love was coming home from the war; or if he was dead at Cold Harbor or Richmond or Bentonville.

Something is coming this way, murmured the grass; and then a thing stirring and strange happened at Lorenzo Benson's. A sudden sound of hoofbeats could be heard coming down the road from Dillsboro, and a military party clattered and splashed into view.

Clutching the younger girl, Nora pulled her down among the long grasses in the fence corner. They peered out Injunwise through the warped gray rails. A tangle of leaves kept Liza from seeing down the road. "Who's a-comin'?" she quavered. "Soldiers!" Nora replied breathlessly.

A Confederate flag bearer, holding a white flag aloft, was riding in front. The horses dripped and steamed from a thick warm shower they had passed through, there was the odor of horse wetness and fresh manure, the rhythmic sucking sound of hooves kneading mud, the clinking of the sabers made a music like the tinkle of broken glass. In the meantime, coming from the opposite direction—from Mink Station—was another party of cavalry. First, a blue-coated soldier on a black mare, also displaying a white flag. Then a small escort and two generals. A lieutenant with yellow straps rode at the generals' left and the smartly dressed staff officers followed, like brightly colored birds. Behind, two by two, came a squadron of heavy horse—tails switching, white foam from the horses' mouths flecking the riders' yellow-striped jackets.

The flag bearers met in the road. Word leapt back mane-over-mane to the hawk-faced Federal commander that the head of the Confederate forces was near at hand. General Blue rode forward and met General Gray. He, too, was riding side by side with a brigadier. The Confederate party fell in with the Federals, and together now they slopped through the mud—through giant soup bowls of red earth mush . . . splashing through broad shallow pools left by the recent heavy rains, from which killdeers rose and circled, whistling plaintively.

"Oh, my Lord God!" yelled Nora. "It's *Yankees*!" And away the two girls went running.

Up at Lorenzo Benson's barn, by the fence, a jackass brayed. The flag bearer's wide black mare flung up her head and started out of the road. He jerked her up and screwed at her bit, but she was a willful fool with a strong neck, gone giddy as a goose over the donkey's salutation.

An order was passed forward. The soldier, shifting in his saddle, faced around to receive it.

"Let her go," said the weather-beaten general in blue with the hawk's eyes and beard of thistles. "It will be as good a place as any . . ."

The flag bearer gave Nellie her head. She struck across the field for the farm, neighing joyously. To keep a love appointment down the wind, and to weave a wide important thread in the destiny of two great armies. The jackass being part of the pattern.

At Lorenzo Benson's gate four generals were passing through. The Blue Thread and the Gray Thread were shuttling together into the cloth of fate.

The Confederate commander looked very tired. "The Monster!" he was brooding inside his weary brain. "The monster I have been trying to kill for years and now here holding the gate open, like an old neighbor. Life's a funny thing."

Lorenzo Benson was not there to welcome them. To fodder the horses at the old paddock fence by the April-green and lilac'd yard. To come striding down with his clodhopper gait. . . . Four generals knocking about in his yard at once and him rotting under the wind-rumpled clover and orchard grass at Gettysburg, with a Minié-ball furrow plowed clean through his heart. Only Maw and the others didn't know yet. His ghost was walking in the rising breeze. . . .

Ever since the girls had burst in yelling "Bloody Yanks," Nancy and Maw had rushed around like the devil at a baptizing. They'd hid the spoons, the fatback, the worn brass breastpin Paw had given her the year they married.

Young Jim was the man of the house now. He'd been gone all morning, had just come back from taking the cows to the river. God a'mighty! He could hardly believe his eyes—the yard all cluttered up with soldiers elegant and higgety as grasshoppers, bigdogs of both sides all mixed up and a couple hundred buck privates, smut-faced Yanks and ragged-ass rebs, outside hanging on the fence and swarming the miry road.

The old hound was barking. "Shut up! you fool, Rock . . ." It was dinnertime, and the big elm tossed little halfmoon shapes of the noon sun down disrespectfully on the broad Gaulish face and ringlets and swaggering pig's-paunch of General Ned Wade Hampton. On the great ears and high three-starred collar of General Joseph E. Johnston, who wore a wan mask of a smile but whose thoughts were slanting back to Missionary Ridge . . . to Mobile and his descending star, to the black smoke rising high in the air and hanging like a pall over the ruined cities' crying doom.

"The Monster of Milledgeville," he kept revolving over and over. Bloody desolate memories sprang up thick as poison mushrooms. "And now who'd think to see us hobnobbing like two fowls in the farmyard—"

The tallest blue one with the sixteen gold buttons on his front seemed to be the head man, so Jim strode straight up to him. He was red-headed and talking with Colonel McCoy. There was something about his eyes that put you in mind of a chicken hawk. Jim had meant to ask him what was the meaning of overrunning a man's home like this, when he suddenly felt the blue-steel shadow of the hawk's swooping. "May we have the use of your house for a few minutes, Mister?" General Sherman said in his quick way. Jim's heart laid low, like the fluttering bird, with fear. The blood rushed up in his face. The voice was firm and keen as sickled talons. Feather-soft courtesy clothed its surface, but underneath lay the sharp brazen fang of military command, of easy casual dispensations of death.

Generals William T. Sherman and Joseph E. Johnston excused themselves from the others and went on into the house.

"It's some kind of a corkus," a Yankee soldier told Jim. "The Old Man ain't ordered no give-out, but 'twouldn't surprise me if the war's over."

The hotheaded little New Jersey bantam, General Judson Kilpatrick, was turning on his heel and walking away so as not to be left alone with that big insolent South Carolina aristocrat, General Hampton. They were mortal enemies, had played hide-and-seek over half a dozen states, he remembered every word of their last exchange of courtesies at Feasterville: "Sir: Nine of my cavalrymen have been found murdered—five in a barnyard, three in an open field, and one in the road . . . your apologies before sundown or I will cause eighteen prisoners to be shot."

In the yard and on the roadbank the soldiers were already fraternizing and playing hustle-cap for tobacco and small belongings. Out in the road Theo Davis, the young artist for *Harper's Monthly* who had been on the march with the headquarters ever since Atlanta, was setting up his easel to begin a picture of the farmhouse. That would feast faraway news-hungry eyes in New York, and adorn the dingy boards of the miner's shack in California.

In Lorenzo Benson's cabin it smelled mint-musty and of tar. White hickory smoke curled up from the black-backed hearth. There was a rocking chair, a homemade walnut bed, and a small black table.

Captain Buckstaff, General Johnston's aide, took the general's gray cloak and gauntlets, laid them on the bed, handed him a packet of papers, and quietly retired from the room.

General Johnston felt glum and dazed . . . Milledgeville—Vicksburg—Bull Run—in grooved alarm his memory crawled back crabwise, seeing shapes in the room's deep shadows. Specters charging black cobwebs of cannon smoke in fire-blasted fields.

"On account of a washed-out railroad bridge I had to ride all the way from Haw River," he said by way of breaking the thick glacial silence.

The Monster shut the door.

In a corner there was a heap of old harness Jim had been mending and greasing of nights. Over the door the flintlock musket shot back gleam and glint of the firelight; it had banged away at King George's men, at Dillsboro and Alamance. "Catnip tea's powerful good for the stomach," said Lorenzo's ghost, haunting a bunch of fuzzy, dry, pale green leaves by the fireplace. But nobody heard. The spring wind whirled and whistled around the house.

General Johnston was a sentimental old man, afraid of nothing but new ways. He kissed his male friends in biblical greeting, had been wounded ten times, yet was deathly afraid of those newfangled coal-oil lamps. He had great fungoid ears. A little goatee and sidewhiskers. Fascinated, at bay, the mouse before the mouser, he paced up and down in the firelight, watching the Monster unlatch a worn saddlebag a lieutenant had just brought in to lift out the long-necked quart of Old Kentucky Bourbon. For an instant he searched, with his pouchy drooping mastiff's eyes, the map of his adversary's weathered and stubble-strangled face. In the flashing fierce electric craters of those eyes he saw the unquenchable funeral pyres of Savannah, of Atlanta, still black-and-purple smoldering there; the crackling inferno of cotton bales, the burning bridges—roaring streaks of lurid red and ocher twisting and hissing down into the Chattahoochee, the Pee Dee, and Cape Fear. It was all stereoscoped there in those hard agates.

Sherman poured out a good stiff drink for Johnston into one of Maw's thick, cracked coffee cups that for three long years had felt cascade of neither coffee nor dram.

Lieutenant Snelling was tiptoeing out. "Wait outside," said General Sherman. "Keep ready to transcribe."

Across the black bow-legged table he pushed a telegram.

WASHINGTON CITY, APRIL 15 1865
PRESIDENT LINCOLN WAS MURDERED ABOUT 10 O'CLOCK LAST

NIGHT IN HIS PRIVATE BOX AT FORDS THEATER IN THIS CITY
BY AN ASSASSIN WHO SHOT HIM THROUGH THE HEAD WITH A
PISTOL BALL . . .

As the gray one read he gulped. The hawk in navy blue and the gold embossed buttons, noting his distress, gloated secretly over having saved his reputation for surprising the enemy. Like strands of a whip, the little paper words uncurling into the brain of the South. O Lord, gone great Abraham Lincoln!—the South's sole hope of mercy. —Broken the strong invincible bulkhead that was holding back the fools and the freebooters! —O magnanimous heart now reduced to the war's common obscene denomina-tor! . . . . . . The Monster was very near now, right across the little table, his acrid cigar-breath warm on the hand shriveling up the sweetness of mint and of tar. Joe Johnston was suffocating, his soul singed with fear—now he would be hanged, President Davis would be hanged. . . .

Perspiration oozed in large drops from Johnston's forehead.

Sherman was elated. I know how to play my fish, he thought.

"It came from the War Office just as my train was pulling out of Walterville," the Yankee general explained. "By the date—it has been two days getting through the lines—they are probably having his funeral this afternoon."

This sad matter called for another drink. "To Abraham Lincoln. —It is bad, but in such times we ride a whirlwind, and must take events as they come."

At first the generals talked all around the question.

"Understand you've got nothing we want," General Sherman said, "—neither your land nor your niggers. Only the return of law and justice from the Potomac to the Rio Grande."

Johnston said that slavery was dead as mutton and reminded Sherman that Napoleon, when victorious at Leoben, had been very magnanimous in his terms with the Archduke Charles. . . .

"One thing I've meant to ask you, General (if I ever caught up with you, haha!)—was how you rebs slipped up on us at Shiloh."

"Oh *there*—well now I'll tell you, General, at twenty minutes past five . . . in the ravine . . ."

"Ha, the first *we* knew was when the squirrels and rabbits came running through the chinquapins and hazels. My horse was shot, couldn't outrun your rebel lead, I mounted another and *that* was killed . . ."

It was a many-threaded drama. They were now turning and examining both sides of the same piece.

The South proposed not merely the laying down of arms, but also a guarantee of amnesty and the North said No he had no power to negotiate except for unconditional surrender. For hours they palavered. Thumped and tapped at the problem, pressed and parried, advanced and withdrew their defense lines of words across the fateful field of the small black table.

In short the job was folding up a war and putting it away in mothballs; lifting the last howitzer, horse, and human from the battlefield; rescuing the final ragged rotting pawn of the war makers—the potbellied bankers and bishops, the lily-handed bluebloods, the senators, corporation lawyers, and jackal judges, all with something to sell: influence, cotton, cannonballs, buttons for uniforms, bandages, weeping black mothers' babies.

The Monster put all his thrusts courteously—thinking, too, of Lincoln. Reflectively he rocked in Maw's chair, eyeing the curl of the smoke from his cigar. . . . The martyred President had given him these cigars just three weeks ago, after Bentonville, the Sunday he'd spent with him and General Grant on the James aboard the *River Queen*. He related one of the great man's maxims: "Cut any fool in two pieces and either end of him would know better than that."

And Rebeldom, sitting in the squeaky slick splintbottom, leaned his bulk back against the foot of the bed, now and again rose nervously, paced, had another drink from the black bottle. He was getting a little cockeyed.

Sherman clapped his hands for more liquor. In the mesh of the amber bourbon, the frayed gray and blue ends of the monstrous feud were drawing together.

There were cobwebs in the dark corners of the cabin, Sherman noticed. A string of red peppers over the mantel halted momentarily—like red lanterns at a bridge—the armies that marched interminably through his brain. His artistic eye was fascinated by the bright inspiriting pepper pods against the gloom, and he thought rapidly, "If it were not for war and these urgencies and I had my sketchbook and color box . . ."

Long crawling shadows reconnoitered through the window. The artist out in the road was trying to finish his picture. The soldiers crowded around him. One was an Indian—probably Will Bear, the famous Confederate scout, Sherman thought. Sherman the Artist, standing by the window, smiled, thinking of *his* painting, of the one in the dining room at home that was Elly's favorite, of a bird dog drinking water. . . . The evening star was rising very bright, and a soldier on a mule with a gamecock perched up behind was reining-up right in front of young Theo Davis's easel. "Will you please back up your asses there?" young Davis yelled, waving his brush frantically.

Sherman the General went back to outlining a plan. Whacked away now with briskness. ". . . I sincerely wish to save the South from further devastation. However, if you ask for it we can be a plague. Poor North Carolina will have a hard time, for we'll sweep the country like a plague of locusts." He thought to himself, I must remember that . . . good line for letter to wife—little Elly, the devout Catholic, cherishing anything biblical—

"Continuing the war will bring ruin." (He still pondered Elly wistfully doing and undoing her hair before the mirror, coming to bed.)

Outside, the soldiers were heaping up sticks and building bonfires. . . . Around and around in Joe Johnston's brain clocked the rotting swollen corpses, the stench of their windrows in the thicket, five thousand dead Yankees lying around in the mud and briars like so many dead bluebirds—piled up in heaps and drifts, the red gore of New York's sons, Wisconsin's, weaving into the hollow insatiable soil of the sunny South, and Willie Hardee the general's only son fallen there with the Eighth Texas Cavalry. The father weeping, the boy was only sixteen: though generals butchered other men's sons they always seemed to have an immense tenderness for their own. The Georgia Boys, Wheeler's Cavalry, Allen's Alabamians couldn't stop . . . fourteen thousand couldn't stop seventy-five thousand. Into the breach he had thrown Stewart's Corps and Kirkland's Brigade, the terrible hell-spit from his batteries, the endless stampeding surf of bristling bayonets. . . . Then seven days ago, at Battle's Bridge on the Neuse, he'd got the news from President Davis that Lee had surrendered the army of northern Virginia: COME QUICK MEET ME AT GREENSBORO Jeff Davis's telegram had said . . . Davis, the contrary wrong-headed old tyrant that had dogged him with bad luck . . . He was still seeing and hearing the dead—picking up his wounded in the black-water swamp and brush like shot birds after nightfall. . . . And now here, having drinks with the devilish Thing that had ravished his fair Southland with cannon and rope and fagot, and left her children crying for bread. . . . Oh! he could have shrieked with laughter. Or wept.

The soldiers outside shuffled coins and threw dice and were singing around their bonfires. A big red-bearded bummer from out west in Montana had found Jim Benson's banjo.

> This year I'll plow the one-horned steer,
>   Nex' year I'll plow the muley;
> Hand me down my hammer-tail coat,
>   I'm a-goin' home to Julie.

Sherman went on with his plan. His voice was coming from a long ways off. "For the surrender of the entire rebel army, from Carolina to Texas, I will give you the same terms Grant gave Lee."

Crows could be heard assembling at their headquarters in the pines. "It is getting late," said General Sherman, unsnapping his watch. "Ha. Old Sol has no respect for the War Department. I really must be getting back to Walterville, my troops may burn up the town when they learn about Lincoln." He opened the door. "Bugle 'em up, Snelling," he called. "What do you say we continue our talk tomorrow, General?"

"Tomorrow at noon," said the general with the large ears.

"Tomorrow," said the other, saluting.

Outside the cabin, the raucous, commanding notes of the bugler died down, horses and men fell in. The Yankee general clucked to his mount and the party was soon cantering out of sight. The gray ones watched the bend of the road swallow them up at the creek; turned their own horses and went off slowly to their camp south of Dillsboro. Joe Johnston sagged a trifle in the saddle.

In the gray of evening the Conqueror noted the fields lying fallow and unplowed. It was as though he moved through a land of specter farms and farmers, everything gone deep in grass and broom sedge. What a capital place, he was thinking, to unsheathe again his invincible weapon! For the old woman to start up her spinning again on her whirling brimstone loom—in case the South didn't accept the terms and had to be smoked out—the Black and Crimson Thread of desolation.

The Signing

Joe Johnston kept the Yankees waiting and chomping at the bit for two hours the next day. He halted his escort out of sight and rode up with only his aide-de-camp—Captain Benjamin C. Buckstaff—and General Hampton. As they reached the gate, the proud and unpredictable Wade Hampton wheeled his horse, called over his shoulder, "Tell the blue-bellied bastards I do not choose to present myself!" and galloped off, his loyal charger breaking wind under him every jump in kindred disrespectful rebel bravado.

Johnston wasn't feeling very well. Alone with Sherman in the cabin, he said that Major General Breckinridge was nearby and he'd like to have him sit in at the parley, if there was no objection.

The Confederate war secretary, General John C. Breckinridge, was soon produced like a rabbit out of a hat, and there was some joking about this sleight of hand and more scattering talk. But Breckinridge admitted, too, that the jig was up. The black god of slavery the South had worshiped for two hundred and forty years was gone to glory.

They'd had some drinks and lit cigars when a courier arrived and handed General Johnston a package of papers. He and Breckinridge looked over them for some time and put them away in their pockets. Then the two maneuvering southerners, going down, grasped desperately at straws of ideas, at the possible impossible, remembered bits of dead diplomatic conversation, strategy, minutes, ancient history, and protocols—tried to trip General Sherman into including in the Surrender a preamble written by John H. Reagan, the postmaster general. But their wary Uncle Billy regretted he couldn't oblige them. It would have guaranteed the South immediate representation in Congress; and so after a brief flutter of nervous jesting he said he'd be fixing up the document with a few "glittering generalities." The Washington red tape, he said, he'd cut with his sword.

He had brought along his chief confidential secretary, Major Hitchcock, whom he now called in. "Dammit Hitch, there's no ink," he said, pawing through his portfolio. "Ask the farmer if he has some writing ink and a pen." And while General Sherman sat there drumming an impatient tattoo with his fingers on the little black old-fashioned table, with time crawling by as slow as an inchworm, and the others staring awkwardly at each other and making surface-courteous conversation, Jim Benson called his boy Renzo to "go fetch a feather from Old Tom the goose-gander . . ." And Maw came and rummaged around in the clock.

In the afteryears, more than one beetle-eyed historian was to wonder why that first draft was written in red ink. Why that famous Memorandum or Basis of Agreement—"entered into on the 18th day of April, 1865, near Mink's Town, by and between General Joseph E. Johnston, commanding the Confederate Army and Major-General William T. Sherman, commanding the Army of the United States," had been handed down to posterity in the peculiar lusterless hue of dried blood.

It was said in fact by some that the monstrous and grisly Sherman, a cutthroat incarnate who dug up the graves of little children, hunting for jewels, had drained it from a dead man into an inkwell. . . . Posterity never knew nor guessed that the bottle Maw Benson took from the flyspecked cupboard clock that dim and far-off day and which she placed before the warriors was, as she apologetically explained, "Jest homemade pokeberry writin' ink b'iled with vinegar to keep it from sp'ilin'."

When the signing was over, they came out bareheaded into the cool fresh air. Sherman's hair stood up all-ways-for-Sunday, like flyaway grass. He introduced them around to his few officers. To Breckinridge he whispered: "You'd better depart quickly; to *them* you're still the Vice President of the United States who took up arms against the government." And thus ended the Battle of the

Bottles. With dram, and drippings of inkberry, they had stopped the barking cannon's mouth—the mug and the split goosequill were mightier than the sword.

Back in Walterville, Sherman took Old Hitch aside, constituted him a special courier extraordinary, and said Now don't lose a minute my boy till you've laid this right under General Grant's personal nose. So battening down the crackly paper, the Pokeberry Agreement, in his inside pocket, the major lit out on the rattling lamplit train to Goldsboro, passed by their lonely silent campsite there, crossed the fishy-smelling bear-haunted cypress swamps of Bogue Sound to Morehead City, hopped the fleet-steamer that was waiting, the *Alhambra,* to Fort Monroe and transferred to the *Keyport,* Potomac-bound—never letting the precious paper, now called Special Field Orders No. 57, out of hand-reach; fingering it a hundred times to make sure it was still there and sleeping with it under his pillow sailing serenely up Chesapeake Bay.

He not only found General Grant but brought him back in person. To save time they came up from the seacoast in the starlight on a flatcar.

To his last rendezvous with the rebels on the 26th Sherman was accompanied by four of his top-ranking gold-stripers. Besides Kilpatrick, with his wolfish sidewhiskers, there were Generals Schofield, Blair, and the gallant reckless Howard, who had left an arm at Fair Oaks. But the dreadful "Ulysses Simpson" he'd kept hidden in Walterville—an extra ace up his sleeve with which to trump should the game demand it. In the lapel of his long brass-buttoned coat that afternoon, the general sported a blood-red rose.

Dogwood and judas trees showered down their tribute of white and lavender pink petals upon the conquerors as they made their progress along the road from Mink Station. Joe Johnston threaded his way between the lines of cocky enemy officers in the Bensons' yard; the weary old Confederate saw them as a chattering gauntlet of bluejays—himself a gray and melancholy thrush. This time a sentry, Sergeant Egan of the Headquarters Guard, the Seventh Ohio Sharpshooters, stood at the cabin door, displaying a big United States flag surmounted by an eagle, gold and rampant.

"It is bad news," said General Sherman as soon as they were

alone. "—Our agreement has been rejected by President Johnson and his cabinet."

What he *didn't* say was that the Christian politicians, Stanton and the rest, and especially the Christian bankers, insisted on an eye for an eye—God's own measure—a tooth for a tooth. To hell with Lincoln's dream, they'd said, there must be dividends to spread on the minutes. Said those heroes behind the moneybags, For what, pray, do you suppose we have fought this war? Above all, they wanted to squeeze some southern gold out of the situation. They were reliably informed, they had grumbled at the council, that Jeff Davis was making off with thirteen million dollars. There could be nothing short of unconditional surrender. . . .

"—And so I must notify you that the truce will expire in forty-eight hours."

"Wait! you can't—" said poor old Joe Johnston, trying hard to hold on to his admirable military bearing.

Sherman's jaw was set like a vise. "Of course, now, if you don't feel like making an unconditional surrender . . . The cavalry's saddled, artillery harnessed up, Howard's column is strung along the railroad. . . . At the drop of a hat Schofield's and Kilpatrick's brigades are ready to tear up the track by God and to burn Greensboro to the ground."

Old Joe looked out the window. In the yard a forest of Yankee bayonets gleamed in the afternoon sun.

"I will," he said simply.

When they came out arm-in-arm and smiling there was a light respectful patter of handclapping. Then Sherman nodded significantly, and a sudden wild rising gale of long-muzzled-up laughter and joyful huzzas broke loose, caught up the soldiers in its ecstasy and meaning. Caps were hurled in air, jigs were danced, and some wept bitterly and unabashed as children. The old southern warhorse was introduced around to all the big dogs and brass hats he hadn't met, and some brandy that had mysteriously appeared from nowhere was drunk to Home, Wives, and Sweethearts, and then to Everlasting Peace and the National Unity. The gold braid and buttons, the kepis of gray and blue, glittered and bobbed in the laughter and elation.

Laying aside his mood of the angry hawk with tailfeathers stiff as a ramrod, Sherman sought out his host, young farmer Benson, and nothing would do but he must come and have a drink with the generals. "Thanks to *you*, Mister, the war's over," he said before them all and patted Jim on the back.

Old Rock began barking and Jim stomped and picked up a stick. "Shame on you!" he said. "Actin' like you ain't never saw a gin'rul."

General Howard had a week-old *New York Tribune* clamped under the stump of his arm. Everybody wanted to borrow it or to devour its news of epochal late events over somebody else's shoulder.

WALL STREET MEETING: A SCENE OF GREATER SOLEMNITY NEVER BEFORE WITNESSED: *Gold Closed at 146⅛ . . . and Prayer by the Rev. Dr. Vermilye: "Our Father, God of heaven and earth we humbly beseech . . ." "—in the olden times Thou hast brought Thy children through the fiery troubles and landed them in safety and prosperity."*

ELLA TURNER ATTEMPTED SUICIDE: *On Saturday . . . a mistress of John Wilkes Booth . . . by taking Chloroform.*

Across the page the black cortege wound solemnly down the avenue, the catafalque drawn by six white horses. First a detachment of black troops, the measured tread of the infantry and the bands, artillery, the long draped guns and the flags, navy marines, the officers on foot, the wild galloping of bad-riding marshals, the New York chamber of commerce, drums muffled, the music of the weeping fife-and-drum. Behind the coffin of the Great Emancipator, piled high with evergreens and white Japonicas, lilies-of-the-valley, and sweet alyssum, walked a riderless White Horse in sable trappings and the California backwoodsman and hunter, Seth Kinman, in his hunter's uniform of buckskin, who a few months since had been the donor of a unique chair, manufactured from wood and stag's horns, to the late President.

The paper told how minute guns were fired, and fifty thousand followed, and the bells of all the churches and the engine houses tolled. . . . How "PROSPER M. WETMORE IS OPTIMISTIC: The gross receipts of the Erie Railway for the first twelve days of April were $1,000,000 . . ."

a mile and a half long, the privilege of viewing from a window was sold for $10.00, the chair appointed thirteen to attend the funeral. Whereas it has pleased Almighty God to take from us Abraham Lincoln, our beloved President . . . NEWS OF BOOTH'S ROOM: *. . . The Carnival of Assassins, Room No. 228 at the National Hotel until last night occupied by Booth had a bare and desolate look. On the bureau, in a brown paper, lies half a pound of killikinick tobacco, a clothes brush, a broken comb and a pair of embroidered slippers. . . .* THE DRY-GOODS MARKET ACTIVE . . .

Acrid little General Judson Kilpatrick chuckled. "Listen to this," he said, reading gleefully aloud: " 'SLAVE OWNER'S CATTLE CONFISCATED. From one of the rebel general WADE HAMPTON's plantations Millwood near Columbia a herd of rare African cattle has been forwarded by General Sherman to the zoo of Central Park.' "

. . . Resolved that members of the Board wear crepe on the left arm for thirty days in token of grief. With the signing of peace the UNITED REPUBLIC PETROLEUM CO. *is intended to combine on a large scale . . . Hamilton Fish, Wm. E. Dodge, Samuel Sloan, Esq., Judge Edwards Pierrepont, John J. Astor—*

High over the Benson farm a flock of buzzards circled lazily. "Vultures," Joe Johnston was thinking. For Wall Street's predacious vultures, all the vast and complicated horrors, hells, and marchings, the price of lives in battles waged for greed. Now they rush the breastworks hand-to-hand over piled-up logs firing into the faces of weary mud-sodden farmer boys, lovers, small-town mechanics, hacking and jabbing slicing jaws eyeballs bowels hot blood-jets spurting like a hogkilling the precious irretrievable and primal blood and fresh young maturity gurgling away to the leaves and ditches. . . . Over stark and writhing forms the sunset slants down through the haze, over broken weapons burning logs and stinking roasting blackburnt skeletons. . . . *For cheap nigger labor. Giant monopolies* (such as Abe Lincoln had foreseen and stood against) *on all the necessities of life. In Jesus' name.* For this they had all been marching: the bright-eyed and the brave, blotted and bludgeoned down now into the red eternal dust of time.

*   *   *

But over Jim Benson's farm and barns the wonderful presence of Peace was sifting down. In that vivid hour the world was very new . . . the smell of the lush, bright grass and lilac and mint by the spring, the dandelions riotously springing, the heavy musical droning of bees on the soft elastic golden-sunny air weaving back and forth to the apple-tree blossoms. Old Rock the hound sighed heavily and stretched out carelessly full length at the august feet of General Frank Preston Blair, commander of the Seventeenth Army Corps.

Eliza was Jim's youngest and it was she who got the rose. As the Great Man chatted gaily with her father and his staff, he unpinned the flame-red flower from his buttonhole. "Here little girl," he said, "—here's something to remember this day by." (Now that the rapids are passed and the boat's in smooth water.)

Inside, the old clock banged six discordant times.

The heavy cavalry horses picked their way delicately down between boulders, scrunching the pebble bed. With slow, arched wingbeats, a heron flew away. In the creek the horses splashed, loitered, bent to drink. The seasoned brown riders, at ease in their saddles, slacked rein. Dodged the sycamore branches. In the alder bushes a troop of tiny bright warblers, aerial marchers from the Argentine on their spring passage north, flitted and twittered. The Ninth Michigan Mounted were also bright momentary migrant birds against the dark woods. The horses clambered out, saddle leather creaking. "Forward!" Colonel Acker ordered, and they were off at a trot, spurs, bridles, side arms clinking; the blue, scarlet, and white guidon flags flapping the wind. . . . Hooves pounded the ancient earth drum, horse tails whipped and swished around the bend.

And they are gone. The last damn-Yankee departed. Along the creek bank there is a restful quiet, a gentle serene waving of the cattails and frog's plume. There is spear grass, bunch grass, and goose grass. . . .

III

The Soldiers

The soldiers poured into Mink Station by a decaying old road that hadn't seen such excitement since the "bloody coats" of Tarleton and Cornwallis had foraged up and down it in the 1780s or since the days of the old Walterville stagecoach before the coming of the railroad.

Following the surrender at Benson's farm, this sleepy old pike was suddenly overrun. Over its mud and ruts, beneath its low-bending boughs of oaks and maples and white-blooming dogwood, rushed a great swashing swirling flood of fighting men. Rifles, artillery, "tail-ticklers" (the bristling bayonet brigades) zouaves—once so gaudy in their blood-red jackets and sky-blue Turkish trousers—but now all tattered and mud-stained. There were cannoneers and cavalrymen (some walking, some bumping the leather), mule skinners, whoremasters, the "jayhawker" freebooting guerrillas, the hungry bull cooks and mulligan mixers with the wagon soldiers.

From both sides they surged upon the town that was the closest railway connection for the outside world—the Yank with the rebel; the rogues, bums and bummers and the refugee black-sheep Negroes with the regulars. What was left of General Hardee's brave little Texas shorties just up from that hell at Bentonville. Many men were deserters, famished and barefoot—some boldly mounted on artillery horses and mules they had "borrowed" from the baggage trains. Their faces smutted from many fires; with eyes tired and sunken. During the parleys, a rumor had spread among the boys in gray that they were about to be surrendered as prisoners; and in five days some eight thousand had gone AWOL. And all—every mother's shaggy sweet swiney son-of-a-gun was fiercely, impatiently raring to start for home.

The village curs were all agog over the sudden influx, the delicious nose-tickling smells of gunpowder, man-sweat, horse-sweat, and ordure, the soup kitchen, the old sores, the new-made gory gashes and shot-holes in human flesh. . . . The children hung on the palings, and old ladies sat on the porch from dawn to dark; for nobody had ever seen or heard of such a might of passing. And the young girls, lonely for lovers and arrayed in their Sunday finery, defied the old folks' croakings on sin and dire disaster to stroll forth in pairs down sunny Mink Street and Depot Street, and along shady lanes.

Mink Station was policed by Kilpatrick's cavalry that, as the advance guard of the federal army, had established its headquarters here several days before the Sherman-Johnston meetings. At that time "Little Kill Pat," as the Yankee general was called by his men, had requisitioned for his billet the residence of the pious Doctor Black. Now the doctor's wife was a whip-cracking kind of a female, and, forgetting she wasn't still the queen of her own parlor carpet, made certain acid comments upon certain fresh red mud coagulated upon certain military boots. Upon which that pint-size, puritanical, and precise general ordered her best four-poster bedstead hacked to pieces. He wanted everybody to know who was running things, and that he'd have no monkey business. He'd also burned down Spratt's General Merchandise & Hardware Store—where by summer the grass was coming out hand-high between the charred planks. But as the war was over and the armies breaking up, discipline was at a low ebb. The higher the deluge of heroes and derelicts; the further receded all regulations.

The veterans were in high spirits. As carefree as weeds in the wind. They all seemed to belong to one common army. Passing one another they would stop to chat.

"Hello Johnny Reb."

"Hi Yank."

"Got anything to chaw on?"

"Naw I hain't, man."

"Not even a chaw tobacco?"

"Nope."

"Not even a hum-ding?"

"Not even a hooper-doo."

"Well so long Johnny, I gotta go locate me some belly timber. . . ."

Everybody, it seemed, was seriously out of everything except vermin, hope, and weary feet. The most had their shoes off. Swung their feet in the creeks at every little bridge and fording place.

Sang:

> Up Grassy Creek,
> Cornbread and no meat,
> Straw bed and no sheet,
> Big belly and nothing to eat

They were all as hungry as rats and ate like horses. "Specially the foot-sloggers," Ira Lemon said. "Stud horses that ain't had their teeth in nothin' more nourishing than stirabout in God-knows-when." And they were all as droughty, testified Mugs Viggers, bartender in Billy Mangan's saloon, as a frog in a church. They plundered Manderson Dismukes's store, stripping its shelves of practically everything save the indigestible cow chains and hickory ax handles. Dismukes had half a bolt of calico hidden under the meal barrel—which, at a hundred dollars a yard, gave them some A-1 legal tender for Old Ab's bawdy house.

"How many titties has your cow got?" enquired one homesick soldier, leaning on the fence to watch Myrtle Sinica milk, and thinking of his own cow way off in Muleshoe, Texas.

"Sev'ral, but not enough to suck Pharaoh's army," she snapped tartly.

The few hogs that had roamed the town had to be put up close; but even so, they all vanished. The soldiers passed and repassed with forage. Requisitioned cooking buckets and kettles of the despoiled, along with their meat. They hunted guinea eggs in the fence corners, stripped down the green cherries, and the telltale crack of spitting six-shooters through the woods announced the execution of the last hidden pigs and poultry. Between long rows of fires in a pine-stump clearing the troopers rested and cooked up their plunder. The gray boys bivouacked with the blue boys; the blue billy-bucks sharing the bottle and their bean feast, and re-picking the bones of old battles with the gray. At night the sky glowed from their campfires, the rude horse laughter roared like cannonry, and the villagers were kept awake with their yowling and singing. With the *oomp-tum-tum, oomp-tum-tum,* of a resolute wreck of a military band. Aunt Molly Snipes came to sell her gingerless gingerbread, and they took it all and dumped her in a ditch for a lark.

But Tysander Warham, a tall and enterprising local farmer boy of eighteen—just back from the Virginia end of the war—had better luck. He had got hold of a little tobacco, crushed it up and put it in homemade paper bags, and, with two Negro helpers, was wheelbarrowing it between the pine stumps of the camps and through the pig-path streets, peddling it out to the officers and men. On the bags Tysander had written in a big bold scrawl

DOVE OF PEACE BRAND

and those who had any money bought it like gold dollars going two for a nickel.

Sherman telegraphed to Morehead City for two hundred and fifty thousand rations to be released from the federal storehouse there. But even that was insufficient to fill for long the vast, growling maw. In their unbridled spirit of high holiday the vagabond vets ransacked every smokehouse, broke into Cox & Son's above the depot, hoisted Zack Wraxbee, a leading citizen, up by the heels because, they said, laughing and whooping like wild savages, he was getting too fat. Caught old Tom Whitehorn, the beggar, and turned his pockets wrongside out hunting pennies, and guzzled all the grog shops dry.

"You kin jest charge that old piss-water to the guver-mint or Cristiver Columpus . . ."

"Now tobacco and whiskey's two things we've got plum blame used to in this man's army . . ."

"And a man's gotta have him a womern—that's another thing, so that makes three . . ."

In the late evenings officers and men danced snake dances in the road out in front of the Morris house—now called the Gaston

P. Morris Hotel—that was a low, dark farmhouse overrun by the military. Singing *Hoop-de-doo-de-doo, the Old Horse Cat,* and getting jass-eyed on anybody's bottle, on anything they could locate to jass up on. The grassy bank swarmed with soldiers blue and soldiers stone-colored and soldiers arrayed in nondescript rags. They gathered in little knots or strolled up and down, chasing anything in skirts that went by. From the grass lot adjoining the rambling old wooden hostelry, a hospital squad would gather up a miscellaneous assortment of the weary wounded who had been put out in the afternoon sun waiting for the train now hours overdue. A lot of heads and legs in bloody bandages; the emaciated; the cankered reeking with rottenness; the gangrened ones that were blue and green and gray with the pallor of death.

Over in Mangan's Bar a big free-for-all fight was going on. "You're a sheep-killing dog!" Hector Robbins, a rebel hero who'd lost a leg at Antietam, yelled at Benbow Barbee, the draft dodger. "Nobody but a lowdown sheep-killing cur would have sot around on a stump, playing-off crazy the way you done," Hector said. "Fishing off a field stump in the daytime between the corn rows and trading cotton with the Yankees at night."

But Benbow's brother Levi took it up; and the bystanding soldiery, both southern and northern—being in a frustrated and highly explosive mood—were soon sailing into the traitor clan and the hurling of bottles and spittoons was following the hurled insult. There were howls, groans, and curses. Shrieking protest from Billy Mangan, the portly pig-eyed proprietor. And the crash of window glass being ravished by rocketing chairs. Coming in at the door a couple of drunks imagined they'd gotten back into the battle of Fredericksburg, so backing out, they tottered across the road and into Wraxbee's Place.

The soldiers were all chomping-at-the-bit to get started home, but it was impossible for the overworked little bullock of a train, which came snorting through the red-clay gullies and pine stumps once a day, to transport everybody. To while away the time, they shot craps, played cards, pitched horseshoes, mumbled the peg, and got down on their knees to roll marbles taken from Cox's Store, like children. They wrestled, fought, made horseplay, and jumped ditches. Some washed their shirts and bathed and seined for perch and hornyheads in New Hope Creek and the "Yaller Bee." Some, lassitudinous, lounged on the railroad bank, chewing grass straws, while others, sick with the mulligrub of love, were wafted away on daydreams in which themselves and Susie Green with the pink-and-blue sashing around her waist—or the girls they'd left behind—or Hot Smoky, the high-yellow harlot—were the only actors. From a thousand pipes and cigarettes of corn-shuck rose the fragrant Dove of Peace smoke.

General Kilpatrick posted the disappointing information that only a certain quota would be issued railroad passes—only the wounded and those traveling great distances. All the military horses and wagons available would be loaned others. The rest would have to walk.

In the plans, Schofield's division of the Yankee troops was to remain in Mink Station; but as the main body of Sherman's army was marching overland from Walterville to Washington, a couple of thousand of the boys in blue were ordered to cross the thickets of Allarbay Creek and fall in with this victorious tide at that place. But those ebbing away were but a trickle—a drink in a thimble—to those other thousands left behind.

The soldier boys hungered not only for food, but were distraught by their primal, pushful loneliness; by having to burn their own smoke, as the saying went, in a well-nigh heiferless world. And now that the iron yoke of discipline had been suddenly removed from their necks and the saltpeter from their grub; now that—after years of privation and slavery to the cannon—the leaden weight of ever-pressing death and boredom was giving way to elation, they were dead set on raising a little bit of bonnie hell and regaining their lost prestige and sweet stallion glory. The first thing they asked, both the blue-willies and the bare-ass johnny-rebs, was "What's this place got in the way of gal-stuff?"

Women in these parts seemed rare as a rooster's egg. The combined population of the three villages of Pinoak, Old Brass Field, and Mink Station was not above three hundred souls—counting the young, the aged, the black with the white—and not over half of that female. Therefore the woman-retrieving part of the program required plenty of reconnoitering, nuisance-ship, and zip. Any hunter must compete with a howling mob of rivals ready to beleaguer, bat, or brain him. Jealous brawls went on day and night, and there was hardly a woman in the community—virgin, spinster, or grandam—who, escaping the rowdy rapist, did not receive some soldier's torrid invitation to a roll in the hay.

"*She's* a pretty good looker for an old chicken," said a corporal from Batavia, Illinois, of Aunt Jennie Reden, well past seventy. Out loud, for her hearing, and winking at her impudently as he passed. And for a black woman who couldn't outleg them it was just too bad. If she wouldn't take off, they took off for her. Tore her stitchery to shreds, like bulldogs.

Oh there was a bad house at Pinoak, all right—with four cut-up girls. "I ain't got nary a gal that's rustin' out," old Ab would brag. On his doorsill the dusty mud of boots from Mississippi and Georgia mingled with the sands of South Carolina, Kentucky, Virginia, as the chatter and shrill swearing, the perfume and sweat and the heathen lamplit nakedness mingled in that high tide of longing and laughter inside. But that wasn't enough for the army, and besides, Colonel Eckelberry had, in his concern for the best interests of the service, closed it up. Posted guards in the road. "Back up, Buddy, you can't go this way. . . ."

When the MPs came to take over the place in the name of Uncle Sam (again the smart and dapper discipline—"Halt! Right dress!"—the bump-bump of rifles grounding), accusingly Abner said to his wife Maver, pointing at the roof: "I been a-tellin' you if you didn't fix that roof we'd have a bad house. Now looky, they're about to git us fer keepin' a bad house."

"Oh it's nothing to worry about," the sergeant said. "Business won't be left in a dead calm. The Department of Public Works is merely taking you over in the interest of public morals for a high-class officers' club."

There were more Yankees in Mink Station now than minksters; and several, staking their entire future on an hour of love in bush or barn, married and settled down here. Decided to become jetsam instead of flotsam. One such "foreigner" was young sergeant Tom Fipps, from Ohio, who later became Mink Station's first policeman. Another Yank who married into Mink citizenship was "Holy Jasper"—said to have come from Connecticut, though until the day of his death nobody ever knew his real name. He was a preacher by trade, and with the New England eye for business, specialized in marrying the freed slaves, who had been living in necessary sin, at a dollar per splice. Isaac Blaylock, of the Vermont "Mountain Boys," Company F, was also citizenized by Dan Cupid, and in time became a large landowner. "Why, with backwoods land selling at twelve-and-a-half cents per acre," he shrewdly figured, "I can pick me up a farm in no-time with my ax!" He would chop and maul wood for twenty-five cents a cord, then invest it in a couple of acres of crawfish land or a hillside with hicker-nuts. Eventually, he got hold of Shady Dell, the old Harrington plantation on the Meeno, with the mill. Over a thousand acres. There had been fifty or so Negroes, but these had scattered and settled away like blackbirds.

Kilpatrick issued orders making looting a crime. Published it on trees at every crossroads. No federal soldier, he decreed, might go beyond the Wolf Den road on the south, Paterson's Mill on the west, or northward past the bridge at Little River. But hunger knowing no law, they kept right on scouring the countryside near and far for hog, hominy, and romance. "That Little Kill Pat musta got out o' the bunk on the wrong side this mornin'," one complained. "Everything and nothing's a crime in wartime," growled another, "and me with a wolf in my stomach."

Three comrades—three drops in the military flood—were riding together. Two upon lame artillery horses and one on a mule. They were coming into Mink Station on the Dog Trot road.

"What is that smells so good?" asked the first.

"Mmm—why, it smells like tobacco," said the second, sniffing the pungent toasty air.

"Say, you gotta pretty good nose for a fart finder," said the third, private Chick Carter. "Yeah, it's tobacco all right. Way over there in that cottage with the smokestack, *I'd* guess . . ."

And the odor and thought of that tobacco came again into the forefront of Chick Carter's mind that night. The breeze was from the direction of the little cottage factory, and the familiar insistent aroma stirred nostalgic memories of his own home town in Virginia. He got out his pipe and knocked it on his shoe heel. "Dammit, my 'bacco is clean out," he growled.

A ragged reb who had been asleep on the clover got up and stretched his gangling length. " 'Baccy?" he echoed. "Well ey-god, thar's a plenty of the stuff right over in old Zachariah Green's prize-house. Yeah, a great big scrush of it all piled up an' a-waitin'. 'Nuff to 'baccy us all a month."

The man in tattered gray was Peck Preece, of Pinoak village. "And we mought's well go git us some, gentle*men*," he added briskly, with sudden decision flashing in his gray cat eyes.

Then they went up—the three companions and Peck Preece— and Chester Cash and Whang Hannah, who had been sitting by the side of the road making a gourd fiddle; and Will Bear, the Cherokee Indian sharpshooter—to have a drink at O'Brian's Bar. There they all imbibed freely of tanglefoot. The fine old rotgut corn. Leaping up on the barroom counter with the agility of a chipmunk, Peck Preece proclaimed that he knew where there was plenty of tobacco and he was aiming to go and make a haul. "Why do 'thout 'baccy when thar's a whole compoodle of it right over thar—mouthfuls, bellyfuls, snootfuls, gutfuls? Now if any other body feels the same way," he said, "I'll be glad to have company. . . . But if anybody's gun shy, or feather-legged, or b'lieves in lettin' the rich draft dodgers keep all the good things of life and the pore man's ass in a split stick, then ey-god the bastard better had stay here and nurse his booze mug, fer they may be shootin'."

The tall Pinoaker's reckless speech brought a round of applause. They swarmed from the saloon like a stream of angry hornets, and soon there were a hundred instead of a dozen. Excited small boys and barking dogs ran along to see what would happen. As the mob moved across Morris's Big Field and horse lot, those who were weaponless stopped to cut themselves stout sticks at the wood's edge.

Zachariah Green was a gaunt leather-colored little man with high cheekbones, a big nose, and the sharp eyes of a weasel. He affected mustaches and a goatee in the style of a Kentucky colonel, and was bald except for a long lock of grizzly hair that rose like a grassy island from the middle of his forehead. When the mob of war veterans led by Peck Preece demanded that he open up and surrender his entire stock of tobacco for their knapsacks, the little man of business became very excited. Like an actor on a stage, he strode up and down the balustraded veranda of his place of business that had until recently been a dwelling, and in his indignation and wild gesticulating, his one lock of hair stood up wildly.

He wanted to argue, but they crowded in on him. "Hell, you

little 'bacco worm, its our'n—everything's our'n!" one shouted. "We *fit* fer it."

"Come on," said another, "we'll smack him down like a sick fly . . ."

"Look at 'im, boys," said Peck, "did you ever hear of a rich man going to war? Did yuh now? Come on, did yuh?"

"Damn right!—it's a rich man's war and the pore man's fight!"

"Nobody's got no right to corner nothin'. . ."

"Smoke's free—ab-so-lutely free. Put that in your pipe and smoke it!"

Zachariah Green sputtered that it was an outrage. But he shivered, facing all those clubs, shovels, and terrible sharp-pointed "Arkansas toothpick" knives. Plus a tomahawk that Will Bear had produced from somewhere and was whooping around with; and the ugly muzzles of several horse pistols, musketoons, and Harper's Ferry and Deninger rifles. So when Peckahiah Preece asked him if he knew what the penalty was for resisting the army, and told him they'd shoot the living bug juice out of him if he didn't "git," he got.

The raiders took all the tobacco there was. They found quantities of the fragrant weed in the flailing and sifting room, where old man Green's black boys had manufactured his Best Bright Leaf. Some was shredded; also some ground up into snuff, or "snooze dust," and several hundred pounds of the great leaves were spread upon long tables. In a dark log storage in back, they discovered more of the golden treasure, packed up in hogsheads. There was also a barrel containing some kind of a flavoring mixture. It smelled like rum; and Joe Snydacker, a Yankee sailor who had skipped ship at Port Royal, tried a swig. "It *is* rum," he said. "Of a rotgut variety, with some kind of yarbs in it."

Then Sailor Joe and Chester Cash and Clyde Freeland fired the building. "Always scuttle the enemy's craft," the sailor said. "That was Farragut's motto." He naturally liked to smell burning deck timbers, he said. It would also let people know to give sailors and soldiers any damn thing they wanted after this.

Fleeing across the fields, old man Green looked back at the billowing smoke. His breath was now coming in sobs, but he couldn't stop, for the broom sedge was on fire behind him, already consuming the fence rails.

Hours after they were gone, he came out of his house a half-mile down the track. Keeping in the shadow of the woods so as not to be seen, he circled back of the Negro George Parker's cabin and entered his factory grove from the rear. It was past midnight. He could hear the little branch babbling peacefully down from Braswell Hill, where he watered his stock and had gotten water for the boiler. He sat down on a rock overlooking the smoldering waste. Sparks were still rising from the charred building. Acrid, low-hanging smoke drifted his way, and he coughed and spluttered. "Ruined! Those devils have ruined me!" he cried bitterly, and with a sob he tore at his lock of hair. "My life's work is now utterly and completely ruined."

Jefferson Warham

Down near Louisburg the last of Sherman's men were swarming and moving. It was said that everybody was fixing to migrate back North to where they'd come from. Some of these troops were already on the way. Heavy feet crunching the road in a shuffling rhythm as they passed. Natives and soldiers lined the road to see them go by. The ones that weren't marching were on a "high horse" and friendly.

"Looka thar comin! We got time to laugh, boys!"

"Hello, Yank."

"Hello yourself, Johnny."

There was one big shaggy middle-aged reb with steel-gray eyes and huge hands. He came pushing his way through the crowd, saying nothing. He was all dusty with the white dust of the road, and his shoes were mostly holes.

"Hey, Reb, got anything to trade?" a Yankee inquired.

From his hip the big fellow produced a frazzled old worn-slick pocketbook and took out a folded five-dollar Confederate bill.

"Swap you twenty-five cents for it in real money," the Yank bid. "All it's good for now's a souvenir."

"Fifty," said the big one with the hard steely eyes and the shrewd steel-trap mouth.

"Uh-huh, if you say so . . ."

The big fellow put the half-dollar in his purse, clicked it shut, and replaced it carefully in his pocket. "It's egzackly the size of my fortune, Mister Yankee," he said with a flickering grin. He spoke rough, like he might have rosin on his voice. "It's the last dern cent I've got in this world."

He was going along, when he heard one of the bluebellies say, "Who wants a mule?"

"There goes an old daddy needs a mule," said another one. He stopped in his tracks. Turned around to see who had spoken, for he had just that minute been thinking that if he and the young'uns only had a plow and a pestletail they could make out somehow.

"That dern Yank musta been a mindreader," Jefferson Warham always said afterward, for, looking straight at him, the Yank called out: "Hi Johnny, they're giving away mules over in that corral. Want one? Like as not they'll give you one. Go over there and see Captain Bodron."

They were a drove of injured army mules. Not worth driving north, so the War Department had ordered them given out to likely looking Carolina farmers. Jeff Warham hung around the corral till sunset, and the veterinarian took a liking to him and gave him two.

As he rode off on one blind mule, leading the other, he shook his big square head soberly and reflectively. "Waal—it's an answer to prayer, it's Providence, as Preacher Lightfoot would say. It must be my lucky day. Double-barreled luck."

As he jogged through Walterville, he turned, at the corner of Lafayette and Hargood streets, to look at the old brick building where they'd all been marched after signing up for the draft in Dillsboro . . . Red Chisenhall, Dave May, Levi Barbee, Lijey Freeland, Jake Sparrow. He wondered where they all were now . . . was sure glad to be alive to pass that way again. He'd been in charge, carried the tickets, and they had eaten dinner at a boardinghouse out there in the town somewheres waiting for the troop train. . . . He'd sure been around the horseshoe since his feet had walked that pavement: to Hat'ras, Fort Caswell, Charleston Harbor, and Richmond. Sure 'nuff he *was* lucky. He thought of the ox eyes and the rat soup the boys had mainly lived on in that Yankee prison at Point Lookout, Maryland. Of the shattering bombshell that had just missed him at Ball Head . . . and they were sayin' twelve thousand Yanks had point-blank *starved* at Salisbury. . . . Maybe it was prayin' saved him. But some of *them* fellers musta prayed too. He scratched his head. Waal, no use botherin' about other folks. In this world, every tub has to set on its own bottom.

He got to Mink Station at last, and plodded on home three miles beyond. He rode slowly up the lane of the old farm that lay in the hollow, clutched in the hot brassy hand of the afternoon.

He stopped his mules and stared, took a deep breath. He loved the hot shimmering sunlight and the baked smell of it off the land and the coming out of it into the cool consoling shade of the old oaks. Walking and riding muleback, he had come a hundred and seventy-eight miles since New Bern.

"Where's my young'uns? Ain't nothin' happened to 'em, I hope. It seems plum naked around here without the children. They must be over at Elvirey's. I'll send and fetch 'em home, right off." But he felt disappointed not to have Tom and Milam come whooping to meet him . . . and Cissy throwin' her arms around his neck and huggin' him hard. And all of 'em squealin' and hollerin'. . . .

And it hurt him to see his fields so neglected, white with daisies and the mullens marching right up into the yard to the well stones, like yellow-capped soldiers. There was his own well of water at last! How many thousand times he'd dreamt of the good cold water sloshing over the rim of that old well bucket. In the prison . . . down on the hot seacoast . . . And the sweet early apple tree he'd planted centuries ago still there by the kitchen, now heavy with fruit. A catbird hopped up on the bucket board and took him a drink from a drip and began to sing.

But it wasn't *his* farm now. That thought stabbed him and stuck in his craw like a nail. Before he went away he'd sold out to Old Man Darwood. The old man had paid him a hundred dollars down and never another cent since. Never another cent. All he had now was two mules as blind as Samson and a cabin full of young'uns.

Old Man Darwood hobbled out to meet him. Jeff could make out the frowzy heads of his family peeking out a window. A bony hound got up from the porch and stretched. There were a few ragged-ass chickens picking about the yard. When he saw who it was, the old fellow plastered his hand to his back. His back was might nigh killing him, he complained; and a rabbit was better able to plow than him. Now where on earth did he get them-thar mules? Didn't he know they was stone stock blind?

Jeff Warham had no patience with shiftless, unlucky people. If Darwood couldn't plow and pay for the land, then how in tarnation blazes could he expect to stay on it? he asked bluntly. Land had to be worked. . . . The sweet smell of the land was coming to his nostrils up through the weeds. But Old Man Darwood said Hold on, the law was on his side. He'd bought the place and couldn't be put off. He said he'd be fair about it, though. He'd tear up the papers for two hundred dollars hard money; or, since Jeff had the mules and the old bull-tongue plow was still in the shed, he'd let him make a crop on shares.

It was pretty hard medicine to have to sharecrop your own land, but as it was the best he could do till he could hire a law-puncher and find a way to get the old codger off, Jeff took him up. Said he reckoned he'd have to dance to the music. He was in the field plowing before daybreak. He would just get in some corn. He wished it was time for turnips. There weren't nothin' better than turnip salet. The Creek Field was edged sweet and thick with wild roses, but he yanked them out and plowed the place under. You couldn't eat roses or put 'em in the bank.

His oldest son Tysander showed up a few days later. From a neighbor, Jeff had heard about Ty's selling tobacco in bags at the Mink Station camps. It was a slick idea. He questioned him. It was so, the youth said, but he'd spent all the money now. His father gave him a lecture on saving, then told him to hitch up one of the mules to the old wagon and go on up to Alamance to Grandmaw's to fetch home the young'uns.

He hadn't seen his kids for over two years, and it would be a happy reunion. Cissy would be thirteen now. Small for her age, but pretty in an Irish way and rosy-cheeked, like her mother. The tears came in his eyes when she came, for she had grown more like his Kate and it made him see *her* again, and think of that day he first set eyes on her singing like a sweet bird in the backwoods choir. . . . Milam was eleven now and looked like his uncle Japhet—tall but spindly and pale. Tom—the baby when Kate died—was eight, and the toughest lightwood-knot of the bunch. He was growing fast, would make a big man. They were all growing like young shoats and had as big appetites. They were barefooted as rats. He'd have to work harder'n a pinerooter to keep 'em "wropped and slopped," he could see that.

But he was full of a new fresh vigor and full of plans. There were so many things to do. He must clear some more land—soon's he got his farm back. He'd save and raise a lot of hogs. Set out some more apple trees in the fall; Winesaps and Magnum Bonums, Summer Cheeses and Winter Johns, Riley Nails and Buffs and Limbertwigs and Creecy Reds. His big hands itched to be planting things.

As Old Man Darwood had a family of his own, he could sleep only one extra head at the house. So Cissy stayed of nights with Ma Darwood, and the rest bunched up and went to housekeeping in an outhouse in the yard. All four slept on a straw tick in a corner. Little Cissy did all her menfolks' cooking and washing, and boiled them pot soap from meat rinds. Jeff told Tysander he'd have to go crop with his uncle Flinthorn Dickey, help get a little money together. Tysander was eighteen, by his first wife. Though he had lived most of his life as a bachelor, Jeff had been twice married. His women had both been short-lived. They had worked themselves out.

The next week Aunt Elvirey followed the children down. She was his dead Kate's sister, a second mother to the young'uns. They had weathered the war out with her back on Cane Creek. The soldiers had cleaned up everything for miles around and hominy and meat-skin gravy was about all they'd had, she said, for the past six months. Aunt Virey said it was so lonesome without her lambs she just had to come where they were. And she brought back Dinah, Jeff's faithful, though now free, slave he had left in her keeping. It bothered Virey to find them living in a place as bare as old ma'am Hubbard's cupboard, and she set right in to fixing up their outhouse dwelling so it would be something a little better than a pig sty. Jeff said they could stay—he'd manage some way. He needed some hands anyhow, and hated to turn away anybody who could work.

When he left for the war, Jeff had packed down what there was left of his tobacco crop in the barn loft. And now, though the Yankee cavalry had been through the neighborhood, he found to his surprise that they had failed to discover it. Tysander's peddling project at the camps went through his head. Maybe *he* could make some money that way too. He smiled. That boy Ty was wicked and spendthrift—he'd never had any raising—but he was clever, and full of common sense as an old bitch fox. . . . So he put all hands to work on that tobacco—even the work-dodging old man and *his* young'uns, stemming and flailing and sacking the driest "bright-leaf."

And now that he had the mules, Jeff was piecing together a daring plan. If they were smart and would hurry and get that tobacco fixed, he told his kids, he was going to light out on a long trip and take the whole kit and kaboodle of them along.

" 'A rolling stone gathers no moss,' " Old Man Darwood threw up to him sagely.

"Un-huh, and a settin' goose gets right shabby-lookin'," parried Jeff. He'd been around considerable now, and he'd decided to take his stuff where there were people with money to buy it. What good to peddle around and wear your horse's shoes out on the Caswell way, or in the Chatham Wilderness. Nosir, he meant to hustle right out and try it all the way back to that faraway town where he'd landed from prison. He had noticed tobacco was awful scarce there, and he wanted to see what he could do trading down that-away. He would take along a couple barrels of wheat flour, too, if he could get some cheap.

Early in August they set out. He had found a lot of the tobacco fixed in twists, suitable for smoking or chewing either one; and had sifted and raked the loose crumbs of the dry hackled leaves into little bags as big as a man's two fists that Virey and Dinah made from some unbleached domestic storekeeper Dismukes had hid away from the looters and let him have on credit. Then under his direction, Virey had cut out paper labels, like for preserves, and pasted one on every sack. And then in his big awkward longhand, Jeff had patiently scratched out with a goose-quill pen on every label the legend:

J. WARHAM
ORIGINAL BEST GENUWINE
MINK STATION SMOKING TOBACCO

Out the lane and down the hill rattled the dingy old covered wagon. At the tail end was a victual box, and you could hear the pots and pans bumping about inside.

They were two months gone. But when they returned, all Jeff's tobacco was sold. They had peddled it all out before they left New

Bern Town. Then he had turned his capital into bacon, which was later sold out on the return trip through the upland. They'd all had a fine lively time of it. Jeff said around the crossroad stores that little old Tom had turned out to be the crackerjack salesman. He had the spizzerinctum, all right. He could sell anybody, seemed as if. He'd trade a dollar for ninety cents just to get the tradin' started, and when there wasn't any money he'd trade for whatever there was. He'd got three hundred pounds of cotton for his flour, and had closed out the last of his cargo to Fapsey Purkins, the store man, in Walterville.

Jeff had a wry surprise for Old Man Darwood. He had seen a lawyer, and Darwood could either take twenty-five dollars and get off his property or be lawed. He also had a surprise for the young'uns. The barrel they'd taken aboard in Walterville which he'd fooled them into believing was vinegar, was hauled out. They lifted it carefully down off the old wagon and set her in the middle of the floor. Jeff pried off the lid with his big old claw hammer.

"Come here, Cissy honey. Here you, Milam and Tom."

"You-uns ain't had enough sugar during these war times," said Aunt Virey, "so your Pappy's fetched us a whole sugar barrel!"

As they went after it like young bear cubs at a bee tree, Jeff talked with Elvirey.

"Virey, I'm rich. I've got all this here and a thousand dollars in the Walterville bank. Yessir, I'm richer'n cream an' tarnation blazes."

Four months had gone by since the last of the troops had left the village, and the air was crisp with fall. Old Mink Station was a bone the Yankees had damn well gnawed. But one thing there was no complaint on, and that was the way tobacco was selling. It was like a tale in a book, the way those soldier boys had been piling letters back to Joel Meek, the postmaster.

"Yessir, they're still coming in by every mail," Postmaster Meek was saying to Tom Warham. He had waddled out to Tom's little bull cart that had just pulled up to the grassy curb, with his leather apron full of letters. "Them letters are comin' plumb from Maine and Californ-i-ay, and all reads the same. 'Dear Sir, please send me some more of that there golden bright kind of tobaccy like I got in the war at Mink Station yours truly.' Some adds a postscript, sayin' 'It was the best tobac I ever smoked.' It looks like every dern vet'ran in Ameriky thinks I've gone in the tobaccy business," he complained.

Two days a week Postmaster Meek turned over his mail orders, on a small commission—measuring them out like potatoes, in a peck measure—to Jeff Warham. The other four days, to Jeff's son Tysander—who, having tired of farming with his uncle, had set up to manufacture tobacco for himself in a barn at the edge of the village; and to Zachariah Green, now over his despair at the robbing and burning of his little log factory and with it built back good as new. Z.G. said now it looked like his misfortune had really been a blessing and good advertising—since it had scattered Mink Station bright leaf up and down the four winds, from Texas to Oregon. From the post office, Tom could see Green's new smokestack puffing away like a corncob pipe across the railroad track on Braswell Hill.

When he got back home that day, he found his usually hardworking father sitting on a stump down by their tobacco barn idly whittling. The sunny October haze hung over their fields, all day long now the grasshoppers chirped, and the cool air smelled tart as grapes.

"I jist been a-studyin', boys," Jeff said, calling Milam from his work. "We'll come nigh to manufacturin' ten thousand pounds of the weed this y'ar. The way things are a-goin' we'll double her the y'ar after. That means we've got to build us a bigger barn—a sort of a little fact'ry—to keep our Genu-wine ahead of arybody else's."

"We ain't ahead," muttered Tom, flinging a wet blanket. "Old Zack Green's done got a sure 'nuff tin smokestack. Had it made in Walterville at Bobbitt's Tin Shop . . . I found out all about it. He's even done gone and got a chopping machine. A thing that works like a feed cutter, and he don't have to flail no more. And Ty, they say, has took on another nigger-woman hand besides old Marthy and her son."

"Green be damned," said Jeff. He didn't often swear, but he didn't mean to let that Green feller or anybody else get ahead of him in the tobacco business. He had a clear vision all painted and framed in his head of "Warham's Best Genuwine" growing always bigger and bigger. Without let-up or ceasing. Leading the ever-augmented pipe smokers' parade right on to the end. . . . He had

dreamt of driving his mules right out amongst the stars, and on up
to the celestial hitching lot and warehouses on the tobacco-bright
Streets of Burnished Gold. "Hm," he snorted, "all smokestacks is
good for is to make smoke. *We're* in business to make money, and
don't you forget it. And tarnation blazes, we'll be a-makin' it when
Zack Green's broker'n a bullfrog. Every tub on his own butt and
the devil take the hindest."

He didn't mention Tysander. They had had a little rippet over
his going to church intoxicated. Jeff was strong against the demon
rum.

Warham and his sons hopped to their new building plans right
away. There was a good sheet of frost on the ground, with the
moon shining down on it, when they set off next morning before
day with the mules and the axes. The Warham boys never minded
work. They went to get Will Garet, and all day they whacked away
up in the Piny Hollow. There were some good straight poles there.
"It takes good north land to raise pretty poles," Will said. The tall
pines came crashing down among the red-berried dogwoods and
haw bushes and tangled in the scarlet vines.

"My God, Milam, my mules is all soaked with sweat," said Jeff
anxiously, going over them with his big hands at dark. "Now don't
you give 'em too much water."

The second day they laid the sills and started the barn up. Will
was a good notcher, and by noon of the fifth day they had the logs
saddled and the rafters up. It was a good stout barn, sixteen by
eighteen, with a loft, and when Jeff and Will had rived out the
white-oak clapboards and all hands had put in a day shingling,the
boys carried water and made mud in a hole, and Virey and Cissy
brought the wet clay in a basket and they had a mud-daubing.
Will said she was snug now as a swamp rat's nest.

The leaves were falling where the boys and Cissy were stretched
out resting after the work. Among the frost flowers and the black-
eyed susies. Tom said all the goldeny leaves were his. They could
have the rest. Gold was the only color he was interested in from
now on. Cissy and Milam laughed, but Tom had a faraway look in
his eyes; looked suddenly solemn, and as tight-mouthed as old
Lazarus Penny.

The Big Money
(1873)

Jeff Warham had been a member of Mount Nebo Methodist Church ever since the time when, as a lad of fourteen, he had been convicted and converted. How well he remembered it all after forty years. . . . He'd been at a dance frolic when the preacher came over from the camp meeting on Muddy Creek to save their lost and wicked souls. A summer storm had blown up and it had grown black, with the trees rocking and thunder and lightning from heaven. He remembered the singing, the terror of the sinners, his own fear of Judgment Day. The shouting and the praying, and then the peaceful overflow of feeling and fellowship, and how he had been filled full of glory and of God and had gone up and given his hand to the preacher. And now since he was out in the world and in business there was no doubt that being a church man paid. Hadn't he prospered like all get-out? It was only seven years since he'd gone into tobacco trading, and now, by dad-jim, he was getting as rich as a honeybee in dry weather. It was plain as the nose on your face, the Lord had sent him showers of blessing. It was religion that had brought him through the bushes of his money hunt. He was manufacturing a hundred and twenty-five thousand pounds of the weed a year now, and he wasn't one to go and act the damn fool in any way to angrify or upset the Lord or his applecart. So he guessed he *had* better begin tithing like Preacher Barlow said. "If you 'spect good luck you gotta pay the preacher," everybody said.

It had got so that Preacher Barlow always stopped at his house. It was now a house of plenty, and Virey set a mighty good fare: with chicken and country ham, and meats all dumpled up in pastry, and liver mush and souse and crackling cornbread in season, and garden truck like collards, turnips, and sweet 'taters and home-made pickled goods and pies and layer cakes. . . . Jeff Warham would get after the womenfolks regularly about their sinful extravagance, just to keep them on their toes, but they knew he didn't want his stomach cheated. "Man," he'd say, wiping his mouth with the back of his huge hairy hand, "jest gimme them greens, and a peevish of milk and bread for supper, and I can sleep my titles clear."

As the news spread of brother Warham's nourishing board, all the Methodist preachers, it seemed, were more and more frequently directed by Providence to travel in that direction. They told it on brother Emsley Chitty that he dropped his false teeth in the creek while on the way to Jeff's one Sunday for dinner, but when one of the kids ran and got a piece of Aunt Virey's fried chicken and dangled it on a string, those ivories rose right off the bottom and snapped into it.

. . . Well, said Jeff Warham to himself, I ain't a-gonta give *quite* a tenth—that would run into big money. (Already he was doing a "land-office" business; was having to buy the tobacco crops of other farmers to keep up with the demand.) That would soon make our little country church too rich—would be the ruin of it; would give folks the swellhead. Money's the root of all evil, he reflected, and far be it from me to put a stumbling block in the way of my fellow-man. It wasn't good business, either, argued the old man, to let everybody know what you made. And they might think you were trying to show off. And, since I can make bigger interest on the Lord's money, he further cogitated, than all them dern impractical preachers put together, it's plain common sense that the Lord had ruther keep His part o' the money invested in my hands.

By the eighth year after his peddling days, the smoking and chewing of tobacco had spread to such proportions among Americans old and young that Jeff Warham gave up farming altogether and built himself a real factory in town.

One day a horse and buggy from Lunsford's Horse and Cow

Barn, driven by Ruffin Arp, the hostler, had appeared suddenly at the farm. A vigorous old Scotchman with iron-gray sidewhiskers got out and said he had come all the way from his home in Scranton, Pennsylvania, to talk about buying an interest in the Warham tobacco business. He said he had been one of those Yankee soldiers marooned in Mink Station at the war's end, and he had never forgotten a certain enterprising farmer boy by the name of Warham that he had met peddling tobacco in a wheelbarrow about the camps, with an old Negro mammy and a little black boy. . . . Inquiring at the Gaston P. Morris Hotel (that had now gone fancy and called itself the Claydon Hotel) for the Warham headquarters, imagine his astonishment at finding that the famous Dove of Peace tobacco was manufactured in a barn.

"Why bless my soul," said Mr. McLauchlen—for that was the gentleman's name—"if I owned that Dove trademark I'd be turning out the stuff by the shipload, for if I'm any judge of a product, it has big possibilities." He went on to say that since the war he had become a successful wholesale merchant, and had found the Dove the best repeater on his shelves. He had an only son in college and was looking for a good business connection for him. His general proposition was that if they would take his son Magnus into partnership and let him handle the business end of the firm, he would invest a tidy sum in the enterprise for expansion.

Now old Jeff saw at once that it was his son Tysander whom the stranger had really come to interview. The Dove was one of *his* brands and somebody had misdirected him. But smelling money, he couldn't now disillusion the old chap and spoil his own chances of driving a trade. In the great Sea of Happenstance this fish had happened his way and, tarnation blazes, charity began at home. And so he let McLauchlen ramble on under the assumption that the two family concerns were the same, and eased his elastic conscience by saying it might be a devious way of Divine Providence to teach his headstrong, impious son a lesson. When the visitor inquired about the boy peddler, now grown a man, his shrewd father led McLauchlen to believe Ty was away on a long business trip—though he *could* have told him how the prodigal's business had flourished like a moonvine until of late he had plunged in recklessly, as he always did, and put himself up a high-class two-story factory, with a gaudily painted turtle dove bearing glad scrollwork tidings of $$$ across its front. . . .

The upshot of the matter was that the transaction was closed without the Scrantonian realizing his mistake. And though he put ten thousand dollars down on the dotted line, he departed with no more proprietorship in the famous Dove of Peace trademark than Buddy Jonas, the black boy; who, now standing six-foot-two on his great bare ebony feet, was at that moment rolling hogsheads and sweating like a bull mink down on Tobacco Street, with his "Cap'n Tysan' "—well lit-up and singing "Roll Jordan Roll You Black Sonofabitch"—right behind him.

In 1873, Jeff Warham's new factory seemed a wonder of the world. It was three stories high, all built of sawed boards, and forty by seventy feet in dimension. Jeff, Milam, and Tom built it themselves. Jeff ciphered it out and bought the timber on the stump and got a gang of carpenters to help and tallied the logs to and from the sawmill, in his old sheepskin-leather account book. There was a log shanty for the Negro hands in addition to the main building, and on the railroad side a little office about as big as a kitchen, with a stovepipe jutting out. Mr. Warham said Tom would be superintendent. He was good at getting work out of people: bossed the hands like it was a game, dared the best of them to race him at the work.

"We ain't a-puttin' up nothin' fancy," Jeff announced at the start. But just in case one of the fifteen hands might happen to oversleep, he ordered a big bell from Philadelphia to roust 'em out of a morning. They hoisted it up on top and put it in a cupola. Lazarus Penny, who had bought out the recently deceased Zachariah Green's business cheap from his widow, came up to look at the bell. He laughed harshly and twiddled his mustache and said it looked like a lot of unnecessary expense to him, a-hoistin' the punkin up on the pie.

It was during the erection of the factory that the elder McLauchlen learned that the brands most popular with the war veterans were those put up by Tysander, and not by Jefferson Warham. Back he hotfooted it to the little hick city edged with broomstraw and patched with vacant lots, to see the real owner and get him to become a party to the arrangements. But in this he had one heck of a time. Tysander was as independent as a tomcat on a fence, and wasn't interested.

Tysander Warham cooked and slept—and sinned betimes with his high-yellow mistresses—up over his factory; and here, intermittently, the troubled promoter spent the better part of two weeks pleading his case.

He would arrive regularly each morning at nine to resume the pow-wow—always to find the object of his diplomacy with his great jumbo feet up on his desk, drumming away with the heel of his hand upon the broad arm of his rocking chair—as oblivious of the visitor as though he'd been a stray cockroach that had wandered in through a crevice in the wall—and singing with abandon. Ty's repertoire of bawdry was immense and bottomless. He would slide easily from vague lyric ectoplasm like

> Diddle diddle dinktum
> Do dar do . . .

to more trenchant roundelays, such as

> I had a little tomcat,
>   And he was double-j'inted;
> I took him to the blacksmith shop
>   And had his cooter p'inted . . .

shocking McLauchlen's rigid sensibilities and intoleration sorely; which, however, only fired the miscreant to further massacres of morals and music. For Tysander Warham was voluptuous and giddy-go-lucky as the Scot was pious.

> Her back was made of whalebone, boys,
>   Her belly made of brass;
> Her love was made for southern men,
>   But the Yanks could kiss her ass . . .

There was one about a frog and a bumblebee that had so many variations it drove the old gentleman wild. But he had to hang on and sublimate his wrath and outraged godly feelings if he was ever to get his money back.

At first the old boy tried threatening: said he'd been tricked, there'd been collusion and conspiracy. (Oh how he boiled inside to see this vulgar, blasphemous fool fiddlefaddling and enjoying himself while *his* financial Rome burned.) But it didn't do any good. When next he called, the carnal nightingale, the indelicate Orpheus, greeted him obliquely with

> Oh he's a stiff old bully cow,
> And worth ten thousand crowns . . .

drummed in slow and stately march time—a mock "Hail to the Chief." In the last days of negotiation the Scotchman's voice took on a whining, and finally a crawling, abject tone. More money was put up, and eventually Ty did come into the partnership. They pooled all interests, capitalized at seventy thousand dollars, and that was the beginning of the firm that was later to become the great U.T. Corporation.

T. P. Warham

"Pa," said Tom Warham one day while the factory was going up, "I think I better go in business for myself. I'm sixteen now, and I've got to be making some money of my own—some real dough."

Mr. Warham threw back his head and laughed. He saw it all now in a glance. The old rooster hadn't realized that the young cockerel was no longer a chick.

"How much you need, son?" he asked gravely. Without waiting for the boy to reply, he took out his checkbook and wrote him a check for a thousand dollars. Stood holding it in his hand, his bushy brows puckered in thought. Then he tore the paper up. "Nope," said he, "I got a better idee." And jubilantly he poked the boy in the ribs with his great horny thumb. "Why tarnation blazes, Tom, I'm a-goin' to take you and Milam into the business as partners too!"

Tom had saved up three thousand dollars, and Jeff lent him eleven thousand more to make up the fourteen each partner had to contribute.

The Warhams had already taken in Mr. McLauchlen's son Magnus as agreed. He had finished at the best college in Pennsylvania, and came with high recommendations as a calculator. There was nothing hit-or-miss about Magnus McLauchlen. Coming from a long line of tight-fisted Scotch Presbyterian progenitors—who for centuries had waxed hard and tall on "flintrock" soup and brimstone; and to whom peeling potatoes sparingly had been an A-Number-One virtue—he began paring operating costs right down to the bone. Mr. Warham had been paying the factory Negroes $1.98 per week, but that was too much, said young Mr. McLauchlen, and he cut them to $5.00 a month and a sack of meal. That was a $2.92 monthly saving in money per person; with an extra $1.98 saved in all months having five weeks. And as the meal could be purchased wholesale for way less than a dollar, this sharp move won him the warm approval of his associates—who rubbed their eyes and wondered why-in-the-heck they hadn't thought of it before. Magnus could add up a whole string of figures in his head right off the bat, and could tell them to the thousandth decimalized part of a cent just how much it was costing to manufacture one bag of tobacco or a million. Oh he was a good solid man, he was; with a long head and a broad backside that wobbled when he walked. And a hard-driving, abrupt, rude, stormy way that gave the hands and clerks the jitters, made them feel small and vermiculate whenever he hove near—all dressed up in expensive tailor-made tweeds and smelling of *eau de lilas.*

There was quite a lot of law business now, the drawing of contracts, chattel mortgages, indemnifications; and it was around this time that Jefferson Warham met Mr. Barnaby B. Fogg. Meeting Mr. Fogg gave him a new slant on lawyers. He was a man with a big bald head, a bristling sandy mustache, and a considerable paunch. He'd been to college, had traveled, had even been some sort of a judge; and was quick and clever as Jeff was slow and methodical. Lawyer Fogg could jump in a jiffy from telling jokes to outlining exactly how to shenanigate any law on the statute books. You could see he was sharp as fishhooks. It wasn't long before Jeff was going to him for advice on all sorts of matters, on things that weren't exactly law business. Mr. Fogg took a great liking to Tom. He said he'd been watching him from a youngster, coming to town in his little bull wagon in the morning to look after the shipping and mail. . . . Said he was going to make a smart businessman and told him about a business college in New York State and gave him a piece clipped from a Wall Street newspaper on the phenomenally successful business methods of the oil man, John D. Rockefeller.

At this time the "old man" Jeff Warham was fifty-six years of age; and while he was still active enough in the settled plant routines, in matters of initiative and bucking the public he was coming to rely more and more on his youngest son. Milam was steady enough, but his health wasn't very good, and, as Mr. Fogg expressed it, he just wasn't the steam engine Tom was.

One winter Jefferson had sent both boys off to a Quaker school in an adjoining county to give them some education; but in a few weeks Tom had come home, saying he'd be damned if he'd waste time from business piddling around over books. Then the summer he was eighteen he packed up unexpectedly and went up to Poughkeepsie to that business school Mr. Fogg had spoken of, and took a course in accounting. When he came back, there seemed to be some huge but vague vision working in him, and he said he would need a whole bunch of lawyers if certain things worked out the way he planned. By now Tom was completely sold on mass production, and John D. Rockefeller had become his mentor; his model of the perfect man, his guiding star. By common consent they all began to look up to Tom as their acknowledged leader and made him president.

The first really big problem Tom Warham ran into in expanding their enterprise was the speed-up. It was an idea he'd got from studying the money-making methods of the great John D. To make the right kind of dividends you had to get plenty of work out of everybody. He had to fire a good many hands at first, before he got it into their thick heads he meant business and any man that took *his* money had to give down all he had. If a hand was one minute late, he instructed Cad Price, the superintendent, he was to be locked out all day. "If you can't do the work, we'll get somebody that can," became Mr. Thomas P. Warham's famous driving motto.

He also set to work to organize a steady supply of the raw material. More farmers would have to be persuaded to wake up and raise more tobacco. How in the gosh-dinged jaybird, he said, could the public smoke tobacco that wasn't out of the ground? (Oh he was a shrewd, horse-sensible talker, like his papa.) As business grew (and in less than two years, J. Warham, Sons & Co. had had to double the size of their plant) they were having to import tobacco from Virginia. And Virginia tobacco wasn't near so good or popular for smoking as Slatterly's pretty Bright Leaf, the kind they raised in the country around Minktown.

Ten years before the war, the Slatterly boys—Eli and Elisha, a pair of hard-headed little Irish farmers over near Rocktown—had discovered that tobacco could be seasoned out by fire, without having to wait for the sun or the air to do it. (That is, one of their bright slaves Stephen Slatterly, had.) This young Negro observed that leaves exposed to burning charcoal changed color—which started them off on the big idea. It was the Slatterlys who introduced the "flue-curing"—the hanging up of the green leaves in a tight cabin and subjecting them for several days and nights to heat from a flue furnace—and tobacco grown in the light gray land of the region had cured up a bright golden yellow. So along with something of luck, something of hard-driving necessity, and the toil of many hands, it was this discovery that had been responsible for the Warhams' increasing harvest of yellow gold.

Tom's plans to organize the farmers sounded practical, so the other members of the company all said to go ahead, and he boosted the price of leaf tobacco way up and kept it there for the next few years to bait the Carolina hay shakers into raising the fragrant weed. And, badly in need of cash, the country people responded. Then the Warhams built in Minktown the first big leaf-tobacco warehouse south of Virginia. It was opened with a Grand Agricultural Jubilee—a free barbecue, and speeches, and stirring martial music by the Walterville Cornet Band.

Tobacco was rolling in now from Swearing Creek, Smithfield, and Penny's Hill. From Weldon, Garysburg, Lumberton; and Troublesome (in Rockingham), Louse Level and Beaverdam and Gilboa and Altamahaw. Clover Hill—in Cleveland County—was contributing its share; and Rocktown and Franklinsville and the Chatham Wilds. Mud Lick came across; and Gum Swamp, and Timmonsville in South Carolina and all down the Wateree and up the Pee Dee, they were now giving-down like Brown's old cow. The quilt-covered tobacco wagons even rolled in from Virginia and from faraway Rip Shin Ridge in Tennessee. . . . And *people,* black and white, were moving in to live. From Walterville, Page's Station, Oxford, Milton, Tarboro, they walked or wagoned it. . . . From Dillsboro and all out in Lemon County. From Manganville—to the north—and Mt. Tirzah, Fish Trap, Knap-o'-Reeds, and Rabbit City . . . arriving to become factory hands and do the stemming, the flailing of the dry leaves on long tables, the sieving and sacking. To open stores, horse-and-cow enterprises, fish-and-oysters, harlot-eries, or saloons. Or to take jobs as clerks and bookkeepers, pick-pushers, hammer-and-saw monkeys, mop-Marys, pimps, baggage-smashers, railroad brakemen, sewing-machine salesmen, bang-away babies, drivers of hacks and drays, etc., etc. All kinds of little businesses were taking root, like miscellaneous windblown seed. Dwelling houses opened up for rent and boardinghouses. Yes, business was blooming—lushly, rank and tall as weeds around a barn or by a lavish stream.

Somebody had recently discovered that even the waste and sandy earth of these parts, especially along the Ridge and out toward Whippoorwill Hollow, was just the thing for raising that bright "golden belt" tobacco, so real estate—that had sunk as low as twelve cents per acre in '65 and '66—had taken a phoenixy raise from the ashen doldrums. And in a few years the shiftless, impov-erished descendants of the old squatter families—the Dossets, Tur-nipseeds, Viggerses, Rileys . . . had turned into tobacco planters or had sold off their property for a good price, and Minktown was crawling inexorably west to swallow up the godless and rowdy old Pinoak settlement.

In the meantime the miserly Lazarus Penny, who had bought out Zachariah Green, had passed away of avarice and malnutrition, and his business been purchased by Colonel Riley Pescud, a Gran-ville man, and Colonel Eugene Owsley, an energetic merchant who had moved to Minktown from up the country. And herein lurked another headache for the ambitious young president of the Warham Company, since these new competitors were not at all of the small-town caliber, but businessmen of vigor and initiative, who plainly meant to give him a run for his money.

The Warhams had acquired Magnus McLauchlen at just the right time. For Milam was beginning to go soft under the corrod-ing pressure of success and spent more and more time fiddling around or pursuing pleasure; while Tysander had become com-pletely irresponsible, and would chuck the most important busi-ness engagement to go on a spree or chase after a woman. But with Magnus to depend on, Tom Warham—or "T.P." as his associ-ates had taken to calling him—now struck out for several weeks on the road to see what was what; to cultivate the trade and undermine competitors. When he returned around Christmas he had been clean to Missoula, Montana, and Rattlesnake, Florida, and the Great Lakes, and had sold such a helluva hatful of stuff that they had to get busy again and step up the output. Now the factory fairly roared: the pulley shafts whirring, the steam exhaust chuffing and puffing from the boiler room, and the whole building a-tremble, as with a palsy, from the jar of the grinding machines. The acrid brown tobacco dust flew everywhere, settled in the cobwebs festooning the low whitewashed beams and ceiling, rained down on the bookkeepers' desks and into their inkwells, dusted the executives' coats on their nails in the corner, plashed Jeff's old black hat that he wore pulled down on the back of his head.

"But whar the dad-jim can we git enough hands, Tom?" old Jefferson queried, in rather a discouraged tone, as they conferred in their little office marked "Private."

"That's just it," whined Milam. "Labor's so damn lazy nowadays . . ."

"We've *got* to have 'em—and cheap," growled Magnus McLauchlen, the treasurer. "If we don't go ahead, Eugene Owsley *will*."

It looked like it was just one damn thing after another, T.P. said. Something had to be done and quick. Pescud & Owsley were running too far ahead with their goddamn Bull. It had just won a gold medal at the Philadelphia Exposition; they were putting up a steam whistle designed to roar like a male cow at a cost of fifteen dollars a toot and that could be heard seventeen miles away; and T.P. had learned through his tippers down in the rival factory that they were going into big advertising and had an inventor working on a machine designed to automatically pack tobacco and knock his business into a cocked hat.

It *was* a snag—how the devil to get enough skilled labor. There were extra processes now: the steaming to run out the bugs, the packing for export, the mixing-and-flavoring department. They had put a spy in Owsley's manufactory to find out what 'twas they put in their "Spanish Flavored" to make it smell so good and it was rum, and all around the Warham factory, now, it was beginning to smell like a barroom. On the trains passing the factory people were wrinkling up their noses and asking what was that peculiar fragant odor. . . . And there were all sizes of bags to make, the inspecting, the getting up of fancy labels for all the new brands (of course all of them were practically the same stuff, but they had to *look* different), the revenue stamping, the building of more and more leaf storage-houses. . . .

But he had a plan. "I've studied it up, down, and sideways, and I believe it's what John D. would do. . . . Listen . . . *we*'ll invent, buy, or steal *us* some packing machines too, to pack our pipe tobacco: the Genuwine, the Wild Rose, Jason's Mule, etcetera—and here's what we'll do, on top of that we'll push our cigarette line like nobody's ever pushed cigarettes before! The cigarette is something new in the United States and 's bound to become popular. Besides us, nobody's manufacturing them yet except a concern in New York and Alloway and Glasner in Richmond. Thanks to the war and the army boys getting on the habit, smoking's picking up fast now, and our bright leaf will make a novel golden cigarette that oughta go big."

The bigness of the idea spurred T.P. to his feet. He strode up and down like a tiger in the little stuffy glassed-in cage of their private office and puffed his cigar viciously. "The American people," he rapped out, "are a bunch of saps that would smoke rat poison or bathe in chicken shit if you spent enough money advertising it." His deadpan seriousness made them—even the proper and pious Scot Magnus—break out in a cackle.

They kept it a dead secret and soon doubled and trebled their cigarette output. To manufacture cigarettes, though, you had to have more and more clever hands with lightning-fleet fingers. Women were the fastest—T.P. had heard the best were the Jewish women from Russia, where this form of smoking had long been in vogue. So they brought down a big cargo of Jew hands—Russkies . . . little gnomish chattery women with their funny boots and soutached garments and garlic-and-Bismarck-herring smell and shawls, who could lick the brown cigarette papers (later it was paste and more sanitary) and pile 'em up like nobody's business. Mamie Borodinsky, the champ, could do almost three thousand in a day, or around three hundred an hour.

At first Tom took on a few Jews for a tryout; then a whole trainload was brought down from the Lower East Side. "It sure look like Palestine has come to Minktown," Zachary-Taylor Hornbuckle, the ticket agent, opined, shaking his head with dire predictions of catastrophe to those twin pillars of world stability—southern womanhood and white supremacy.

Mink Street (now Main) took on the appearance of the Bowery, or a sidestreet in ancient Babylon. There was a continuous babble of strange tongues: from all the flashy city-slicker young men in their horse-blanket-check suits and dilapidated, tobacco-dusted brown derbies; from the old rabbinical graybeards; from the swarthy young paint-faced Rebeccas and Hittite Cleopatras and Jezebels, with tawdry sweaters and hug-me-tight skirts worn in loudness. There was magpie laughter. There was the saturating odor of sweat and garlic with the sweetness of rummed tobacco, as they strutted their stuff to and from the ghetto T.P. had set up down on Turpentine Street, in Niggertown.

To Minktown's pure and sacred Anglo-Saxon soil, down in the misery and mud of Irish, Turpentine, and Israelite Streets, came the Jew's fears, the Jew's wit and wisdom. To the sordid social silt of East Stogie Street arrived the Yiddish newspapers, the battered old silk hats and long greasy beards and wild unworldly eyes of the rabbis. Ex-slaves and old hillbilly grandmas too old to work in the mill got themselves little Jew-jobs building Sabbath fires and were called "fire-goys." Entered the "fire sales" as well and felines trained to knock over lighted lamps. The goings, under the morning star, of the Jews to prayer up over Moisheh Solomon's store—there being their temporary place of worship. The ringing singings of the Jewish anthem and the fervent Asiatic chantings and wailings, the solemnly intoned Kaddish.

The Jews spilled over into the Halfway-to-Hell District: into the concentrated grossness and stinkingness of Big Punkin and Pig alleys. Into Abraham Lincoln Street in Jigaboo. Intermingled with the ignorance and hellish poverty of Paradise and Success Streets, out on the West Side—where the Messrs. T. P. Warham and Magnus McLauchlen had put up a cottonmill called Erdmannton, after Colonel Cass Erdmann, the big bully of a man they had picked to run it. Mixed in with the beast-quartered and fierce bad-whiskey-spiked murderous truculence, squalor, and degradation of the Black Belt, about the fetid fringes of the town.

Among the lacklustrous Minktown "smart set," the Weber and Fields Jew-jokes became all the smart rage. Over the whist and tacky-parties and masquerade balls, the rummage sales to the colored for getting rid of old clothes, the exclusive rollerskating levees, ran much chaffy small talk of the new-come "kikes." And even some of the age-old Shylock slanders and sucking-the-blood-of-Gentile-babies vilifications.

And then—in pushing Magnus's decimal and millesimal cost-per-cigarette points just a peevish farther left, T.P. decided that since some of those avaricious Jew-gal "swifts" were now making as high as $1.75 per day—and since he had suddenly discovered that the female sex's fingers weren't the only pebble on the beach and that black or tan fingers were as usable as white or gray—it was time to put on bright young nigger boys to take their place. In this way he could save 1/1000 of a penny in no time.

Let's slap a big poll tax on the Dirty Masses, T. P. Warham suggested to his mentor Lawyer Fogg. That was the way to do it—put the clamps on the radical masses of low-lived poor-white trash as well as the niggers. Keep their dirty hands damn well off the ballot box. Voting ought to be based on property anyhow.

He could now see the practical value of Lawyer Fogg's suggestion about getting the legislature to carve off a slice from the county and incorporate a new one. As John D. Rockefeller said, you could get away with anything if you were a corporation. That way he could run the county like he and Mr. Fogg were already running the town through Mayor Dismukes.

"And why *shouldn't* I run it?" he said to himself and Mr. Fogg. "It was my old daddy that made the place—this humming big old town."

One day after they'd been manufacturing cigarettes for quite a while, and were building up a good trade, Tom Warham heard that a machine had been invented in Virginia that could roll cigarettes. He didn't believe it, but went over to Lynchburg anyhow to see the Anstack people. It *was* true—the miracle had happened—and before he left he'd worked out a deal providing that if the Warham company would install a couple of the machines it could have them for half the royalty to be charged any other manufacturer.

At first, though, it looked like that cigarette machine was going to be a flop. They sent over the best machinist they had, but it wasn't perfected and for the first month the contrary monster chewed up more material than it rolled. T.P. ranted and raged and said it wasn't worth a high-class fart; but with a young mechanical genius he got hold of, Donald O'Malley, he continued to stay up with it like a sick baby day and night, weekdays and Sundays. He had trailed this O'Malley through a New York detective agency and traded him off the Manchester Locomotive Works in Glasgow, Scotland. And after several months, O'Malley got the thing really going, so it would run smooth as silk for a ten-hour day without a stop.

The Anstackers could roll around two hundred and ten cigarettes per minute or twelve thousand six hundred per hour. One machine could do more than fifty humans could. They spit 'em out so fast it hurt your eyes to watch 'em coming, but that clever Irishman O'Malley said faith-and-begorra he knew he'd have those two machines turning out a quarter million a day soon and bless Pat if he didn't. And then they struck it double lucky. On the third day of March, 1883, President Chester Alan Arthur, that big-bellied, bluffing Yankee lawyer—hoping to win influence among Southern politicians—reduced the tobacco tax in Congress. The act was effective as of April 1, but T.P. showed a certain ruling senator how he could make some money, too, if he would kindly keep the matter hush-hush right up to that date. Then, while his competitors were rubbing their eyes and wondering what effect this new law would have on business, that slick Warham boy rushed out telegrams and letters to every listed dealer in the United States offering to accept orders immediately at the reduced-tax price.

It was a great scoop. The orders poured in and the Anstackers roared and rattled and hummed and poured the cigarettes out by the millions. In a week they had cleaned up a hundred thousand dollars.

T.P. laughed a big belly laugh then, kicked out all the nigger boys rolling cigarettes by hand, and said they were now really getting down to something like brass tacks. But there were still a lot of stumps in the road. First thing, all this mountain of cigarettes had to have a steady outlet. "We've got to whet the world's appetite for 'coffin-nails,' as the fool 'anti's' call 'em," he said, and sent their Mr. Cyrus T. Badger, of the sales department, on a trip around the world. And he made a deal with Frank Neugebauer the church decorator (who was later to become famous under his sign-painting nom de plume of "Salvador Salt") to tail his star salesman with a crew of painting punks and daub the Warham advertising up everywhere. "On the pyramids of Egypt, the royal backhouse, the Rock of Gibraltar, or just anywhere historical or conspicuous you can sneak a paintbrush in," he directed. "Wherever you can slip in and slap it . . ."

But it took money to splash around like that, putting salt on the luck birdie's tail to keep ahead of the others, and, notwithstanding Treasurer McLauchlen's good Scotch money management, there were times (especially in the shy-money times of the late 1880s) when they needed hard money in big chunks to finance their cash purchases of tobacco at the warehouse auctions or to pay off maturing bonds or obligations in the Baltimore or Richmond banks. In these emergencies they would coin-comb the town for the metal. T.P., dressed in his Sunday best, with a flower in his buttonhole, a big cigar in his mouth and lots of them in his pockets for give-away purposes, and a bottle of Old Hunk's XXX Superior Tennessee Corn on his hip, would sally forth in person as briggety and full of brass guts as a brass monkey to round up the necessary true spondulix. He would solicit short-term loans from any and everybody. Go through the warehouses, on the big sales days when they were glutted with the leaf and all the farmers were in town. And would go after the hillbillies, merchants, carpenters, gamblers, barkeeps, bookkeepers, barbers, bricklayers, mule skinners . . . giving Warham Company "due bills" or his own personal I.O.U.s at 10 percent interest. Minktown had every confidence in their godlings of the tobacco machine and their paper was as welcome to the storekeepers as greenback, or more so. It is said that on a pinch T.P. even extracted solid money from those good-natured and obliging whoreladies Big Blondie Lola and old Nan Mahler. Old Nan boasting that she was really a lot smarter than T. P. Warham. "I don't have to paint signs all over the world to get business and I never take anything but the hard stuff," it was said she said. But she thought so much of Mr. Warham she'd go through her place making all the help shell out, too. Luring the money out of their hideaways and explaining how much more convenient the script was for stocking-banking. . . . And it was during one of these money famines in the late '80s that that wise-as-a-hoot-owl Magnus put over one of his most acuminatious feats of fiducial statesmanship.

Colonel Belo Van Buren McCubbins, the banker, had early seen the big profit possibilities in the Warham enterprise and had invested fifty thousand dollars of his wife's money in its common stock and first-mortgage gold bonds. Arabella Schulze McCubbins was from one of the best families in Georgia, and her father, a gentleman of the old school, had squeezed a fortune out of nigger sweat, cotton, and naval stores; and by the time Sherman's army came marching through, had safely sold out and salted it down in the North.

But soon after the Warhams had enlisted the banker-colonel McCubbins as a financial angel, he had lain down and died. T.P., Milam, old Jefferson, and Magnus went into a huddle then, and it was decided that the Scotch-Presbyterian partner, who was also the big dominant dog in local Presbyterian circles—to which faith the McCubbinses also adhered—must give the doughty old financier the most elegant and spectacular funeral money could buy, or that had been, or ever would be, staged in Minktown; and charge it to advertising. By such a grandiose gesture of honor and crocodile affection and grief it was hoped that his wealthy widow would be sufficiently impressed and pleased to let her lot and capital stay cast in Minktown and tobacco. That she would not pull up stakes and take her stuff back to Atlanta, when *they* needed it so badly.

It was a bright day in late March that this grievous event took place. That a dull little office memo of Mr. McLauchlen's blossomed into magnificent brilliant reality and being. The streets were still muddy but the birds were singing like sixty that morning and the peach trees were now in full bloom.

The distinguished mummy had left the stately Victorian McCubbins mansion for the church sharply at ten o'clock. Magnus McLauchlen was a stickler for punctuality, so even a dead man mustn't be late. Two weeks before, foreseeing the trend of events, he'd had a hearse specially painted gold by old Heindrick Anders, the German carriage maker, and it was now surmounted by a fine silk U.S. flag at half-mast and a gold eagle and a pure white wooden angel. The four black hearse-horses wore plumes of white and scarlet; and the poor old corpsed Colonel's fair blond widow (and her victoria) was swathed in deep mourning. She was accompanied by the family and dear thoughtful Mr. McLauchlen in his black jim-swinger and top hat as master of ceremonies, and the Rev. Marcus Wilber Dargan. Ten of Minktown society's best equestrians on ten fine horses (oh it was a big day for the Pulaski Livery Stable!)—each wearing elegant mustachios and sideburns and a sable sash emblazoned in red with the letters B.V.B.M.—rode as a guard of honor. The superefficient Mr. McLauchlen had synchronized the whole town by his watch, it seemed, and as the cortege debouched from the regal gateway, all the factory whistles in town, and all locomotives that were within the railroad yards and Minktown's corporate limits, let go in a wild ecstatic frenzy of roaring and tooting that was supposed to cacophonically represent grief, but that some wag said sounded like the poor old town was blowing its nose. Then the noise subsided and seemed to cease—but opened up again in full-mouthed glorious fortissimo at intervals of every three minutes, making the parade horses snort and sidestep around. When the procession reached Magnolia Street, the military company—Captain Henry Celadon Crow commanding—was drawn up, according to the master plan, in review formation and fell in immediately behind the crepe-hung carriage. Held bravely aloft by the young color bearer, Heygood McNeith, was a flag bearing the black letters B.V.B.M. on a field azure. And when Stonewall Jackson Street was crossed, gathering strength like a stream in flood, the cavalcade took on the Masonic Lodge—plumed in admiral hats and drawn up with swords at salute. And as it flowed into Main Street, the red "Boston Steamer" fire-engine, drawn by four horses and with all the firemen aboard in full fire-fighting regalia, was waiting there all steamed up to take the lead of the procession—a moving and tooting *avant garde* just ahead of the golden death wagon. Which caused several of the saddle horses to ramp and rear in fright and tried the mettle and skill of their riders, but added greatly to the drama.

The factories had all let out for the day, and a large throng of idle Minktowners were there to take in the free show. The Minktown Brass Band awaited them, too; and marched along out of step, botching up Chopin's funeral opus.

The wooden bank building, at the corner of Main and Baltimore, was garlanded, too, in heavy mourning—with black bunting steamers and rosettes—and *its* Old Glory flying, too, at half-mast; and another and larger flag, also mournfully half-masted, unfurling to the breeze those cryptic, ubiquitous and this time bright crimson, letters B.V.B.M.

And thus at last arrived the splendid royal catafalque to the simple small church with a small white steeple; to the halfway station of blessing and oratory. It was met by the elders and deacons wearing black clothes and the deceased colonel's monogram broidered in gold on sashes of purple; by the Presbyterian preacher come up from Walterville to assist Reverend Dargan; and by an honor guard of Sunday-school children all in white.

But the secret thoughts and comments of bystanders— disregardful of the solemn doleful bong and tolling of every bell of every church in town—weren't entirely elevated or respectful.

"Oh he'll fry in hell all right, hee-hee!" (This from Tabby Tolloch, standing meekly and solemnly beside her dour and redbeared lord-and-master, Angus Tolloch.)

"Ain't life funny? Last week he was a moneycratical man, nursing all them dollars and nickels he had squirreled up. Now I may be poor as a coot and dodging the rag man, but this week I'd a damnsight ruther be me!" (Oma Gossett, the weaver.)

"It must have been his liver. The last time I saw him I said to myself, 'He ain't healthy—he's yellow as a pisspot.'" (Dr. Jehu Viggers, the fever doctor.)

"I'd sure like to pick up what the old boy has laid down." (Young Sherman Josephburg, the reporter—thinking of the rich and pulchritudinous blond relict as he was taking notes for the flossy obit he would be turning out that night.)

The partners said it had cost more than they'd figured on, but had to admit that Magnus had "done things up brown."

The Chinaman

By 1885, Mink Station, incorporated as Minktown for several years, was in her Golden Age. There were five new tobacco warehouses and ten manufactures of smoking and chewing tobaccos and snuffs, bombarding the world with choice home-grown nicotine: Eureka, Orange Blossom, and Buffalo Bill, Indian Chief and Gypsy Girl, Pescud & Owsley's Southern Bull; Warham's Best Genuine, Drummer Boy, Grizzly Bear, and Dove—and all the other brandmarks, crests, and insignia of Minktown's dollar-questing sons.

The town was still like a big lump of bread dough, sprawling and crawling out everywhere over the edges of a pan. It boasted the Elite Pharmacy now—a popular meeting place for the dandies and their donnas, its arty cheese-colored walls sporting a marvelous gallery in large colorful chromos of current events. It also boasted a brick church—for Jefferson Warham, who always had the spiritual welfare of the laboring man at heart, had generously put up a House of Worship near his factory. He noted with regret the rotten potatoes among the sound, who preferred getting extra sleep or getting piffercated on the Sabbath to getting right with God.

Spring came to Minktown in that year naturally and peacefully enough, yet summer was to see strange and momentous events foregather. In June a Republican shot a Democrat through a knothole. In July, like an ocean wave, the tail end of the Great Mississippi Revival Movement hit the town. The Second Coming was

not more than thirty days off and everyone knew the Beast de-
scribed in the Book of Revelations had surely come—it was Jack
Powderly in Chicago, with his anarchist talk of an eight-hour day.
Discreet and sober citizens went hog-wild under the frightful
brimstone rousements. Practically all mundane business fell to a
standstill. (Except of course at Q. Septimus Rawky's Racket Store,
where there was a rushing trade in white muslin and sateen resur-
rection robes, and in the tobacco factories and fertilizer plant—
where business would be business right up until the dawning of
Judgment Day.)

And then in August the Chinaman came.

Charlie Wooden, the greengrocer, was daydreaming in the doorway of his store when the crowning wonder of that singular summer passed by. With a loose and shuffling gait. With long
fingernails, slanted eyes, large strong prominent teeth, and a pigtail slipping down from under his second-hand brown derby.

"Saaay!" bleated the grocery man, rubbing his nearsighted eyes
and wrinkling his brow into a question mark.

Jack Mulkey, the barber, who had been shaving no less a personage than Mr. Tysander Warham, glimpsed the Thing over his
shoulder by way of a mirror and left his soap-bound victim in a
fresh spindrift of lather to run to the window. "My *Lord,* my
Lordy!—whatever kind of a man is that?" he gasped.

And thus came to Minktown the strange and delicate Wah Sing,
the alpha and incipience of her later large and flourishing laundry
business.

This enterprising Oriental workingman was no time-waster.
Soon he had rented from Cyrus T. Badger a small store building on
Firehouse Street with dirty windows full of dead flies. Although—
since his supply of American words was exceeding small, and as
he had not a compatriot in three hundred miles who might have
acted as interpreter; and as Mr. Badger never, never, under any
circumstances, told his business—it was always something of a
mystery, a Chinese puzzle, just how these two struck their
bargain. But the language of profit has its own peculiar power to
impart the general drift. And is not improbable that the secretive
Mr. Badger (who had just started his famous collection of the
choicest corner lots that were to turn him into such a wealthy

nabob later) had, during his trips to the Near East as a whirlwind salesman for the Warhams' tobacco company, got onto that curious bastard Esperanto called pidgin English.

Wah Sing's Chinese Laundry was soon a going concern; a ship well launched in a sea of suds. The laundryman did particular work and his prices were low. And after the town had taken a second glance at him, it decided that this tall, lean exotic was really a distinguished-looking fellow, if not handsome. By the time another spring had rolled around and Minktown had wriggled out of its red flannel "long handles," the Chinaman had been accepted as a necessary and integral thread in the garment of local cultural progress and cleanliness.

A real estate brochure of this period, composed by a versatile go-getter named W. T. Iserman, used Wah Sing's auspicious arrival in Minktown as an advertising peg. Printed in Johann Anders's Job Room on canary paper, it was suitably entitled: CAME A STRANGE AND YELLOW BIRD FROM FAR AWAY . . .

> It took, it seems, a foreigner from the other side of the world to see the vast possibilities of our City. Which, from a small "hayseed" hamlet of a mere 2,126 souls four years ago, can now boast a population (taking in the mill village, the settlement of Possum Level, and the darkey section) of 3,384 . . . another railroad, a bank, two hotels (the Claydon and the Turnipseed House), a Military Company, two Brass Bands (one white and one colored), a Market House, and now a LAUNDRY. . . . Let the Chinese Gentleman be an example to all of us to "Stay at Home and Keep on Sawing Wood!" To "Keep on Buying Minktown Mud!"

Oh, certainly the Chinaman had his few little early discouragements. At first he was as alone as though marooned on Juan Fernandez or the Galapagos Islands. But not for long. The laundryman's waiting days were, in a way, like those of the young lawyer who has just hung up his shingle and must possess his soul in patience and divide his glut of time between reading the Walterville *Athena* and *Harper's Monthly* behind a deskful of deep-looking tomes and galloping back and forth to the courthouse to convey an impression of busyness. Since Wah Sing had nothing to read but his one Chinese newspaper (many months old), most of the time he just looked out his now-spotlessly-clean window or prepared his scanty repasts of rice and tea.

And at first there was some hostility on the part of suspicious and ignorant elements. Even after he was approved and accepted as a public servant by the Best People. The small boys particularly—passing on their way to school or Sunday school—were not to be dissuaded from their pastime of baiting him with "Chinaman, Chinaman, eat more rats!" After which insult they would scamper away in great terror and glee: as though all hell's devils were on their heels. But the Chinaman had the patience of Job. Knew that in heaven's own good time whatever was his would come to greet him.

In the beginning, Wah Sing only blinked at this barbarity; he even tried to look amused. And could the boys but have read the look in his oblique and liquid, lonely eyes, it was all sweetness and light and wanting to be friends. But, to add zest to their sport, the boldest of these young citizens took to venturing inside his door and throwing mud or offal upon his spotless, sacred ironing board. At last the milk of long-suffering human kindness turned to blue acid; the worm turned with a howl and came after them a screeching celestial berserk with pigtail a-flying. And giving forth such a flow of invective in the unknown tongue as to fairly make the air sulphurous and their respective heads of hair stand endwise. All of which vastly sharpened the joy of their game.

Even in those early hard days, though, Wah Sing the Chinaman had much to smile over. Minktown was a land of plenty and here he would eventually find peace. He had come from a hard, competitive place where he'd had to wrestle for every grain of rice or cast-out vegetable from the gutter. In fond or detestable visions of his native village, he recalled the stinking slum; the foul green drinking water from the canal; the wild dogs and jackals digging up the dead; the one family bowl traveling around to their many mouths, young and old, sick and well . . . so that this crowded laundry room of his emerged from his dream as a gracious, spacious room in a palace, and he rich, and Minktown a haven little short of the ten spheres of Paradise.

In the beginning, people called him John Chinaman, or the Chink, and associated with him only for reasons purely commercial.

Farmers stared through the window.

"Sump'n I never 'spected to see, brother: a *man* a-ironin'! I always *heared* them Chiny people done everything bass-ackards. Reckon their *women*folks be the vigorous ones . . . the plowin', cuttin' them's wood and hay, doin' the horse-tradin' . . ."

Now and then the overbold ones, impelled by curiosity and a life anemic for drama—and wanting to tell about it to wife and kids around the supper table—would poke their hayseedy heads in at the door. They ventured in fearfully at first, like cattle coming to strange feed. Rarely risked a sparse bit of brushy conversation. As "Hot day, hain't it?" or "Got any drinking water, mister?" No word of which ever percolated through to his understanding.

He was humble and friendly, and you could see he'd been a poor hard-working guy all his life.

But Wah Sing was a man of high hopes and single purpose. Of firm fatalistic faith in his luck. And before a single patron had flitted across his threshold—a first cherished swallow in the sky of spring and a first triumphal nickel in the sock—he'd tacked up his schedule of

VELY FINE PRICES

Shit 5 cent
Undershit & drawirs 5 cent
Hankyfif 1 cent
Cuff & colar 2 cent

Which tariff had been laboriously copied under the midnight lamp with much reflective gnawing of pencil, from a model furnished him by the Sing Me Hong of Brooklyn which had taught him his trade and put the dragon claw of mortgage on his earnings for years to come.

He was deeply perplexed, though, when his long-awaited first customer *did* finally arrive. For after reading his prospectus, the man roared with laughter and ran away—forgetting to leave his bundle of soiled linen. Puzzled, Wah Sing shook his pigtail. Now what could be so funny about a simple business price list? he asked himself. In *his* country, prices were a serious business. These 'Melicans were sure queer ones.

And then the man came back, bringing several others with him. And they all read the sign and all guffawed together. But it somehow started business rolling. For a throng of these strange, happy people flowed in and out of his place now for a week. In the crowd he recognized several of the bad boys coming in to pore over his prices, as though they might now be an important part of their arithmetical studies. And these, too, began bringing him custom. But everybody must first go take a look at his advertisement and have their laugh.

Wah Sing's first welcome into the social life of the town came, though, from that multitude of mostly black citizens that passed his place of business on their way to and from the various work shifts of the tobacco factories.

From the first, the black people had seemed more interested in him than the white. Many stopped to peer in his window, and pretty soon the tobacco "stemmer" women got to coming in to take a look around. To spy out the land of Cathay. For they, too, took in washing when the factory laid them off, and were curious to see if he had any trade secrets or paraphernalia they didn't know about.

One October day at noon a large-bosomed, dimpled, and kind-hearted young black woman came in. Ostensibly on business, but tarrying for a friendly "chin-chin." Observing the big Chinaman, she had shrewdly guessed that he was womanless; and having no racial scruples whatsoever, reached certain conclusions and instigated open negotiations leading to a certain definite and desirable consequence.

At first she hinted and quibbled. "You got anything I ain't got, mister? . . ." But by the way he hung his head, by the vacant look on his face when he *did* look at you, she gathered that he wasn't "getting it." However, this particular lady was an enterprising and indomitable soul; one full of bounce and buxom valor. She saw that if she was going to arouse consumer interest she would have to talk frankly—and in his language. For a thoughtful minute the conversation bogged completely down. Then she seized old Opportunity by the horns. Putting more sparkle into her brown African eyes, she grinned ingratiatingly, leaned way over the counter and whispered huskily.

"You likee poontangee? You comee to my house tonight, huh?" ·

This thrust of sales talk galvanized a toothy smile, but Judie Odums's woman's intuition told her she was still missing the target a mile and that he didn't understand a word of what she was saying. Nevertheless, miracles do now and then happen; and the lonely Chinaman being more desperate for feminine company than she had ever dreamed, her sharp intent and his deep hungers suddenly came together like hammer and dynamite and he read at last the subtle ancient meaning in her eyes. He had heard the call of the hormones, and she could see he was really quite young and pulpy.

There was no one else about the place, so, having no more compunction, ethnic or moral, than she, her newfound lover drew her into his private nether Chinese bachelor's apartment. Jabbering, the while, in her ear something hot and foxy. Only this time, it was she who must intuit *his* breathless need.

Afterward, Judie Odums remembered that in her flusteration she had forgotten to collect. She hadn't meant to leave without reward—it then being between the panic of '84 and the boom of '89 and money very scarce among Minktown's lowly. But she philosophically concluded as how it was all right to now and then give a new customer a come-on sample.

It was none other than Mrs. Colonel Pescud, one of Minktown society's loveliest Presbyterian ladies, who introduced Wah Sing to the smart set.

Not, of course, that he was ever accepted socially. Heavens no. Only commercially. Though who knows (with his exotic looks and mysterious, magnetic personality, plus her beauty, *entrée* and know-how) but what she mightn't have given him, in some later decade, all possible social latitude.

It was in October, just as Wah Sing was getting settled, that Mrs. Colonel Pescud, back from one or another summer of spas and resorts, and strutting the latest bustle, was seen one day about the hour of high noon coming to halt before the Chinaman's house of purification.

Now, this distinguished social leader and lovely peroxide blond had, among her many other charming attributes, a large bump of curiosity. And so it befell that instead of bidding her coachman (who was dressed like a monkey in stovepipe hat and gloves of bright geranium red) deliver the bundle she had brought, the great lady herself, with an enthusiastic bounce of her silken, curvaceous rear, descended into Wah Sing's place of commerce and pervasive steam to see for herself, with her own lorgnon, what the inside of an opium den was really like. . . .

It is one of Colonel Pescud's least expensive dress shirts that she offers up for experimental purposes. So to the Chinaman's lean and catlike hands it goes to test his magic manipulations and prices current.

She studies him and his habitat as he studies her husband's *distingué* underpiece. He is certainly tall for a Chinaman, she thinks, contemplating his sensitive and variable features tautened over prominent bone. There are shelves halfway across the wall . . . boxed in like at the post office, and on the shelves are packages with laundry lists brushmarked in his kind of brush writing, odd as chicken tracks, in very black ink.

On another wall a Chinese calendar; a worn Chinese newspaper lies on the counter. How on earth can he make head or tail of it? and the air smells dried up and funny, but fascinating: kind of like heliotrope fried with garlic, though there is a lot of steaminess, too, from the pressing irons. . . .

Ai! she is a goddess, he is thinking, in Chinese. With real golden hair eighteen carats fine! Which has the splendid yellowness of the sacred lily, of the inside of a China squash, or medicine made from the galangal! Shades of my ancestors, how I adore this type— with the fat hips, cow's eyes, and large fine milk bags! . . .

She recalls Dykes Pfusch's telling at a party that when a Chinaman sprinkles the clothes for ironing he puts the water in his mouth and spews it on them. But she doesn't see him doing it. The fellow has fine large teeth. . . .

Mrs. Colonel Pescud gave detailed instructions how she wanted the shirt-tail job done, but all the time she was talking he kept his head ducked. His pigtail showing from under his tasseled silk bowl of a cap was carelessly coiled, and she wanted to take hold of its beautiful satiny blackness and show him how to fix it.

She didn't see any weird idols about, but she thought he had kind of a dangerous heathen eye.

Graciously he presented her with a ticket and pointed with pride and a flat, taloned finger to a legend he had lately added to the price list.

NO TICKEE NO WASHEE

"How perfectly delightful! What a scream!" And Mrs. Colonel Pescud could hardly wait to tell all about it around her dinner table.

In a few days, the lady's regal vehicle came again. And once again the wonderful princess, as fragrant as a rose, alighted herself to negotiate the business in hand. She had on a new dress of rich, ripe bishop's purple and a pair of little cut-glass *flacons d'essence* dangled on a long gold chain depending from her nice fat neck.

He grinned in recognition and laid aside his ironing.

. . . How firm and even his teeth are, she notes. And his delicately stained yellow fingers have such beautiful long fingernails!

. . . This time he is better dressed. Yes, he is real good-looking for a foreigner; and if I could dress him in a tuxedo or get him encased in a Carlovingian velvet jacket and sash and a cavalier's hat with a plume, or mount him on a charger like Napoleon or that bronze general of the Ming dynasty I saw in the Louvre, he might even be "dashing." That fresh-laundered orange mandarin coat he is wearing looks like real silk!

On the coat there was an interesting design—the symbolism of which was, of course, the deepest Greek to our good Presbyterian lady. It represented the Chinese good-luck phoenix: with the forepart of a goose, the hindquarters of a stag.

And there is that same baffling incensy odor. She takes another sniff. What *does* it smell like?

Florissa Pescud came a bit closer to him this time, and noted that he had a most pleasant personal aura and that her heart fluttered like a flag. There was a certain personal, indefinable, charm; a potent physical chemistry that was releasing warm and vivid curiosities as rowdily as little black imps of mischief rising from Pandora's box!

Also his gleaming hair was today done up somewhat differently. As if he'd read her thought about it. His crow-black queue—done in a sort of Psyche knot—had a most attractive glint.

But he hadn't done the shirt at all like she had told him.

. . . He noted again that she had fine fat hips. Now he was looking at her strangely out of those black slant eyes and she felt weak and deliciously dizzy.

La me! Can it be that odd, eluding fragrance is some kind of aphrodisiac? "Spanish fly" or something?—like Colonel Owsley had insisted on telling her about when he was in his cups the other night at the Foxes' and the talk got on breeding horses. It gave her a body blush to think of it. Why, Colonel Pescud, her own husband, would never think of discussing such a subject! Oh yes, he had appeal all right (no, not the colonel her husband—this Oriental boy). He *was* young—couldn't be over twenty-five. . . . She was conning him in a calculating mood.

. . . Muriel Sweet had said that Cytherée Warham—Mrs. Tysander Warham the fourth (who was Continental and had lived in Cairo, Egypt, and certainly ought to know if anyone did)—said that there was nothing like a Chinaman or a nigger they practically never did give out . . . for hours and hours. . . . Then she awoke with a start.

It was as though a rattlesnake had rattled in her path. A poor laundryman! And she a lady—so rich, so pure, so proud.

"My God, I must be going crazy! I must be careful. . . ."

But softly that night he came on slippered feet, past all the manifest barriers and decorums; past the bedroom of her old snoring husband-dragon; to the secret room of her dreams. In a trance she rose to meet him, as if by levitation.

Wah Sing never quite knew what happened. That the handsome pickup in his business thereafter was due largely to that visit from Colonel Pescud's talismanic shirt and large, fine lady, he never guessed. All he knew was that all of a sudden a drove of ladies of high degree descended upon him like so many whinnying mares and became his customers; and that after that he was set up as solid and snug as a rock in the lively current of the town's economic river.

For what the rich and fastidious Florissa Pescud did, all others of her set—those lesser elite—always strove to do as well.

In the wake of the ship came the gulls. Came ultrafine ladies in mauve and gold and garnet and green and their victorias, phaetons, gigs, and sporty traps and froufrou and flower scent. Came some with modest, shrinking-violet eyes. And some as bold as brass, more hussy than the rest, seeking to break down the fence of his privacy.

Where were the idols? (They all wanted to know.)

The opium pipe?

What did he eat and where and when did he sleep and do the washing? Some from crude country curiosity would have stridden right behind the scenes and into his purgation parlor.

Incessantly he ironed. By now Wah Sing had so much work on hand he was forced to get an assistant.

Yes, everything was going quite well with Wah Sing.

He never had "a Chinaman's chance," of course, of crashing the wealth-encrusted walls of Minktown's top social circle. Nevertheless, the fruit of the Chinaman's hands and sweat; the wispy steam of his tubs and his irons; and even his spittle, danced vicarious attendance upon their pleasures. And though he never knew it, his alter ego hopped in and out of several fine ladies' dreams.

And as for his solid self, did not his new helper Ah Ling prepare him fine cakes of green bean flour? and the first Minktown chickens ever martyred with fried noodles? And bean-jelly dumplings? And had not Wah Sing, the poor laundryman, recently put his mark to a paper up in the rich and formidable Mr. Cyrus T. Badger's lawyer's office that gave him title to the building he occupied? And did he not, after the reciting of all its wherefores and whereases—and to the whole town's amazement—plunk down twenty thousand dollars cash on the barrelhead? (Oh yes, a Committee of Citizens waited on Mr. Badger for selling business property to a foreigner; but he humphed and said "A Chinaman's money's money, ain't it?" Whereupon the committee closed up like a clam.)

But as there never was a son of Adam but had his pesky private problems, certainly there were a number of things the Chinaman could never figure out. Why was it, he asked himself and the heavens, that Large White Cow of the Morning never came any more? And why, oh why, when he went to visit with Little Midnight Flower on Sunday afternoons in their secondary shrine of love down in Blackbird Bottom, did her five blue black brothers always pick their teeth as one, and look at him so hard, and never say a word? He paid the woman twenty-five cents each visit, so didn't that make her *his* woman?

* * *

But now it is a Saturday evening in autumn. Something of the American bigness of advertising method, has been achieved by the Chinaman. With a bucket or two of good 'Melican house-paint, he and his helper have made the reception chamber as brightly blue as a robin's egg. A string of ting-a-ling bells has been added; to sing delicately with the breeze or be brushed into beautiful crashes of lingering dreamy tinkle at the touch of a hand.

Now, too, the customers can hear, behind the portiere, the orderly homelike ticking of a clock. But isn't that just like a Chinaman, people say, putting the clock where no one can see it?

And they have made yet another fine 'Melican innovation and refinement, though *this,* too, is a thing the General Public cannot see. The workroom—where the Chinese gentlemen bunk, dine, and on gala nights smoke a pill of the sociable poppy—has been industriously done in a nauseating brown.

Certainly it cannot be said that the master works less than his ox. Though surely now he is a man who will soon be very rich. Ah! then he may buy himself once in a while a little white rice liquor— or even a bottle of Sam Pen's Medical Brandy.

In a weedlot adjacent to the laundry the Reverend Noah Guntzel and his congregation were raising revival hymns.

The reverend specialized in Saturday-night preaching, when the poor working boobs had just drawn their pay. He knew just when and how to dangle before their bleary eyes the horrible retribution of that hot and bottomless hole-in-the-ground bound to follow ambitious living or doing any loving whatsoever without the sanction of clergy.

Reverend Guntzel—dishing out religion red-hot—spake with a wisdom and certitude acquired by a lifetime of constant conversance at the lip and ear of the Almighty. And when he had got the brains of his congregation well scrambled with wild and mournful singing, and sufficiently sodden in gore, he proceeded to take up a collection—purportedly for the heathen.

Wah Sing and his assistant toiler, Ah Ling, didn't know what that doleful, over-and-over singsong "Washed in the Blood" meant. Any washing other than the regular tub kind was beyond their ken and, insofar as they knew, God was still a Chinaman. They were working their overlong fingernails off trying to catch up with the weekend rush.

Long after the evangelical ecstasis broke up that night, and the
worshipers, washed and unwashed, had scattered, and that faithful guardian of the holy roundup, the Reverend Noah Guntzel, had
gone to the Claydon and was snoring away happy in the Lord that
he was richer by $17.63 for the evening's vineyard labors—the two
lone sons of Mongol still toiled away at the tubs. Their bony unbe-
lieving hands and the scrape of resistant alien fabric on fluted
metal making their own monotonous sloshy music.

That Sunday morning Mrs. Colonel Pescud remembered with a
sinking feeling that the colonel was leaving on the ten o'clock train
for Washington, at the special invitation of Congressman Swink,
and that his favorite senatorial-style collars were not yet packed,
were not, in fact, yet retrieved from the laundry. She thinks of
those distinguished, dignificatory "chokers" and of her lord-and-
master, that leading southern manufacturer and perennial expo-
nent of democracy, white supremacy, and cheap labor, of the
gauntlet of banquets he will have to run, as soon as President
Cleveland and Congress learn he is in the national capital, poor
dear. So she rousts out Sam the coachman and sends him off to
the Chinaman's, posthaste, riding the colonel's bay gelding.
Which simple domestic gesture is soon to set off a chain of reac-
tions that will riffle down, like dominoes, a whole series of hidden
and sensational phenomena and goings-on, and will send chills
and thrills through the town's backbone, and hold it by the ears in
gossipy thrall for many a year to come.

The Sunday-morning sun and the steaming dew were fresh and
fragrant upon the old brick sidewalk of Firehouse Street that
passed before the Chinese laundry.

Sam found the door not yet unlocked, and knocked upon it. Having no success—after rattling it and calling out—he put two
fingers to his mouth and gave a piercing whistle. Then shouted a
couple of "hey-o's" besides. Then he went around by the alley back
of the wash house to arouse the good-for-nothing, born-tired
Chinks. To let it be loudly known that the emissary and dispatch
rider of a very important personage and a very impatient military
man was without, and not to be trifled with by any low-lived rice
belly. And that his valuable time was of the essence.

But the haughty speech poised on Sam's glib tongue was never delivered. Getting no response to his importunations, he shoved open the back door and walked in: and the sight that met his eyes startled those orbs nearly out of his head. And also sent tremors of dread to his brain and caromed panic down his marrow, for mightn't he in some way get blamed for it? For the two dead men. For the horror—fresh and grisly.

When Sam returned to Mrs. Colonel Pescud's presence, he was weak as water, hadn't the package she'd sent him for, and his neat white teeth were all in a chatter.

All he had fetched was a hair-raising story that he couldn't half-way tell and which was in no way useful to her exigency; so the colonel's lady stood wringing her hands trying to think what to do next. She went and awoke that worthy warrior. Tore him rudely from a sweet and double-jointed dream of riding beside General Stonewall Jackson at the Battle of Manassas, and of being received by the young and beautiful wife of a South American ambassador in the City of Magnificent Distances From His Own Wife. Which in turn caused him, impulsive man and capable executive that he was, to reach for paper and pen and work an order to Captain Lemuel Rambo, Minktown's Chief of Police, to proceed "im-*me*jetly" to the scene of the crime. After which he shook his handsome head sagaciously.

"You never know what's in a bean patch," quoth he, borrowing one of Mr. Jefferson Warham's famous saws.

There was a considerable difference of opinion about the murder. For murder it clearly and incontrovertibly was. Messy and premeditated, too; with the bodies of both coolie-American businessmen barbarously mutilated at the hands of a person or persons unknown and their neck veins slit. And they were, when found, entirely unclothed. Which latter fact, though it threw no light on the crime or criminal, *did* clear up that oft-speculated-upon mystery: when did they do their washing? And seemed to demonstrate, beyond a reasonable doubt, that Sing and Ling had been doing their tub work at night and in the nude.

Here was a side angle vigorously dwelt upon by the *Minktown Advocate*. Its astute young editor-reporter, Mr. Sherman Josephburg and other amateur sleuths thought they saw in the victims' nakedness proof of some sinister though impalpable, lurking import; too deep, as yet, to be exactly defined, but which would in time—any moment now—burst and burgeon into the Grand Solution. But outside of proving that washing is hot business, this guess continued to remain profoundly problematical. Chief Rambo, however, clung tenaciously as a leech to his original starting point that since the Negro Sam had discovered the knock-off, he must, per se, be the guilty party. Though in so doing, he still risked the lightning bolt of that great man, Colonel Pescud.

The police department—all three of it—wanting to make a name for itself and wanting to believe the worst of any and all "furriners"—hugged to its broad and honest bosom Theory No. 2: the belief that the yellow man had been raping a white woman, and her menfolks, catching them in the act and in *déshabillé*, had obeyed the "unwritten law"—the chivalrous southern pattern of honor—and rightfully taken vengeance.

However, the killer had used a peculiar cordage to bind his prey. A small, but stout, silken string that was a plait of red and black. Even detective Lem had to admit, "No, I don't b'lieve I ever *have* knowed of any one stranglin' a man with strings. And snarlin' up his arms and legs with 'em to boot." And moreover, as though to purposely complicate and multiply the poor policemen's problem, the victims' tongues had been removed.

Next above the nebular horizon rose a lovelife hypothesis. Some mean woman. Jealousy. *Cherchez la femme.* . . .

The police called in for questioning everybody who had ever done business or had the slightest intercourse with the Chinaman or his helper. Except, of course, those supergenteel and impeccable ladies from the refined and upper air of McLauchlen's Hill. Heaven forbid that the Minktown Police Department should ever so far forget itself as to subject such snow-pure souls to such a harassing and low-life ordeal!

The police drew their dragnet very thoroughly—almost down to the old battle-scarred black-and-white tomcat that nightly visited the Pigtail Alley garbage pile, to dine *à la Chinois*. And in it they landed poor Judie Odums, the late Wah Sing's Dark Cherry Blossom and ebony flower of delight.

Standing at the stern white bar of justice, accused—if nothing more—of criminal conversation with a man, the dusky courtesan easily confessed to having been in the laundryman's back bedroom and his bed. Shockingly it came to light that the laundry had been a place of improbity as well as purification; a veritable snake den, where black and yellow serpents entwined in both Occidental and Oriental wickedness and hit the pipe. But Judie's personal alibi for the night of the murder was airtight.

So then they started in to incriminate her five very big and very burly brothers—who all had large white eyeballs and were of a shade of black like unto the shimmer of new-mined coal.

Ah, now at long last, soliloquized Chief Lemuel Rambo—a new light breaking in his dark gray matter—we are on the right track and getting somewhere! The situation was made to order: a sister seduced, a houseful of no'count, ruffian, grizzly-bear brothers to right the wrong. To avenge *her*—and to rob *him*.

Vigilantly he rounded them up, all five. Here were precisely the proper vehicles for the chief's peculiar talents and previous, preconceived postulation. He would now pin the crime where it had all along belonged—on a nigger. Preferably, several. Here, he nimbly rationalized, were involved brute strength and kinship to the ape, inferior self-control, false notions about a low-down nigger wench's "honor"; his correlation of which would make him famous and get his picture in all the papers. And oh yes, one of them had a police record! For being caught in a game of craps.

But when the Odums boys retained Lawyer Fogg as counsel, he made Mr. Rambo look like a monkey. Made him admit the improbability of these one-hundred-percent Ethiopians leaving their respects in Chinese writing. "Remember those several small bangles attached to those fancy cords?" Lawyer Fogg reminded him. "With Chinese signs and signatures?"

Though the doer or doers of the horrid deed were never apprehended, the final deductions reached by Mr. Fogg and accepted by the court were probably correct.

"Our respected Chinese citizens," said the cosmopolitan Mr. Fogg, "may have been ex-members of an opium-smuggling ring. Gentlemen, this tragedy may well be one of those tong murders. . . . A tong is a kind of Chinese secret society. Something on the order of our Ku Klux Klan."

Everybody perked up at that, listened for some kind of a pin to drop.

"These Oriental killers were always very careful not to leave any clues. They probably had their feet tied up in something soft, like grass, so as not to make any noise or tracks."

The chief, however, thought it funny that no one had *seen* such a conspicuous and peculiar foreigner wearing only a bunch of grass on his feet "slinkin' around. Gettin' off the train, or hangin' around the fruit stands and pool parlors. I reckon these here tong fellers can be seed, can't they? Same as other humans?"

"Oh yes," said Mr. Fogg. "They were most likely in disguise. On crutches, perhaps, so that they would pass for cripples. Or blacked up like darkies, wearing kinky wigs. Maybe even dressed as old ladies with sunbonnets, who knows? And then, in the dead of night, they stealthily stalked the doomed and undone men and did their bloody work fast and well. These criminals were probably very strong as well as cunning. . . . *Sing and Ling never knew what happened.*"

Lawyer Fogg was convincing. His auditors could feel the drama as though it were all happening before their eyes, in a "ten-twenty-and-thirty" melodrama on the stage in Stoeger's Hall. The sons-of-bitches entering the room . . . tiptoeing villainously about in their muffled footgear with their hands full of tongs and tools of murder, and the strangling strings . . . the gong on the old clock dragging and wheezing getting ready to strike . . . Oh it was a thriller! *Count of Monte Cristo*-stuff: swift-moving, breathless and tight with suspense.

"You mean, Lawyer," said Mr. Rambo, "that the way them tongsters kilt our Chinks is the way they alluz kills 'em? Cuts their throats, drowns 'em, and ties 'em with them little strings and fancy fangles?"

And so the Chinese Laundry case was closed.

To be sure, they were no ordinary Chinese laundrymen.

Neither was Minktown any ordinary town in those days.

Sherman Josephburg, on the *Minktown Advocate*, summed it up editorially thus: "In all towns, and in our fair Minktown no less— do not all blocks, buildings, and alleyways harbor wonders, strangeness, and secrets? Yes. Endings to far-off beginnings [there without a doubt he meant the untimely ending of the local laundry] and beginnings born to ripple, boom, or break like bubbles on a foreign shore."

Some say Sherm was also thinking of Jefferson Warham's to-bacco business. How the leaf was manufactured in Minktown and shipped to all the foreign shores for smoking.

(Sherm kept a copy of Walt Whitman's awful book *Leaves of Grass* in his desk. But he wasn't fired, for that was before anybody else in Warham had ever heard of Whitman. Or his book.)

Minktown wiped its eye. The mysterious citizen that nobody really knew had washed-and-ironed his way into its tender, sentimental heart. And yet that warm heart chilled to marble and its tenderness grew tough as rhinocerous hide when it came to donating six feet of ground for his burial.

Among Minktown's several modern improvements was a public cemetery—Cedardale—of which it was justly proud. And as much as Minktown cherished her First Chinaman, she had no intention of interring him and his employee in this sacred municipalized ground. Nup, nixey, no indeedy—they positively could not count their daisy roots from there, said Mayor Dismukes and the aldermen in so many words. Indeed, they were in a tough quandary as to *where* to deposit them.

At the first intimation of the unpleasant, polite society had hurriedly lost all interest in its one-time protegé and washed its un-calloused, lily-white hands of the matter. Some of the Chinaman's colored acquaintances, however, offered to plant him in the old slave burying ground out at Branchtown, where they then buried; but the Law again stepped in and said no. He wasn't exactly a white man but he was nearer white than black, and if you started burying dead white with black, the live black might start pushing to get on a level, and, after all, you wouldn't want a dead nigger lying out there by your beloved dead daughter, would you?

Oh, it was quite a problem. And certainly no good churchman wanted a pagan buried in his private Christian burying ground. Who knew but what there might be some mixup at the Last Day and the souls and bones of all be snatched up and thrown indiscriminately into hell or the heavenly rest together?

And just imagine, if you will, what might be the puzzlement and rage of a Colonel Ashley Rutherford or other good risen planter, counting his good old risen darkies and finding among them a Chinaman!

Then there was the doctors' college at Temple Hill. Always as hungry for cadavers as an ogre or ogress or *loup-garou*. But when it tried to get the Chinamen, to be on the safe side, Lawyer Fogg, who was also the town attorney, looked up the law and it specified "executed criminals." Henry Clay Brassbone, a member of the town council (who was a Temple Hill alumnus) said, Oh well, why make an issue of such a trivial detail? After all, a Chinaman is nothing but a foreigner and a heathen and a foreigner's nothing but a criminal but—Oh well, to be on the safe side . . .

And then the vexing question was suddenly settled by the large-hearted and unprejudiced farmer Willie Gare's coming forward and offering them sanctuary and a bury-hold out on his farm. Whereat the carpenter Jass Cates, contracting the contagious malady of charity, and having on hand a surplus of locust planks, constructed and contributed two plain, but good tight boxes at half-price. And Colonel Eugene Owsley—always a man of ideas and never one to shirk when any civic enterprise was afoot—was moved to contribute shrouds. The idea came to him, as his best ones often did, in the middle of the night. He had the details worked out down to the last fidfad . . . they must be of the finest genuwine luteolous silk—the shade of a jonquil—he would telegraph Richmond in the morning to ship the material direct by hurry-up express . . . and oh yes he thought it would be nice to have a little yellow flag to plant on the grave (Mr. Harper Yarbro, the undertaker and cabinetmaker, who was taking care of the corpses, was making a stick for *that*) and maybe a little procession, which he would lead personally on his horse Dixie.

And so they were at last laid away in an old cabbage patch overgrown with sheep dock and ragweed, out west of town. Young Preacher Luther Riley (suspected of having more than one hole in his theology, and who was said by some to have once been a Quaker) offered to officiate.

Mr. Badger, that rugged and rapacious businessman who never missed a business chance, smiled a sneering smile at all this folderol over a couple of dead Chinese. And under the momentum of his resistless craft and greed, went to work to gobble up Pigtail Alley—together with its bloody legendry, its runic ratty recollections—and to reacquire, in the court of chancery, the laundry building for a third of the robber's price he had sold it for.

*   *   *

But even under the green grass there was to be no rest for Wah Sing. Nor for Ah Ling, his helper. For thirty years later there came another son of Cathay—one Chung Tung—to take up where the Messrs. Sing and Ling had long ago left off. And on hearing of his countrymen's sad snuffing-out, one of the first things he did, after getting his washboards up and operating, was to have them dug up and shipped back to the Flowery Kingdom. Under the primordial Eastern belief that, had the living failed the dead in his sacred duty, not only would their spirits have been doomed to wander, troubled and without rest, through all the ages and levels of eternity, but he himself would have become an outcast devil.

The expense was borne by the Restless Bones Society (the Sue Yep Kong Shaw), in New York City. Which sent its special representative, a withered but stiff-hearted little old man with cat eyes, down to Minktown. Napoleon Sparrow, the jitney man, drove him out to the old Gare homeplace, where he set up a little tent in a clump of bushes near the grave for his peculiar work.

First, in the presence of the exhumed dead, he burned the gold and silver joss paper—in the form of ingots and coins—with apologies for its not having been done earlier. (Buddha only knew what these two had been using for money in the spirit world all this time!) Then he peeled off the sticky silk bags that had once been yellow and cut away the dessicated flesh from their bones; and whatsoever he might, by prayer and imprecation, of the pagan 'Melican burial ritual. And boiled the bones and laid them out in the summer sunlight. On newspapers. On news items about Peruna and Tanlac and ladies' night at the Warham Kiwanis Club. And Lew Dockstader's coming Minstrel and the bargains in ratiné and georgette crepe and boys' caps at the Q. S. Rawky Department Store. Concerning the sinking of the *Lusitania* and the rise of "war baby" stocks, the Warham Chamber of Commerce, President Wilson's second marriage and the building of the O'Lannigan Hotel. . . . And packed them for shipment in two very special metal boxes.

The local boys had buried the Chinaman's stretch of red matting with him, thinking it some kind of a prayer rug. And now the old man smiled a small shadowy cat-smile at finding this unholy furniture extant in the coffin of yellow locust. The old sage (knowing all the known history of them—and maybe more . . .) knew this for a poppy-smoker's mat . . . how they loved to get prone, to wallow on the dreaming-floor. The old man thought: What matter now? What does it matter what they smoked or what they dreamt? Or whether it was five minutes to midnight or seventeen minutes past three when their hearts ceased to beat and enliven these little heaps of bones?

The metal boxes were decorated all over in lacquer: with curious charms and emblems of ghosts, spirits, and demonic powers. Prominent among which was the Fum, or good-luck phoenix: which has the forepart of a goose, the hindquarters of a stag, the neck of a snake, the tail of a fish, the forehead of a fowl, the down of a duck, the marks of a dragon, the back of a tortoise, the face of a swallow, the beak of a cock, is about six cubits high, and perches only on the woo-tung tree.

The old man prayed. And hoped for them some harbor of rest and peace after the storms of life.

Sunday School
at the Fifth Avenue Presbyterian Church

Johnny Anders was on his way to Sunday School. He always took the longest route for getting there, and was now dawdling along on Kehoe Street, avoiding the cracks in the long boards of the sidewalk and mumbling morosely to himself:

> Step on a crack
> Break your mother's back.

It was a lovely, fresh, dewy spring morning; and, feeling overwhelmed by life's beauty and wonder (and feeling like a wild young deer being shooed into an ambush), Johnny longed for the enchantment and freedom of the woods. He hated Sunday school and despised everybody connected with it. His day was being wretchedly wasted, going to that old jailhouse. No telling what he was missing. In the thick pine woods where the crows roosted, he knew where there was a wren's nest in a horse's skull . . . and just the day before he'd seen a great blue heron wading in Farmer Glenn's pond.

But his strict Scotch-Presbyterian mother thought there was only one place for her son to be on a Sunday morning and that was at the Fifth Avenue Presbyterian Church. At least he didn't have to wear that darned old big Scotch-plaid butterfly neckpiece any more, that his mother used to tie on him after scrubbing hard behind his ears and slicking his hair with water. And here he kicked a rock out of his path in vicarious revenge.

Then suddenly there dawned upon him a delightful whiff of perfume. And looking up, he saw beyond a low wall, in carpenter Clark's yard, the most beautiful cherry tree. It was ablaze with fragrant blossom, the bees humming and ravishing its bloom with velvet touch. And a warbler was singing, singing and darting out after sawflies. This glorious apparition of April loveliness thrilled the boy. Blew through him like a sharp wind. He would ever afterward think of the thoroughfare he was on as Cherry Tree Street, though officially it was named for a dead politician.

And now passing Mr. May's house on that same street, he remembered with delight that time when he was very young and riding by here with his mother and father and Dan, their sorrel driving horse snorted and shied so bad the surrey almost tipped over. For there beside the road was a short little man with long mustaches and big brass earrings, and with him a big shaggy moth-eaten-looking bear—a dancing bear! The little man had taken off his raggedy hat and bowed. Then jabbed the bear to make him dance around and around a long stout pole he held in his paws. That bear was sure funny, and he had wanted to jump out and stay watching him all day; but his mother had caught him by the jacket and told him to sit down. And Papa had had all he could do to keep Dan from running away. But he had squirmed up to take one last look out the little isinglass window in the back curtain. He had always hoped to see that bear again, but never had. Now a picture of a circus clown—that funny one in John Robinson's Circus—drifted into his daydream. And then he thought of Anna the Circus Girl and was glad Mr. Pulaski had settled down in Minktown.

Anna had such a foreign, out-of-this-world look. She never braided her long golden hair (that made him think of a princess in a fairy tale) back in tight ugly pigtails like the other girls did, with a crooked part in the back. She wore a shining band around *her* beautiful hair; and a bright red dress printed with queer little flowers, and high-button kid shoes. He wondered where Anna was this morning. At the livery stable? Or going with her father to the Catholic Church? If she was going to his Sunday school, it wouldn't be so bad there.

He looked along the tree-lined street. The Fletzer twins Tom and Fred were ahead of him. They were all scrubbed up, too—with their Sunday suits pressed shiny, and wearing their new shoes hurting their big feet. Tom turned around and whistled for him to catch up.

When they got to the church, they joined a lot of other boys standing on the sidewalk outside the Sunday-school-room door. The boys always joshed each other and bragged a lot and made bantering remarks to the cuties who passed; and some of the older ones—like Cullen Mathis and Dutch Pace, with fuzz and pimples on their faces and gosling voices—made lewd male speculations as the girls orbited out of earshot. But mainly they were waiting to see Mr. McLauchlen, the millionaire, arrive and alight. (The Negro sexton Joe was waiting, too, as he timed the ringing of the take-in bell by Mr. McLauchlen's arrival.)

The top moment of drama was when, with a smart slap of hoofs, the big victoria came rolling around the corner, drawn by the fine matched bay horses with docked tails and their glistening necks reined up so short that the veins stood out and they were forced to take short prancing steps. There was a proud, fat black driver in a high hat and livery sitting up on a high seat in front. The showy brass accoutrements on the shining black harness were all a-jingle, and the horses held their stumpy tails so high Johnny guessed they'd had a shot of ginger to make them hold them up that way. And Mr. Magnus McLauchlen was sitting back in the cushions large and lordly beside his little sickly looking mouse of a wife.

As he stepped briskly out of the carriage and handed out his lady—dressed in fine lavender silk—the take-in bell was ringing loudly and the more timid of the boys went on in the doorway. But Johnny waited with the others to see all the show. To be beamed on, but sternly, by the famous tobacco, cottonmill, and fertilizer magnate; and to watch the royal pair go up the granite steps. The great one had a wide behind that wobbled as he walked, but a back as straight as a ramrod; and his weak little wife clung desperately to him and his enormous vitality.

Inside, it took quite a little time for things to get settled. Everybody was waiting for Mr. McLauchlen's grand entry, as he was the ruling elder of the church and the head man of the Sunday school. First (as his wife sank into a seat on the long bench at the back wall) he went along to where the very dressed-up and sweet-smelling "society folk" of Swelldoodle Hill were sitting—shaking hands all around and stopping to chat a moment with his favorite ladies, who were always very excited and doing a lot of chattering, giggling, and toying with their smelling bottles hanging from their necks on little gold chains, as the millionaire, who smelled like lilac and had a huge diamond-horseshoe stickpin in his big fat purple cravat, came their way. It made them nervous because he owned so many factories and mills. (And he owned the church too, thought Johnny Anders, soaking up the scene like a sponge and remembering what Papa said.) Dear Mr. McLauchlen was so interesting, and *so* strong and good-looking, and he had a sickly wife who didn't look like she'd last much longer, and—well, if God did see fit to take her up to Heaven . . . there was always a chance . . . one never could tell.

Mr. McLauchlen was a hard man, and there was one thing these ladies dreaded, and that was his hard handshakes. When he shook hands with you, it was something to remember, for he had a grip hard enough to wring a chicken's neck.

There were also several men that Mr. McLauchlen specially greeted before he started up the business of God and Jesus. They were old dry, stern, ugly men, but they owned a lot of the town.

And there were three or four younger men who smollicked around or tried to stop Mr. McLauchlen to bleat him a word. They reminded Johnny Anders of sheep, the way their faces looked and the way they followed him so meekly. (When he mentioned it to Papa at home, he said these were fellows who wrote down the money matters at Mr. McLauchlen's different outfits. Bookkeepers—but Papa had funny names for bookkeepers, such as book-juggling-billy-ho's or assetainers-of-the-assets. And Papa said if they didn't go to Sunday school and kowtow around like they did, Mr. McLauchlen might drive them out of their bookkeeper pens to starve.)

When Mr. McLauchlen finally got up on the platform, with all faces turned his way like sunflowers to the sun, he tinkled a little bell up on the Bible stand with the flat of his big impatient hand— that meant "Turn off the talking!" and everything got so hushed Johnny could hear a robin singing out in the alley. Then Mr. McLauchlen said: "We will now sing Number Fifty-seven—'Stand Up, Stand Up for Jesus' "—and everybody stood up like he said and shattered the silence into smithereens. Then Mr. McLauchlen said, "We will now have a reading of the minutes," and took his seat and crossed his black broadcloth legs and put a wise and fiercely sanctified look on his face. Then Mr. Ezekiel R. Hammer—a burly, hayseed-looking kind of a man—who was the head of the Building and Loan Company weekdays, but was Sunday-school treasurer and bookkeeper on Sunday, would stand up and read in a harsh growly voice from a long black book all about what was said, done, sung, and collected last Sunday.

It was then that Mr. McLauchlen would make another lecture (with a map on the wall and a pointing stick) about his latest trip to Egypt and the Holy Land. . . .

When the others stood up, Johnny stood up too. But he never sang—just looked around at the singing others, his thoughts fluctuating between the dreary and the dreamy. He was wondering What Made the Rich So Religious and Rambunctious? and Why Did the Heavenly Father Make Some People So Poor and Others So Super-rich and Snorty? He had noticed that if any of those cottonmill women from Erdmannton, Ruby Mill Bottom, or Shit Creek, with their shabby shawls and pale sorrows, chanced to sit down near that bon-ton crowd, they would stare at them through their funny spectickles-with-handles as if they were some kind of bugs.

Now Papa was an outspoken man; and in the bosom of his family and to Mother's horror and the flouting of her ingrained religious convictions, he sometimes irreverently referred to the great Mr. McLauchlen as the King Pin and Angel Gabriel of the Fifth Avenue Presbyterian Church. *He* rarely went to church (only now and then when he was trying to make up to Mother about something); but on Sunday mornings, after a lot of cheerful singing in the bathroom, he would don his dignified tailor-made Prince Albert suit, put on his high beaver hat that he called his "topper," slide his walking cane out of the front hall hatrack and hie him away to Vann's Drugstore. Evidently Mother didn't mind too much, though; knowing that he would be collecting a lot of interesting town news there.

Now Johnny was reflecting on all those silly and poodely old men—the big "pillars of the church"—whose faces had been pounded, carved, and intagliated for always upon his senses. Their names he mostly knew, from hearing his mother describe them to his father at the Sunday-dinner table. Mr. Kerrigan, with a long bushy beard and a glint of black hair about his cheekbones, who owned the iron foundry. Mr. Rawky, who ran the racket store (he had been there with his mother to buy dress goods, but he couldn't see why it was called a racket store—there weren't any tennis rackets and no one was making any big noise there). Mr. Peyton, the tax collector—who smiled and laughed like a loon when Mr. McLauchlen came around handshaking, but frowned and looked mad if any of the kids asked him questions. . . . Mother always told Papa about church: who-all were there; what the leading who-alls had on; and lastly, what the preacher preached about. And then he would tell *her* what leading citizens—lawyers, doctors, saloon proprietors—were at Vann's Drugstore. What-all was said; what kind of cigars they smoked; and who had on what latest New York thing in men's haberdashery: jim-swingers, cutaways, or pepper-and-salt suits. Also the financial news: what the tobacco Warhams were up to on the New York stock market; how much business International Fertilizer (that had been started in Minktown by Silas Crenshaw and Mr. McLauchlen) was doing, and so on. One noon he heard Papa telling Mother that Mr. Ezekiel Hammer had stolen everything in the Building and Loan, but would probably get off light on account of his being the brother of Colonel Edwin Speight Hammer, the banker; and Colonel Hammer being the son-in-law of Mr. McLauchlen. "That old blowhard ignoramus Zeke Hammer," Papa called him. And after that, Johnny noticed, Mr. E. R. Hammer didn't come to the Presbyterian Sunday school any more. One of the Sheep young men, or the tall, baldheaded, lady-shy bachelor, Mr. T. B. Hotchkiss, who whistled through his teeth when he prayed and who was Mr. McLauchlen's head man at his bag factory, now read from the long black book.

After a couple more sings to liven things up and get everybody in the mood of Sunday-morning righteousness, the main gathering splintered up into classes and scattered off to the different classrooms.

Johnny was now in Mrs. Euphemia Buckner's boys' class, and she was droning away in great certitude and solemnity, telling all about God and Heaven and Hell and how the Loving Heavenly Father sent unbaptized babies there. And what was going to happen to the boy who doubted even one word in the Bible or Catechism. She looked at Johnny, and Johnny knew that the widow Buckner meant him; for ever since he had dared to ask her Who made God? (and she had flared up angrily, her gray eyes glowing with detestation, and declined to come out with any answer but a snort) she had had it in for him. If she was always talking about Getting Right With God, oughtn't he to find out about somebody he was supposed to get chummy with? And since she had never been anywhere nor got beyond the fifth grade in school—and was only a clerk in Rawkey's Racket Store—how had she got so wise about everything in Heaven and on Earth? Oh the widow was a crusty character—except when Mr. McLauchlen came around, when she suddenly got as sweet as pie. In a way, Johnny felt sorry for her. She'd had a hard life and you could see she wasn't exactly satisfied to be a "bride of Christ." One of the older boys had said that p'raps all the old hen needed was a rooster. . . .

But still Johnny took little interest in what she said, and he often went off into dreaming. One thing that set him off to seeing airy pictures—that kindled his imagination—was a bird in one of the stained-glass windows. It was the loveliest white dove on a bright blue background, and represented the Holy Spirit, the widow Buckner had once explained. Every time he looked at it his spirit flew off to the far-off deep woods; went hiding in that hollow tree on that cool sweet place on the creek where willows dipped over the water and elderberries grew and you could hear doves cooing from the pines.

One of the Sunday-school scenes floating back to him was that day when, as a small tyke, he had won a Bible for reciting the shorter Catechism. It had a gold topping and a black leather back that had a good doggy smell. To win a Bible that way, you had to go up on the platform. Mr. Magnus McLauchlen asked the questions and you said the answers your mother had made you learn. He'd felt just like a parrot being trained to say a lot of funny nonsense.

Then he got to remembering his earliest induction into the fold of Presbyterian goodness—right over there beyond that closed sliding door—in the infant class. After the first song was sung out in the Big Room, that sliding door had been shut to keep the kids from hearing what the grownups were saying and singsonging back and forth all together so solemn out there in the Big Room, like katydids. With Mr. McLauchlen, the main katydid, standing up on the platform leading the racket. Then he had heard an interesting swishing sound. (Thinking back on it now from a big boy's viewpoint, it was a sound like that big blue heron made flying up out of the marsh.) It was Miss Lizzie Mulhouse, a lady with a face like a horse and a big behind, rolling Jesus down. All the rest of the week Jesus stayed rolled up in His white sheet.

It was always stuffy in there, and some of the kids were always bawling. Some bad kid would be making bad smells; and there was another one that pulled a little girl's hair every time they sang "Jesus Loves Me."

Painted on the ceiling were young angels flying around with no pants on; nothing but a little strip of ribbon where their monkey-doodles were.

Miss Allie Hannigan, the old-maid lady with the long nose, was the one who told the infants all that stuff about devils. Devils had hoofs and horns and tails and pitchforks, she told them. Miss Allie looked like a crow on account of her long beak, and while she was telling about the devils, Johnny was also listening with one ear to the distant seashell katydid roaring out there in the Big Room. You could see Miss Allie was scared spitless of those devils by the way she talked about them; and the way the whites of her eyes showed. He understood that devils' wings were skinny with hooks on 'em like bats' wings, and not feathery like angels' and white leghorn chickens'.

He had asked Miss Allie if she'd ever seen any devils. Her red hair bristled and her catlike green eyes gleamed in her pale bloodless face. She said it took spiritual eyes to see devils. Said only the pure-in-heart could see the glory of the Lord and his handiworks. But Saint Paul and Saint Stephen had seen devils, plenty of them. Miss Allie was probably the reason, thought Johnny, why he had always sort of liked devils. Anyway, he respected them. They must be pretty tough hombres, and know their stuff, to have sassed the Lord so long and gotten away with it.

That poor old lonely spinster loved to tell the little boys and girls her dark and doleful fantasies. She lived in a vale of gloom and loved to dazzle their little noodles and piously transfer to them her fears and obstinate credulity. It was she who told those young tykes about the dead people stepping out from their graveyard bury holes. He knew, even as a child, that it wasn't so; that people like Miss Allie were leaning on weeds and reeds. But he liked to listen to any kind of a fairytale. The Great Gruesome Resurrectum Day tale caught his imagination and got him quite excited inside. What a day! It was something to give you bad dreams at night. A wild-eyed angel-bird way up in the sky would begin blowing a big long horn and thousands and millions of dead people who hadn't had time to pull themselves together or wash their gray bony faces, or even comb their sloppy hair, went flapping about like crows, like chickens just let out of a coop, like big Carolina buzzards. Up from the graveyards they rose—all the graveyards looking like ant heaps with the winged ants coming out of the ground in spring—only the ants were people. Up from the ocean too—for a lot of dead people were in the ocean. Some of them had been sunk in the mud ten miles down for a thousand years and had turned to mud, but that didn't matter one bit. . . . A great big old three-headed God, as tall as a poplar tree and with a big gold sword as long as a telephone pole lying cross his lap, was r'ared back on a huge Golden Throne as high as a hotel; with angels picking harps and playing on juice-harps all around him. And so on. . . .

Funny, Johnny discovered, but everybody in the Sunday school had a special smell. (Maybe everybody did all the time, only in Sunday school you had more smelling time.) Miss Allie had smelled like a pickle barrel; Mr. McLauchlen was perfumy like lilac, and you could notice it five feet away. You could catch a whiff of pine on clean, neat Mr. Gilligan, from the Gilligan Lumberyard, and poor frumpy Miss Mulhouse reeked of a washtub. The tall, bald, sleek Mr. T. B. Hotchkiss was flavored with the slight incense of a billy goat; Mr. Kerrigan's smell was more like a rusty iron pipe; Mr. McTurf, the old Pennsylvania Scotchman who, in the summer, came down to distill tree extracts in the woods, had a fragrance of witch hazel mixed with pipe tobacco; Miss Tonkerson made him think of wet chicken feathers and Mr. Septimus Rawky of weak tea. Most of the Sunday-school ladies smelled like good homemade bread with perfume sprinkled over it. He liked to sniff the dressed-up little society girls; they were sweet as honey and all-day suckers. That little Debbie Winbrook now, with her dark red hair and gray blue eyes the color of his mother's iris flowers—she was so dainty she reminded him of the little satin bags of sachet his mother kept in her dresser drawer. But she turned up her pretty little nose if any of the boys in his class spoke to her.

But aw, what the dadslapped-dingbang-tarnal-boggered-walleyed dickens did it matter, thought Johnny, remembering some-thing of an old Irish sot's long string of picturesque ejaculation he had heard leaning out the window of his father's printing office over Caudle's Big Nine Bar. Now what *I* like is the smell of good earthy things, like burning leaves in the fall; the sun hot on my Irish setter Sut's hair when we rest together in the woods, old Sut leaning heavy against me. And he liked the smell of cow barns too and horses wet from the rain.

There was one thing, though, that Johnny *did* like about Sunday school. The last thing, just before the boys' class was dismissed, one of the teachers would hand out "golden text" cards. They had pretty colored pictures on them of the whale swallowing Jonah; of Abraham about to cut his little boy's throat; of Queen Jezebel being thrown out of a window for some dogs to eat; of Queen Esther watching the hanging of bad old Haman; and of Absalom hanging in an oak tree by his hair with his mule running off . . . Johnny had a collection of these cards and kept them in his sacred shoebox, along with his Confederate money and his tobacco tags.

As soon as he got his cards, Johnny Anders got ready to make his getaway. As fast as he could, he ducked out around the corner of Garfield Street and without saying pea-turkey to anybody, and yanking off his collar as he ran, he skedaddled like a rabbit till he was winded.

The Livery Stable

When Michael Pulaski made his impetuous vow to abandon circus life for the sake of his daughter Anna, he assumed that the Mother of God would be satisfied if he went into any kind of a settled, honorable business—such as groceries, a candy store, or even maybe a saloon. The chances were that She wasn't overly interested in livestock anyway. But as he loved to live around horses, the dream of having a horse hotel and livery rigs—with several head of bushtails, dobbins, and pert ponies—had spontaneously taken root in his mind and grown like a mushroom.

At first both he and his daughter Anna had been like fish out of water in Minktown. They had taken quarters at the Turnipseed House; and when Anna contemplated their trunks and boxes standing in the bare little rooms, a wave of frustration and homesickness overwhelmed her, that was almost as awful as when the *Jacobus* had run off with her before the wind. She felt as though a sea wave had tossed her up on a desert isle. Oh how could she ever get used to living without the crowds, the band, the train travel from town to town (with the elephants pushing the cages on board with their heads), and her friends the animals and troupers, and most of all without Uncle Toby?

She buried her face in Papa's vest, and he hugged her close.

"Well we always gave 'em a great show, Anna. At least *you* did, my *roza bialy*. But I've lost you up in the clouds for the last time—

and we've landed safe together here, little pigeon. So this will be Home Sweet Home to us now."

He looked around him with satisfaction. "I've got plans for us—big plans. And all our savings are right here in my grouch bag."

Anna brightened up. "We're going to have horses, Papa?"

"Sure. We'll have everything from baggage stock to fancy driving horses—high steppers. And you'll have your own pony. How would you like a calico pony?"

"No. I want a big horse, Papa. Like Black Beauty."

Her father laughed and shook his head. "Oh I might have known you'd want something big and dangerous . . ."

She took it all in, the morning they started building the livery stable. The fine rosiny smell of the lumber being unloaded and tossed with reverberant *whang* (or a flat and solid heavy *whump*) in a pile by Mr. Blake and Jass Cates, one of the young carpenters. It smelled deliciously like the circus sawdust. Then all the preliminary pacing, followed by the more accurate measuring with a metal tape line. Talk over the plan sheet: Papa and Mr. Boney discussing this and that provision for ramp, stalls, hay space, feed and harness rooms, drainage, and a place for Papa's office.

Now this was something like, Anna thought, standing wide-eyed and quiet, clutching her doll Molly. Things were going to begin happening again.

She was fascinated by all the sawing, chipping; the scrape of the drawing knife cutting the bark off the base logs; the getting ready to raise tiebeams, staddle, and stanchion. She marveled at their tools: the granny bar, the plumb bob, the doosenwhacker, the rabbet plane, the jack plane. . . . Her fingers itched to work with the carpenters' tools—to be one of them and no mere onlooker. At first she tried snitching a hammer merely to play with, but was soon pounding away on thirty-penny nails among the mud sills.

She was grown up enough to know she shouldn't bother the hands, but so strong was the compulsion to be in on everything and not to miss a trick that she left Molly at home now—put her away gently in a trunk—and wouldn't go home with Papa to dinner, but began bringing her lunch so as to eat with the workers and listen to them talk.

Talk of nervy people and smart horses stuck in her head best.

". . . Boys, I see by last week's paper that Jack Powderly and the Knights of Labor is sticking right up to old man McCormick, and Armour, and them other money hogs, out in Chicago . . ."

". . . They tell me Colonel Pescud's little old Chocolate Gal, right here in this town, can beat anything 'tween here and Texas . . ."

". . . Whaddya know about Mrs. Annie Laurie Lochs getting fined fifty dollars out in Saint Louis by that goddamn judge (pardon me, Miss Pulaski) for just throwing a battercake in Mrs. President Cleveland's lap! . . ." . . . Dave Duck talking.

". . . Well she ain't no *queen,* is she? I say Grover Cleveland oughta be splintered-and-burnt, if you ask me, the way he's raisin' taxes, the son-of-a—" Big Sam Tate cut his eye at Mike's tomboy girl that was always hanging around, and planed down the rough cussword to "biscuit-eater." They all laughed. Anna too.

She loved to ride in Mr. Blake's wagon. Driving, of course. And standing up, of course. Catching the breeze bareheaded with her legs planted apart like a seafaring man's . . . going with Uncle Flag to the shoals and willows of Ullowee Creek for sand. ("Most folks calls this here crick the 'Allarbay,'" the old man had said, "but *I* names it same's my gran'pap—that was Injun-blooded— did.")

Now and then, in the evenings, Mike Pulaski and his daughter would go buggy riding around the town. One place that always interested Anna was a famous house called "Jethro's Joke" behind the owner's back. It belonged to Doctor Jethro Mink, who had given the railroad its right-of-way and was thus responsible for Minktown being on the M.R. & P. map. The doctor's father had been a large landowner—another one of Minktown's "land luck-ies"—and *his* father, "Muleshoe" Mink, had started out with only two little old bull calves, but in time had parlayed these into houses and horses, big river farms and a big store over on Ephraim's Creek. Back then, the settlement that had now grown into a town was called Mink Hollow. And after that, when the railroad came—and Sherman's Army—it was Mink Station. The house was an overfancy, rambling structure, three stories high, with too much banjo work and too many cupolas, set back from the railroad track. She remembered seeing it from on high, but then it had been but a blob, a bubble of brown, no bigger than a cow-pie. (Oh but she was now down in the whirling hive of the town and she and Papa were now part of it.)

Little by little, she had joined in the lively banter of the workers, gotten her hands on their saws, planes, chisels, and friendly heartstrings. Had, in her unladylike boldness, cut loose and demanded a job as assistant to Sam M. Bowles, the fast-working, tobacco-chewing black brickmason. For some weeks her soul's salvation hinged upon learning to mix mortar, to snip off pieces of brick or the jagged edges of rocks with one deft clink of the trowel. And, with her great gift of persuasion (having happily thought of a way, too, to get up high again), she found herself, by February—when the Great Blizzard of '88 began to fall—stretched out up at the comb of the livery stable's roof with a cut-off pair of her papa's pants on and her mouth full of shingle nails, tacking away for dear life as one of the roofing gang.

And then at last, when the huge, rambling, double-decked horse-and-hay barracks that in its shape and form looked like some giant insect with hay sticking out of its mandibles, had been completed and a big black-and-white signboard nailed up front bearing the legend

PULASKI'S LIVERY & FEED STABLES
M. Pulaski, Proprietor

she had helped Papa pack up the *Jacobus,* sold now to Smolka Brothers & Rosen's "Slightly Used Amusement Specialties," in Philadelphia.

And oh how that unhappy closure—that final formality between the two fellow sky-travelers, who had shared so many exalted journeys, the shrieking winds, the high altitudes of hope and thrilling, desperate dangers—had tugged at her heart's inmost cordage and loaded a leaden ballast upon her blithe spirit. It was like nailing up your childhood in a coffin. She was the wild bird having its glorious pinions permanently clipped; and now she was shut away forever and completely from the skies.

Mike Pulaski's Anna had a time getting started in school. What to do with such an unusual youngster was a problem for her teachers. She was so poised and sophisticated for this small town; she knew so much of travel and famous people. Yet even though she had been tutored by Catholic sisters and by Toby Lolo, the famous clown, her education had wide gaps.

Her use of exotic and profane expressions absorbed from associates of every nationality often sent her teachers to the dictionary and caused laughter and shaking of heads at teachers' meetings. But the little circus girl tried hard to fit in with the new order.

When she was put back with younger children it was a heavy blow. But she did not mope—only worked fiercely to climb into a higher grade. She caught on quickly—except for arithmetic, which was so much insurmountable Greek to her and which made her feel foolish and hopeless, and caused her tears.

The Circus Girl was different, but being different came naturally to her. She never seemed to worry about it or even try to be like the others.

The children called her Circus Anna, or Balloon Girl. At recess they would bring her cookies and apples and beg her to tell them stories from her wonderful life with the "big top." Then they would gather around her, forsaking their games of jacks or marbles or tag. Many of her stories were about horses; and more than once she told them of what a thrill it used to be when she was a tiny child and her father, a famous trick rider, had taken her for rides around the ring up on his big strong shoulders. Of that awful night at the Dublin Fair when Blue Lady tripped while he was doing his head-standing act.

Johnny Anders and other town kids hung around the big horse barn as much as they could. Watching to see what horse would be led down the ramp, its dancing hooves making a hollow thudding on the boards. They craned their necks to see when a loud-talking drummer, or a land shark or a lover-boy was renting a surrey or a buggy to canvass the country stores, or show customers some real estate or take a sweetheart for a drive out into the country. But most of all, they hoped to see Anna. Young as she was, she helped the grooms exercise the saddle horses, one after the other. And always she waved to the kids and called hello. When she smiled at him, Johnny felt the way it is after a dark rainy spell when the sun suddenly bursts out, winking on the wet grass and making everything new and fresh and glorious.

The boys got so they knew all the different horses in the stable.

There was Colonel Eugene P. Owsley's famous saddle horse; Dixie of Marlborough Villa, who could do a brilliant Spanish walk and the parade gait. Dixie was a spirited five-gaiter who, like his illustrious master, was a born actor and exhibitionist, as proud as a unicorn, fierce of eye, very fond of sugar, and who craved lots of attention from the lady horses.

Among Anna's favorites was Dent, a bright chestnut with elegance and disposition. She was named for Mrs. General Grant, born Julia Dent. There were several horses in Minktown named after Presidents or their wives.

Mr. Milam Warham had a big white mare named Martha Washington. Martha was handsome and carried a stripped tail and roached mane. But she had been cruelly teased by the boys of a former owner, and now no one but Anna could get near her without being bitten.

Young Anna had chosen for herself a gleaming, high-spirited saddle horse—five-gaited black Belle. And though she was lively and often shied, Belle was gentle—Mike Pulaski saw to that. Anna loved to curry and brush Belle to make her shine. She braided her mane tightly so it would be curly. And she snitched sugar lumps at the boardinghouse, hiding them in her pocket to give to Belle, who nickered softly and nosed for more.

The stable hands like to lounge on an old harness chest, which was worn slick from the swabbings of all their backsides. Anna loved the things in this chest and all the horsely appointments on the dusty shelves: the brushes and currycombs, hames, bits, bucking straps, and cruppers; the blinders and lazy straps; the breeching stays and bellybands . . . their scent of horse-sweated leather and brass. And there were the resting carriages. The way they stood when off duty with the shafts fastened up to keep the kids from riding them. And sometimes one of the widow Jones's hens would slip in and nest on a padded carriage seat, or a cat would have kittens there.

Another thing that was interesting was to watch a horse make manure. The lifting of the tail, the gases coming, the steaming biscuits bobbing out—a most remarkable performance. You weren't supposed to notice such things, but Anna had no mother to tell her it wasn't "nice" and not to, and it was all a part of the wonder of life about her. Also she liked to watch their big haunches grinding;

to smell the fine strong smell from a horse. She was greatly interested in horse colors, too: the bays, salt-and-pepper whites, blue or strawberry roans, the chestnuts and the sorrels (not much difference in these), the dapple grays, and the blacks.

Sometimes she played dolls up on the seat of the melancholy hearse. Rode up there, too, beside Mr. Buttonwood when he took it out to a funeral.

"How'd you like a ride on the old meat wagon?" he'd say, and she hardly ever refused. But on such occasions she was very sober and quiet. Riding on the hearse, it seemed you were cut loose from earth and body. Sort of like the passenger in the black box back there. Same as when you jumped off a balloon and went riding off all by yourself up in the sky.

A little wrenny bird was singing happily near the livery stable the morning Anna wheeled out the new bicycle Papa had given her for her birthday. She had practiced and practiced on it till she could ride it now as well as anybody—except, of course, people like Samson Swift, the famous pedal-pushing virtuoso and speed demon. Yesterday she had gone with Papa to see his thrilling exhibition: riding backward a mile a minute, jumping ditches, doing handstands and standing on his head while going full speed—in a roped-off area on West Main Street.

"Well if he can do it," she told herself as she wheeled her bike toward the ramp, "I can too." She had dreams of maybe going back with the circus someday as a daredevil bicycle sensation.

Papa had ordered her bike all the way from Boston. It was an Overman—the new Victoria model for girls; made with a drop frame so it could be ridden astride. The wheels had thin, solid-rubber tires, and were equipped with mudguards. There was also a guard laced with twine, that almost completely covered the chain and wheel-spokes so her skirts would not get caught. The fine slick bouncy leather saddle was stretched over several coiled springs; and, when coasting, she could put her feet up on the footrests, while the pedals kept flying around.

She came whizzing down the ramp that morning, ringing the little warning bell on the handlebars that startled the hands and horses alike. But her pet cat Snowflake took a notion to run right across her path and knocked her ambition of becoming a bicycling star sky-high and put the brakes on her dream of a circus come-back forever. For Anna's back was broken, and for sixteen long weeks she lay strapped to an orthopedic board.

It was a grim and lonely business for the child. Her father couldn't be with her all the time, on account of the livery-stable business, so he hired Genevra, a Negro woman, to be her nurse and take care of her in their rooms at the boardinghouse. And of course he had the best doctor in town—old Doctor Mack Smith—at beck and call. But as he believed one horse doctor to be worth several fever doctors, he also brought in the young veterinarian Carl Hostetter, who had very satisfactorily attended animal patients at the stable.

There were no fluttering banners now. No thrilling band-music or cheers. Oh if she only had Uncle Toby to josh and say foolish things to make her laugh, and bring her his funny little presents. Like that time he brought her that trick drinking glass that dribbled water down your chin. But she had a darling funny letter from him in the shoebox of treasures on her dresser. The circus was in Hartford, Connecticut, now. Uncle Toby wrote just like he talked.

> *Sure Mike it's easier to take care of 100 fleas than one young girl. . . . . . but you're lucky that Mazie the elephant didn't sit down on you, or you'd be a permanent paper-dolly. . . . Say, we're all coming to see you the next time we get to town. And we'll bring some animals (a monkey or two and Oliver the chimp maybe) and the horse-piano, right up to your room. How'd you like that? And we'll bring the cameraman so you, and all of us and the giraffe, will get our pictures in the paper.*

Papa bought her a canary that sang and sang. And when the cat wasn't around, Anna insisted that Genevra let the bird out of its cage. She got hours of pleasure watching it flying about and perching on every sort of place.

The livery-stable hands brought flowers and stood awkward and embarrassed to see her all crippled up, the pale little girl in her snow-white bed with her blond hair done in two long braids (for 'Nev found it easier to care for that way). And most always with her big white tomcat Snowflake curled up on her pillow.

Mr. Josephburg, the reporter for the *Minktown Advocate,* interviewed the cat as well as Anna, for a laugh; but Snow wouldn't admit his part in his mistress's accident. Was evidently trying to forget it. And when he asked *her* to tell the public about it in a few words, she smiled. "If I could ride a balloon," she said, "I figured I could surely ride a bicycle."

As soon as Anna began to get better (it was young Doctor Hostetter who had introduced the helpful orthopedic board into the case), Miss Mamie Rankin, her teacher, came every day after school to help her keep up with her lessons. Anna had hated arithmetic so, and had always closed her mind tight shut whenever anyone tried to explain the problems. But now she tried harder, with her new patience—and being alone helped—not having a whole class grinning at you when you were near tears over being a dumbbell on long division. Miss Rankin tried to explain things in terms of the livery-stable surroundings. "Now if you had twenty-seven bales of hay, Anna, and sixteen bags of oats, just how would you divide it among ten horses and how long would it last?" (Mr. Pulaski had suggested this approach, and it worked.) Anna brightened up then and applied her quick brain. But like people, she pointed out, some horses ate more than others.

From the first, Doctor Hostetter took a great interest in Mike Pulaski's pretty little daughter's case. He stopped in often to cheer her up; would sometimes bring her a box of candy or other small present. And he promised her, if she did her exercises faithfully so as to get well and strong again, he would take her along in his buggy on some of his trips out into the country.

After sixteen interminable weeks, she was at last able to get up. It was necessary to learn to walk all over again, step by step; but the shock and thrill of her good old-time life came rushing back as she pushed a chair ahead of her for support. She wrote the old clown: *I'm up! I'm up! I never realized that you don't have to be a mile high in the sky to feel so happy.*

And then one day the circus was in town again, and Uncle Toby Lolo *did* come to see her, but he didn't bring all the animals and the steam piano like he promised. He only brought Auntie Stell and a beautiful Scotch collie named Prince, that was for her. And Auntie Stell brought her a Mexican bracelet and a big box of salt-water taffy. She was still wearing her lion-taming outfit—the high boots and officerlike cap—because, she said, she had to be back with the cats pronto. But she didn't have her whip and her pistols.

Something seemed wrong with Uncle Toby, though. He wasn't as funny-talking and gay as usual. Something had happened to sober him down.

Several years later, when the old clown Lolo was really old and had retired from circus life (and little Anna was Mrs. Carl Hostetter) he came back to town on a brief visit. (He said it was very upsetting, though, to come back to a town such as Minktown and find it all shrinkled away and its name changed to Warham— it was like having the ground slide out from under you; or making friends with a nice tame white sheep and suddenly having it change to a great big floppy overbearing gray whale.) Anna and Papa were sitting out in the sunshine down at the livery stable with Uncle Toby, talking old times, when he reminiscently turned the talk to the time when he and Stell had come to see a certain spunky and brave little bucko who'd been in a fight with a bicycle.

"Did you notice anything wrong about me that day?" he asked Anna.

"Well yes, come to think of it, I did," she said. "You seemed sort of squelched, like something had got your funnybone."

Then the wrinkles around his dark-ringed eyes twinkled and he laughed gaily and painted in his own funny words a picture of what had caused his gloom.

It happened during the parade. Mayor Manderson Dismukes was riding majestically with the unshaven and shrewd-eyed Old Man John Robinson himself, in a sporty trap behind a pair of smart docked bays. The clown, coming along not far behind, was imitating the horse-prancing and getting laughed at, when he noticed the mayor doffing his hat to a large potbellied man of importance, who was reared back cross-legged in his sumptuous carriage. He wore an English bowler hat and a frock coat and one of those over-size watch chains that were then the height of fashion and almost bulky enough to tether out his old bossy. Scenting a chance to make some hooptedoodle, the jester tarried to stick a witty pin in this solemn distinguished personage. Not knowing that he was frolicking before the lord of the bailiwick, Jefferson Warham—the local A number-one tobacco tycoon (that old Minktown had changed its name to honor). The crowd sensed something in the air of drama, and pricked up its ears. "By gosh," Toby Lilo popped suddenly, rudely pointing his finger, "if it ain't me old Uncle Josh!"

A gasp came from the people around him. Then a shocked silence. Toby Lolo had put his big flappy foot in his mouth this time—trying to make a laughingstock of the town's greatest man! Miss Elvira Mooney, Mr. Warham's housekeeper and sister-in-law, who was lolled back comfortably in the soft cushions eating chocolates and who looked a lot like Queen Victoria (or so she had oft been told) held a chocolate drop suspended before her mouth and apprehensively blinked.

Then a bystander (it was Gus Harten, the race-horse man, they say, who with his father ran Colonel Pescud's race track and private stables), sprang instantly to arms at such an unheard-of, traitorous breaching of the town's proud wall of custom, and outstepped truculently to take a poke at Sir Funnyface. If he said anything further along that line, he was advised—or along any line—he'd be ridden out of town on a rail. And the tough guy Gus further turned the jokester's little joke to Dead Sea tomatoes by addressing him as a striped-ass son-of-a-horsethief.

Whereupon the common, or vulgar, part of the throng whooped and hollowed. "Go it clown! Go it jockey!"

The great Jefferson Warham pulled a great wide grin, and Miss Mooney resumed her candy-poking.

It was with gusto that the crinkle-eyed veteran of the slapstick related this little story on himself. " 'Anything for a laugh' was my motto," he said, "but that was one time the applooze fell on yours truly's poop like a brickyard."

The God

Just when Jeff Warham, T.P.'s daddy, was translated from a mortal man into an idol is one of those fine points in history that may never be settled exactly. Certainly the process had been going on some time prior to the date when the grand old name of Minktown was erased and the municipality and county renamed for the distinguished peddler-manufacturer.

In 1893, the United Tobacco Company was incorporated at $25,000,000 by T.P., the family's guiding genius. It took in a dozen of the largest cigarette manufacturers, then extended its monopoly to cigars, snuff, plug tobacco, and snuffed-out two hundred and fifty lesser manufacturers.

T.P. made plans to move up to New York and open an office and factory there. He'd decided he'd better enlarge their credit sources and keep in touch with the stock market and world market. Also he was hatching up a plan to latch onto all sources of supply of tin foil, licorice paste, cigarette paper, etc., etc. If J. D. Rockefeller could corner everything in oil, he was confident he could do the same thing with tobacco, and make some real mazuma.

Then came the Panic of '93, with almost every town in the U.S.A. feeling the pains of unemployment. Coxey's Army, a band of twenty thousand unemployed workmen, marched in angry protest from the Midwest to Washington to try and wake up the Congress and President Cleveland. But as everybody in the country now had to get their tobacco from the Warham combine;

and as men out of work used more tobacco than when working; and as foreign countries, too, had taken to smoking Warham cigarettes, *cigarillos,* and *cigarros,* the Minktown factories were kept busy all day and night.

It seems it was about then that the local citizenry got the notion that old brother Jeff—who had started this keep-everybody-humping business—was either a wizard or a god and they'd better go to doing him obeisance.

It was in 1894, during the height of the popular excitement over all the big money T. P. Warham had cleaned up in the combine deal, that certain Minktown citizens started a movement to change the tacky old name of the town to the more up-to-date one of Warham, in honor of Old Man Jeff. It was a big growing town now with 5,885 inhabitants, and time to leave a lot of old-timey things behind. So happily and rapidly did the idea take shape (perhaps with just a little sub-rosa prodding by Mr. Barnaby B. Fogg) that soon the city fathers decided it ought to be done. Some wagged their heads, as heads will wag over anything new or strange. But when it was put to a vote, the innovation carried by a considerable majority.

Some of Jeff Warham's earliest idolaters were women. Many an ambitious damsel or dame thought of the hulking civic demigod with high-flying incandescent desire, and worshiped him from afar. There were the pallid, proud, and Episcopalian Misses Saundras (those deft and jolly sempstresses who sewed only for the carriage trade, and whose nimble thimbles were always booked for months ahead by the Best People up on Swelldoodle Hill)—Miss Priscilla, Miss Guinever, Miss Tex, to whom everything was all attar of roses and the fragrance of God's will, and in whose credulity the saintly old sodbuster and dividend-dispenser—even though a Methodist—inspired an ardent (but high-toned, you understand) pragmatic Christian devotion. And more than one loverless and discouraged little birdie of a schoolmarm harbored snug and surreptitious reveries of becoming the wealthy old widower's young-darling wife; or even his doxy, it mattered not which.

Martitia Henshaw, a bedraggled weed of a gentlewoman uprooted by adversity's winds from one of the haughtiest old family flowerbeds of southern aristocracy, conjured him up in her disorderly fantasies as a wonderfully potent ringtail incubus that came nightly to make unholy tomcat whoopee, with bump and thump, upon her rattly bed. Again he would appear as a big buck demon rabbit, always chewing rabbit tobacco and never removing his hat. At times he came guised as a bulbous-beaked and great-footed brazen clucking cock. . . .

Also a prime mover in the enshrining of Jeff Warham was the Reverend Amos Gragg, first pastor of the Mink Street Methodist Church before its transfiguration to the Warham Memorial. For a time the good parson had strictly remembered that his flock were straight-laced God-fearing Dixie-loving souls—not decadent adorers of earthen gods or sticks and stones. At first he had steered them carefully around those sordid snares, those devil's deadfalls, of Worldliness, Covetousness, Vainglory. Had preached simply in sound bucolic vein, of Heaven's loft and Hell's cellar, and had eulogized the church's rich ruling deacon and mortgagee but sparingly. Had allowed him to blaze no brighter at first in the sermon than the smallest of stars. But that was before his surprise salary raise. After that, the Man of Golden Leaf Tobacco bloomed out in the preaching like a watered geranium. Grew taller and taller, by subtle steady steps and notches, as the wild gourd vine; whilst around his head there pretty soon appeared a halo like unto the Star of Bethlehem or a locomotive headlight.

"That fellow Gragg's a man of good understanding," Jeff told his sons. "I wish thar was more like him."

Once the preacher dredged up a text from the Book of Luke: "Soul, thou hast much goods laid up for many years." And preached, "Oh what a fine thing, what a wise thing, what a noble thing, for a man to replenish, conserve, keep unto a rainy day, lay by, and gather into storage houses the riches and materials for doing good."

"I'm not sure Christ was against smoking," Gragg told his flock. "Didn't He put spit in the blind man's eye? Well, how do we know it wasn't *tobacco* spit? Certainly the Indians were well acquainted with the medicinal value of tobacco." And so the purity of the man and of the U.T. Company was permanently established and the U.T. smokestacks became the town's altar fires.

In his later years, old Jeff had a large imposing chair made and put in the vestibule of the Sunday-school room, where every Sunday morning he silently sat, like a king on his throne.

All his words, his lightest drippings, were rare philosopher's meat and fresh manna from the sky. Let him but proclaim that it looked like rain; that the 'bacco-worms were a-gittin' too dadblum numerous; that "hard money" was better than "rag" (the whyfor of his voting for Buchanan in preference to Polk); that he preferred cidey to whiskey and turnip greens to all your fancy city-fixin's; or croak from the mouth of wisdom some pithy, moss-covered proverb—like "Beauty never pulled a plow," or "A little money makes the wheel roll," or "A bird don't fly so fur but what his tail always follers him"—and in no time it would be all over town—a spreading crackling prairie fire that onward raced and rolled by way of butcher, baker, and barber's chair, via beauty parlor and Big Blondie Lola's bagnio down in Punkin Alley (they called her that because this popular little whorelady was only four foot three)—that their oracle, the Sage of Hayseed, had spoken.

Even though the Warham County farmers had bad years when the U.T. Company didn't halfway do them right—all they knew was that the town was Mr. Warham's plantation, his personal hog wallow, and had to be run the way he wanted it.

This was also the way Hazah Obey, the hogshead roller, and Phedoniah Blue, the stemmer, saw it. The big wise money men like Mr. Warham would always be on top, be the "masters of the bread." Thus they talked in the early morning as they hurried along, two chips—one dark mahogany, one a light yellow-pine— borne on the dark human flood tide running to the mammoth new Cheltenham cigarette plant out toward Jigaboo Town. And so thought black Hump Bodack, Minktown's earliest printer's devil, washing up the job presses in Johann Anders's printing office and singing in a deep, bemused bass of the Lord's great chariot swinging low.

Had the box of Lady Luck only opened to *their* touch. Had things—the pattern of chance, chronology, and change, deflectible by the weight of a fly's dropping and from which depended the heavy fate of a million small men's small-town lives—been ever so slightly different. Had the cards of circumstance only been differently stacked. If one single tiny turnip seed of event had come substanced or packed in the pod slightly otherwise, otherwhere, otherwhen.

Say if those snaggled old dames of destiny, Clotho, Lachesis, and Atropos, had dropped a few drops more of melanin in the sap of certain family trees—had there been a slight shift in the chemics of coloring matter: in the shade of chocolate or of Angle-Saxon peppermint pink exuded by certain now-mouldered flesh—then well might the Obeys and the Bodacks have been the Warhams or the proud Southern Owsleys. That jungle boy snared in a banana grove by the Arab slave catcher . . . that woman sold for a bag of salt at Zanzibar . . . not Hump's great-great-grandparents but Jeff's.

With Hump's illustrious family buried under the never-was, and *their* oil portraits hung in the marble cool of the college library; whilst those ragamuffin others, such as the Warhams, merely rag-picked or danced the buck-and-wing for small coins or barbered, perhaps, or shoveled the horse-muerda, maybe, out in the hot dusty dirty workers' world, to get along. Or cleaned up some un-born printing press after closing time, in a town named Obeytown or Bodackville, hopping around on floppy old shoeleather.

Take back, as never having been, the sunset light on a face or a fence; the hanging out of a certain long-disembodied and time-tat-tered Monday's wash or the baking of a loaf of barley bread; the deflection of a kiss; a step thrust here, not there; one sailing schoo-ner boarded and another missed; or catching a ride in a wagon going west at Hagerstown in the spring of 1848, or being in that last Conestoga wagon passing through Mink's Hollow on the Walterville pike the night of the Great Star-fall of '45; and the Warham boys could have come out in the cosmic wash as pale and poor-white-trashy as Oakey France or Cauline Riley's brats—or swarthy macaroni-eaters the same as the "Eyetallies"—or dirty and hopeless as the old Jews sorting rags at night under a lamp in Rocco Manzatti's ragpicker's loft—or been named Pflugfelder, Philpotts, or Manzatti.

Or if Dilcey O'Lannigan, pink-cheeked and wild Irish soul, had had some other lover than Crigger Warham, the Methodist back-woodsman, climbing bearlike to love's little naughty game in Mr. Warham's mother's cord-slatted bed. Had another pawn of a progenitor than Dilcey been moved by the Finger of Fingers to sift old Crigger's hairy bruin's joy—to receive into her sod the electric seed of his embrace—in a certain cold leaf-skirling dawn of early spring in the year of 1819; yes, things would certainly have been

different. Or had *her* old grandam Betsy Buckner's ego and in-
ertness been fanned into flame by other bellows of affection than
Enoch Strowprack's, in her youth and in the dim leafage of some
other far-past, time-whirled-away firelight or forest cow barn or
cabin. (A key is oh such a weak and shakelty thing. A lock a thing
so unportending. But only the woman-lock and the man-key may
open the door of tomorrow.)

Cyrus T. Badger

It was Cyrus T. Badger, the famous collector of corner lots, Warham Tobacco's star salesman, who put Warham Tobacco on the foreign map, spreading the great name around the globe as he thumped his way—he and his old cherry walking stick—from London to Shanghai, from Finland to Capetown and Madagascar. He was on his way to South America when Old Man Warham announced he wanted to retire and gave Cyrus T. an option on his holdings in the partnership.

It was during Cyrus's trip, however, that T.P. decided to form the gigantic United Tobacco Corporation monopoly. And foreseeing how valuable all the stock was to become, T.P. fixed it up with his partners to keep Mr. Badger in the dark about the coming expansion and for Old Man Warham to buy his stock back. T.P. said Badger was a good salesman all right, but never would get away from his picayunish Hetty Green habits. "I don't mind a man's being a shark—that's good business and I'm one myself," he said. "But let's say I'm a broader-minded shark, like Rockefeller—willing to let a few of my key men make money too."

At first the deal the Warhams offered suited Cyrus to a t, for Old Man Warham was to let him make a handsome profit on this switch-back, and secretly Cyrus had been figuring on launching a company of his own—where he'd be top dog and not have to divide the winnings. He was also confident he could swing most, if not all, of those valuable sales connections he'd made to his own outfit.

But right there was where he slipped on the banana peel. For the outcome of this transaction, instead of following the happy trajection planned, took a kinky turn and became a new dog-eat-dog act in the drama of Minktown tobacco.

In a few months, as soon as Mr. Thomas P. Warham got his ducks in a row, news of the big tobacco combine suddenly flooded the papers; and shortly thereafter came the announcement that those on the inside track had cut themselves a melon of nineteen million dollars.

When poor Cyrus T. discovered that he'd been taken for a donkey ride and had let a great golden bonanza slip right through his fingers, he saw red with rage and disappointment. He yelled that he'd been swindled and was going to bring a million-dollar lawsuit; but the hard-headed young Napoleon of tobacco finance said Sue and be damned. So, seeing he'd never get anywhere on that tack, Cyrus Badger pretended to bury the hatchet. He played possum with the Warhams for a while, while privately nursing his grudge—that was to grow and redouble itself like Jack's beanstalk. That was to guide his plans and purpose all the rest of his life. He'd heard that that big robber T.P. had said he had the social viewpoint of a gnat. Well he'd show the dirty young bloodsucker. He'd get even if it was the last thing he did on earth . . . he'd strip them down to their socks and union suits, no matter what it took, or how long.

And then, like an inspiration from the blue, he spotted the soft place in their armor. Machines.

Heretofore, Mr. Badger's one and only hobby had been collecting Minktown corner lots, but now was added another. Carefully, patiently, foxily, secretly, relentlessly, Cyrus T. Badger began his search all over the world for tobacco-processing machinery. Machinery perfected; or machines whose unshapen cams, cogwheels, and levers were as yet latent and no more than the cryptic scrawls of genius. Whose blueprints were still in the brain-placentas of inventors and the misty web of the future. He was after anything and everything that double-crossing Warham gang of thieves would have to have. If the thing looked good, he'd finance it for a controlling interest.

In no time at all, he'd located in Cleveland, Ohio, a new type of cigarette machine that was destined—after being fertilized with fifty grand of his money—to grow into the famous Casson-Butler-Kuntz patent. By the time the U.T. got wind of it, Cyrus Badger had everything under control; and though T. P. Warham put up an awful bluff—waxing first indifferent, then bellicose, and swearing by all the gods he'd never use it unless they'd sell him the infernal dad-rotted contraption outright—Mr. Badger knew he had to have it, so simply sat on the bank and played out his line and waited for the great man-eating, but now well-hooked, shark to wear himself down and sign up for his machines at $20,000-a-year royalty per each, plus a percentage on the number of cigarettes produced.

"And that's only a beginning," said the bold bad Cyrus Badger, out loud, as he danced a jig—in spite of his defective foot and reputation for dignity—and grinned into his mirror like a laughing hyena when he was alone with no one to see.

The man seemed to have a sixth sense for smelling out exactly what the Warhams were going to need years before they needed it; and when they did, to be sitting on it. He was a whiz at weeding out the workable from the worthless. And he had a way of latching onto the right brilliant-but-starving mechanical geniuses and soup-kitchening their souls and bodies together until their brainchildren got hatched. Sometimes this took years, and they weren't always world beaters. Every now and then they would hatch him a duck . . . on that bag-stringing machine, for instance, he had to pony-up a hundred and fifty thousand for infringing. But his general average was patsy; and in a few years he'd amassed a fortune on his near-monopoly of cigarette, cigar, and plug-tobacco machinery and had gone on to grabbing up patents for the packaging of tea, bread, chewing-gum.

One night in the early 1900s, Mr. Badger was in Richmond, Virginia, and had gone to bed at the Murphy Hotel in his old-fashioned nightcap and nightgown (made of a pink peppermint-stripe flannelized material, that had been sent him for a Christmas present by a favorite niece).

The next day was going to be a busy one, with a big showdown battle with his eternal adversary (case of *Badger* v. *U.T. Company et al.*) before the February term of the United States Court of Appeals for the State of Virginia, so he had retired early. His exclusive patent rights on the Casson-Butler cigarette machine were expiring, and from all he could find out, it looked like certain new features originated by Galeoto Patzer, one of their young mechanical men, had him beat this time. But you never could tell, and anyway he guessed he'd flogged a-plenty gravy out of T. P. Warham's ornery hide on that one.

Midnight came, and a rap on his door. "What the hell?—this time of night," he muttered, all his vulpine faculties and wolf instincts wide awake. He rubbed his eyes. He had a lifelong fear of robbers, and it was only when he was sure it was Mr. Barnaby B. Fogg, the lawyer, on the other side of the door, that he unlocked it. To his surprise (which he carefully camouflaged) in came not only Mr. Fogg, the Warhams' chief counsel, but John W. Gates, the big speculator, market manipulator, and race-horse addict; Bill Butler, one of Thomas F. Ryan's men Friday; and W. C. Whitney. Mr. Badger's brain was clicking fast, and he recognized in them the several financial interests that, over the years, had become associated and interlocked with the Warhams'. "*Gen*-tle-men," Mr. Badger said in a perfectly level and unperturbed tone—though for a fleeting instant he wondered if they mightn't have come to give him a caning—"what can I do for you?"

He didn't invite them to have off their hats and fine fur-lined overcoats; and Mr. Fogg said they hadn't long to stay. Then, after a little beating about the bush with insincere pleasantries and legalistic hemmings-and-hawings (they pretended not to notice *mein* host's weird get-up), Mr. Fogg, who seemed to be the spokesman, said they'd been having a little meeting in regard to the morrow's pending litigation and just thought they'd drop up to see if he'd be interested in selling his Casson-Butler patent outright—lock, stock, and barrel—and calling it quits.

Mr. Badger did some quick calculating. The U.T. crowd had bought up the Ardway and the Emerson machines, but probably neither had turned out to be even as good as the Anstacker. . . . The Anstack people had turned down their $250,000 offer. . . . They figure they are going to lose my lawsuit and are sunk unless.

"Well . . . I . . . might," he said slowly, and you could hear a distinct composite sigh of relief coming out of them, and they (all but Mr. Fogg) sat down. Mr. Gates on the only chair and Messrs. Whitney and Butler on the bed's edge.

"And have you ever thought of an approximate figger?"

"Not approximate—exact," the bold brusque Badger replied. "One million dollars and not a red cent less."

"Will you put that in writing?" Mr. Fogg asked.

"Yes."

Whereupon the lawyer produced from his pocket a long envelope and his fountain pen.

When the inscrutable Mr. Badger had scrawled a few words signifying his willingness to part with his patent rights for the compensation stipulated, the U.T.'s man took out his checkbook and started to write.

"Wait a minute," interrupted Mr. Badger. "You know I'm a 'hard money' man."

"You mean you won't accept our check?"

"That's right. Not from J. P. Morgan himself. Only the hard cold cash will suffice in a deal of this magnitude."

Mr. Fogg grinned. "Yes Cyrus, I forgot your aversion to modern monetary methods. You sold me a horse thirty years ago and I distinctly recall your putting up this same objection then. I can't quite understand how a man whose machines are the last word in up-to-dateness can still cling to the financial mores of the money sock and the iron kettle, but we can fix that. You shall have your money in cash—in nickels and dimes if you've got a prairie schooner outside big enough to haul it. . . . But let me finish my horse story. I *will* say that horse you sold me, Cyrus, was a good one, and I only hope this trade will prove as satisfactory.

"And now Cyrus," Mr. Fogg said—discarding *his* frigid-fish attitude and waxing once more warm and playful—"if you will change to street dress from that—ah—er—mother hubbard, shall we say?—and accompany us to the bank . . ."

"Yep, better change your wrapper—it's snowing like blue blazes outside," said Mr. Gates. (Whose thought at the moment was What the hell difference does it matter what the old pirate wears? He's a man will always come out on top—even if he was naked with a ring in his nose.)

"My personal habits of dress and finance are none of your business, sirs," said the irascible old wizard in the *sac de nuit*, as he started getting into his red flannel longhandles, mittens, overshoes, ear warmers . . . picked up his heavy cherry walking stick.

Which choler was of course feigned—he had found it paid to keep up his legendary pose of being a boor and hedgehog on all oc-casions. "And what is this anyway I'd like to know—a snipe hunt, or April-fool joke? You know the banks are all closed this time of night."

"No—we know one that's open, don't we, boys?" said the un-suppressible Mr. Fogg, in high good humor and winking at the others.

Outside they had a surrey with two horses and fur lap robes. They took him to the Branch Banking Company, with President Branch himself there chafing his hands in welcome, nervously, in the immemorial manner of bankers. The institution had been held open all night for the big deal. "And how will you have it, Mr. Badger?" asked Branch.

Old Cyrus had brought along a suitcase, and into this he packed in the gold and large-denomination yellow-bellies as matter-of-factly as if he were stowing away mere shirts and socks. And when he had finished his packing he wasted no time in amenities. "Well," he said, still wearing his cryptic stopped-clock expression, "I must be getting back to my beauty sleep." And everybody but Mr. Badger laughed.

They watched him out the door, and then Mr. Fogg slapped Mr. Gates on the back. "Well it looks like everything's in the bag, John W.," he crowed.

Back at his hotel, facing his own broad grin in the bureau mirror, the boyishly buoyant Mr. Badger was shaking his large head and saying: "Ha-*ha*, old chum, I believe that's the first million-dollar deal we ever made in our neg-ly-gee. Ha—what's that old axiom about 'catching a weasel asleep'?" Then he added: "But get a move on, goddamn it—we got to hit the grit!"

He snatched up a few pieces of clothing from the bottom bureau drawer and crammed them into his other suitcase. Sleet was rat-tling hard on the window, a gust of cold air blew in through the window frame. There was a mixed freight-train going through to Washington at 3:15, and he would just have time to thump through that dadburned snow, and the wolfish wind howling down the deserted streets, and hop it. He put back on his mittens and ear warmers and left word that if anyone wanted to know his forwarding address they could get it from his office in Warham. In Washington he caught the early Pennsy and shortly after noon was in New York, depositing the money in the Guaranty Trust. Then he went on up Broadway to the Grand Hotel and took a dollar room for the night. He was lucky, and, by taking Cabin 13, was able to get passage the very next morning on the little fast Cunard packet book *Umbria*—that would land him in Liverpool within two weeks. Before leaving the Grand he had impressed very carefully on the manager that he was sailing for Cherbourg, France—just in case anyone should inquire. And had sent off a wire to his Warham office to get it put in the papers that he was in France.

At the appellate court back in Richmond that day—Judges Duddell, D'Arcy, and Rutledge, presiding—the legal outcome in the case of *Badger* v. *U.T.* was somewhat startling. Barnaby B. Fogg, of Warham, North Carolina, for appellants United Tobacco Company, chartered under the laws of New Jersey, exhibited the papers executed in the bank the previous night by Cyrus T. Badger, in which all rights in the Casson-Butler-Kunz cigarette-machine patent were forever sold and assigned to the said Tobacco Company; but attorney Fogg nevertheless prayed the court to pass on the merits of the case. Whereupon the court unanimously held that the famous patent they had purchased was now null and void and automatically superseded by United Tobacco's Patent No. 1,313,186: with its several improvements made by inventor Patzer in the guts of the machine which constituted a novel, meritorious, and sempervirent new invention. Which was to say that Mr. Badger would have lost the suit, and the U.T. Company had therefore unnecessarily lost a million dollars.

And as if it were not hard enough on poor Mr. Fogg to have been so outrageously outsmarted, by the time he got back to New York—where Mr. T. P. Warham was walking up and down chewing his cigar and waiting to lambaste him unmercifully and forevermore about going around buying dead dogs at a million dollars apiece—he, Mr. Warham, had received a tip-off from the patent office in Washington that old Cy Badger—goddamn his dirty stinking carcass—had just taken out a new patent on a completely new type of cigarette machine that had everything on the market completely paralyzed, bumfuzzled, invalidated, dollymolished, and skinned a mile. And, learning that the old scoundrel was on the ocean on his way to France, Mr. Warham had put two and two together and cannily deduced that he was on his way around the world to peg down this new patent in the foreign countries before the U.T. could patent theirs. T.P. was mad enough to bite twenty-penny nails in two; and just as fast as he could grease a ship purser's paw on the liner *Adriatic*—that was all steamed up and ready to lift anchor and put them aboard—rushed his Mr. Fogg and inventor Patzer off to London. . . . If he could just beat the enemy to the British patenting, he would be automatically covered in all the British dominions.

("Oh what a battle of Titans!" privately exulted that learned and undrooping lawyer, Barnaby Fogg—enjoying the time on shipboard at whist and wowing the ladies. Old Barnaby had always liked to see a good fight. "From now on, it's Fafner Warham versus Fasolt Badger," he thought. "With good blackthorn shillelaghs and no holds barred.")

But that slippery eel and sharp old dog-fox Cyrus had laid his false scent well. Mr. Warham's emissaries picked it right up and when they got to England found he'd been before them. They jumped over to France and it was the same thing there; and as they circled the globe he stayed a jump ahead and patented his new Yankee Whizzer in every country where they had a patent office, including China and Japan.

The day after Mr. Badger got back to Warham from his foreign travels, with several million dollars in his bank account, he walked into the Watkins Pharmacy, at the corner of Wraxbee and Main. He bought a couple of two-for-five La Belle Jasminola cigars, and then as he was leaving, remarked casually to the proprietor: "By the way, Watkins, I'll have to go up on your rent next month."

"But my God, Mr. Badger, I can hardly make a go of it at the two hundred and fifty I'm paying you," cried the drug merchant in pained surprise.

"That is no concern of mine, Mr. Watkins," said Cyrus T. "This corner lot I acquired when it was a cow pasture in 1893 is getting valuable. You can pay me four hundred per month or get out."

Johnny Anders

Right in front of where Johnny Anders lived down on Cackleberry Street, there was a large deserted brickyard site. Most of the bricks for the Warhams' big tobacco factory had been made here; and now the place was just an ugly red-clay desert crisscrossed by deep rain-rounded gullies and pocked with water holes. There were a stagnant pond, with cattails and bulrushes, and an old green-scummed well called "the graveyard well" where the inhabitants of the Negro slum on the low hill just beyond drowned kittens, deposited dead dogs—and sometimes a dead unwanted baby. All the kids had been cautioned by their papas and mammas never to go near it.

The middle part of the Gully was a place of red-clay dust in summer and red-clay mud in winter; but to Johnny and the neighborhood youngsters it was a grand playground. It was too rough and uneven for a ball field, but bang-up for running and jumping and all kinds of adventurous play, like Washington Crossing the Delaware, or Indian warfare, or Buffalo Bill pursuing buffaloes, or Battle of Gettysburg or other heroic carnage. One of Johnny's most memorable victories took place one day when two opposite gullies were forts out west getting ready for battle. Johnny and Caddy Parker were the redskin army, and Butch Wilson, Pinky Deems, and Chicken Webb—the 75th Cavalry—were down in their hollow rolling mud cannonballs to throw at the cruel savages; but J and C, the bold Indian scouts, pulled off a brilliant sneak attack and poured a big hatful and tin-can-ful of sand right down on the un-suspecting enemy's bare heads.

"That ain't fair! That ain't fair!" yelled the cavalry, pawing sand out of its ears and eyes and hopping mad.

One twilight time in late summer a big flock of bullbats came to catch mosquitoes about the pond, and Papa had great sport shoot-ing them. As the strange sickle-shaped birds hawked low toward the ground, calling *peent peent* and making a hollow, booming sound, he banged away; and Johnny had all he could do picking them up; and Sut, his dog, worked hard retrieving the ones that fell in the water. Papa said it was fine practice for quail-shooting. He said he'd heard these big-mouthed birds were good eating; but nobody wanted to pick and gut them, so Papa told Cuffy Taylor, the hired boy, to feed them to the pig, unless he wanted to take them home to eat. "Law-zee!" Cuffy said. "I wouldn't eat one o' them things fer nuthin'. Doan you know dey's witches' chickens?"

On summer nights when Johnny's folks would be sitting on the front porch listening to the katydids sawing away in the trees in the big front yard, and Papa smoking cigars to keep off the mos-quitoes, they would hear singing coming from over on the Hill. Such songs as the tobacco-hogshead rollers had sung since the days of slavery to lighten their loads; all the good old spirituals that the women at the wash pots and the tobacco-stemming women in the factories sang to ease their hearts with sweet intoxication.

And from over on the Hill would often come, too, that doleful, ancient music of the deathwatch. It was weird and disquieting; since you knew that in that room where they were singing a dead person lay: but it fascinated Johnny, because in it he could distin-guish the deep bass voice of Noey Brown.

Noey Brown was a big strong bare-armed blacksmith who worked at the Howrigan Wagon Shop; and who always had a kind and jolly word for him. On his way home from school he often stopped to watch him nailing an iron tire to a wagon wheel, or shoeing a horse, or pounding red-hot iron on his anvil.

There was a well-worn path across the Gully; on which came, through the years, the many cooks, garden diggers, wood chop-pers, and children from the niggertown to Johnny's home. Willie Jones, a black boy of nine, was Johnny's first boy friend. He had been hired to look after him when he was just learning to walk;

and as soon as he was big enough to go with his young nurse to the grocery store, Willie had taught him his alphabet from the Celluloid Starch and Arbuckle Coffee signboards. Among the cooks there had been Long Liz, Big Dora, Slowpoke Jane, old Aunt Emmeline. . . . And there was Uncle Miles Heart at hog-killing time.

It would be cold weather when Uncle Miles came; and he always brought along a little humpbacked dwarfish white man he called Arch—who slobbered at the mouth and was dumb—for a helper. Uncle Miles would knock the hog on the head with the ax and Arch would jump in and cut its throat. And when it was scald-ed, scraped, and split open and cleaned inside, and lifted up on the kitchen table, Mother would pay Uncle Miles three dollars. But all the little white man got was fifty cents and the chitlings. What Johnny liked best about a hog killing was to get the bladder that he blew up and hung up to dry so he could bust it with a loud bang on Christmas morning.

One day when old Aunt Emmeline cooked at Johnny's house, something bad happened that he never could understand. Or forget. That day the slow, sad old woman had seemed gayer than usual—went about her work singing, like there was something happy on her mind. Aunt Emmeline had a little grandchild, Teenie, who was dearer to her than anything else on earth. This little girl had filled the empty place in the old woman's heart that had been left when her daughter went home to glory; and today was Teenie's birthday, and Aunt Emmeline's head was full of beautiful thoughts about a birthday supper she was going to fix. And so while she was baking the big blackberry pies, Emmeline had made a beautiful little pie, with a beautiful little fork-pricked heart on it, for the child. And that was what had sparked her singing—that was the magic that had lightened her day and made her old worn-out heart beat lighter.

But knowing only that you had to watch all colored cooks to see that they didn't steal your flour or meat or sugar—didn't "pan-tote" when you were paying them $2.50 a week and money so hard to get—Mother was rummaging around on the pantry shelf among the meat skins being saved for soap grease, and there discovered the little extra pie put away neatly in a paper bag. Then a great wrath arose and walked about in Mother's eyes, and she lit into poor Emmeline with a torrent of abuse. "As good as I've been to you . . . I don't like this one bit, stealing from me when I'm paying you more than you're worth and more than anybody else would ever pay you!"

The old woman stood silent and stunned. Felt that old smothery feeling coming back. Dear Godamighty! Can't black folks ever have nothin' a-tall—not even one pore little pie to make a pore little orphant child happy? It was more than she could bear, and she buried her withered old face in her berry-stained apron and wept.

And wicked though it was, from that moment Johnny never loved his mother quite so much again.

On Saturdays Johnny would sometimes get Papa's horse and buggy and go out for an all-day explore to the Rutherford Plantation. Papa said it would be all right, just so he took along Cuffy Taylor, the Negro boy who looked after the horse and cow and worked in the garden. Cuffy was two years older than Johnny.

Johnny's interest in the vast, but run-down, old slave plantation pitched in several directions—the foremost being the wonderful joy of roaming the big woods and the pebbled barrens in search of killdeer and turkey-buzzard nests. The boys knew where there was a certain tall dead pine in which the buzzards roosted, and if they got there early, say as early as nine or ten o'clock, they could see the big slothful birds with wings outstretched to the sun, luxuriously drying themselves off from the night's dampness.

If it was summer, they'd go swimming in the Goose River. And on bright August days they loved to lie deep in the grass by the river's edge to watch a wood duck or muskrat swim by.

In the dark deep woods was where the vultures nested. The mama buzzards just scratched out a hole under a rock or a log and lined it with dead leaves. The eggs were large and beautiful; cream-colored with lovely purple splotches. From the first nest he found, Johnny took one for his bird-egg collection. But never any more—he only collected one egg of a kind, and all the other huntings were just for the fun and challenge of finding something hidden—of matching wits with these grotesque wild sky-soarers. Once he and Cuffy found a nest with two fluffy, pure-white infant buzzards; and when Johnny picked one up, it growled and hissed energetically and then spattered the most awful-smelling puke, compounded from a decayed rabbit, all over him! It was a smell that just knocked you down; and he had to go to the creek and take a wash and scrub his shirt and put it on a rock in the sun for a long time, and even then it stunk so that when he got home his mother made him take another all-over bath before he could come to supper.

Cuffy had a grandfather living in a cabin at the edge of the big woods who, in slavery days, had belonged to the Rutherfords; and when he went to visit the venerable, white-haired old man, Johnny was always glad to go along. Uncle Eph was a fine story-teller, and Johnny loved to listen to his "befo' de wah" recollections.

Now as Colonel McBrander Rutherford, the inheritor of the plantation's thirty thousand acres, lived in Richmond and rarely set foot on his domain, the ex-slaves and their families continued to live there on the only home earth they had ever known. They lived by a little sowing and reaping, raising pigs, and by hunting. Under the old slavery rules, they said, a Negro was forbidden to even carry a knife, much less a gun. But nowadays these independent survivors had guns a-plenty.

The old Negroes made vivid and frank talk about those wicked old Christians the Ole Massa and Ole Miss, whom they had pretended to adore but had despised. They would recount the myriad small meannesses of their masters that stemmed from their heartless and senseless "southern traditions." They recalled with anger and with sorrow that the barbarous and main business of the plantation had been breeding slaves for sale; and told how their precious children had been sold off like cattle. But now, thank the Great and Good Old Marster up Yonder, one said, that was all over; and the proud, mean Ruddyfuds had been humbled down. And then the wise old black man passed on to the boys an axiom that was ancient when Archimedes was born: "All that goes up must come down." It was a saying that Johnny Anders never forgot; and as he grew older he realized that up and down was the natural rhythm of all human activities and ardencies.

Uncle Eph had bright eyes and a young old face, and could scrape a little on a homemade fiddle. He told of how, in his boyhood, it would often be ten o'clock at night when his mother got home from her hard day's work in field or swamp and how hungry he and his young brothers and sisters would be. They would eat field mice or lizards and anything they could catch, he said, and rummage in the garbage box at the Big House kitchen; and if they got for supper a meal cake cooked on a hoe in the cabin fireplace they were lucky.

And then there were weird and wonderful folk tales. Uncle Eph would bite off a fresh chew of his twisted homemade "natchel leaf" tobacco and spin his stories by the hour. The Woman That Ran With the Hyenas, The Monkey in the Koma Tree, The Hoo-zick-in-a-ma-den. . . . His were a folk who lived near the wild heart of life; and though their ancestral times in the African jungle were past and far away, their minds kept their fathers' rhythms and knew their indestructible imagination and vital flame.

There was one old man out at the plantation—Uncle Pompus—who had run away in slavery days and joined the Union army and been in the Battle of Petersburg. Uncle Pomp remembered how it was when Sherman's soldiers were camped around about the village of Mink Station, singing "Hang Jeff Davis on a Sour Apple Tree"; and General Joe Johnston's beaten and ragged-ass boys fraternizing with them and some of them showing them where the tobacco was.

There was an old pipe-smoking, toothless crone, Aunt Minnie Jule, who was full of stories and recollections of certain strange or solemn things that had happened in her youth. Pictures from her long, hard past came crowding. The pigeon seasons—now where on earth did all them pigeons come from? Millions would come down out of the sky in the fall and cover the scarlet oak trees and break down their branches up on Riggs Hill. They roosted on the low cedars, and the overseer would take several black boys and go up there to kill 'em at night with sticks and they'd come back with a wagon load. . . . How her mother had been whipped for "sassing" Ole Miss, and salt brine rubbed into her lash cuts.

"Nat Turner. Now him a fine nigger preacher. Him git up a big rebelium one time in Verginny an' dem-dar rebelium boys dey slewed a might ob white folkses, young and old. But O Lawdy, bimeby dey ketch 'im, an' pore ole preacher Nat, dat tried to free we-alls—an' nigh'bouts to a hunderd other niggers, five ob 'em 'omans—got hunged on dem ole white mens' chains." She told how Mink village was so scairt it sent out a posse ten miles down the road to see iffen any of them turrible escaped slaves mought be coming.

They laughed at that. The old woman cackled high like a hen.

Then Uncle Pomp told about the white preachers coming to visit Massa Ashley Ruddyfud and their preachings to the slaves. " 'Slabery am God's holy will,' dem preacher-mans say. 'Hit be etarnal and wrote up on de sky in letters ob gold.' But none ob us niggers ain't nebber seed no sich writin' up dar." And he giggled. " 'You slaves gotta be obejunt an' be satisfied wid de condishum whur God hab put you,' dem mean old lie-tellin' preachers say; but us niggers knows hit's one big damn lie."

When Johnny heard them sing the sad and homesick plantation songs, putting all of their heart into the singing, a wondering, inquisitive kind of pity surged over him. Steadily there formed within him a resolution to someday put on record something of their story. He felt a complex longing for the power to express—to state himself and his times, the old times and the new times—to achieve loving understanding of people, of places—even of inanimate or fantastical objects—an inspiration begun that was to go on all his life.

One day when Johnny was in his early teens, Papa bought a set of Dickens from Mr. Izador Luckman, the book agent. Mr. Luckman was a good customer at Papa's printing office, and also a very convincing talker. " 'Turn about's fair play,' Mr. Anduss," he had said, "and now I've got here a wonderful bargain in the printed word as dripped from the pen of a topnotch English arthur in a gen-u-wine and bona-fide Morocco binding *for you to buy from me* . . ."

Johnny was soon deep in *Barnaby Rudge;* and it gave him a thrilling look-in on history and left him with a ravenous appetite for more books like it. He was carried away in the excitement of the Gordon Riots; he lived the life of the half-witted hero boy with the tame raven that went everywhere he went—even into battle.

Now about this time, that volcanic and public-spirited citizen, Colonel Eugene Pericles Owsley, partner in the "Southern Bull" tobacco factory, and ever a fiery fountain of ideas, decided that Warham needed a public library. And as the colonel never jog-trotted but always went at a gallop, it wasn't long before he had remodeled a cottage on Main Street, perked it up with a coat of courageous canary-yellow paint, filled it full of books, and presented it to the town with due ceremony.

When Johnny Anders came in to look around, he told Miss Harriet Pettigrew, the librarian lady, that he wanted to read more books about riots, ravens, and wars, such as were in a Dickens book he had. She smiled knowingly and led him to a shelf containing a row of brown-bound, musty-smelling tomes on the Civil War. "If you're interested in history," she said, "then why not start with some history that has happened, not in faraway England, but right here in Mink County?"

History in this sleepy little place? Johnny's eyes brightened at such a brand-new proposition; and from then on, all that summer, all the time he could spare from the other boys and his roamings, he spent in the library hanging around the Civil War books. He liked to keep after one subject for a long time—he devoured it, slept with it, and dreamt it.

One day there was a meeting of Confederate veterans in the library. The place was crowded; and the now-aging men had their chairs banked closely in front of the shelf where Johnny's favorite books were, so that he was completely blocked off. Patiently he postponed his research—but then, thinking it might be a good idea to listen in, he took up a book and pretended to be making notes.

Captain Buckstaff was speaking. He was a slightly built man with a finely wrinkled, tanned skin and a genial expression. His small, lively, dark eyes were set under wisps of brows which contrasted oddly with the wide gray mustache that completely covered his mouth. In his loosely fitting wing collar his neck looked thin, and his black string tie was carelessly knotted. In his lapel he wore a violet, and Johnny could see the tips of two cigars in his coat pocket.

Referring to a diagram he had drawn on an envelope, he said, "The South was really up against it that day. We were in a tight spot." The captain's face was serious, his shoulders stooped as if the urgencies of that vanished day and time were still with him. "With our supplies gone, Atlanta in ruins, Richmond fallen, and General Lee already passed under the yoke—it was the end."

Jack Crabtree, of the Lemon County Grays, spoke up. "I was there myself, Captain Benjamin. I saw you go into the Benson cabin and I felt for you and General Joe—we all did." And he touched his empty sleeve.

Captain Buckstaff went on. "But gentlemen, I've mellowed a lot these past few years. The Yanks didn't treat us too bad, considering." He glanced around the group.

"Well *I* ain't mellered any!" shouted Sergeant Misner, jutting out his chin, unwilling to be convinced. "I left a leg in the Wilderness and my two brothers was killed at Shiloh . . ."

"And I got a Minié ball right here in my hip!" barked another unregenerated reb.

Then the librarian coughed a delicate little diplomatic cough, and the captain took out his big gold watch and smiled around. "Why boys, it's already closing hour for the library—so I guess we won't have time to fight another campaign." And his old eyes twinkled.

The others limped out by twos and threes, but Captain Buckstaff lingered to take one more look in a big worn volume. As he was reaching absent-mindedly to gather up his papers, he noticed Johnny, craning his neck, eagerly studying the diagram on the envelope.

"If you don't want this, sir, could I have it?" the boy asked timidly. "You know I've just been reading about the Surrender. I hiked out to the Benson place the other day, and I've been wondering how the reb soldiers and the Yanks were placed—to keep 'em apart, you know."

Captain Benjamin chuckled. "Well son, I think they got pretty well mixed up that day. But I was in the cabin most of the time, with General Johnston."

And the two walked out of the library together—the boy listening intently to the man's every word. He was on fire with admiration and with questions—for now it had dawned on him that this man was Captain Benjamin Cassius Buckstaff, one of General Johnston's own aides—whose name was in the big book.

"It's odd," the captain was saying, "but two little things stand out most clearly in my memory about that day. The tears in General Johnston's eyes, and the way General Sherman's hair stood up like porcupine quills as he signed his name to the document with a scratchy goose-quill pen. . . ."

They walked up Main, still talking about the War, and as they came to the courthouse—the sun being still quite a ways from down—sat on a bench under the big spreading maple tree there.

The captain took out one of his cigars, bit off the end, and lit it. Then blew out a puff of fragrant smoke.

"Yes, history was being made in that little farm cabin," he reminisced. "We were living history." Thoughtfully, he sent out another cloud of smoke, savoring the cigar and his eager audience.

"Oh I wouldn't have missed that day for anything," he said. "And the longer I live the clearer it comes back."

The Printery

It is six o'clock of a winter morning in the home of Johann Anders the printer. Johnny—bemused and dreaming as usual—is at the breakfast table. Papa is saying something to him, but he is afloat in a blue whirling mixture of reveries and longings, musings over a peach of a book he has been reading. In which a boy finds refuge from a war in an Alpine cave, where he lives with another boy, who turns out to be a wonderful girl named Laurence. Then he falls in love with her, but as he is studying to be a priest, he gives her up and beats it. Sure sounded like a dumbbell, but that's the way it was in the book. . . . Laurence is a little like Anna the Circus Girl and a little like Essie, that girl in the bookbindery. . . . He thinks of going several blocks out of his way this morning just to walk to school the same way Anna will be going. What would she say to him if he caught up with her? And what would he say back? What if he just got tongue-tied? Anna got him all confused, she was so pretty.

At first he didn't hear a word Papa was saying. Not until his lively, fun-loving Uncle Jake called to him across the table: "Hi, old Rip Van Winkle, it's wake-up time!"

Papa was in a big hurry this morning—said something about a special order for labels that had to be bronzed and delivered to the Southern Bull factory today; and also he seemed to be trying to tell his son something important. "John," he said suddenly, looking up over his plate, "it's about time to decide what you want to be in life."

This took the boy by surprise and his dream guffed out like a candle. It was certainly an awkward time and place to be settling such a momentous question; as if it were no more important than grabbing up a shirt for the day or hefting a bag of potatoes. Why he hadn't yet even glimpsed all the wonderful and exciting ways down which life could lead you!

But he had to say something, so he said the first thing that came into his mind: "Oh—well I think I'm gonta be an artist and an author."

His hair was standing up perversely and his heart beat fast, like that of a bird caught in a corner. Uncle Jake grinned, Mother was shaking her head, and all at once Papa smacked the arm of his chair with the flat of his hairy hand and exploded in a roar of laughter. "Author, eh?" he gasped when he could calm down. "Well—" and he wiped the grease from his mouth with the side of his hand. "Why son, whatever makes you think you could be an author? Don't you know authors have to be born that way? And highly educated. Why you've only been to the seventh grade—though that's three grades more'n I ever got," he added a little ruefully. "And besides, there's no money in writing—you'd starve to death. Only the great geniuses like Shakespeare or Mrs. Henry Ward Beecher Stowe ever made any money at writing."

Young John Anders didn't mind so much stopping school and going to work in the print shop. ("Seven is all the grades I can give you, son," Papa had said; "and you must come in the business and learn it now . . .") But never again did he confide his secret hopes and aspirations to his father—or to anyone else.

He liked the printing office. It was not exactly new to him, since he had been going in and out of it all his life. To see Papa for advice, or to borrow a quarter for this or that; to get drawing paper or colored paper for kites; and sometimes Papa would get passes for a circus when the advance man had to have extra date stickers printed to paste over the big colored posters and wanted them in a big hurry. Or now and then it would be tickets to the ten-twenty-and-thirty shows in Stoeger's Hall—when some theatrical "stock company" got stranded and had more tickets than money.

He liked to watch the men feeding handbills and big paper sheets into the clanking job-presses and the great roaring cylinder press; to listen to the whining pulleys and slapping belts; to inhale the strong vital smells of the trade: of printer's ink, paper and cardboard, the bookbinders' steaming glue.

He had already worked some in the shop on Saturdays: mostly as helper to the "printer's devil"—that big, strong, black man Hump Bodack—who washed the ink off the press rollers with cottonmill waste and benzine; wiped and oiled the gasoline engine when it was stilled from its heavy pumping and thumping that shook the floor. Who swept, handled heavy boxes and bales, filled and emptied the big banging garbage cans, delivered jobs around the town in a pushcart, fetched beer and trotted errands for the men, and put out poison for the rats.

And one Saturday, when Papa was short of hands, he had put Johnny to work in the bindery, folding papers with a slick bone folder.

There was a pretty girl, a girl older than he, working there then—Essie Green. Her eyes were full of merry light, and he fell violently in love with her; though certainly by his precipitous manifestation of affection she would never have suspected it. As they were working together at the same table, a sharp, strange thrill overwhelmed him and he suddenly grabbed the glue brush and daubed it, loaded with hot glue, right down into her bright golden hair. And when the tempest was over—the lightning words and great rain of tears—and Essie Green had stormed out with a twenty-dollar bill in her purse and profuse apologies from Papa; and Johnny had been called on the carpet for his wild misdeed; he just stood stock-still and silent. Wouldn't say a word, though Papa gave him to understand that the hush money would be deducted from his pay envelopes. But to himself poor Johnny was saying plenty. "Oh she oughtn't to have looked at me that way!" and "Gosh—she was so beautiful!"

There was a row of barrooms right across the street from the typesetting side of the printing loft—with its four tall windows—and in those early boyhood days Johnny would stare down, fascinated, at the men going in and staggering out. In Caudle's Big Nine, when the weather was warm and the door open, he could see the customers sitting on stools; and the bartenders with all the fancy bottles behind them. It was a hangout for gamblers, and sports with their bulldogs, and at times there was considerable singing.

> Oh beefsteak when I'm hungry
> Whiskey when I'm dry,
> Money when I'm hard up,
> And heaven when I die . . .

But now that he had come of working age and was one of the "hands," instead of just a visitor, gawking out the windows was out. Now Papa was making a real printer of him: he was learning to set type, to do bookkeeping, to help out in the bindery when help was short (and Lord, when he remembered that earthquake with Essie he was sure glad she was no longer there!), to meet customers, and take on responsibility. He was getting some spending money in his pocket, and since it was good to be learning new things and meeting new people, the printing craft soon won his enthusiastic attention.

Sometimes funny and unexpected things happened.

There were the tramp printers. Competent type-slingers were scarce, and could demand a good wage. So some of these nomad ones were very independent and foxy; and all seemed to have a yen for change, for moving on. With a week's or a fortnight's pay in pocket, they would turn up missing the day after payday; having taken off with notice to no one—legging it down the railroad track and heading for another town. They knew they could get work there if the place had a newspaper or print shop, and they were always gandering hopefully for less work, more pay, and new love affairs.

The prize peripatetic printer of them all arrived one hot day in July, with his pants rolled above his knees and on his head a straw hat that in its day had been sporty, but now was nothing but a brim. His dirty brick-red hair poked wildly up through the vacant space and he introduced himself to the boys as Sam McCound. Inquiring the way to the drinking water, the next thing they knew he was up in the zinc sink taking an all-over bath—to the amusement of everybody. Then, hat brim in hand, he went into the office and came out a full-feathered member of the type-assembling fraternity. All afternoon he stood at the case, filling and emptying his composing stick industriously on "The History and Necrology of Grand Lodge No. 522," that was a rush job.

At quitting time he borrowed a quarter here and there and got Papa Anders to advance him five dollars to get a haircut and pay a deposit to the landlady.

"Looks like you know your stuff," said Papa, looking at his output tied up neatly on the composing stone.

But the next morning McCound was nowhere to be found. He had skedaddled and was never seen again. And when a proof was pulled of his precipitate labor, some 1,863 errors and "wrong fonts" adorned the page. It took a man all day, and then some, to untangle the types he had conflummoxed and get them back in their right boxes. But Papa had to laugh. He had the proof sheet framed and hung on his office wall—somewhat as a curiosity, and as a warning to himself never again to hire a hobo without first testing his know-how.

The Anders Printery had come a long way. Papa Johann hadn't had an easy life. He was the son of a German immigrant with a large family, who had apprenticed him as a boy to a Chicago newspaper. Here he worked for a year without pay, but managed to learn the printer's trade. The Anders family had landed in Mink Station soon after the Civil War—just in time to get in on its industrial rise. The old man—Heindrick—was a carriage maker, and he and his son Jake had started Minktown's first shop for the making of wagons and fine vehicles; while the other son, Johann—on capital borrowed from banker McCubbins at 12 percent—had launched its first printing office. At first it was only the Anders Printing Room, in a single small room upstairs over a grocery store. Then, its custom increasing, it came down into a store building on Mink Street. By and by it had gone upstairs again—to occupy a large loft over a Main Street clothing store, at which time it was rechristened the Anders Printery; and Papa said in a few more years he hoped to have a building of his own.

The job Johnny liked best of any was being sent on errands to the tobacco factories that provided most of their business—now to the J. Warham factory, now to the Southern Bull or Z. R. Zachary's Pride of Warham, or maybe to Tonkerson's Old Virginia Snuff & Cheroots. . . . It was this activity that taught him there was more to the printing business than the workings of machines. In going about among the men of tobacco he began to glimpse the bewildering mechanics of life.

The first "big wheel" customer that Papa turned John loose on was General Eugene Pericles Owsley. "Be careful," Papa said. "General Owsley is one of our very best customers. He never considers price, just so he gets what he wants. And he always knows exactly what he wants; so *never* make any suggestions. Also he's proud as a turkey cock and really turns purple in the face if anybody dares to cross him. And as he talks very fast, and like he has mush in his mouth, be sure you understand all the details."

General Owsley (lately promoted from colonel by the politicians commanding the United Confederate Veterans) was a small man with a potbelly and a ruddy, wine-fed face. He always wore a carnation in his buttonhole, and liked to keep the common scum at a distance while he played the heroic and patriotic potentate. To the general, there was nothing like the antebellum South and slavery days. He had several Negro sons—all very handsome—by various upstairs maids.

"Ump-ump-er-humf!" said the great man, clearing his throat. He always said that before giving orders.

What the general wanted was a superfancy program folder for a district meeting of the United Daughters of the Confederacy.

"Now this is the way I want it, young man," he said, reaching for a dummy he had prepared. "Must be printed in dark purple ink on a heavy lilac-colored stock that I've telegraphed a firm in Richmond to ship you immejetly. Then a Confederate flag in full color on the front, with a cut of General Robert E. Lee. And on the back a drummer boy with drum, and a portrait of General Stonewall Jackson. And now in the upper right-hand corner I want a bow of gray and red ribbons entwined—the red to be about the shade of an American Beauty rose. Submit proof in color—and, oh yes, this is a rush order, of course."

A few days later, when John carried his distinguished military customer the assembled proofs—ribbons and all—the general was dictating to a pretty young stenographer with flirtatious blue eyes—leaning back in his chair with the tips of his fat fingers joined. But he swiveled around from his "In reply to yours of the sixteenth," and with his preliminary "Ump-ump-er-humf!" reached out the imperial hand.

He smiled and twisted his short neck around in its senatorial roll-wing collar as he read, and then waxed enthusiastic. "I must say, young man, that you have a most admirable capacity for following orders."

This was like an accolade to the gangling young John; and he smiled back as he picked up his hat and said "Oh thank you, sir," and backed out toward the door.

But if General Owsley was pompous and particular, John's next contact, Mr. Tysander Warham, was a giddy-go-lucky and most inelegant. John had gone to his office in the Tysander Building to collect a bill of seventy-eight dollars that was a year past due. Mr. Ty Warham was in a gloomy mood that morning. His life had been lived in a high-rolling way, with many a purple passage, and his big bulbous nose was very blue.

At first John was awed. Here was the ogre that owned the wonderful woods where the owl lived. Rared back in his swivel chair, with his oversize feet up on his desk, he was bewailing in vulgar song the present ineffectual condition of his male member and the unreasonable demands of the female tribe. As was his habit, he had reduced his thinking to indecent doggerel, and was singing in a thin quavering voice:

> Pore old pecker—
> My pecker won't peck;
> He's got no spezaza,
> No git-up, by heck.

Then he brightened up. "What you want here boy? Did you bring me any booze?" And when John presented his bill, he laughed. "I never pay bills, son," he said kindly.

"I know one you paid," said John, a sudden burst of commercial confidence coming up out of the compost heap of discouragement.

But the bawdy tobacco baron didn't hear him; was too absorbed in his music.

> My name is Joe Baker,
> My ass is a Quaker;
> My bollox weighs forty-four pounds!

"I said I know one bill you paid, Mr. Warham," John repeated, somewhat louder.

"Wha's that?—Why, I'll get me a tin bill and peck shit with the chickens before I'll pay you one penny, boy."

"Well sir, you paid my Uncle Jake Anders two thousand dollars the other day."

The tough old reprobate's face took on a truculent flush. "So— you're one o' them goddamn Anderses, eh?" His interest seemed to deepen, and he gave John a sharp looking-over. He put the palms of his hands together and gave his swivel chair two little reflective rocking squeaks. Then he called over to his secretary Bill Brandley at the bookkeeper's desk: "Hi Bill, pay this-here little gazoop his swindle-sheet."

When John told at the family supper table how he had collected money out of hardboiled Tysander Warham, his Uncle Jake reminisced in detail on his own encounter with that incorrigible, who had run through several fortunes and half a dozen wives. "Why, he had owed us that money on a victoria we built for him for over three years, and I thought it about time to collect. I just asked him if he was going to pay it, and he said 'Not by a damn sight.' Then I took off my coat, rolled up my sleeves, and said: 'Then I'm gonna beat the holy hell out of you.'"

He slapped John on the shoulder with his big, strong he-man's paw. "Looks like we're pretty good bill collectors, don't it?" he said.

The poorest of all the print shop's patrons were the poets among the Negro factory hands. Almost every Saturday, when the hands were paid, some shy and inward-seeing old man would come in to "git a ballad struck off." Rudely scrawled in pencil on tablet paper would be presented the ballad poem on "Moses on the Mounting," or "Old King Faro," or "I'm a Gwine to Heben on the Wind," that he had mused on all week and saved his money to get published. To those humble authors, their "ballads" were treasures of creation that gave them absorbing, noble uplift from drudgery—the same happy genius-feeling as that experienced by authors much more celebrated.

And since Papa had impressed upon John that the small orders and the small customers must be handled with the same consideration and service as the large—and being even more interested in the poetic than in the bag labels and the myriad "special offers" and other tobacco advertising matter—John took particular pains to help such illiterati get their brainchildren straightened out. It was a real pleasure to see the light in their eyes when he'd get their words perfected and ready for the world in black and white.

*   *   *

Uncle Jake played first clarinet in Sherman Josephburg's band and orchestra, and one day he suggested to John that he, too, learn the instrument. Also there were several fellows in the printing office who belonged to the band, and who made quite a bit of spiff on the side playing at land sales, patriotic gatherings, dances, at Mr. J. Warham's Gragg Street Methodist Church, or Mr. McLauchlen's Fifth Avenue Presbyterian Church Sunday schools, as well as in the theater—so before long John was also caught up in the musical tide. And, with a little starting off from Uncle Jake, was practicing furiously in the evenings and on Sundays. After a while he was allowed to sit in at orchestra practices at Stoeger's Hall; and in a year, so ardent was his application—so many thousandfold were the experimental ups and downs, trillings and cadenzas with which he improved his practice hours—that he was taken in as a member.

The theater enchanted young John. Everything about it. The music, the keyed-up feeling in the perfumed air, the dramatic scenes unfolding. On stage, the rare and rapturous actors and actresses, and the dancers in tights and spangles singing away and wickedly showing their gorgeous legs. . . . He was intrigued by all the secret machinery of illusion. Loved to listen to the excited chatter, the buzz of calls and conversation coming from the dressing rooms with their lamp-bordered mirrors, the calls and curses of stagehands pushing painted rosebushes, mountains, or palaces into place. And, out front, the gala, clean-washed aura of the audience—hushed and expectant; held in thrall by the first yearning, long-drawn liquid notes of the violins beginning the overture.

There was big excitement in Papa's office one day when a Mr. Arthur D. Savery, of Brooklyn, New York, a self-assured and portly man with a honey-and-beefsteak voice and chewing on a big cigar, came to see him. He was an executive in the Mergenthaler Linotype Company, and was out to sell master printers the idea of setting type by machinery instead of by hand. Papa had seen something in the printers' magazine about the invention, but didn't see how on earth a machine could set type. But so deep was the salesman's knowledge, so catching his excitement of sales talk, that before he left, Papa had signed up for a typesetting machine—

five hundred dollars down and the rest on time—costing ten thousand dollars.

That night at home young John asked his father: "And who's going to run it?"

Mr. Anders scratched an ear, cocked his head to one side, and, with a twinkle in his eye, replied: "Well—why not you?"

And so it was to be.

No sooner had the big, wonderful, complicated machine of brass and steel arrived and been set up by the expert mechanic who came with it, than another expert, the operator, appeared and began to tickle the alphabetical keyboard with swift and nimble fingers. To make the little brass matrices come tinkling down from the magazine in endless cataract to the casting mechanism on the pot of hot lead. And in a few weeks—when the rest of the boys had got the hang of the new system—John began taking lessons from "the Chief," as he called the fat and jolly operator expert. There was so much work coming in from the rapidly growing town that the business needed two operators and two shifts. Papa got him a dummy keyboard from the factory, and on this John practiced hard at home of nights and weekends; and it wasn't long before he had himself a regular job.

For a time, John's zeal in learning this new technique of the printing trade made him neglect his clarinet practice, but once he got it under control, he found that the two occupations—the graphical and the musical—mixed up beautifully and went along together like harmonious strands in a weaving.

But the long rush jobs and the book jobs weren't always coming in, and during such lulls, the night shift he worked on was discontinued. Then John's education in public relations—in dealing with the golden ones, the "top dogs" of Warham's business world—went forward.

Came a bright October morning when he went to wait on Mr. Magnus McLauchlen in his downtown office in the McLauchlen Building. It was the first time he'd ever entered that royal red-leather-appointed apartment on the mezzanine floor. Papa had sent him to get the specifications on a blankbook that the great Mr. McLauchlen wanted made.

While he was waiting for him to come out from an inner sanctum, Mr. Milam Warham came in. He was just down from New York. Now this multimillionaire tobacco man kept a small desk in a corner of his partner's office to use when he wanted to open letters, or write a check or a note to some pretty girl who had charmed him. Without noticing the young printer any more than if he had been a speck of dust or a peanut hull, he stood his gold-headed cane up against the settee, picked up his telephone with pale and nervous fingers, and called the Fiducas Bank. "Smiley, come over to my office," he said, as bluntly as though addressing a dog. And then in a few minutes there came hot-footing it, all out of breath, the bank's cashier, Mr. John Smiley. He attempted some fawning pleasantries, but the impatient Mr. Milam Warham wanted none of them. "Put twenty-five thousand dollars to my son Dismukes's account," he said. "That's all. Good day."

An overwhelming sickness of awe struck young John, facing Mr. McLauchlen in his own den. The domineering magnate with the predatory eyes, the granite voice, the shoving bullish will, offered no straw of courtesy or link to his Sunday-school warmness. All hymn-singing was gone down the drain; business was business, and the infant damnation business could damn well stand on its own bottom. He was seated at the big Napoleon-sized desk of polished rosewood with mellow brass bindings that looked like pure gold. His face was florid, heavy-jowled, and he wore a fifty-dollar be-diamonded cravat. His suit of gray tweed was impressive—with maybe a million dollars lying at that very moment in one of its pockets, John thought, and he carried the same old-time Sunday-school aura of lilac.

The big book he gave the order for: *Private Record of Stock Transactions:* was to be bound in red morocco with his name stamped on it in big gold letters, and all ornately embellished and hand-tooled in gold.

The town's Grand Old Man, Mr. Jefferson Warham, was easier to deal with than any of the other tobacco kings. But he didn't have much printing to do these days, as the active management of the business was now in the hands of the younger generation and old Jeff had taken to loafing and getting up late. He went out to Gilchrist College—where he had donated a few hundred thousand in tobacco stocks—now and then to be lionized; and he had spent the summer in Europe, "jest to see what it's like on t'other side," he said.

Soon after his return, John went up to his mansion, Grand View, that looked down on the great J. Warham factory, to take an order for a booklet of poems that his sister-in-law and housekeeper, Miss Elvira Mooney, had composed.

The room he entered was brightened by a cozy fire that cast flickering shadows on a couple of oil paintings the old man had bought at a bargain in Otterburn, England—one a Jesus and one a flock of sheep; and the warm light glittered on an ostentatious chandelier and heavy red curtains. And on old Jeff, sitting stolid and cross-legged in his leather chair. Beside him was the be-bosomed and heavily perfumed old lady.

"Come on now, Jeffie, and help me tell this young man how we want our poem book fixed," Miss Elvira cajoled the old codger, who might have been a stuffed man in a museum for all his stiffness and silence. "You know," she explained pleasantly to John, "Mr. Warham's going to get my po'try printed for my birthday present."

"Waal," rumbled the effigy, in a slow, deep voice as rough as a crosscut saw, " 'A fool and his money's soon parted,' and that's no lie." And he launched slowly into reminiscence of how he had started out as a plowboy at five cents an hour. Expounded on the virtue of saving money and hoe-chopping and following a mule. Especially two mules, and both of them blind. "And what's meaner than a mule with shoulder galls?" he philosophized.

But Miss Elvira wasn't to be sidetracked. She knew his love of lecturing, and headed him back to the subject. "Come on now, Jefferson—we've got this busy young man up here to see about it, and he ain't intrusted in mules; ner how you planted them little ole six-weeks bunch beans, neither. Come on now—give him the order."

"Tarnation blazes, Virey, I don't know nothin' 'bout these doo-dabs," he muttered. "I'm a farmer." And he tried to get back to talk about farming. But seeing that Miss Elvira was beginning to cluck and bristle, he scratched his big Roman nose to readjust his mind, and began to melt. "Well now, young man, I want you should fix up them pomes right purty and proper fer her. But jest how, I can't tell you—no more'n I could run down a rabbit. If 'twas me, though, I'd put a picter of a 'bacco leaf on it—'bacco leaves is luckier than four-leaf-clovers any day—but she ain't me, and mebbe Virey druther have a rose or a magnoly. Or a johnny-jump-up. Mebbe with a leetle per-fume sprinked on it, jest a smidgen."

Then he looked up, alarmed. The imperial beard on his lower lip moved with sudden force, and he said: "But say, young man, you ain't said what you gonta charge me fer it. I'jings, I made my money the hard way—with a wagon and a mule. The Lord'll provide, all right, but we've got to do the hustlin', yessiree-bob. And I jest kept a-hangin' on, like a puppy to a root . . ."

One evening when John was leaving the printery, a scrawny little black girl who looked to be about nine, stepped off the plank sidewalk and came timidly toward him.

"Yuh want some cock, mistah?" She spoke so low he didn't at first understand what she was saying.

He was too shocked to say anything. His first impulse was to cuss her out—you little black bitch, or something; but then compassion came and he saw in his mind's eye the devil that was driving her. He found a dollar bill to be grabbed by her eager little claw, and told her to run along home. It was all he could think of to say; and then a vision of what her "home" must be like came upon him heavily. A squalid dilapidated shack in a fringe-of-the-town settlement by a smelly, green-scummed branch. . . . A drunken stepmother—or stepfather—and more children swarming about, with nothing in the house to eat. . . . Bean Pole Beulah being sent out to bring back some money or take a beating. . . . And he knew there were many other young skinny girls, wilding things, and not all of them black, out in Warham tonight trying to bring back a little money.

There had been a lockout at the Erdmann Mills. First a strike over the miserable pay and conditions. But Colonel Cassius A. Erdmann, the Warhams' mill factor, wasn't the man to ever give in. "We'll show 'em who's running things here," he bellowed, and closed everything down.

The workers were cocky at first; built fires and sang songs to bolster up their hopes.

> Like a tree that's planted by the river,
> We shall not be moved. . . .

But when their groceries gave out and they got good and hungry, they marched in ragged disorder to the courthouse to picket there to try and scare the politicians into setting up a bread line. In this they were successful for a short while, but the colonel brought pressure to bear and tonight was the last night the "lintheads" were to get any free food. "The very idea! Making the taxpayers feed these anarchists and bums!" had howled the Warhams' local lawyer, Mr. Barnaby Fogg, to the city fathers.

Each day had its night, and John Anders, who had a habit of wandering about the town after dark, found himself out at the Erdmannton mill village, going about among the slowly moving men and women and the children who had worked in the mills, who were awaiting the arrival of Whitmire's bread wagon. There was a drizzling rain; and a bitter feeling of failure and frustration—a brooding sense of calamity—pervaded the crowd and clutched at every heart. Bewildered, sodden with disappointment and fatigue, they were wondering what was going to happen to them tomorrow, when there would be no more bread. What will we do when they stop throwing this measly little dog's gulp to us? What *can* we do but go back to work on the mill owners' terms?

John saw Oakey France, a young tobacco-factory worker, going about among the outcasts, too. Oakey was a workingman's poet, and he had written a long poem about old Cass Erdmann.

> He's graduated from the school of brass,
> To bash the strikers with a rifle-butt in the ass . . .

he was singing to a guitar.

Standing among the poor shabs, listening to their singing and talk and mutterings of fear under the fitful curling gusts of rain, John Anders felt himself one of them. His people had all been working people, he thought. Tonight he deeply felt their dull anger and despair.

War
(1898)

John Anders went to the J. Warham factory one February day to answer a hurry-up telephone summons. T. P. Warham wanted a figure on five million little sample cards—"They're to go in cigarette boxes and will picture the Navy's different battleships."

T.P., flashily dressed in a checked jim-swinger and sporting his usual brown derby, was chewing a big cigar. John sensed that some big excitement was fermenting in the brain of the financial wizard. "You know," T.P. was saying to Mr. Trenton W. Titcomb, his executive man-Friday—talking loudly above the rumbling din of machinery as if he didn't care who heard him, "a war with Spain is the very thing this country needs. I'm having our senators see McKinley to put a bug in his ear, and if necessary, a doodle bug in his pants pocket. President Buchanan was right," he declared, turning his rapacious eye to a spider web on the ceiling, "when he said Uncle Sam ought to seize Cuba if he couldn't persuade Spain to sell it." He strode up and down with his hands behind him, and John noticed what a big man he was. "Oh, some of the crazy milksop preachers don't want war. But it sure-God would help business."

Then he turned to John and grinned. Shifted his cigar with his tongue. "We're going to be in the market for millions more boxes, sacks, and labels—in patriotic red, white, and blue. Our sailor and soldier boys will be needing a lot of smokes. You printers will be in on the boom too, young Anders."

*   *   *

And now it has gotten to be the morning of February 16. See how splendidly the dawn comes. Observe that a warm breeze is blowing o'er the lea, although it is midwinter. Over the winter weed stalks, the chicken houses and churches, the back yards and the leftover shivering cornstalks of Warham. Know that it is a Wednesday, and notice how skilfully Phoebus the charioteer drives his famous golden vehicle up over the fertilizer factory down in East Warham; how he holds his nose and the sky horses sneeze and that the wind is south by southwesterly.

Before dawn the Warham carrier-boys had whizzed some 1,558 copies of the *Morning Bugle* over gates and picket fences, past aristocratic ironwork and heads of haughty dogs yapping, and small front-yard patches of cinders or mud. Each fresh, inky-smelling newspaper, as it struck and fell against the front door of a subscriber, carried concealed within its neat and innocuous-looking folds a precariously ticking time bomb whose impact multiplied by 1,558 and spreading out to the households and the countryside, would make it a day in old Warham's history to be remembered. It was only a six-word headline:

THE BATTLESHIP MAINE IS BLOWN UP

At nine o'clock in the evening, while on a "good-will," but uninvited, voyage into Havana harbor, the good U.S. warship *Maine* had been, with a villainous thunderbolt of TNT, blasted, buckled, and bent like any tip bucket—her decks, mainmast, and turrets torn and disrempted from her hull, and all her sailors and cargo sent into the long, long ago.

But the cornstalks and winter weeds of Warham stirred no faster. Nor the wagons and ox carts rolling in from the country. Life seemed to be jogging along at the same old tempo, and it was not till here and there a front door opened—till there and here a pair of eyes were rubbed and opened wide—that the town's pulse began to rise and hometown hearts beat faster as that early morning newspaper started pouring out its deadly jingo thought.

An undying Seed Thing of so destructive and resurrective a substance, and so charged with power for evolutionary blight, that it was to go on bearing fruit for years, even for generations, enlarging its potency and range and wreaking its havoc. And not until

long afterward would Americans begin recognizing the relation between the seed of an original folly and the tree of an eventual fury.

But happily, no man on earth (much less in the minuscule town
of Warham) had, that February morning, the slightest knowledge
of these future eventualities. The mild soft weather, the sweet
rosy-golden clouds sailing the sky, the redbirds singing in the
hedges, gave no clue. Though, as soon as the town began to
awake: began hopping out of bed and saying morning prayers;
began to stumble over chairs and kid-vehicles and to say the matu-
tinal goddamnits; began to cross itself and go to the synagogue; to
light up the morning corncobs and slice off chaws of plug tobacco;
to wax up handle-bar mustaches and scissor beards; to fry sowbelly, sausage, chitlings, eggs, and oysters, and to toddle out in slippers and bathrobe for the paper, there were no waiting milk bottles
on Warham porches yet in 1898—there began a communal buzzing.

At first people were merely bewildered; then angered with a
dull and frustrative ache. As though they had been lushly spat
upon by an unknown in a crowd, or had a cow maliciously turned
into their garden, or been cuckolded.

By ten o'clock the town was a swarm of fiery fractious bees—
whose buzzing core was centered, as if by some fundamental
swarming instinct, at the great wooden hive of the Jumbo Tobacco
Warehouse.

John Anders was shoving through the crowd on his way to the
warehouse office to deliver a big checkbook and some cardboard
pile tickets that Mr. Bowling, the manager, had telephoned about.
"Some of these boys have been down to the side-street joints taking
on plenty of corn and 'Cape Horn rainwater,'" John thought. It was
giving the inhibited their tongues and making the uninhibited
more quacky. At times, the surge of the crowd and the talk was so
heavy out in front of the warehouse that the plank sidewalk's old
worn backbone seemed like to break under the burden of all those
determined hotheads' feet.

"No sirree—nobody's gonta sink a battleship belonging to the
United States and get away with it!"

"Well, I'll tell ye *this* much—that old whats-his-name—Premier
Shagaster—Sagasta—oughta be kilt!"

"And that Queen Maria Christina, too—the whole kit and

boodle! Why I was talkin' to a sailor that's been over thar, and he said the queen was a-tiddlin' round with the palace help and the gen'ruls and ossifers same's a common you-know-what."

"How did they do it?" asked Schoolboy Number One.

"Oh they had the harbor mined, so they could jest push a button," said Schoolboy Number Two. "That's what the *Bugle* sez."

Mr. Titcomb, hurrying by to his office at the J. Warham factory, was asked by Miss Murine Gannett, society reporter for the *Morning Bugle*, what he thought about the situation. Oh, what had to be done had to be done, he said in clipped and measured words. And reminded her—flinging out a pure golden apple of discord—that, as Cato the Censor said, *delenda est Carthago.*

At last came 2 P.M.

And with it to Stoeger's Hall on Main Street, up over A. Marx's Bargain Store and Fergus-Robinson's Hardware, the multitude of Warham's fretful citizenry. Two thousand pairs of feet—taking along with them two thousand pairs of lungs to lap up the pap of the politicians—clumped noisily up the dirty wide reverberating stairs.

Ahead of the shifting storm center went the Warham Light Infantry and the Warham Brass Band. And head of *them* the three moving mountebanks of the meeting: the Honorable Inzer D. Wyantt, the lawyer; Reverend Luther P. Funderburg; and mayor pro tem, M. B. Tubson—who were already upon the stage, seated on a high-backed settle borrowed for the occasion from the Boykin & Rawdon Furniture Company. Sitting in their best black Sunday coattails with all their legs crossed in unison (two pairs of long and one of short); their black hair, what small amount they had, brushed slick enough to slide a fly; and selfsame solemn, glowering expressions hard-packed upon their faces.

All was backgrounded, and the stage set. They had got out the old fetish bundles. The national flags and the sacred colors of the Lost Cause and the United Daughters of the Confederacy were amicably crossed, and there was red-white-and-blue bunting draping the side walls and backstage and engarlanding the speakers' lectern in brilliant folds and pleats. (The elbow grease having been furnished free by Morlock the signpainter, flags by General Owsley, the bunting by Mellis-Doan Dry Goods, and the red and white carnations in a big blue vase contributed by Dalberd the Leading Florist.)

A number of other prominent bigwigs, manufacturers, and females had by now also arrived upon the stage—by the back entrance, so as to avoid the *profanum vulgus*—and were dispersed in prayer-meeting folding chairs to flank the Three Wise Old Crows in serried semicircles. There were the city fathers—in whom love of country was ever uppermost, and exceeded only by love of country ham and cabbage and buttermilk and boodle—and the choir, hurriedly recruited from all the church choirs in town and from the highways and the byways of choicest and purest southern womanhood.

A vast assemblage having now flowed and waddled up the Stoeger's Hall stairs, the meeting was called—from a pandemonium of buzzing, yelling, foot-stomping, coughing, and piercing whistles—to order.

The chief and canniest crow, the Honorable Wyantt, stood up and looked sharply about, and held up a black, white-cuffed wing for silence. But noise and snake medicine was what was wanted. The Honorable motioned to his music crew and that little jumping-jack, Professor J. Russell Horsmayr, was right glad to jump into this breach and the public eye and shake his music stick toward the choristers and his prominent bottom toward the assembled excited audience and soothe its savage breast somewhat with the rolling strains of "The Star-Spangled Banner." In which, of course, it was urged to stand up and chime in.

Some of the mob's angry hissing steam thus let off, Chairman Wyantt now launched ably and confidently into his oration, which he prefaced with a patriotic poem hot from the versatile head of that industrious, imaginative citizen, Johann Anders the Printer (ere 6 o'clock, it would be launched upon the streets and porches of the town in the form of a "throwaway").

It opened with the stirring words:

> Sound the tocsin,
> Wake the nation,
> Cuba shall be free!

Chairman Wyantt's eloquence was considerably bulwarked by a brace of telegrams in his pocket. They had come early that morning: one from Senator Cloverman, in Washington; and another, treasured even more highly, from the great tobacco magnate, Thomas P. Warham, in New York. By a peculiar coincidence, their substance and sentiments were as like as two pie-prints, as two stripes on a zebra; both urging him to get busy in a hurry and transform public sentiment in his neck-of-the-woods into a loud demand for rapid and aggressive governmental action.

Chairman Wyantt cut loose with all his guns that day. ("Just think what a war would do for the tobacco business!" the still small voice of his tender tycoon-loyalty kept whispering.) It was the most powerful orating he had ever put forth, loaded with synthetic sincerity and frequent references to Liberty, Christian Civilization, the Founding Fathers, Southern Womanhood, and Almighty God. Sowing the dragon's teeth, Wyantt referred effectively, and ever and anon, to the elite chewing-and-spitting heroes in gray aslouch on the front rows. Those worn old warhorses seated beside the modern spick-and-ramroddy Company B.

Rabble-rouser Wyantt played on his harp of cajolement, sang his siren song to fan the fire. With his grandiloquence and invective, he appealed to every prejudice, introduced the finest denunciations and philippics from Cicero, Saint Paul, and Shakespeare. But as his eagle eye looked down upon his rapt listeners he was shuffling them into a mergence with something else; lining them up in the plans of the Messrs. Warham and Cloverman; and J. P. Morgan and Havemeyer and Spreckels for the embryonic Sugar Trust; Armour of the Meat Trust; Carnegie's Iron and Steel at Bethlehem and elsewhere; and the Rockefellers, ra'ring to expand Standard Oil's export of kerosene and lubricants and to put their National City Bank in charge of Cuba's finances; and the Du Ponts; and the railroad kings James J. Hill and Harriman (already plotting how they were going to crisscross even faraway China with railroads)—all the hard and raptorial merchants-of-death who had never cared how murderous a thing was, just so there was money in it. ("I'm a clamorer for dividends," Saint John D., the patron saint of the monopoly capitalists, had said.)

By the time the chairman roared out his last thunderous diatribe, rolled his eyes upward for the last time to a bloody choleric God of Tooth and Claw in an imaginary celestial city located upon the dinged and cobwebbed ceiling, shook his shaggy locks out of his eyes, parted his coattails and sat down, there was hardly a cool brain, a calm breath, an unjaundiced eye, or an unhardened heart in the house. The hoi polloi whooped, hollered, howled, and hurrahed till it was husky. The various isolated angers that had begun earlier in the day as small individual whirlwinds were now, by the magic of demagogic cant and red-hot words, compacted and fused into one furious raging hurricane. So far as the town of Warham was concerned, the war that was to be launched by Washington a few weeks later was already detonated.

Commander Owsley, that gallant and intrepid colonel in the "Department of the Confederate States Army," who was, of course, together with his red carnation, prominently seated on stage, got up with the old lightning in his eyes and got in a few electric licks on how all Carolina hearts were beating as one, from Manteo to Cherokee. This aroused more thunder—notably in the front-row contingent. For though every man-jack of them knew that the general's military exploits in the late war, or any war, had been limited to valorously riding in victorias at the head of Confederate Veterans' Reunion parades, it didn't make any difference. Didn't he send them all turkeys from his big stock-and-fancy-fowl farm at Christmas? And though he had never been on any but postwar battlefields and his ardent innumerable skirmishes had all been with the skirts—they one and all admired him for a brave and horny old tomcat and two-mamma papa, and when any of them needed help they knew where to go to get it.

Colonel Cass Erdmann then did his usual bullyboy act for a minute or two—which consisted of striding up and down like an angry bull and wagging his broad posteriority while he sputtered some pompous prolixities on "Southern Womanhood." And when the mayor pro tem got up and mentioned the horrid names of Sagasta and General Weyler, it brought such a cannonade of catcalls and boos, you'd have thought the Battle of Bull Run or Shiloh was being refought all over the place.

The mayor was confident our boys would be in Madrid by the Fourth of July at latest. It was a pity the Spanish nation didn't know the invincible virility, the galvanic get-up-and-git of mighty America when once aroused.

There wasn't much left for Reverend Funderburg to say, except "Me too." Though his was the sacred task of affixing the seal of heaven's approval to all that had been said, anathematized, and done. Avenge our dear and sacrosanct scuttled battleship. Tear their guts out. Sack, ravish, swoop down upon all their islands and seas, and all will then be serenity and Christian brotherhood and freedom and free trade and democracy and Uncle Sam on top of the heap and God's holy will, forever and ever amen.

The Warham Brass Band played stirring agitative Sousa marches and the young men of Warham—rampant to shed blood—began looking around for an enlistment office.

But with all the orating, praying, singing, certain dark bedrock facts and stark fecund realities that underlay that day, that year, went unremarked.

Only a few deep-sighted Americans, the delvers after truth, had, then, discerned our catastrophic trendings. The blood-soaked probable outcomes: the sowing of the wind and the whirlwind-reaping.

Thorstein Veblen, a mind as clear as a crystal spring, was one who had seen the strong American nation being strangled by Big Business and the Big Military; its Bill of Rights and dedication to minding its own business being subtly replaced by monopoly's "systematized delusions" of dementia praecox and conquest. Edward Bellamy was another who saw it straight. "As an iceberg floating from the frozen North is gradually undermined by warmed seas," he had mused, "and becomes at last unstable, churns the sea to yeast for miles around by the mighty rockings that portend its overturn, so the barbaric . . . system which has come down to us from savage antiquity, undermined by the modern humane spirit . . . by the criticism of economic science, is shaking the world with convulsions that presage its collapse." An ex-President, Benjamin Harrison, had opined: "I do not look upon territorial expansion as the safest and most attractive avenue of national development." But there was a rough and ready cowboy-in-a-silk-hat—Theodore Roosevelt—who was likewise Assistant Secretary of the Navy.

"T.R." was a devotee of strenuosity. Of jump-into-everything-in-all-directions-with-both-feet. He was a bear for wood chopping, for jujitsu, for jumping fences on a horse, writing books, boxing, rough-riding lickety-split in a big wild-west hat after wolves, wild-cats, or hummingbirds, and he was an egoist who loved the limelight. Outside, the man looked quite sane and steady, but inside he carried the blood taint and social superstitions of a dozen generations of overprivileged Dutchmen who knew for sure and certain that the set and rise of suns, the westward rolling of the seasons and the stars, were planned exclusively for the enjoyment and profit of the English and the Dutch. And he was deeply religious and haunted by the Old Testament god of battles and the blood sacrifice. T.R. was for doing first and thinking afterward; and he bared his formidable stallion teeth and fiercely pish-tushed at the sissy pacifists and divinated: "Every expansion of civilization makes for peace" . . . "Speak softly and carry a big stick" . . . "McKinley has no more backbone than a chocolate eclair." . . . So to our Teddy the war-to-be was "bully."

In Congress all the corporation lawyers were doing their screwy stuff too, for the aggressive expansionist millionaire monopolists. The old Romans and lone lions (all fat flunkies of the ruling businessmen) tearing their togas and roaring platitudes for freedom's holy cause, and W. R. Hearst and his nineteen newspapers and Fitzhugh Lee (son of General Lee) and Senators Albert Beveridge, Henry Cabot Lodge, Mark Hanna, and many more, and the naval strategist Captain A. T. Mahan, working for the spread-eagle imperialists, and General Miles (the great Indian killer), rattling the saber and beating the war drum.

The good goofus citizenry of Warham, up in Stoeger's Hall, singing

> Onward Christian soldiers,
> Marching as to war . . .

were ignorant of those unvarnished truths about Spain and Cuba and our Wall Street supergovernment that should have been unequivocally blared forth that day.

. . . *How the 260 brave and salty seagoing lads who went down with the* Maine *had been scuttled and drowned like rats by a monopoly-captained War Department on Machiavellian command—to create "an incident," when all her officers but two were safely ashore.*

. . . *How, on April 10, the queen of Spain met all the U.S.A.'s harsh, humiliating demands, but President McKinley, the tool of*

Wall Street, said hardly a word about it to Congress and let it declare war on April 25.

. . . How in Warham and all over the land, amid the patriotic songs and sacred hymns and sacrificial chanting, never a word was said about Old Man Typhoid waiting in glee at Jacksonville. About Señor Yellow Jack, who was to be a guest of the army in Havana and Luzon. And who, between them, were to slay eleven times more American young men than the Spaniards' Mauser rifles and dum-dum bullets. Never a word was mumbled either about the embalmed beef of the Chicago Meat Kings (old stale stuff "rejuvenated") or Armour's deadly rotten pork-and-beans, that also slew the assembled companies and platoons and the unassembled epidemic throng.

In years to come, some who were then small boys would remember the day the Warham Light Infantry (Company B) and a new company of volunteers entrained at the depot, with the girls kissing them goodbye and weeping and waving and the tobacco factory across from the depot all decorated in red, white, and blue with whistles shrieking and the soldier boys bravely singing

> Goodbye Doll, I must leave you
> Though it breaks my heart to go!

as the engine tooted and the Southern train, with its old wooden coaches and the old brown paint peeling off, pulled out. And the day the coffins were unloaded by the Southern Express Company on that same identical platform and hundreds of other platforms. And all the little flags and flowerpots that were to stand ere long in mute and frozen celebration among the sere grave grasses of the mowed-down or poisoned youth.

The Opera House

But a town corpus must also have some glory and pride, beer and schnapps, fool notions and feather-minded moments; music as well as meat. Thus it came about that in the year after the sinking of the *Maine,* the municipality of Warham caused to be erected a new and resplendent Warham Opera House—not to mention a Municipal Meat Market. If the upper half of the opera house symbolized life's higher values, its lower level, sacred to the Lares and Penates of cold cuts, chitlings and chuck, catered to man's more ephemeral and fleshpot drives. "Art and Fresh Meat" might have been carved over the main doorway. The reality-escapers, lotus eaters, and matinee mammas were succored in the building's higher atmosphere. And in the less rarefied and blood-stenched air of the nether and baser story, convened the carnivorous, the matron and the butcher, haggling over remnant bones to go in the soup.

The new meat market as well as the rendezvous of the Muses was adorned with the first Italian Renaissance facade in town.

It was Ogden Undergrift who answered the summons of the mayor's building committee to construct this magnificent edifice on the site of the old Jumbo Warehouse. For some time the Ladies' Civic League had been ding-donging to get that historic, monstrous structure done in. Though to be sure they'd had plenty of opposition—especially from the part of the population that equated theatergoing with perdition. Reverend Lish D. Wingo, leader of this particular flank of the good folk, used a rather quaint argument to pull the rug out from under the civic ladies. "The good old Master up there must have made tobacco for a purpose," he opined, "so I'm in favor of leavin' Ole Jum a-settin' right where he be."

"You could say the same of rattlesnakes," the Anti-Cigarette League ladies parried. And it was an esthetic crime, so those other esthetic ladies said, to let that old wooden eyesore continue to sit right in the center of the new and greater Warham the Beautiful.

With his main office speedily transferred from Walterville to Warham, Builder Undergrift set the stage for action—for wrecking the old and mixing concrete for the new. He was to make a neat little fortune clearing away Warham's dirty small-town cobwebs and dreaming up and hammering out handsome new metropolitan buildings. Later would come a time when Warham's architectural cup would be running over with pilasters, pinnacles, and porticoes—in the Florentine, Roman, and Bolognese manners. A time when also the Gothic, Tudor-Gothic, Neo-Gothic, and near-Gothic would be heaped upon her in abundance.

This Undergrift was a high-class man—handsome, spruce, and a good red-blooded American—so that even the very-select Tarheelia Club (Warham's pre-Rotarian businessmen's elite fraternity) opened up and took him in right away. He was a regular boiler factory of bang-up mass-production ideas and wouldn't have anything but the fastest and most-up-to-date machinery and power gadgets around him.

And so, with hard-working gangs, lubricated public relations and a lot of shoveling, dumping, and raising-of-walls, the Undergriftian masterpiece was finally and beautifully achieved. And not only that, but Warham was then given her first concrete sidewalk alongside. A crowd stood in the sunshine outside the cusped and foliate Lorenzo di Medici arches, watching M. Hoegger & Son, from Philadelphia, work at the strange forms, smoothers, blocking tools, and lineators. Watching the autographing of the Hoegger's handiwork, printerwise and semiceremoniously, there before the new and pilastered meat market, with an imprint block. Some later immortalized their own footprints, and small boys enstamped the paws of pooches.

Everybody—or almost everybody—was satisfied. The opera house would be a joy and pride to the Warham citizenry (for the two decades in which the cold-hearted gods of Chance, Commerce, and Orthodoxy would allow it to exist); and one local politician and a banker accomplice, holding an option on "Old Jum," cleaned up a tidy ten thousand dollars on the deal.

On the gala opening night—for which the management had booked *Lost in Africa,* a lively show with lovely, funny Hattie Williams as leading lady and a lot of snappy lady legs besides—the hometown orchestra played "The Awakening of the Lion," by De Konski, with its loud heroic, long-flown roaring.

Sherman Josephburg, now editor and half-owner of the *Morning Bugle* and a very versatile musician, led the noise on the baritone horn and did himself and the lion proud. The bass fiddle growled, the cornets yapped, and John Anders's and his Uncle Jake's clarinets snarled away like everything. Sherman's buddy Boozer Bobbitt throbbed the snare drum and gave the bass drum hell, building up the body of the big and increasing bellow by fierce and *sostenuto* rataplans.

There were orchestra, dress circle, and parquet divisions, and all the king's horses and all the king's mares were present at the opening. A special gallery was Reserved for Colored—just above the first gallery, where sat the ragshags and the cottonmill hands.

Downstairs, a universal flutter of programs. The flopping down of the patent seats, the settling of the ladies in place—done thoughtfully with nice southern manners.

A patting of lady hands to hair and a general titivating of noses. Some chatted or sat silent and expectant. Some stared at the curtain, upon whose center was emblazed a big, strange, and grandiose device—ASBESTOS—but which, as soon as the house began to fill, withered away upward to give the ad curtain a chance to play *its* part: with boast and brag of clothiers; penny-pinching advice from various banks; the Southern Railway, the Hot Shot Pressing Club, and Mrs. Isadore Fern the Florist respectfully coveted everybody's patronage.

Upstairs the eyes of the small-potato audience feasted on the aristocratic and moneycratic shirtfronts, diamonds, and furs in the boxes.

"Did you ever notice how much like a baboon Gladys Erdmann looks?"

"In spite of their money, those Dismukeses always manage to look disreptile, don't they?"

Up there in a box for all to see was old Mr. Tysander Warham with his strapping hot-babe latest bride. His seventh conjugal gamble, all decked out in jewels. Every sophisticated body was thinking of the old rounder's innumerable sexperiments and escapades. Especially of his recent sensational rescue from his wild sixth wife by his brothers T. P. and Milam, who—with Tysander's wastrel son Dudley—had put him in the crazy house. To "save" him was what they said, but to prevent him dragging the family name any further through the mire was their real motive. And to save what they could of his money for his children. But they muffed it bad and found they had the wrong bull by the horns. For old Tysander's smart lawyer, Bill Brandley, got him out pronto on a habeas corpus. And what a story, though unprintable, the old buzzard gave out.

"It's my dough and my dick, and I'll do what I damn please with both," he had snorted to the newspaper men.

Ten minutes before the ring-up, the wonderful snuff-colored, azure, and gold tapestry curtain—the "scenic"—rolled down with its Louis XIV lady with her big hat and panniers, her adoring shepherd and his carefree sheep. And after that came the awaited, enchanted moment of the lowering lights, the dusky violet dim-out, the curtain's revealing upward roll. Then there is a velvet hush—chatter suddenly stilling and the quick lively music breaking off at the tap-tap signal of fiddle bow on music stand. The magic theatrical air glows red and copper; and a little draft stirs backstage—a sunrise breeze through a castle hall.

To the opera house that year and in other years, came many godlike stars. Came Joe Jefferson: with his bushy eyebrows and Dutch dialect . . . the putting of his famous foot to the local concrete pavement after wiping off the grease paint and shaking off Mynheer Van Winkle's autumn leaves and worn leathern rags. And that sparkling little high-kicking, heart-squeezing Mitzi, laying aside her smash-hit and stellar role in *Sari,* to click her sweet French heels to Warham earth in smart-tailored Broadway mufti. And Alois Burgstaller and Madame Ternina in *Parsifal.* Oh Wagner was hard on the band boys and the electricians! The juice gang sure had to work fast in that scene where the Holy Ghost arrives. . . . Came Laurette Taylor in *Peg o' My Heart* (that poor orphan girl with big staring wistful eyes and swift, sad, haunting smile) and Prince Charming Chauncey in his tall gray Irish beaver and great coat—singing "Sonny Boy" and "Ten Baby Fingers and Ten Baby Toes" and always stepping gallantly on or off stagecoaches and being so kind and courtly to the old ladies . . . coming out the stage door into the night air throwing his great silk muffler with a careless grace and twist about his divine tenor soundbox that was worth a million dollars. That could turn the tears and the laughs on and off like a tap and make the tickets hop and that kindled rare and noble feelings that would stay lit in many a secret heart, to burn and flicker, till their lamps were turned low at the edge of their graves.

Will Kettlewood was keeping the door when William Faversham passed by. "Rather a cold evening, sir." And Will Rogers, with the common touch and the hearty, funny, crowy voice, "Betcha boots, buddy!" And Gus Klein, the midget, stumbling over an empty matchbox and exclaiming *"Got-*dammit to hell!" George M. Cohan—good old nifty George, kindling another fag with his hand cupped against the wind, and talking East Side fast from the corner on his prattle-box and spinning his bamboo cane with a flair. "Get a hustle on, girls!—C'm'on gals! Snap it up girlies!" The klieg lights spotting him dancing in all colors with the 2,400-watt "rifle" spotlight throwing an adjustable beam to follow his action: always surrounded by all-colors-in-the-rainbow of pretty high-stepping sisters, and the "grand old rag"—from which he milked such handsome red-white-and-blue royalties. Sherman Josephburg talked to him a bit backstage in person, that is, listened respectfully to George's gab. Afterward he let out to Boozer Bobbitt, "Now *there's* a musician that's really took his ducks to town! That little red-blooded dude American with the pale face, that prances around like he's got the Saint Vitus dance But boy-oh-boy has *he* cleaned up on patriotics at the piano!" Came trooping from the New York booking office of Klaw & Erlanger, *The Chocolate Soldier* and *Abie's Irish Rose* and *The Wizard of Oz* (with the tricky "Scarecrow Dance" that had to be played right to a click with the hay-bag's floppy, off-beat hopping).

Thomas Dickey, the Walterville baptist preacher, playwright, and Negrophobe—who had made so much money on his hate-play, *Big Buck Nigger*—made a fiery curtain speech when it came to the Warham Opera House. He dumped out the certitudinous, excited oratory for White Supremacy, now and forever, and for the noble Knights of the Ku Klux Klan.

Young John Anders was so disgusted and furious at this brazen demagogue's outpouring of prejudice and lies that he could scarcely keep from crying out in protest from the orchestra pit.

Almost as soon as the noble building was done and dedicated, its nether portal took on a battered, scuffed, and grimy look. A hard look, too, with its belligerent legend of KEEP OUT—POSITIVELY NO-BODY BUT ACTORS. And, being situated at the intersection of several alleys and streets, the wind whipped against the stage door constantly with a touch as gritty as sandpaper.

To lend teeth to the forbidding words displayed upon the pale and bluish cracked-paint door, just inside a burly bear of a door-keep sat always tilted back in a cane-bottomed chair. To see to it that you *did* keep out unless you were an actor or on actor business, was Clement Hafferty's job. And you got the idea almost immediately, as he rested his truculent eye upon you, while he whittled on a piece of soft pine plank with a big frog-sticker barlow knife.

Editor Josephburg boldly thrust his nose into this civic situation. In his wisecrack column, he proposed transferring the warlike palace guard to the department of meat—"where some valuable properties are really at steak." He went on to ask what-the-hell did the city fathers think they were so urgently guarding up those narrow and dirty back stairs? Was it (1) some holy golden chalice of the Middle Ages or the Knights of St. John? Or (2) were they afraid some yokel youth might endanger his immortal soul by getting a peep at the back side of a leg-show; or a love-smitten stage-door Johnny smuggle up a couple o'dozen red roses to an actress's dressing room? Or (3) could it be they were guarding the virtue of some Brooklyn or Chicago Sleeping Beauty? Was *that* it? . . .

That little piece of editorial sarcastigation got the town to laughing and the alarmed city dads lashing around like a whale with a harpoon in its back. They held a special meeting—at which, looking about for a scapegoat, they bounced old Clem the bounder.

That old stage door saw much in its day. John Barrymore's famous feet scraped upon its baseboard. Mary Garden leaned upon it briefly to fumble in her bag for a Smith Brothers coughdrop before stepping out of the court of Pharaoh and into the unlovely pouring-down night. William Jennings Bryan paused ostentatiously upon its steps to wrap the draperies of his dark blue cloak about him; yawning heavily and taking a deep sniff of the sweet tobacco-and-demon-rum Warham atmosphere, he departed with his host, General Owsley, for an after-theater soiree and pleasant presidential dreams.

There were, of course, the stage-door Johnnys. The easy-dough boys hanging around on the old sidewalk in back after the show, hoping to interest a carload of chorine sweeties in a little steak supper at Nick's and a joy ride out into the country afterward.

Backstage, everything would be in a buzz and a hubbub. A regular anthill of animation and excitement. The huge open prop trunks, the motherly old wardrobe mistress coming and going with cloth and costumes, the sketchily clad chorus girls rushing for repairs. Girls, girls, everywhere: moving, gabbing, swearing, making dirty cracks, woo-pooing with the lavender boys and scene rats. Girls going rampant and staging hair-pullings, girls snake-hipping and acting all over the place, mugging their lines against the band out front, arguing, reading fan mail, overflowing to dress out on the runway for lack of dressing-room space. . . . And that special *mise en scène* smell—composed of many little scents and sub-scents, tiny curling wispy scentlings of perfume, feathers, fabrics, the pitchy scent of flambeaux. Odor of canvas stage sets, the dye, wax, and mothballs of artificial flowers. Aroma of coffee, cigarette smoke, grease paint, depilatory, shoe polish, hair tonic, and magnetic musk of male and female; the steam heat popping and the banana-oil-smelling gilt paint of the radiators, American Beauty roses and pink and white carnations arriving by Western Union boys.

The orchestra boys, when not playing, loved to dart through the pit door backstage and stand around, and it was all quite soul stirring, exciting, and very risqué to the quiet young printer Anders.

. . . Patricia has just received a mash note. "To the tall goodlooking redhead on the left end," it says; and the girls gather around to see what's what. To help her lay out the gold-dig.

"Why, the little woman's gone and hooked a 'tobacco king'— just fawncy that!"

"I'd give my kingdom in hell to snag a rich play-daddy with a steam bundle-buggy . . ."

"Now don't forget who lent you that fiver last week, Titian-top."

"If I can only get the giddy goat off somewhere where *we* can be alone together . . ."

Shrieks, giggles, ga-ga noises, and naughty animal anticipations.

A gawky messenger boy with a pimply face stares, open-mouthed, at a luscious chorine standing in the aisle in her scanties. With the wardrobe madam coming and going with her arms full of fluffy stage dress. In the babe's lips a cigarette adroop. "Hey, kid," she drawls, smiling and exhaling through the nose, "ain't you never seen nothing?"

All about were placards reading POSITIVELY NO SMOKING.

But sometimes, in one of its morbidly moral moods, "The City With a Warm Handshake" tendered the poor troupers a rather fishy mitt and a frigid, even hostile, hospitality.

It was thus when Amelia Bingham, the popular New York trage-dienne, came to town.

A Board of Theatrical Censorship had been set up— following a particularly deep-washing revival wave in which a couple of the city fathers had got "saved"—and Miss Bingham's brilliant acting in Sudermann's poignant "problem play" *Magda* was its first suspect. They called her on the carpet to defend her show that some reverend had called "nasty." To run the ferocious gauntlet of their ignoramus authority. But Amelia the Brave brought along a dramatic little surprise and a powerful friend-at-court, in the person of Mr. Milam C. Warham (who in the Big City always attended her opening nights and sent her flowers or gave her a party). And before that awesome millionaire and his gold-headed cane, the erstwhile august tribunal wilted like wild honeysuckle and could only gape and gulp and extend the handsome actress unanimously, and with a rising vote—the key to the city.

But other thespians didn't fare so well. When *The Girl From Rector's* came, the censors demanded a private performance to determine if it were "obscene"; and after sitting agape on the edge of their seats for three hours, enjoying that racy bedroom farce and

the shapely Parisian scenery to the fullest, the three honorable aldermanic asses piously decided it *was*. . . . And Gaby Casadesus
was also declared *verboten* because it was rumored she'd been
known to show her navel. . . .

X

John and Anna

A sudden storm had come to Warham on the first day of February. Had piled snow in drifts and bowed and broken many of the town's old trees, making a white wreckage. John Anders, roaming the streets in the afternoon to survey the damage, wandered far out along Livery Stable Road. No paths had been tramped out here; the snow got into his galoshes, packed into his shoes, and forced him to duck under heavily laden boughs.

He was just passing the Pulaski's big old two-story frame dwelling that had once been a farmhouse, when he noticed a young woman out in the snowy yard tugging at a heavy limb the storm had torn from one of the big maples.

"Why, there's Anna!" He had not seen her for several years, since her marriage to Doctor Hostetter. Local gossips were gabbing that they had already separated—and what could anybody expect from a circus girl anyhow? Well there she was, all spattered with wet snow and, as usual, cheerfully doing something unconventional. In spite of himself, his heartbeat quickened, as it always had whenever he saw her; and without waiting to be invited, he shoved open the gate and waded across the yard.

"Hi! Don't you need some help?"

"Hello there, Janka!" she exclaimed, her dark eyes sparkling. "Wherever did *you* come from? How tall you've grown since the last time I saw you!" Her voice had a slight huskiness that reached right into his heart.

"Oh, I just happened along like the old gray mule that barged into the Sandy Street schoolhouse that time, remember?" He grinned.

She laughed with quick amusement, a rich ringing laugh, showing her white even teeth. "How could I ever forget that? I was so tickled—because I was at the blackboard and all mired up in a problem . . ." Her cheeks were tingling from the cold and the strenuous work. A loop of blond hair had slipped from under her green wool cap. She tucked it back unceremoniously.

"Say, it looks like you need a horse to tote that one."

"It *is* a heavy old thing," she admitted. "And look at all the rest of them—broken branches everywhere."

"Let me help you—here," and he gave the branch a yank. "If we tackle 'em together then it won't be so hard."

"You're hired, as of now. I've just been fussing because I couldn't handle this alone."

They made a game of sliding the big awkward piece of timber around to the woodpile in the back yard. "This can be cut up for the fireplace," Anna said. "We've been needing more wood."

"Sure, and maple burns fine; one of the best," John agreed. Gee, she's pretty, he thought. I've got to find some way to stay longer. "Anna, now we're at it, let's drag 'em all back here."

"Suits me! I was about to give up, and that's something I just can't bear to do . . ."

The exercise was warming, and despite the cold shifting wind, John shucked off his overcoat and put it up on the porch banister. Anna, flushed and enjoying the activity, pulled off her brown leather jacket too. She was wearing an old green corduroy riding suit and gloves scuffed from much wear. But she'd look good in anything, John was thinking.

They tugged and gathered and dragged until all the breakage of the storm was neatly stacked on the back-yard heap. By the time they finished their self-imposed chore it was coming dusk and beginning to snow again—a soft powdery snow that clung to Anna's hair and eyelashes.

Soft yellow light streamed from the kitchen windows. "Let's go in," she said. "I'm getting the shivers out here. We need a rest—we deserve it. And why can't you stay for supper?" she asked eagerly. "I told Edna she could leave early, so we won't have anything fancy. But we could eat it by the fire—and it would be fun. Please do!" Her dark eyes shone mischievously, her smiling lips seemed to promise more.

John gulped. "I—I—why sure! I didn't know how hungry I was. I'd—I'd like to. But don't go to any trouble."

"Well, come on into the kitchen and let's wash up."

The big old-fashioned kitchen was warm and comfortable, with the odor of spices and simmering stew. John sniffed the good smell of some home-baking that was cooling on a board under a red checked cloth. There was a canary in a cage, and house plants arranged around the steaming windows. But what caught his eye was a shining brass samovar standing on a heavy oak sideboard. A small teapot was perched heating on top of its tall chimney.

"Reach yourself a clean towel up there on the shelf," Anna offered, as she dipped hot water into the basin from the reservoir of the wide range. She turned back to John, smiling. "Papa went over to Temple Hill today to trade some horses. He just can't stay away from horses, you know. . . . We might as well have our supper now."

"Where's Doctor Hostetter these days? I haven't seen him for some time," John ventured to ask; remembering rather ruefully that Anna was still the doctor's lawful wedded wife.

"Neither have I," and her dark eyes went somber. "We've separated, you know."

"No I didn't—sorry to hear it," he lied brazenly, his heart taking a hopeful bound.

"I'm all damp from the snow, aren't you? Here, let me dry your coat by the stove. And some hot tea will help us. We're tea drinkers, are you?"

John nodded, though he had never before had tea made with a samovar. He watched as Anna poured the strong tea essence from the little pot into two tall glasses and added boiling water from the spigot.

"Want a spoonful of raspberry jelly? That's the way we like it."

A cat came from around behind the stove. He stretched up tall and yawned, turning his whiskers forward. Then he tapped her on the foot with his paw, purring roughly. "Oh, so you want something too, Toby. He's named after that old funny-geek, Uncle Toby Lolo. And this Toby is a kind of clown too—aren't you, fellow?"

She bent down and rubbed the cat's fur back along his neck, and he purred lustily, rubbing against her ankle.

Oh she's a darling, John mused. The separation couldn't have been *her* fault. Oh anybody would be lucky just to be near her!

As he drank his steaming tea he watched her setting out the dishes, moving with an easy assured grace. When she was done, she excused herself and came back dressed in a long blue green dress with her flaxen hair brushed up in a sleek new way and piled high on top of her head.

She put on a small yellow-sprigged apron. John wanted to tie it around her waist for her, but was too shy. He blushed. "You don't wear your hair long anymore? I used to love it. But it is something to see you this way too."

"And less trouble," she said, giving that pale shining mop a pat. "I wore it hanging down a long time, just because I liked to feel it blowing behind me when I rode."

"Don't you get lonesome out here all by yourself?" he asked suddenly, his expression catching up belatedly with his emotion.

A wistful look came into her slanted eyes. "Not exactly." Her voice was low, almost sad, but she gave her chin a lift. "You see I've still got Papa, and Toby here, and the horses." Then teasingly, with raised eyebrows: "But how about *you*? Are you the lonesome kind? Why I'll bet you've got several girls. A dozen, probably." And she laughed the laugh of a bantering young witch.

Then abruptly bouncing the cat away, she got down two big trays and filled them with supper things. "This isn't much, but as farmers in Poland used to say 'Let's have an omelette of a *whole* egg. Now that we've sold our grain, we can celebrate!' "

Said John, "Oh yes, it *is* a celebration. We're celebrating the new woodpile."

"And our new friendship," Anna said. "Let's go into the front room. You take this tray and I'll take the other one."

It was a charming firelit room, friendly and full of color. Books— many of them in Polish—were stacked about everywhere in happy disarray. Books could never be out of place, John reflected. There were many interesting paintings, lithographs, and signed photographs of famous people to awaken memory. Photos of the Old Country and of her mother and father when young—several showing them standing by their sleek trained horses, and one as bride and groom. She was petite and pretty and he in traditional Polish costume, with a cock-feathered hat and fierce drooping mustaches like tusks, and a big flower in his buttonhole. John instantly recognized Anna herself, as a child star, sitting in her trapeze on the *Jacobus* with her sweet little legs crossed, a grin on her face and her black rag doll wearing a striped cap hugged close to her heart. There were two comfortable settees drawn up on either side of the hearth, where the warmth of the glowing coal fire could reach them.

John felt completely at home, as if he belonged here. If he could only *stay*. For the first time he realized how alien the other rooms he had inhabited had been to him. They had all been so uninspiring and commonplace. No gay colors and delightful hodgepodge of books and papers. The books in other houses were always set stiffly away from dust, behind glass bookcase doors.

For a long time they sat in the warm firelight, talking over their glasses of hot tea. Of the circus and her travels, and how it felt to go kiting up into the clouds in a balloon.

"I was on a shed roof with a bunch of kids and watched you go up that day. I can still see you with your long princess hair and those red tights."

"Yes, and with Molly, my mascot," she added, moved by the memory.

"You smiled at me—or I thought you did. I nearly lost my balance and fell off the roof."

She laughed merrily. "Of course I smiled at you, Janka. I was trained to smile at everybody. But a little girl's smiles are not so professional. I think I remember you smiling at me."

He studied her lovely mobile face and the delicate modeling of her high cheekbones. She was even more delightful than she had been in her childhood days, with all the excitement and glamor of the circus about her.

He found her so easy to talk to, her warm husky voice so sympathetic, that he came out with a confession he'd never made to anyone. "Look here, Anna,"—he hesitated—"that was a big wrong guess you made about my lovelife. I have no sweetheart, and I've never had a woman in my whole life." He felt his face reddening.

She was amused by his ingenuousness, but also touched. "Why, you are very young yet, Janka," she observed. For a moment she was silent and thoughtful. "Have you ever read Jean Jacques Rousseau—his *Confessions*?"

When he admitted he had not, she went to her crowded bookshelves and picked a small volume. She hunted through it and wrote something on a margin of a page, before closing the book and handing it to him. "When you read it, Janka, remember I am older than you—yes—two years or so: and a marriage and separation beyond you. One learns from these—even if the marriage doesn't work out."

He started to ask her if it was true that the doctor had been brutal to her; had been running around with other women—but thought better of it. Instead, he told her shyly about his writing, his passion for it. How he wrote after work in the print shop night after night. How he listened to anyone who wanted to talk, had a story to tell; gathering their impressions, their experience; forever trying to find out what was underneath, or inside, everything and everybody. How whenever he passed a graveyard, he regretted, even more than the dead folk under the gravestones, all the stories that had been buried with them and forever lost.

Anna leaned toward him, her black eyes warm and tender. "And now I will tell *you* something, Janka; but don't you tell a soul. I am writing a *play*!" Her face lit up with enthusiasm. John was completely captivated by her rare and vivid personality. Without a doubt, he decided, she is the most fascinating and cultured woman in this town!

When it came time to leave, and Anna went to the door with him, the moonlight outside threw curious lights through the stained glass on the door panels and on her uplifted face. He tried to fathom the expression in her eyes. She was so beautiful; sophisticated, yes—but also so enchantingly childlike. He wanted to obey an impulse that had been building up in him all evening—to catch her in his arms and overwhelm her with kisses. But no—that wouldn't do. She might resent it, and he mustn't do anything to shatter this enchanting friendship.

"Anna," he said, "I've got to see you again. Tell me—when."

"Well—well—we'll see. Soon, maybe." She opened the door. The wind swirled the snow about them—carrying little stinging pellets of frost.

He thought her eyes more glorious than he had ever seen them. He seized both her hands and kissed them.

"Ah, Janka, you must be part Polish. You have talent, Monsieur Rousseau." She laughed softly and called after him, "Janka, I like you! I really do!"

He turned back impetuously, but the heavy door had already swung to, misty colored lights shining through its side panels.

Far into the night he read her copy of Rousseau. She had marked the chapter "Madame de Warens' Proposal," and he found scribbled on the side: *Better let these experienced women alone!*

He hot-footed her a note asking to come again—at once— When? Where? She wrote back immediately, a small note on soft gray paper: *Not too hasty, Janka!* But it ended by saying: *Sometime—maybe. But remember that Madame de W. was more interested in instructing than seducing, and required a wait of eight days for prayerful consideration.*

John could sympathize with the fervor and impatience inherent in the words Jean Jacques had penned: *"The novelty of the situation has taken complete possession of me . . . eight days seem eight centuries."*

The Lovers

It was a few weeks later that a capricious and totally unexpected shower of artistic blessings descended upon Warham—a performance of the great Mira Chernevskaya and those other divine female forms and ballerinas of the Russian Imperial Ballet, as well as the first symphony orchestra ever to set up music stands in the Warham Opera House.

The Warham Orchestra was firmly pushed aside—lock, stock, and bass fiddle—like bantling birds boosted overboard from a warm nest for their own good. Chernevskaya's musical director didn't tell Mr. Josephburg that his pastoral crew of fifers, tootlers, and catgut scrapers was ridiculously inadequate and *gauche,* only pointed out that for Madame "everything must be oh so verree pear-fect." His musicians had all kinds of bizarre and unknown instruments: the English horn, the bassoon contrafaggotto, golden French trumpets like morning glories, with their long twisted tubes and widely flaring bells, and even the balalaika. No artistic pains had been spared.

All during the performance the muted Warham musicians sat in the front row, spellbound. The whirling bobbling ballet skirts, the goddess wrappings of purest feathery white . . . now spinning dizzily as fireworks wheels, now teetering like killdeers, and all the lovely legs and loins. . . . John Anders was inundated in wonder. Charmed and ravished by these unearthly creatures from the

Milky Way. His entranced imagination carried him so far along that, when at the end of Chernevskaya's Swan Dance, the graceful white bird so calmly gliding upon the coolness of water dropped with drooping pinions and began her last fluttering movements— her wild free life ebbing away, her moving stilled in quiet death—he was feeling such a poignant sympathetic sorrow, her sadness and charm had so wrung his sympathy and love, that the arrow that killed her struck into his own heart. All beauty and life and love were dying! The emotion the great ballerina had uniquely created and transferred was devastating, overpowering, and it moved him so, excited him so excruciatingly, that after the falling of the curtain and the deafening applause, he slipped away from the others.

Out in the street a soft snow was falling. People in evening dress were waiting for their conveyances, or turning up their overcoat collars and going out to find them in the whirling snow and confusion. A policeman with a whistle was trying to untangle the snarl of carriages. And there was General Owsley's victoria, with his Negro coachman up on the box—a blanket drawn over his knees and his high hat and livery whitening.

A huge hum of talk and laughter was to be heard, and callings back and forth. The air was alive with excited salutations. "Oh wasn't it marvelous! . . ." "Perfectly stunning! . . ." "Did you ever see anything so lovely as those dresses!"

John Anders felt a powerful urge to roam away from the lights and the crowd, with only the blowing snow for company. To see the snow falling on the cracked and dirty sidewalks, covering up all sordidness and ugliness. He wanted to walk for hours under the night's moon-drenched clouds, the strange romance of life and life's possibilities flowing around him.

As he was pressing through the chattering crowd, burrowing this way and that in the stream of people, a familiar husky voice said close beside him: "It was a grand performance, wasn't it, Janka?" And there was Anna, looking lovely and quite regal in a long brown wool coat embroidered about the shoulders. She carried a small fur muff; a white wool-lace scarf, its ends tossed lightly back and partly covering her shining hair, and John caught the gleam of antique gold earrings. Love enters a man through his eyes, he realized, but there was also an alluring flower-fragrance about her that charmed and elated him.

In his happy surprise, he felt like a prisoner freed from his dark cell of loneliness. "Oh I'm still under Mira Chernevskaya's spell," he answered her, appropriating her arm and holding it tightly, "but under *your* spell too, Anna Pulaski." Then adding in a low voice, "Madame Pulaski de Warens."

She gave him a radiant smile. "I'm only talking ballet tonight, Monsieur Rousseau," she said in mock sternness. "But you know, it was so beautiful and splendid—that I don't want to go home. I'm all excited and I just have to get out and walk it down."

He laughed in pleasure and excitement in meeting this unexpected echo of his own mood.

"Madame Pulaski-Ballerina," he said, "if you have no palanquin, no coach-and-six, no Pierce-Arrow waiting to carry you off, may I have the pleasure?"

"Why yes, I would love it! But monsieur, a troika with sleighbells is what we should have—though really, I would rather walk. *Do* let's take a long walk. I'm so keyed up—my head is fuller of fancies than it can hold."

"Are you sure that is what you want—in all this snow?"

"Oh monsieur—the snow's not deep, it's just beginning." And she lifted her skirt to show him a small furred snow boot.

A pair of pinch-faced spinsterish ladies going by turned to look, too. "Well I never!" one sniffed to her companion. "That young woman is too forward—showing her ankle like that! And by the look in that young man's eyes, I'd say she's going to need a hatpin before this night is over."

The other one craned her thin neck. "Hm-m! foreign-looking," she opined dryly. Then catching a whiff of Anna's perfume and a word or two of her talk, "You never can tell about those foreigners . . ."

The lovers didn't catch the comments, though; and with the ballet music dreaming through their blood, they linked arms and stepped away into the whirling whiteness.

Around the windy corner of the opera house, and through the thinning crowd, they went. The on-foot home-goers were humming and laughing and talking of the great extravaganza as they passed. A man went by softly whistling a waltz. It was Boozer Bobbitt, the drummer and bookbinder—taking his drums, packed in their cases, back to the print shop to store until the next orchestra practice. His eyes brightened when he saw the unseeing Anders go by, engrossed in a pretty young lady holding her muff close to her cheeks against the wind. He pivoted his head around to look back at them.

"So John's stepping out tonight. Wonder where he found one like that in this town?" He squinted through the blowing snow. "Saay—that's Doc Hostetter's wife—Little Anna from the circus. That boy had better watch his step—Doc's got a high-rollin' temper, they say." And feeling old and wistful, he went on.

Behind them the lights from the opera house glowed up into a dazzled plum-colored sky with leaden low-hanging clouds, and here and there a yellow street lamp bloomed and flickered dimly behind a wind-tossed curtain of snow.

"Why is it, John, we always meet in stormy weather?" Anna was asking, squeezing his arm for a question mark. "See how it feathers down, the feathers going here-away, there-away." And she hummed a bit of the nostalgic Tchaikovsky score, smiling to herself like a child lost in a happy secret.

"Oh the great Chernevskaya! Wonderful! Overwhelming!" she murmured. "And to think I should have a chance to see her again. I saw her in Paris, you know, when I was very young. That was twenty-odd years ago, but she doesn't look a day older. She's just as enchanting now as she was then. And isn't it a miracle that one of the big-city opera houses should burn down so she could alight like an angel here in our little old tobacco town!"

Walking on, they exchanged confidences. "Papa and Mamma once wanted me to study at the ballet school in Poznan," Anna told him. "But I was too young. I would have had to be eight or ten years old before starting. A child's foot bones are too soft before that. I would not have been allowed to start dancing on my toes until I had had three years training, with several more years' study to come. From Mademoiselle Doreen, in the circus, I did learn some of the classic positions, though. But, oh my aching legs! They're done with the knees turned sidewards, you know, and it makes my legs hurt to think of it."

"Well Lord, I'm awfully glad you didn't become a ballerina! Then I would never have had a chance to get near you. It was bad enough to have you go kiting up into the clouds in a balloon. But at least you had to come down sometime. Do you know, it couldn't be more than a mile from this very spot to that field where the circus was; where you sat on the trapeze that day swinging your legs in your red tights and the band playing and me adoring you."

"Was it love at first sight?"

"It sure was."

Anna looked serious and shook her head in amazement. "Ah yes, it was those red tights of course. And do you know, I still have the jackknife I carried in case I had to stab the balloon to let the gas out. It's a keepsake."

Down an avenue they went into a sidestreet, in a quiet, everybody's-gone-to-sleep section. Rarely a pale window light gleamed behind a tracery of white branches. A hack drove down the street, its wheels singing with frost. And once a distraught old man hurried past them, his shabby coat held together by a single oversize safety pin. His thin beard and coat were splotched with wet snow, and he was muttering to himself.

"The poor always have the wind in their faces," Anna murmured, her dark eyes somber.

Then when no one was passing he suddenly caught her to him and kissed her mouth emphatically.

"Here, wait! Stop it, you rascal!" And she broke away from him. "Why you're as bad as Jack O'Dare—the way he gets fractious on the way home. I can hardly hold him in, the big bay devil."

Then she smiled mischievously. "*Cuckru,*" she said. "That's what you both want, I take it."

"What's *cuckru?*"

"You just guess, *najdrozsy.*"

"Now what's *that?* Anyway, I love the way you say it. Say it again."

"*Najdrozsy,*" she whispered.

The snowfall had now abated somewhat, and they were going through other little fast-asleep streets out toward the edge of town. Past vacant lots and weed fields, hushed pockets of misty darkness. For a time they walked silently without touching each other. But the cold and the snow seemed rather to help than to hinder their lovemaking, and, as they walked along under the low-hanging branches, that come-and-go feeling would every now and then throb them to each other and they would stop and embrace. Once in a wood, they lingered to lean against a rail fence and catch their breaths as an interlude to the strenuous hiking. It was here that

Anna revealed the meaning of those mysterious Polish words. "*Cuckru* is sugar and *najdrozsy* means sweetheart. And if you want another one, *kochany* is darling. And now are you satisfied?"

When they had nearly reached Anna's house, they peered into the blowing white murk, trying to make out the old shingled building. Caught sight of it, etched darkly upon the shifting snowscape.

Anna stopped and touched his arm. "Wait—there isn't a light on, except the one I left in the kitchen for Papa."

John's heart felt a catch of excitement. "Your father isn't home?"

"I'm not sure. He went away today on business. That's why I came to the ballet alone. . . . Papa would have loved it."

The blood was beginning to pound in John's temples. He was thinking suddenly and nervously of the promising possibilities of this lovely night.

They stomped the snow off their feet and she took her key from a small brocaded bag and opened the big front door. "Papa!" she called up the stairs. "No, he's not here."

John gave a sigh of relief and caught the sound of one from her as well.

"He must have stayed in Walterville for the night, on account of the storm."

A mighty exuberance swept over him. The old house, like his heart, was full of music. Into his vitals marched a big surge of man-power, and he knew his luck was going to hold.

The hall was dark, but he could make out a tall hatrack on one side and the dim glow of a mirror. From the front room came a soft glow from the hearth. Anna reached for a light, but he caught her hand. Drew her to him roughly.

"Why, Janka," she gasped. "Who'd ever suspect? You look like such a quiet one. But you're just the way I hoped you'd be," she said softly. Then, "Come on in. I left a good fire in the grate, and thank goodness it's still burning."

"I'm burning, too," he said, warming his hands at the grate.

"So you don't want any apple strudel and good strong hot coffee after walking so long in the snow?"

"Woman," he said, "you're getting me off the track. But yes, of course I want that coffee and stuff too."

"Well how about pulling my boots off for me, *kochany*?" And he did—liking that, too (he liked everything she did or let him do), and put on her old wool slippers that lay handy by the settee, after warming them at the fire. Then he followed her to the kitchen.

"Now here, sir, you grind the coffee. I'll let you off the tea tonight. We'll need six heaping tablespoonfuls . . . and don't talk to me, because I'm counting cups of water."

John ground away vigorously with the little square grinder on his knees, thinking raptly of the lovely name she had called him. Then, she brought out a bottle of elderberry cordial from the big sideboard.

"I found those elderberries growing out by the creek last fall. The bushes were hanging full and I couldn't bear to waste them. It isn't too bad."

She smiled as she filled two old Polish goblets, one garnet and one green.

"To us!" she cried, and their eyes held each other as they drank.

When they had finished their coffee they loitered deliciously at the kitchen table, warmed by the wine and savoring the time, the tremulous excitement. Each knowing well enough what was in the other's mind and expectation. He put his hand over hers, and, leaning over to his nearness, Anna looked down at her hand captured in his as if she were gazing at a songbird held by a hawk. Let this enraptured moment live forever, both were dreaming. The snow was coming fast outside—and sleet, with its rattle-rattle— built a beautiful wall of privacy around them.

Then he said: "All right, Madame de Anna, come on now, your eight days are over."

"Well—well—" she whispered, "I think it would, it would be— simply lovely, *moj kochany!*"

The Loss

It was on a day in late June of 1905 that John Anders sat at his desk in the printery brooding and figuring at the same time, thinking how much he hated the cut-throat competition that was said to be the "life of trade." He wished all this scheming and foxing just to get enough business to keep your plant running could be laid to rest. It looked like everything a man wanted somebody else was after. He sure would have to keep on scratching and pushing and competing if he expected to ever get anything or anywhere. Especially with that goddamn Van Damm Supply Company that T. P. Warham had organized to purchase all United Tobacco materials other than tobacco.

When John had put in an order for a certain kind of yellow paper his father had long used for the Warham's Best Genuine sacks, he'd been informed by the mill that its entire output had been contracted for. The same thing happened when he tried to get the special black paper the Anders Printery had been using over the years for the labels on Southern Bull. To his dismay, the nearest source of supply for that was now Holland. In addition, a certain big printing outfit in Baltimore seemed hell-bent on grabbing all the label printing—the most profitable part of his business. And all printing orders were no longer placed locally but bought from New York—thus throwing him into collision with many other printer-dogs contending over the same bone.

It was pretty clear he'd have to go to New York to get that order for those fifty million Genuine labels he'd been given the chance to bid on.

It was a lovely warm day and he wished he could spend it with Anna. Love kept getting mixed up with his thoughts of business. His life had taken some dizzy turns since that walk in the snow the night of the Russian ballet. Like fire, Anna was comforting, dangerous, and necessary. His thoughts kept returning to the last time they'd been together—how her eyes had sparkled so full of tender understanding, how she'd held his arm for a moment after she'd said goodbye as if telling him how much she wanted to stay and be loved by him forever.

Even by this time she had not been able to locate her runaway husband. But despite all his urging that she try to get a divorce on the grounds of separation, she still always hesitated for some reason he didn't understand. He realized how little he knew about Anna's feelings for her husband. Perhaps she still had some special affection for him. He remembered how the sympathetic young doctor had gone in and out of the boardinghouse for many months when Anna had been a little girl with a broken back lying painfully on a straight board. He'd seen Doctor Hostetter carrying presents there to lighten her suffering and boredom: books, toys, a box of candy done up in ribbons. He'd been a handsome man in those days, with his healthy ruddy face and mustache and dark brown eyes that women found disturbing. Then, as the young girl convalesced, he had often taken her in his buggy on his rounds out into the country. Even then, when more than one attractive woman in the town was "setting her cap" for him, he'd fallen in love with Anna and waited for her to grow up. Though they'd had a stormy marriage (with many violent quarrels, as Anna had told him), there must have been some tenderness—such love as an older man can give a beautiful young girl. . . .

He forced himself to stop thinking of Anna and focused back on the order. Maybe the DeLonge Company in New York would be a good bet for the Genuine paper—his father had dealt with them sometimes, he remembered. Here he was thinking of marrying—he certainly needed to make some real money.

He decided to go immediately. He'd have to be gone at least a week. He scribbled a note to Anna telling her he'd be leaving that day. There was a train at five-fifteen.

On the way to the station a little later, he noticed a legend, "Jesus Never Fails," that one of the town's religious zealots had painted in white upon a rock. He decided he'd accept it as a favorable omen.

John Anders walked everywhere in New York that week, when he wasn't doing business. He was shy about city ways—such as the elevated, the long monster cable cars, the bright red-and-green taxicabs lately come from France. He flowed in the tremendous stream of pedestrians up and down the Great White Way, breathing in the city's gassy, asphalty smell, the stray whiffs of perfume and tobacco smoke, of peanuts being roasted.

Broadway was a street of novelty and excitement—a horde of people pushing, jostling, dodging in and out of theaters, restaurants, jewelers, haberdashers. Fire wagons raced past and church bells bonged the sunny air. He saw a sign atop the nine-story Normandie Hotel that towered above Herald Square advertising the new Edison phonograph. On a wall there was a painted advertisement that was more familiar:

PROTECT YOUR TEETH!
CHEW WARHAM'S BLUE WHALE TWIST!

In and below the square, there were congested long lines of drays and wagons, with the cable-car gripmen clanging their bells and pushing, inch by inch and foot by foot, to get through. And to complicate matters, many gas buggies were dashing around frightening horses with their queer noises.

On one day that was fair and hot, he was lured to roaming by the deep hoarse booming call of an ocean liner getting ready to depart. He walked down to where he thought he'd see it, but missed it somehow and found himself in the warehouse district.

On the riverside were the freight and ferry houses and cold-storage warehouses of the great railroad lines, with a lot of traffic of unloading passengers and cargo, a swarming nest of wagons, hansom cabs, and tooting autos. Since boyhood he had loved to wander about and look on at the world; and this day, this hour, was a rare delight. He marveled at the great dapple-gray Percheron horses with their huge hairy hooves that clopped heavily over the hard, tarred Belgian blocks, pulling trucks piled high with beer barrels, or crowded with cattle. Oh how Anna would love those horses!

There were strange and provocative odors as well as the gustatory good ones. Bananas and coffee, garlic and cabbages, the perfume of apples, flowers, and pineapples; the gust of horse sweat and tarred new ropes and spicy pine boxes. Oranges blazed in peddler's carts; cloth and old brass were for sale, second-hand footwear and potted geraniums. In the glinting summer sunlight hundreds of yellow and blue butterflies that had come in with a ship from the tropics flitted about, and a wind was rising and blowing up Fish Street from the dazzling blue waters.

The glutted streets and alleys ran down through a maze of materials and confusion to the masts of ships. Argentine sails talking and flapping to Swedish sails, and some from Greece and Holland and even Hong Kong. Oil tankers, sloops with racing sails, fore-and-aft-rigged schooners with three masts and square sails, fire and police boats and coal barges. . . . Whistles blew, tugboats bellowed. Big longshoremen in overalls were loading and unloading, pushing trucks to and fro on the docks.

Oh the world was full of stir and adventure! And as long as Anna was in his world, he thought, the world would always be enchanted.

It was very lonely up in the oppressive gorgeousness of his hotel room later. What a lot of things and excitement he could share with Anna if she were with him. If she were only here tonight, he thought, staring at the big empty bridal bed, he'd make big love with her, hurl everything she wore to the winds, to the leather chair by the window. He'd bury his face in her long lovely hair, unbraided and flung over the pillow, and hear her husky laughter. . . . And then they'd sleep together profoundly.

He thought of all the other honeymooners who must have been here. Their coming back to this opulent love-base from the wonderful city to begin all over again their adventures of passion and discovery.

There was a concert at Carnegie Hall the following night. The New York Philharmonic playing Beethoven's Ninth Symphony, with Walter Damrosch conducting. The house was crowded, and he climbed the steps to the gallery with many other eager, chattering music-worshipers. High up there he had a good view of everything: looked down on the tall gray green walls; on the students, lovers, musicians, odd costumes and expectant faces coming in; on the stage, with its rows of faraway music stands and empty chairs. It was all very exciting, the anticipation of beauty.

As the lights went down, the first thrilling bars of the great symphony flew out into the darkness like strange wild birds. They hung in the air as a mist, the flowing sounds of strings and the cutting sharp notes of the horns. At first it was all a mysterious mixture of confusion, groping, and restlessness. With fragments of melody snatched hastily together, from the strings. Then suddenly these fragments were hurling together, miraculously like flakes in a snowstorm, like a rainbow gathering up light and color out of a fog or from the sea, and the bold and joyful theme was bravely shouted forth by the whole orchestra. The trumpets fading into the tremulous tones of violins and violas, all the horns with their mellow mysterious beauty. There was a sweet little meditative song from the oboes and clarinets about the joy of living, and then the sound of throstling blackbirds, and a soft and distant voice that was Anna's, and her laughter. Now they were together—happy— their happiness was a river rolling into melody.

He was aware then, was apprised by the music, that happiness was something as elusive as his first frightened long-ago little minnow that had slipped through his childhood fingers.

Then the master composer painted passionate yearnings, a wistful melancholy that brought tears to your eyes.

In the final movement, the great hymn to joy, there were thrilling human voices in solo and chorus arrangement—all joy and none of the sorrow and storm of life. The cellos and basses were dancing together, and the end came in a great blaze of jubilation and exaltation.

Walking down the street with the night's enchantment around him, John continued to feel that strange and joyous madness, that wild silken sobbing.

Back in his room, he wrote Anna a long and ardent letter.

Meeting Mr. DeLonge was something of an adventure in itself. A large well-dressed man with a trim black mustache, he exuded vitality and good fellowship. He had a smiling, but discerning, gray eye with a quick, authoritative flash in it.

"Oh yes I remember Johann Anders well," he said. "We did considerable business together and had several pleasant meetings here in New York."

No, he didn't have the paper John was looking for, but would be glad to help him find it.

"You can find anything in New York if you know how to go about looking for it," he pointed out; and then put in a few telephone calls.

"Ah!" he uttered triumphant and beaming, after the last one. "Go see Hubert Lindenmyer and Sons, at Thirty-four Bleecker—Nathan Woolcock's the fellow to talk to."

So off John trotted once again to the grimy business of buy-and-sell—to carry his battle with T.P.'s Van Damm Supply Company a step further. And got what he had come for: plenty of that yellow label paper at a fair price.

He left for home on a balmy midnight, with a moon shining among swiftly moving, inky clouds. Under the high sooty roof of the railroad station, the big locomotives chugged and steamed restlessly as he picked his way through the embarking crowd, looking for the right Pullman car.

A monstrous din of construction was going on night and day where the great Pennsylvania Station was being built nearby. Being brought "out of the nowhere into the here": that is, being transferred from the architect's sorcerous brain and drawing board into solid steel and stone. It was going to have the biggest waiting room in the world—so high of ceiling that a small skyscraper might comfortably nestle there. Five hundred old buildings had been cleared to make room for it and all the trackage and walkways beneath it; and thousands of men were working on it.

Oh, New York was really a wonderful place, he thought, but he was glad to be getting out of its dazzle and going home. He felt as if he'd been away from Anna for months, as if he'd been around the world.

He awoke at dawn in the hurtling, clattering train. Along the ridges and ditches beside the tracks the sun was painting the butterfly weed with orange glory, and, in the marshy places, putting red on the long coarse grasses. He was feeling very elated. It was going to be one of his happiest days—he knew it in his bones. His daydreams of Anna flamed like a fire run wild. Over and over he rehearsed what he had to say to her.

"We must marry, Anna. It's the only way. We've got our lives to live and it's nobody else's business."

It was evening as the train neared Warham with hiss of steam and clanging bell. The hometown rum-and-tobacco smell had already invaded the train—he could smell it by the time they reached Erdmannton. Passengers crowded at the car's end clutching their grips and packages. A group of young girls was giggling and whispering.

He had it all planned—how he would bypass the station crowd by slipping through the express office, how he would stop at the florist's and get her some valley lilies. . . .

But outside the station in the dusk and traffic, there came a quickening of heartbeat. He was smitten by a vague uneasiness. He had to go to her at once, he decided—before he went to the shop or anything. He had sent her a telegram from New York and she would be expecting him.

He dismissed the hackman at her gate and rang the bell, listening intently for the quick fall of Anna's footsteps.

But it was not Anna who opened the door, but Edna the cook. "Mr. Anders! You sho' is a stranger these days."

"Yes, I've been away, Edna. Where's Anna?" He smiled, embarrassed because there was no way of suppressing the eagerness in his voice.

The old woman seemed to hesitate. "Law, Mr. Anders, if you're lookin' for Miss Anna, she ain't here."

"Well, where is she? I sent a wire."

"Yessuh, a telegram did come for her, but she never did git it. It's right over there on the table—an' a letter too. She never did git it, Mr. Anders. Miss Anna's been gone for sev'ral days an' Mr. Pulaski's been off too. This ole house sho' empty."

The hall clock chimed seven o'clock and the little one on the parlor mantel verified the big one's statement half a minute later.

"Well, where *is* Miss Anna? What's happened?" He dreaded the answer.

Edna wiped her hands on her apron. "That doctor man, her husban' Doctor Hostetter—well, he done had a accident in Richmond. . . . A elevator fall with him . . . sev'ral people was killed—and

Doctor Carl got hisself hurt so bad he ain't never gon' walk no more."

John caught his breath. He waited, as if expecting a blow.

"Yessuh, he telegrammed Miss Anna beggin' her to come to him."

"Did she leave any word for me?" he managed to say, his voice sounding far away.

"Yessuh, Miss Anna tried ev'ry way she know'd to reach you, Mr. Anders—but you kept movin' about. She left you this letter." And she reached it down from the high oak mantel. "She sit right there in that very chair and cry . . . Miss Anna look p'int-blank like a ghost, po' thing."

Mechanically he took the letter, tore it open. The writing—crowded and blurred in places—was difficult to read.

Janka, my dearest,

How can I tell you? Carl has had a dreadful accident. Janka, he will never walk again. He needs me now. He begs me to come to him. And how can I do otherwise? I am still his wife. In his way he has been good to me.

This is the hardest decision I have ever had to make in my life. To give up our love. But I must go to him. This is good-bye. When you come again I will be gone.

But you must always know that I love *you,* alone. Only you. You must never doubt this. Perhaps it is better we will not have to go through the agony of parting.

Now it is time to pack my things.

All my love, Janka dearest. *Dearest!* My heart's choice.

Anna

He folded the letter carefully and put it in his inside pocket. "I may as well be going," he said dully. And passed through Anna Pulaski's door with a funereal feeling of forever.

 **XI**

Mrs. Elbridge J. Holt
(1922)

Time was flying, but Mrs. Elbridge J. Holt still dawdled before her mirror, undecided whether to wear the hat with the daisies or the pigeon one.

"Come on, Mother dear, let's get started. You look perfectly stunning." It was her second daughter, Diantha Holt Anders, speaking. Her mother had been primping and daydreaming now for two solid hours, and something had to be done or they'd *never* get to the library.

"For heaven's sake, let's!" burst out Mazara, the tempestuous one. "Octavia told the woman you'd be there by eleven."

"Tst-tst, I look like a witch, that's how I look," Mrs. Holt deprecated—dabbing a last little dab of Chevalier de la Nuit under her ears and fishing for another compliment. "I look as old as the book of Genesis." But now something has decided her, and she is stooping before the glass to settle the chic little felt hat featuring the fowl.

"Oh drat it," she says, "here is where I need that three-way mirror your father has been promising me for the last forty years. How can I ever see how it looks in the back!"

The new Warham Public Library sat back from Main Street, and on that October morning the maple leaves made a pretty tesselation in gold and scarlet upon its broad esplanade and walkways. They—Mrs. Holt and her three daughters (oh, how she loved to

have them all about her, like a hen with her chicks) found Miss
Inez Beaver the librarian having a sandwich-and-thermos lunch at
her desk amid the musty smell of books and a compounded aroma
of coffee and some yellow roses in a large, lemon-colored vase.

The October sunshine, entering by a lofty window, spattered the
smooth hardwood floor with profligate cheerful gold, and also burnished into mellow glory the pigeon on Mrs. Holt's hat.

Tall, erect, with silvery hair, and giving off the elegant and refined screep of silk, Mrs. Holt had on a smart Sally Milgrim
frock—a leaf print in bold design. Three-quarter sleeve . . . brief
shoulder bertha . . . white gloves—which caused the bookish
Miss Beaver to think of Shelley's line: "lovely lady garmented in
light."

The season is on now for the literary clubs, and Miss Beaver is
much sought after as a writer of club papers. No, it's not as open-
and-shut as that. You—as a member of the Ivanhoe, the Ne Plus
Ultra, Less Douzes, or Globe-Trotters or the Up-to-Snuff club, say—
confer with Miss Beaver about helping you "gather material" for the
paper you have to write. And if, during the interview, you happen to
sigh and say, "Oh dear, how I hate to waste time writing these dratted things!" Miss Beaver may casually remark that she just *loves* to
write papers, and would be glad to "assemble some notes," and will
you just come back on a certain day. And on that certain day you
will be agreeably surprised to find the material all put together for
your approval.

Mrs. Holt, who wishes club papers had never been invented, has
chosen as her topic: Queen Elizabeth. "You see, the Up-to-Snuff-
ers program this season is Famous Queens, and would you believe it, we have the same birthday. September seventh, I
mean—and my husband is in the tobacco business."

Miss Beaver, who'd promised her plenty of material the previous
week, has a sheaf of papers ready this morning—which means
Mrs. Holt will have to pay her five dollars. She is thinking of that
with some dismay as Miss Beaver clears her throat and starts off:
"The Virgin Queen."

"I don't like that," Mrs. Holt says. "Sounds too much on the sex-
ical side."

Miss Beaver presses forward with the desperate boldness of a
baited Elizabethan bear: *"Elizabeth, Queen of England and Ire-*

land, was the daughter of King Henry the Eighth, by his second wife, Anne Boleyn; and was born in Greenwich Palace, on the seventh of September, fifteen thirty-three."

. . . The same as me, thought Mrs. Holt, proudly; only mine was September seventh, eighteen sixty-eight, and in that outlandish old green farmhouse at Rabbit City. She has a perfect vision of Anne Boleyn's bedroom. A royal four-poster bed with a royal baldachin, and a fancy royal mosquito-netting thing hanging down, and the British Lion embroidered heavily in gold, and white and red rose bouquets on the wallpaper. Vaguely she remembers something about a war over some roses. . . . And there is a lovely royal fragrance of real American Beauties. (And comes a trashy, warring remembrance of that time those two tacky ladies from the Ladies Aid brought her two wrinkled oranges and a bunch of wilting roses when she was sick, and having Toosha the maid dump them in the ashcan.)

And there are lavender-colored lace curtains, massive mahogany furniture—two royal chairs with golden lion's paws—and many mirrors and a polar-bearskin rug and a larger beige rug with the initials *A.B.* worked in it. The bed has a formal purple velvet coverlet with a valance, and on the valance little red British lions. And she imagines with horror vulgar King Henry the Eighth bursting noisily in, waking the royal girl-baby and rudely disturbing the femininity of his second wife's bedroom. (Myrena's imagination was like that. It picked up bits and elaborated and fancified upon them.)

And now the near-past and the far-past jostle each other, blur, become one. Myrena Holt falls to thinking of the old green farmhouse. Overlaying the American Beauty fragrance of the royal boudoir are the old home scents of sun-kissed scuppernong grapes, of tobacco hanging in the barn, of hickory smoke and meat in the smokehouse. Comes the scent of musty winter bed quilts pulled up around your neck in the cold upstairs bedroom, and of the shut-up parlor opened for Sunday-morning prayers. The sage scent of sausage frying with sweet potatoes on a wintry morn . . . the aroma of the cool earthy cellar at noon, in July, with the apples, the pickle barrel. The jimson weeds in the hot sun.

Her remembrance picked over a bright and indiscriminate assortment of treasures like a playful raven: pebbles of ancient slick-worn prejudice; snail shells of self-admiration; broken teacup handles of disappointment and doubt. Here and there she plucked at a shimmering fragment to be hoarded against time.

How could she ever forget her Sunday-school class and that strong muttony smell of Rabbit City's small boys? That was where she first saw Ople Goble, with his red hair brushed back, reminding her of a young drake.

Her eyes are fixed on a sun fleck on the library floor, on that gold-shiny puddle.

She sees an old red road . . . and Ople Goble. It was the year she was seventeen. She almost married him, and it was the nearest thing to true love she'd ever had. Ople, the farmhand, had "borrowed" Mr. Smith's buggy one Sunday afternoon, and they had slipped off and gone buggy riding. Over the old red road through the green woods : . . . out the Wolf Pond pike. She groped her way back through the years. . . . There were still those sepia cows on that sap-green meadow. (Somehow the frail rose-breath from Miss Beaver's roses was unlocking the door to long-lost latent Sleeping-Beauty Land, to memories graceful, tender, nostalgic.) It was spring, one of the loveliest of bright days near the end of May, and she could still smell its delicate sweet burgeoning. The spiced and earthy scent of meadow and blossom and grass, of fields deep in red clover. The meadows were white with the daisies, bees stirred murmurously. In the air was a magic stirring, and the creasy mustard was in bloom. ("An ox-eye daisy's one of the finest land-builders in the world," her farm boy said, trying to appear responsible and wise.) A thrasher sang in a mulberry tree. ("Cold weather's over after the cornplanter bird comes," he had said.) The new corn was up hand-high in the fields. ("The first week in May is the time to plant corn—on the full of the moon; then it won't grow so high for the wind to be tearin' up.") However did Ople know so much?

Again she breathed in the new-grassed bank that sported phlox and the shy tiny bright-eyed iris and the pink-tinted bloom of dewberry. And though she was embarrassed now remembering it, she had also inhaled—at first gingerly, then eagerly—of that indecorous but rousing he-man reek that healthy, wild, red-headed, freckle-faced and sweat-moisted farm boys have, like the lower animals.

Now she was two people at the same time: she was that tacky, inexperienced country girl riding in a buggy through that haunting, delicate springtime and she was also a smart, well-to-do socialite sitting here in the Warham Public Library. She could refeel the buoyant tang of youth that was in her that day; her rash and uncalculating virgin fancies; the sheer animal delights and desires racing impetuously through her like leaping, startled deer. Oh there was just too much beauty for one day and one heart to bear (so that young girl had thought then): with her first real beau, the pink azaleas and calico bushes spreading the hills, the musky wild grape blossom everywhere in the woods and along the creeks: "I am young!" she had exulted and shouted within. "I needn't worry about death yet awhile—I have long, long years stretching before me." That was what she was saying to herself when she was young and bloomy—at seventeen.

Mr. Smith's jaded old workhorse was very slow. The evening breeze rose in the branches and the lightning bugs came out. The bars of pink and green and primrose (foretelling that pastel ice cream she was to eat two years later at General Owsley's lawn party) faded out in the west as the dusk fell. . . .

It was way after dark when we got in and Mamma was furious. Questioned me for over an hour. "Now if a man puts anything between your legs and you get in trouble, don't blame me!" she snorted, and ran from the room in embarrassment.

Yes, Ople *had* to kiss me, but I never told. He hugged me so tight, so close . . . he was trying to reach up under my dress, but I pushed him away. . . . What if I hadn't been able to hold out against him? Things might have worked out very differently. There have been times when I wished I *had* let him. If I hadn't gotten so scared; with awful fears plaguing me then, of Mamma, the Devil, love, and sin. . . . Oh why does it all remain?

But the next day Mamma gave me a lecture on Casting Your Nets Wildly and about taking your ducks to the right market. She told me straight out that Ople was just 'common gully dirt'; it was calf love and he was no better than a snake in the grass . . . and I cried. Oh, Mamma meant well enough, but she didn't have to go around telling all sorts of things that were just plain lies to break it up. And she kept nagging poor Papa till he packed me off to the Blaxton Female Seminary and got Mr. Smith to run Ople off his place. It was too bad, but Mamma knew best. Women have to stick together. I know now, I was never meant to be a poor man's wife. Young girls can be such fools! And even yet, sometimes in dreams, that buggy ride with Ople Goble leaves me so up in the air, that I'm just spinning around on my toes.

Feeling giddy, she struggles to regain the present.

"Mr. Holt has promised that, if the foreign demand for tobacco is back to normal by next summer (which it ought to be), he might take us all to Europe!"

Myrena Holt had never been to Europe like her daughter Mazara. She didn't really know about castles and royalty, except as glimpsed in movies; could only feel and guess around here and there. "After all," she was thinking, "I'm only an ignorant old woman. But I have to do all I can to keep people from finding it out."

Miss Beaver, who was continuing to read, glanced at Mrs. Holt's large pensive eyes, and "blue, darkly, deeply, beautifully blue" popped into her bluestocking mind.

But Myrena wasn't listening now to a word about the Virgin Queen. She was thinking her own thoughts and they had wandered off to John Anders, her daughter Diantha's husband. To his perfectly terrible remark about all the ghost writers and librarians being kept busy nowadays "writing speeches for that dim-wit President and papers for illiterate clubwomen." John Anders is always coming out with things like that, showing disrespect for authority. *I* was taught to accept whatever is—the established order—but he never does. He has the most disturbing ideas. Even says *Napoleon,* one of the greatest men in history, has been proved by H. G. Wells to have been nothing more than a little runty rooster that strutted a while on a manure pile! And worst of all, John's always looking into one's mind, where he has no business."

To rechannel the unhappy current of her thoughts, she switched to Mazzie's wonderful new house. Everything so elegant, with the curved drive, the terraces. It was wonderful how thoughts of gracious living, the refinement of quiet beauty, dissipated her worries. Yes, despite John Anders, she knew in her heart-of-hearts there was no higher destiny for a woman than to be a lady of fashion in a neat, sweet hat. She could just see the dark green walls of Mazzie's drawing room. . . .

But now her vagrant attention was caught up by the reading:

. . . *"When Queen Elizabeth was but three years old, her father, who had executed her mother and married Lady Jane Seymour— his paramour—declared her and her half-sister Mary illegitimate . . ."*

After noting that "paramour" was a bad word, Mrs. Holt's mind again went woolgathering.

. . . My goodness, all these books! (Though she hadn't *read* a book since that thrilling novel about the Chicago fire by the Reverend E. P. Roe, she loved books—they were so decorative.) The library shelves were so colorful with all the green, blue, yellow volumes patterned in rows. But these weren't near so pretty as those red-leather ones in her son-in-law Grimshaw Johnson's sporty study. Grimshaw was delightfully clever, too. He said he cared a lot about Italian art but not about dagos.

In Miss Beaver's reading, that bad word *paramour* again rang out raucously, indecently. (Hmm—that'll have to be changed too. Funny how old maids who know nothing whatever always . . . Miss Beaver looks so sweet, so pure, and yet she has such thoughts.)

There was a regular gallery of Warham notables on the library walls. Jethro Mink, who had given the land for the depot, long ago when Mink Station was just a grassy place in the road. One of Colonel Ashley Rutherford . . . now *he* must have been a really and truly great man. He wore a gold stock buckle. . . . One of Judge Carroway—*such a* cultured and refined man! . . . Ah, there was her beau ideal, General Owsley, in his rakish Confederate fedora and red carnation.

> Oh yellow's forsaken and green is foresworn,
> But blue is the sweetest color that's worn,

she fished up from the many wise maxims of Grandma Starflax. And remembered that she'd had on a blue dress the day General Owsley spoke about her to Papa. She saw herself helping Mamma make lye for the homemade soap. Papa had made the ash hopper: using wooden pegs, no nails, and I gathered heart leaves from the woods to scent what soap was to be used for bathing. She glanced at her hands with satisfaction. They were soft and white and well manicured and no one would suspect they'd ever fed hogs. Well, anyway she'd never made any hog-gut soap, though Mamma had. But she had helped grind the sausage-meat and singe the pig's-feet to get the hair and the toenails off. . . .

Diantha glances at her beautiful, well-preserved mother. Sitting so upright, so calm, she made you think of Mary Pickford or the Mona Lisa. And on her face, in her large eyes of green blue mist, Diantha could see that abstracted, thoughtful, refined look that marked her as a true patrician.

And now Mrs. Holt is two people again—half of her listening to Miss Beaver; and the other and spiritual part hearing again her father's voice . . . that time at the supper table—that proud and happy time—(she can even recall what they had that night for supper—hominy grits and pig brains) when Papa said to Mamma: "Guess what Eugene Pericles Owsley said to me today, Cassie? He said, he did—'Mr. Mazara, that daughter of yours—Myrena—is certainly the handsomest thing in town.' " Her jubilant heart had been like a mist cloud rising to the morning sun and it had made the world all over fresh and new, as in childhood. But it was all her secret—a secret that had nestled for over thirty years in her breast; a secret dream that she had tended and watered like a flower. Ah, the General, her hero and secret love! He'd never given her any love-words except compliments, and was old enough to be her father, but the drippings of his every word had lapidified over the years into matchless rubies, diamonds, and pearls of romance. But perching on the pedestal to which he had long ago lifted her—sustaining the role he had thrust upon her—hadn't always been easy. I am now an old woman and it is not easy to keep playing the part. "Ugly stays, but beauty fades away," as Aunt Lorinda Peeler used to say. (Aunt Lorinda that had bad eyesight and did her sewing with a big coarse needle she called a "baby-threader.")

Oh how time mixes and botches things up, changes things, piles up the worries and the bothers! But always that night hovers before her inner eye. It is the rabbit always running just ahead in the hound's dream.

And now she was wading deeper and deeper into the past. She was remembering Grandpa Peeler. He'd been very rich but lost a lot in the War. She could hear him r'aring-and-charging now about that-scoundrel-Abraham-Lincoln-that-stole-all-my-niggers!

. . . And there was Cousin Gabriel Harris, the preacher—who, preaching at Old Zoar Church, had prayed God to strike Lincoln dead. (And He *did,* too. God certainly answered Cousin Gabe's prayer, though a trifle late.)

Grandpa Peeler had never become careless of his personal appearance, nor forgot his military bearing, even when killing hogs. I guess I took some after him; for, even when I was a small child, they say I tried to look as much like a paper doll as possible. . . . Yes, Grandpa Peeler *did* behave a little queerly in his latter days: took to wearing his dead father's knee breeches, cocked hat, fancy embroidered jacket, and shoes with the gold buckles he had won in the Revolution as an officer in Captain William Hurst's Troopers of Granville. He would ride over the narrow creek roads through the woods, followed by his free-Negro lackey as though he were still managing a vast estate. Grandfather Peeler always smelled of coffee or cheroots. And Grandma Lizzie dried bunches of sweet clover to make her clothes smell good. . . . How she was dreaming of both Grandma Lizzie's carrick-ma-cress lace collar and of what General Owsley said to Papa. Ah, how little things like the general's gracious, fateful words can turn the tide of your life!

Papa was a True Southerner. Believed in keeping the nigger in his place and that it was a sin for women to vote. Mr. Jefferson Warham also believed that. Which made it one of her favorite argument-clinchers. It gave one such a fine exalted feeling to let people know you were blood-kin to the most successful family in town, in North Carolina, in the whole South. . . . But Cousin Jeff did one thing she could never forgive him for: he'd put notions in Jack Mulkey's head—Jack Mulkey the nigger barber (that Mr. Holt says shaved him many a time)—and lent him money to start an insurance company. And before he died, Jack got to be a millionaire, and now just think of it—the United States government has named a ship after him (through Mr. Holt says it's just a trick to catch the nigger vote).

Niggers. . . .

Papa had excellent southern judgment. In his opinion it was better to get rid of the bad ones they couldn't handle and were afraid of—those kinky-heads like Becky, Gloster, and Cicero Sam. Just set them out on the road like a dog. . . . She had often heard Papa tell about how he went with his father to take away dangerous niggers (well I really should say "darkies" it would be more refined)—anyway the vicious ones, that wouldn't respond to kind treatment. . . . They herded them all together, a whole carful and took them clear to Ohio and dumped them out. Served Ohio right, Papa said. Let them find out what we've been up against. . . . That was before the War of 'Sixty-one. (When she thought of Papa, she thought of hot iron dipped in a blacksmith's barrel, for that was asthmatic Papa's exact smell.)

The net of her memory reached so far back she could even remember the first train she ever saw when she was three or four years old. When the train pulled in from Walterville I clung to Papa's hand in absolute terror. And I can never forget my first ride on one. With Mamma to Giptonville. When we got to the Haw River bridge, Mamma pointed out the big river the train had to cross and said "How do you suppose we are going to get over it?" They say I said "Don't worry Mamma"—and later when we were safe over the bridge on the other side I piped up "We made it" and everybody laughed. And Mamma remembered how at first there was only a boxcar for a depot.

I saw in the morning paper where Muleshoe Mink has been dug up. Well they had been hunting for him a long time . . . they say it was an old darky was able to point out the forgotten sunken grave in an old burying ground at Spring Branch Baptist Church up on Ephraim's Creek. They say it was only a low spot in the deep grass and Mr. Howrigan, the undertaker, probed with an iron spike and felt the contact of an iron coffin. He must have been buried ten years or so before the Civil War. When the outer lid was opened, there was glass over his well-to-do face (Mr. Mink was a slave owner) and his face was in almost perfect preservation . . . had on spectacles, the glasses much smaller than those of today. An old-fashioned waistcoat and stock (but they say the fool undertaker rammed a bar into the lower part of the coffin to "give the body air," and Old Mother Nature then went to work releasing the chemicals kept in captivity for eighty-some years and the stench was like unto the Day of Judgment). There was his portrait on the wall, too, right up there beside General Owsley. . . . (Oh how she'd drunk in those few words the general had said to Papa about her beauty—they'd entered into her very soul, like wine. . . .) Mr. Mink's portrait was what they *thought* he looked like from an old tintype they *thought* was him.

Sometimes she almost wished Mr. Holt knew how hard she worked at trying to look like she had looked to General Owsley thirty-five years ago. For years—ever since she had seen Serena Warham's—she had wanted a new three-folded modern mirror, but Mr. Holt thought it a foolish waste of money. "Since you're the most beautiful thing in town, I don't see why you need *any* looking glass." And so, rather than tell him that much of her beauty came out of a jar, like a jinn—was artist's work—and that it took plenty of varnish and gilding, she had just worried along with the old glass and the old walnut dresser where she had faced and admired herself as a bride. . . . Mr. Holt was tight as the bark on a tree, she was thinking, though you had to give him credit for wanting his wife and daughters to look dressy and paying the clothes bills with less scolding than the other bills.

Oh I could have married others. There were others who looked my way. (There was Mr. Tom Warham himself. Now had I known that big awkward country boy with such big feet was going to start the great U.T. Company . . . I did very well, but if I'd acted right—made a few sweet eyes his way—I might have landed even *him*.) She thought of Isaac Jones Benson, who had gone to work for Thomas A. Edison and gotten rich. Edison had given him a job of authority in his factory. But after he retired and settled up on Pansy Creek, he kept buying up machinery and experimenting with it till he went clean busted. (Lord! what if I'd married *him*? She shivered at the thought.) And there was George Pescud, Colonel Pescud's brother. A good dresser, and a man of money, though a little absent-minded.

There was that splatter of sunshine—that gold-shiny place—again on the floor in nearly the same place. It lit up Mazzie's silk flower-print dress from the knees down and her elegant and very sheer Humming-Bird-hosed legs, and the new blue Perugia shoes, but threw Diantha, who was sitting back of her, in the shade.

"I suppose I ought to give the dress I have on to Diantha to make over for herself, poor child."

. . . And now, going on at the same time with thoughts of Mr. Holt, and those enchanting words General Owsley had said about her being a beauty, when she was eighteen—and moving beneath Miss Beaver's drone—ran the Unpleasant Thought of John Anders. . . . She just knew Mr. Tom Warham never would have stood for that nigger-lover in his family—it makes me sick to think he's married into mine. Now the Lord knows I'm not one to make humdudgeon over nothing, but his taking up for Stephen Slatterly that way, and saying the town ought to erect a monument to him in his old rags and barefooted, right in front of the courthouse; or better still, at Five Points, where all the factory workers pass— because it was that old black slave that found the way to cure tobacco a bright yellow color, which was as good as saying that a nigger slave built this town and not Mr. Jefferson Warham. Ugh! Well Mr. Holt had given him as good as he sent. "The day this town puts up a statue to a nigger," Mr. Holt had said, "that's the day I'm leaving it." (Oh they had hoped to make a good Methodist out of John Anders. Had given him a big church wedding. They would have changed his ways and transmuted him into pure gold, but he was so hard-headed it was like throwing good seed down on a sandbar. There's something radically wrong with a man who can't or won't—learn to play bridge.)

But here Mrs. Holt's strayed attention was jerked back to the reading.

". . . *Her next favorite was a handsome young captain by the name of Walter Raleigh. After distinguishing himself in the Irish War by his dash and daring, he conceived a clever stratagem to attract the Queen's notice. One day when Her Majesty had to cross a particularly muddy place in the royal grounds, he managed to be present and astonished the gentlemen and the ladies-in-waiting by stepping forward and throwing his expensive new cloak in the mud for her to tread on. This so pleased the Queen that he became her Favorite.*"

("I shall say 'stepping *fowward*' when I read it," she thought. "That is the more elegant *Virginia* pronunciation we learned at the Misses Blaxtons' seminary . . .") Then she recalled how Serena Warham, when with her old friends, would lapse into her rural and illiterate talk, which still came natural to her, as in her adolescent days. Though Milam and her daughters had about ironed it out for society purposes. . . . It shows good breeding to talk Virginian. The general spoke Virginian, although born and bred at Ahoskie, North Carolina. He said *fowward* too; and *cam* for calm, and *onnly* for only, *immejitly* for immediately and *coo-cumbers* for cucumbers. . . . Some say he was only a "chicken general." Now that really makes me mad.

(Miss Beaver stole a glance at Mrs. Holt to see how it was taking. She was listening spellbound, her eyes faraway and misty. You could see she was entranced. Her eyes really *were* lovely—matched her sapphires. . . .)

"*At the time, Dudley, Earl of Leicester, was her Favorite, but he was getting old and was not so brave in war as Raleigh, and had got mixed up in some trouble with the widow of Walter, Earl of Essex, which made Her Majesty very angry, as she had inherited her father's jealous nature, and so she heaped her favors upon Sir Walter Raleigh instead. She knighted him and gave him great estates. It was he who later discovered tobacco in Virginia.*"

Great estates! Myrena Holt said to herself. My my, wasn't it wonderful how little events could change one's fortune and future. Couldn't you just *see* Sir Walter, so well-off and handsome? With a feather in his hat. . . .

She could also simultaneously see her son-in-law Grimshaw Johnson, Junior—not exactly handsome, but well-off . . . his handsome new tailor-made tweed suit and bat-wing collar and Malacca cane. . . . Oh you could always tell when a man was successful—nobody but successful people dared carry Malacca canes! And she could see (though she didn't want to) that John Anders again, Diantha's little unstylish, unsuccessful husband. It really gave her a kind of malignant delight to dwell on John Anders and his shortcomings. He was neither rich *nor* handsome, and he'd *never* be successful, that poor bookworm, nor carry a Malacca cane.

"*He was twenty-nine and Her Majesty was forty-eight.*"

Well, I married a man who was older than I, but not *that* much difference. Mr. Holt was thirty-seven when I married him . . . I was eighteen and General Owsley around fifty at the time he had said to Papa: "She's the handsomest thing in this town." Ah, how little things, little words as light as thistledown, can stick in one's memory, can go to one's head. Why, I'd have married the general in a minute if he'd ever asked me to—and could have gotten rid of his wife—even if he'd been seventy-five! Oh he was quite a ladies' man. And evil gossipers—all those old gossipy, quizzy old women—said he had quite a way with colored ladies. Said the Owsley boys had more colored brothers and sisters than white. And she had heard tales about her fascinating hero's affair with a preacher's wife. But if he was such a lover, God made him that way and she just knew God would forgive *him*. And besides, all that was now far, far away—"in the eighteen-ninetyzoic past," as her daughter Diantha would say.

"Pardon me, Miss Beaver," Mazzie was saying. "Couldn't we put something in right there about women smoking? I've read somewhere that Queen Elizabeth tried it once with Sir Walter's pipe."

"That's a *splendid* idea, Mazara," chirped her mother enthusiastically. She was very proud of Mazara.

"Yes, that's true, Mazara," Miss Beaver was saying. "And Mary Bell Washington, General Washington's mother, always kept pipe and tobacco by *her* rocking chair. As Galsworthy said, 'Manners change and modes evolve.' "

"Now don't they!" Mrs. Holt exclaimed.

Mazara was smart all right—in college she had been in theatricals and the Gamma Gamma Sigma sorority. (She and Mr. Holt were firm believers in education and had given all three of their daughters a good education—all three could speak French.) And Mazzie at least had married well. Grimshaw Johnson, Junior, was making at least twenty-five thousand a year, probably more than any young man in Warham. And what a sweet nature he had. He didn't care a hoot how many dresses she gave to the Junior League rummage sale. And a stylish rubber-shod pony pulled the up-to-date lawn mower over Mazzie's lawn . . . while poor Diantha's pitiful little yard out on Glendale Street was always in a perfectly horrible mess, unkempt as a barber's dog. Oh you could tell successful people by their lawns, too. You could tell the difference in the *quality* of the man who lived there. Well, John Anders had had his choice between mediocrity and being somebody, but he muffed it. . . . The Lord knows we were all charming and gracious enough to him at first—till he began to talk radical talk.

"I wish more women *would* smoke," said Mrs. Holt with energy. "That's what Mr. Tom Warham always said. Maybe the U.T. Company should put good-looking *men's* pictures in cigarette packages—say Sir Walter Raleigh and Douglas Fairbanks and Rudolph Valentino. You remember how Mr. Thomas Warham got men to smoking by giving away pictures of Lillian Russell and Ada Rehan and Anna Held in tights."

They all laughed, until a pale young Jew who was looking

through a stack of books stared in their direction. Had she said something out of the way? Undignified? She didn't like Jews. He reminded her of John Anders, his hair not half combed and his trousers out of press. . . . The cloud shadow came back. It came back to her how Mamma thought it awful indecent, those cigarette pictures of actresses: Lillian Russell, Olga Netherole, Lillie Langtry; but if Mamma were alive today, she would of course understand it was smart advertising and that anything is all right that's good business.

She thought of the hundreds of queer-looking factory Jews Mr. Warham had imported to roll cigarettes, before the cigarette machine was invented. At that time nobody but Russian Jews seemed to have the knack of rolling them; but they thought they'd take the town and started to organize a union and Mr. Warham quietly got an old Jewess to teach some darkies and then suddenly kicked them all out. . . .

After they laughed, the librarian had clamped her mouth to like a rat trap and arched her eyebrows, which signified Please everybody let's not forget to whisper, and resumed, in a low voice.

"Sir Walter Raleigh was now a very rich man, with great estates, and cut a noble figure at court, in his doublets of silk and satin."

Myrena Holt, as Queen Elizabeth, lifted up her head a notch higher, stepping over that muddy place on Sir Raleigh's new purple plush overcoat lined with sarcenet and with a silk slash. (Though her elegant color sense was for an instant confused, choosing between pink, cerise, and rose Du Barry for the slash, but it compromised a scarlet.) And the drums were beating, the flags flying, the guards saluting, and the glorious royal brass band playing the *Tannhäuser* wedding march. Underfoot, Sir Raleigh's cloak felt soft and turfy like the Warham's luxurious floor coverings. And Sir Raleigh was tall and tailor-made, as good-looking as Colonel Hammer, that married the McLauchlen fortune. . . . She put up her lorgnette to stare at nothing in particular, though a vision now hovered of Mazzie's evening bag of silver and watermelon pink, and her new long evening wrap of black wool fastened at the neck with gold frogs. When Warham was young, when most of the women still wore sunbonnets, a lorgnette was a thing as rare as a blue diamond. Mrs. Colonel McCubbins had the first, then

Mrs. Magnus McLauchlen. But now there were at least six in town. . . .

She glanced at Mazara. Yes, Mazara was the brightest of her daughters. Though at times a bit too hard-headed. She had been warned against ever making the acquaintance of a farmer and here she had gone and *married* into a farmer family! That is, Grimshaw Johnson, Junior's, father was chairman of the board of the Southern Farming Corporation, but of course he really was a "gentleman farmer," not a "dirt farmer." Yes, really there was a difference: he was *really* just a big landowner and banker—with a persistent, pounding personality like Mr. Thomas Warham's, and was always wanting to know when Mazzie was going to have a baby. Mr. Holt said Mr. Johnson's Southland Farmers' Cooperative wasn't *really* a cooperative, or anything socialistic, but a sales outlet for his feed mills. It was quite a family joke. Mazzie said: "Now that was one time it paid to disobey my parents."

Thinking of self-made men made her think of Mr. Jefferson Warham. He was sure a wise one. A regular Solomon. She heaved a sigh, looking at his portrait over on the far wall. She just *knew* her people were kin to Mr. Warham, the way Mamma thought; no matter *what* those New York lawyers said when they were investigating to see who could share in Mr. T. P. Warham's big bequest to his kindred. She could feel it *spiritually,* and in her bones. . . . When he was a young fellow, just starting out, Mr. Jeff used to plow for people, and on Sundays would often trail wild bees with stink-bait to get his winter sugar. She had heard him say that when his son Tysander was born, before the War, he was that poor he had paid the midwife for her services with a bushel of beans and a bushel of crow-egg apples.

Poor Mamma, so stiff and prim in her threadbare finery, her slick-with-age brown Sunday dress, her heavy jet earrings and jabot of homemade "spider-point" lace. . . . Mamma had cold watery eyes of iceberg blue, and how poor dear Mamma loved to claim kin with the well-off and the bon-ton! Though some of her family connections—such as that to Colonel Rutherford and Flora Macdonald—I realized as a child, were quite in the realm of fancy. Mamma always said the Peelers were related to the Proudfoot family of Charleston. She had our ancestors carefully arranged (so as to bypass the horsethief branch) and spoke of "us Proudfoots." But that didn't sound right to me, so I always corrected it in my child mind to "us *Proudfeet*."

Cousin Gabriella Maria Proudfoot, that married one of her great-uncles Peeler, owned a chair thought to be from way back in the time of Queen Annie. (She must remember to ask Miss Beaver if she'd ever heard of a Queen Annie.)

And Mamma would tell about the cousins Snodworth, said to be descended from Robert the Bruce. "Cousin Ibbie Ida Snodworth, had a son named Bruce, you know," she'd say, and picture them residing in the fine old family mansion in Rome, Georgia. . . . "They raised a lot of rice in their fields and indigo at the edge of the marshes." Once Mamma's unspeakable brother—our Uncle Bill, with the unseemingly big Easter-bun nose and coarse animal nature—said "Nooow Cassandra," in such a tone of voice that it was like calling Mamma a liar, and obscenely referred to our grand relations as "them Snotworths." Which is the reason we never had any use for Uncle Bill after that.

But though poor Mamma's highest goal in life was to be a "carriage-lady," it just never worked out that way. She had to walk to the end of her days. But she had been well instructed by *her* mother in putting the best foot forward, and she never betrayed all the scrimping and makeshift at home. . . . And she never did give up trying to link our family's blood to that of Colonel Ashley Rutherford, the richest man in the Carolinas in his day.

But oh how poor we were after Papa got mixed up with that evil scheming widow-woman, Mrs. Ellen Buckhammer, and had run through with his property. After Papa went broke, Mamma vowed her *daughters* should all marry rich. She just couldn't bear the thought of her daughters being poor men's, or farmer's, wives. Even if *she* never could, she prayed that *they* would dress in silks and satins and have their own carriages. Well I have a nice Lincoln motorcar, haven't I? So you see, prayer *does* pay. But right away, almost, she thought sadly of poor Mamma again—because Mamma never got to ride in an automobile. . . .

It was at Mount Tirzah Church that that Buckhammer woman repented. Said she'd been caught in sin like a bird: sin was like a partridge trap. But she must have truly got religion, for she stopped wearing openwork stockings. . . . Myrena Holt remembered when *she* was converted. There was a blood-red sunset and someone said it meant Judgment Day was coming and the whip-poorwills were crying. She always *was* afraid of whippoorwills and screech owls and thunder-and-lightning. Of course she wasn't superstitious *now* (except about lightning, ladders, breaking a mirror, and cats). But Mamma had been; and Grandpa Peeler, too. Which was one of the pushed-back things—one of her unrespectable skeltons-in-the-closet. Oh how ashamed she was now, of their poor country ignorance.

In her dreams she often saw the yellow kerosene flares about the preaching ground, the lightning flashing fearfully that night and the reverberant roar of thunder rolling away to the far distance—surely the voice of the Devil or God. And just to think— that sacrilegious John Anders saying the god of the U.S.A. is not Jesus and the Holy Ghost anymore, but bathtubs and autos.

Now the Unpleasant Thoughts were beginning to buzz, whirl, and prowl. The day Mr. Holt had given her the new car. . . . "Now you won't have to run your legs off doing a few little things," he'd said. . . . The chauffeur had driven her downtown to see the human fly climb the seven-story skyscraper Warham National Bank building. It was a beautiful morning and I had on a new foulard dress—blue trimmed in green. . . . And who should she see among the hoi polloi, gawking up at the little foolhardy Italian, but a whole flock of her horrible country kin from Rabbit City! She'd tried every way to avoid them: laid low and turned her head the other way—but that awful Arlie Adkins had spied her and yelled: "Hello Myrena! How do you like flies?" Then they had come over and Willie Ridge even put his big dirty bear-paws on the new machine. She could feel the old anger crowding through her. "Iz-ern-tit lovely?" Dave Ridge said; and there was big fat Effie Cooter (she that made baskets of skinned honeysuckle and they always said had Indian blood), and that old hatchet-faced Beulah May Adkins, and Joe Dickey; and I was never so ashamed in my life, for there was half of Warham society seeing me with those horrible louts. And the general was there gawking, too. . . . She had wondered if he remembered. But he didn't see her, and doubtless his words had meant nothing to *him* in the first place.

Then there was that horrible time in the winter of 1905 when Madame Chernevskaya, the great ballet dancer, sent all the flowers showered on her at the opera house to the hospital. . . . As chairwoman of the McLauchlen Hospital Visiting Committee, she had put on her new wool suit in rosy beige, with her little Dobbs hat to match, and gone to the hospital next morning. The flowers had been distributed with the breakfast trays, and Miss Nc-Naughton, the head nurse, took her through the charity ward . . . and oh I was never so insulted in my life! For there on one of the beds—with an American Beauty rose pinned to his bed gown and a possumy grin on his face—was propped up that old rummy reprobate Buck Sam Goodloe!

"Why hullo, Cousin Myrie!" he said, looking hard at me with his piggy eyes under those thick, shaggy eyebrows. Then he bleated out, right before Miss Nora McNaughton and all those people: "Now Lord a'mighty, hain't this a treat? Danged if here hain't my good-lookin' Cousin Myrie Mazara a-comin' to hop in the bed with me!" And that perfectly horrible, loathsome old incorrigible laughed like a wild hyena. . . .

Oh Lord, how I wish Diantha had made a more genteel match. Hadn't gone daft in love with that impossible John Anders, with a few thousand dollars in the bank and his tacky little bungalow out on Glendale Street and his *ideas*. Mr. Holt says poor men don't have any business having ideas.

After Papa went broke we were never more than nigger rich: we'd get a few dollars and spend it all. But Mamma *always*, as far back as I can remember, said we were kinspeople of the Warhams. Through Jeff Warham's mother's folks, she said; and in the bosom of the family, she referred to him as "Cousin Jeff." What an awful shame she didn't record what she knew! And if only she hadn't lost that old letter and tintype out of the clock! It was bound to have been so, for Mamma was a truthful Christian woman.

She was sure Mamma would have understood—if *they* didn't— why she'd had to lay down the law about the Rabbit City relatives coming to see her after she was married to Mr. Holt. Some of the old ones believed a toadfrog, boiled, would cure the consumption . . . that chips from under a gallows, boiled into a tea, was a sure cure of chills and fevers. . . . Though you couldn't help laughing at Cousin Hat Adkins's or Prissie Barstow's sayings. . . . Cousin Hat never would understand China. "They tell me Chiny's down under the ground . . ." And there was her way of stopping at a neighbor's around noon, and when she didn't see any dinner preparations going on, saying: "Folks, I'm hongry as a b'ar, and I want you to either feed me or shoot me." But that type of people could pull you down socially like a rock around your neck . . . . Grandma Starflax, now, who lived to be very old and came to live with them in her last days, was different. *She* had owned slaves and been a lady, and also she had a little property to leave. And *she* was picturesque. That is, you could dress *her* up in a lace cap, with a kerchief and a cameo, and use her for old southern antebellum atmosphere.

But there was that one time I let down the bars—let Cousin Becky Bullock spend the night when she came to Warham as a church delegate. And oh my Lord it *would* happen!—who should call that evening but Mr. and Mrs. Milam Warham! And Gloria Warham was with them. How well I remember it. . . . And that unspeakable Becky thing—who smelled like vinegar and wet ashes and was forever talking about cows—was there when they came. (Oh there was always that ugly world one couldn't leave behind and was always waiting to trip you up!) That old Beck, she monopolized the conversation talking about her dratted old cows—her muleys, hawkies, three-titters—when Mr. Warham was trying to tell us about the horrible strike at their Gastonia mills . . . how it looked like labor never would learn . . . and now just when earnings were going onward and upward and skyward, this had to happen . . . but he said fortunately the mayor, chief-of-police, and the county attorney were all on his side and putting the guns and the American Legion on them again.

But oh no, that country fool Cousin Becky had to keep butting in, telling how she cooked 'taters for her cow; how a young orphan pig had been "dreening" her cow. How when a cow comes fresh, you must get a piece of white flint rock and rub her bag with it to help her make good clean white milk. How, in November, they always turned the cows in the corn, and about old Bess's getting hold of some dog-hobble and getting awful sick. . . . The old hayseed didn't have sense enough to keep her country mouth shut. . . . Oh that dreadful moment when she asked Gloria, that grand heiress to all Mr. Tom Warham's millions, if she'd ever seen a cow "vomick!"

But all the same, she thought of her poor farmer kin out on Rabbit Creek with a little stab at the heart. She remembered Uncle Malachai, gentle and sweet, who made her first and dearest doll.

She had walked beside him through fields of summer flowers. He had also shown her the proper way to root grapevine cuttings. "You take the cutting and stick it in a 'tater—so—before you plant it; and it will never perish for lack of moisture." He was the slow one, too. Always took his time. (Took his time about dying, too; was the last one to go.)

And there was Cousin Ike Ducker who discovered Buzzard Oil—he was from Rabbit City, too. I was only a little tot—seven or eight years old—but I remember him by his bushy black whiskers. Cousin Ike always did have an inventive streak. He moved to Warham when the boom started there; and for a while it looked like he was going to be a millionaire. Only his supply of buzzards ran out after the Blizzard of '88, when most of them were killed.

It was just before that, though, that some rascal put a sheep bell on a wild buzzard and that bell would go dang-a-langing up in the sky. *That* buzzard got to be famous, in Warham, Rabbit City, and elsewhere. It had everybody scared or laughing. Got in all the papers.

Anyway, Cousin Ike went broke and took a job selling flavoring extracts for the C. I. Taggstadt Company at Kokomo, Indiana.

. . . And there was old Molly Bird Spinks, a "johnny-come-lately" in Rabbit City, who had the brass and disrespect to go around speaking of Mr. Holt as "Jehoash" instead of Elbridge. How on earth, now, she found it out, the Lord only knows, but she was always busier than a bumblebee in June when it came to poking her nose in other people's business. She was one that could nose out just about anything. But thank God she never did dig up that awful buggy ride I took with Ople Goble!

I always did hate Mr. Holt's middle name—it sounds so "country" and also Jewish. So I got him never to sign his middle name and Mazzie was a great big girl in the third grade when she asked: "Mother, what's the *J* in Papa's name stand for?" They were studying proper names, surnames, and "given." And I had the gumption to say "Jevons." It was the first fit name that popped into my head; I think I'd read about a Lord Jevons somewhere.

Well, my wedding day was my one great day of triumph. . . . All in white—like a princess—high above all those poor tacky country kin; soaring away superior above the life of rude, smelly farmers and crude working people.

And it was probably the happiest day of Mamma's life, too, to see her vow coming true and *one* of her daughters, at least, marrying money. For even then, Mr. Holt had a good start. He had inherited quite a little nest egg from his father, Judge Lemuel D. Holt; and we didn't have to start off exactly poor, as Mamma did. He owned a tobacco prizery and no telling how many nigger houses.

Professor Vernon D'Argan played the *Tannhäuser* wedding march with so much expression, with such sudden sharps and minors. He *was* a little put out, though, that he had to perform on a plain old cabinet organ. Of course I *could* have been married at the First Methodist Church where they had the grand new *pipe* organ given by General Owsley, instead of at the Mink Street Methodist; but the business feud between the general and the Warhams hadn't yet died down, and Mamma thought it would look like disloyalty to Cousin Jeff for me to be married in General Owsley's church. (I never argued about it, for what the general had said was a sacred matter—just between him and me.)

Cousin Jeff Warham sent a lovely family Bible, all padded and scrolled and bound in black with red corners and imitation gold hasps. (Oh how mad it still makes me just to think how our chances of a lifetime rolled by and all those Garots, Rileys, and country jakes got in on Mr. Warham's bequest, while we, who had known his father so well and been neighbors and called him cousin, didn't get a smell.) Mr. and Mrs. Milam Warham sent us the loveliest cut-glass carafe. And Mr. Tysander a whole case of the finest French champagne. General and Mrs. Eugene Pericles Owsley sent a perfectly wonderful set of china dishes handpainted in purple and gold, and Mrs. Colonel Belo Van Buren McCubbins, a beautiful ormolu clock. . . . And would you believe it, Aunt Effie Jessie Adkins sent a pickle dish, and sister Lillie sent a ham. And I was told afterward that several of that Rabbit City riffraff had come, entirely uninvited, and nearly filled the back pew! The brass of some people!

I was wearing a pale summery dress and feeling so thrilled and so triumphant—and *he* came right up to me—with his famous diamond-peacock scarfpin, and smoking one of those sweet-smelling El Roi Tan Club House cigars that Mr. Holt said cost fifty cents for three—and I guess he'd had a drink, for several little devils were dancing in his eyes—and what a blushing blaze I was when he, my secret love, colored up red in the face and said,

"Miss—Myrena—how charming you look tonight, my dear!" (Oh I knew he meant it; and he gave a little grip to my arm, and a squeeze.) And I also knew that moment that he was too much of a gentleman to have nigger babies. Oh it was a sin, I know, but I sure wished he didn't have his old ugly dried-up wife . . . how I'd have liked to put a spider in her dumpling! . . . and had his wife Miranda died that night, before my marriage to Mr. Holt, I'm sure I'd have broken our engagement.

Mrs. Myrena Holt's reverie was automatically startled to a stop by an unexpected doomful note in Miss Beaver's monologue.

". . . *Queen Elizabeth, one of the greatest rulers of all time, died in her seventieth year, on the twenty-fourth day of March, sixteen-o-three.*"

Oh couldn't you just see her? Her piles of wonderful jeweled skirts; folded and tucked artistically about her in billows in the special oversize royal casket. (They'd have to have one very big, wouldn't they, to hold a queen in a hoop skirt?) Her sweet delicate face framed in her proud and stately starched ruff of pure white—lying still and dead. And Myrena Holt felt like crying.

Curious how life is largely a thing of *boxes,* an impression flitted in the top of her mind. From the time of one's baby clothes, one's wedding clothes, one's last and simple clothing of the grave. First you're boxed up in a cradle, then all your life you're boxed in by the old folks' sayings and what-will-people say? . . . and finally there's a box of pine or mahogany or a $20,000 bronze one like Mr. Jefferson Warham's, all nested in a box of marble in that perfectly wonderful family crypt under the chapel of Warham University that used to be just plain old Gilchrist College until T.P. bequeathed it fifty million dollars under the condition that it would change its name.

Oh yes, they'd moved Mr. Jeff to the university to lie in solemn eternal state, so his grand and noble Christian life could be an example to young men and women for ages to come. (Ty of course had been left high and dry on the mausoleum shelf out at Cedardale cemetery because he'd feuded with Tom and Milam.) Mr. Jeff's effigy was all very formal and correct, with his smooth bronze hands folded across his hard bronze chest. It seemed a bit unnatural, though, if you'd known old Mr. Jefferson's big horny paws that had held the plow handle and the reap hook. That had peddled out the fish, hog meat, and tobacco. Had planted, wormed, and weighed such a mighty mountain of the weed in his life; had scrabbled his pennies and nickels, built a factory, caressed and cuddled-up his women. . . . And when it came time for *their* effigies, what would they do with the soft fat hands of his sons Tom and Milam that had guided a little country business into the big money? Hands that had once so jauntily swung their gold-headed canes, had handed out ten-thousand-dollar checks at Christmas to loyal political people like Senators Hodapp and Mulhooley, and felt their diamond scarfpins and fingered the ticker tape and directed secretaries how to clip the coupons or "take a letter" to the politicians in Walterville or Washington on how to do in the silly child-labor laws, or demolish those horrid cottonmill strikes or anything or anybody that stood in their way. (Oh, she'd always loved all the Warhams—except that awful vulgar Tysander.)

She thought: "Now what kind of an effigy would *I* choose if Mr. Holt and I were millionaires and going to have one? . . . My hands crossed under a lace collar, a single gold chain, and my lorgnette."

Before the mirror at bedtime, Mrs. Elbridge J. Holt was smacking cold cream on her face and rubbing it with lemon juice, preparatory to putting on her rubber sleeping mask. She was happy as a child dabbling in mud, and her eyes sparkled with joy. Being a little nearsighted helped minimize the flabbiness, the crease in her eyelids, the wrinkles marring her eyes and neck. She knew they were there—knew the years, marching across her face as across a battlefield, had left their tracks—but her motto was "never say die" when it came to beauty. She had already finished with the Peach Blow Beauty Balm Treatment and the Beauty Turtle Oil for firming up the face, neck, and hands, and was reflecting on the comparative dermatological merits of Cream de Beauté and d'Illusion.

She was still excited over her club paper, but she would be truly glad when all this great mental strain was over.

Mr. Holt was asleep and snoring. She was glad. She'd been married to him thirty years but still felt awkward doing her beauty routine in his presence. I must order some of that Luxury Crème de Jonquille like Serena Warham's—but good Lord it costs twelve dollars a jar.

Her mind hopped back to the paper Inez Beaver was helping her with. It sure was wonderful to have a mind like Miss Beaver's— that could go back all those ever-so-many generations and fit history together like a puzzle picture. . . . Then, as she was taking a last little peek in the mirror; as her persistent, graceful, aimless, frightened hand flitted caressingly from her precious patrician nose to her wrinkled cheeks to her thinning eyebrows; there came back her bothered and beleaguered frame of mind, and she said to herself, out loud, "I think it's an outrage! Five dollars is entirely too much."

The Rich

Warham's big modern mills are out beyond the town limits, but the old cottonmills like the Ruby are located at the edges, in the slums. They were built there when the town was two-thirds broomstraw field; before the land boom of the '80s. The slums followed the mills naturally, as the tide the moon, the flea the dog.

In the big tobacco manufactories there is the eternal rapid tinny slapping shuffle of the cigarette-rolling machines. And in the cottonmills the heavy dynamic searoar, with the intricate close-up levels of drone, thread hum, and clacking from the looms and spindles in the long interior lanes. Aisles as clean swept as church aisles. As windswept gravestones. And amid the clatter, Warham's factories forever fabricate and roll out from the workers' sweat and toil, from their nights and days of bitterness, from their penury and heartbreak and the half-formed hands of captive childhood, the dividends for their absentee owners. Amid the sour filth and dreary desolation of mill villages, they weave the unvarying high rate of income so indispensable to large-scale gamblers and the lives of richly scented luxury being lived up on McLauchlen's Hill, or in Paris, Palm Beach, Rome, Manhattan, Switzerland—in the strange faraway floating palaces and gilded ballrooms.

Throughout the long bleak vigils of the night the workers have worked and the machines have raced. The looms, the bag machines, the clicking and speedy knitting machinery. These working men and women—these bobbin hands, weavers, cigarette

spinners and cigar packers—are ladies and gents of little leisure
. . . no time at all, don'tcherknow, for horse racing, travel, or
bridge. Being busier than a one-armed paper hanger with the itch,
they have little time for garden fêtes, or *chemin de fer,* or yachting.
And as for fine new wearing apparel, they have to make out with
"head rags" for millinery and let their old things do.

With all the cloth you've made, you "lintheads"—isn't it bizarre
that you possess only the old worn gingham, the sleazy rayon
dress? Or thrice-patched pants and the scuffed and run-over second-hand shoes?

But Mrs. Milam Warham and her lithe and lissome daughters,
those dark imperious beauties, Hélène and Margaretta, had their
acute clothes problems too. Though they carried trunkfuls of special seagoing things, with two maids to look after their brilliant
flannels, nobby tweeds, and ravishing décolleté evening gowns
that they doffed and donned and promenaded to knock their fellow
passengers cold; when they approached Europe's historic shores,
Hélène would be sure to say to Serena, "Good Lord, Mamma, we
haven't a thing to wear!" And they would be seized with panic—as
though awaking from a dream and finding themselves American
savages going down the Buckingham Palace receiving line without
any clothing, and from their luxury liner would leap frantic S.O.S.s
across the leagues of watery waste to amplify previous dress de-
signers' orders, to change the details on a hat.

"Just a stitch in time, Mamma," Margaretta said while they were
having fittings. Knowing that one might bump into *any*body on
the quarter deck or at the captain's table: from a horsy Vanderbilt
to a British lord.

And once at the beginning of the World War, when more and
more epaulettes and gold braid were brightening the table the
captain, casting his sea-eagle eye around, boomed heartily—and a
little louder than he intended—to General Pershing on his left:
"Ah! today we have beef, tobacco, and oil . . ." Whereupon Mrs.
Rockefeller—at his right—and Hélène and Mamma and
Margaretta and one of *the* Swifts from Chicago, had tightened
their lips and tried not to look self-conscious. As if they didn't feel
important—though they felt warm and embarrassed like being
caught naked under the glare of a navy searchlight.

There were the moons of enchantment at sea, the eerie encirclement of fog, the rapturous night breezes—but inside, all those highballs that had to be drunk. It made you dizzy—the jazz band with the niggers from St. Louis diked up in Louis XIV satin britches. You had to bet on how many knots a day and promenade in the Queen Elizabeth saloon and sit in the "diamond row." And the grand balls, the lights, of that floating palace! You had to keep dressing and undressing. There was forever the work of buying more clothes.

Rarely did the restless, swift-darting daughters, the Warham princesses, wear anything more than twice. It being one of the hardships of those caught in the flood of machine-age opulence that you can't get around to everything, there was nothing to do but grin and bear it. After all, one frail human frame simply couldn't put on and take off but so much; and so Mrs. McKlosky, the custodian of the armoire, was always digging up something that, as she expressed it, had "never been given a past."

Mamma was a damned good sport, considering her raising—although it almost took a chisel, at times, to pry a dress she'd taken a fancy to off her back. Stingy as she was, there were three things she'd always shell out for: more shoes, more ornaments, and more statuary. The girls had to laugh and shake their heads, and Papa would say tch-tch-tch, when they got reminiscing among themselves about that morning Mamma had haggled half an hour over a head of lettuce and then gone to Tiffany's the same afternoon and paid $250,000 for a ring.

The girls got a kick out of going around with the horse-crowd to Longchamp, Deauville, and Epsom Downs. To bet on the races. To wear the clothes. Papa entered right into the spirit of the thing. They had to laugh when he lost seventy-five thousand smackers on the tail end of Jupiter's Fairybell. Why the hell hadn't he *bought* the damned plug? he said, scratching his distinguished dome. Or bet on Mudhopper? Which was something to think about. And though perfectly horrified, they couldn't help being amused at the way Papa went around slapping nobility on the back, but in spite of this, Lord Northcliffe took to him right off and introduced him to the Prince of Wales.

They kept on society's giddy round, all over Europe. Papa had

his picture taken at Deauville in a bathing suit with Lady Astor.
. . . It was rather a bitter pill to Serena, though, that Milam soon
lost interest. His *vivacité* eventually collapsed—his weak stomach
was wrecked by the long and late alcoholic hours—and cablegrams
began arriving concerning business urgencies in New York.
Serena was naive enough to think her Milam indispensable to the
business—never suspected that foxy, previously arranged signal to
his personal factotum at the Office: FOR GODSAKE GINIGER GIVE US
THE HEAVE HO. Really, Milam cared no more for society and royalty
than a hog.

The Warham women took a chateau for "the season" in France.
But Papa could hardly ever get off to go with his wife and daughters anywhere, he was so tied down in the United States with important business (she was a vivacious little black-eyed charmer of
twenty-three). But now and then he would break away from routine affairs and come to Paris or London to go "Continental" for a
time and fornicate with the maids. In London, they bought a town-
house near Mr. Morgan's in Grosvenor Square.

They moved around so much that Serena sometimes forgot
where she was. One day, to a Cockney workman helping around
their London residence, she absent-mindedly said (her thinking
not moving around much): "Now you want to be sure and vote for
Mr. Coolidge."

"Mister 'oo, ma'rm?" the man said, looking up with knitted brow
and scratching an ear.

Sucking in the nectared breath of tropical night, Serena and her
daughters dawdled upon exotic, expensively exclusive hotel terraces, eating ices as full-dress waiters hurried about.

"You can never trust a maid," reflected Serena gloomily. (She
had missed fifteen cents out of her purse, but maybe it was that
cabin stewardess. She wasn't sure whether she had counted the
change when she'd tipped her a crown and told her to take out a
shilling.)

"Oh for godsake, Mamma!"

On their intermittent returns to the States, the Warham women
were also in evidence at important sporting events. The Westches-
ter Women's Golf and Tennis tournaments. The yacht regattas off
New London. And religiously did they attend the Church of the

Holy Trinity and the Waldorf and Newport bridge clubs. And everyone said that the Warham girls with their raven type of beauty looked perfectly stunning in their silver blue minks.

They had been shopping at Altman's one day and Papa had been along and when Mamma asked How much? and the salesperson said Only twenty-one thousand, six hundred, plus tax, Madam, Papa said We'll take three. One for Sereny and one for each of the girls. He said they deserved a "pretty" after all the Red Cross and Junior League war benefits they'd suffered through.

Besides, he told himself, what good was all the goddamn money the goddamn war had dumped in his lap but to keep his women happy? It poured in so fast you had to spend it to keep from getting covered up. Everything his brother T.P. touched turned to money. T.P. was sure a wizard. Their Burdex Explosives was now busting all over the place with war profits and today's mail had brought him a quarterly dividend of $402,675 from a couple of their Carolina mill properties. Their Beargrass Mill topped all the others, though, and was referred to in the bosom of the family and among financial cronies as "the good old Bear's Ass," on account of Dismukes, when little, misunderstanding the name that way. Brother T.P. had put in a postwar speed-up and efficiency system, and it acted like fertilizer on a tobacco plant and production was shooting way up. . . . So on the side, he had instructed the sales gal: "Say, sweetheart, make it a foursome on those mink coats and send the other one to Miss Janet Browne at the Barbizon-Plaza."

Back home in Warham, Dismukes (he was Serena and Milam's only son) and his attractive sisters had lots of big houseparties. Especially in their college days. They'd run down from New York in Uncle T.P.'s private railroad car, the *Coronado,* loaded down with football stars and prizefighters, perfumed playboys and debs and fresh-water mermaids and Broadwayites. Uncle T.P. was simply swell about lending his car. He thought the world of his brother Milam. He never would let them pay the railroad's bill, either. Said Hell, he owned enough stock in the Southern Railway and the Pullman Company to make up for a few little debit memos; and besides, anything he gave anybody was f.o.b. But he kidded Dismukes and his nieces to their faces about not being worth a damn.

*   *   *

Ah, but old Jeff Warham's descendants were privileged children
of the sun. Their lives held together by a stout black guardian rubber band: that held a magic packet of crisp paper certificates with
scrollwork engraving and pictures of eagles that guaranteed them
plenty of everything without working: life, liberty, and all the time
there was to pursue happiness. They resembled nothing so much
as a fairy-ring of tiny fungi risen after rain, out of the ash pile of
desolation, from the musted and festered overripe and feculent
manurage of war. Strangers were they to those unpublished peas-
ant years of old Jeff; little they knew of his hard-scrabbling struggles, his dreams, passions, and cold calculating scheming. All the
small and incidental footings of luck, of elemental drift, that had
gathered under his great square-toed No. 13 manure-saturated
shoeleather; under his life and destiny.

His horny unrelenting hand had clutched his fortune like a vise.
(Within the great man's greatness this layer of miser's littleness
lay.) In his lush last-will-and-testament, the manufacturer-
philanthropist overlooked entirely his fellow-townsmen, as well as
the workers in the great Warham enterprises. He had not remembered any of them by so much as a nickel. It had been all his, that
ambitious amorphous lump of something that had sprouted and
spread, like the town, into the large and unlikely cabbage from the
rich and illimitable muck. The roots of the great Warham financial
empire were grounded in low-priced labor. They delved down into
the patriarch's fortunate inheritance of the vitality of an ox. Were
traceable to the invention by others of the tireless, remarkable machinery from whose deep rich potentiality of patent fruited now the
sweet and mellow dividends as from a proliferous vine. (As a matter
of hard cold fact, the workers and citizenry of Warham possessed no
more stake in the great Warham fortune than did those mud turtles
sunning themselves out in Gare's Lowground or bedded down in
the winter mud beneath the slues of Buck Creek.)

All year round Jeff's grandchildren played; doing their loafing
and highjinks in Warham, France, De Funiak Springs, or Den-
mark. In solariums, on February's tropic sands and tennis courts,
in the perfumed private baths of Manhattan's or Piccadilly's
hundred-dollar-a-day hotels. In their Florida home the Milam Warhams took their gin with orange juice and played the market in the
bucket shops and attended the dog races, and for mental stimula-

tion, talked of the great American Calvin Coolidge and What would the masses do with leisure if they had it? and the price of stocks. In their New York home they drank everything but the cocktail shaker and worried over the servant problem and talked of that great American and up-and-coming savior of the country, Herbert C. Hoover.

But Mamma seemed happier in Warham than anyplace else. There she had been born and there she was the flower in its natural sod.

In Warham the old jokes and the old superstitions and the old hymns and jolly personal anecdotings, and ancient games of her childhood, returned—especially when she was with her girlhood chums Emily Vann and Myrena Holt and Minnie Marshwood Jackson. Sometimes Serena would try to describe for Warham ladies, who had never traveled, the soul of Vienna or Gay Paree. But, words failing her, she could only tell of the robber prices charged Americans, and of her fear and contempt for the horrible peasants and dirty masses that were crazily trying to go "red"—only our brave engineer Mr. Hoover, in charge of the Belgian Relief, wouldn't let 'em—and the arbitrary austerities of fashion.

"The styles are very tricky in France this season. Last season we covered up our busts and wore short sleeves, but now if you're going to be fashionable, you've got to wear long tight sleeves with lace and your tiddies must almost be showing."

Buttressed by her Cinderella millions, Serena would outdo them all in frank confessions of her early poverty and lowliness. That is, when her proud and formal daughters weren't around to cramp her style.

"Sure I used to pick the worms off tobacco. And I've tried dipping snuff, too. But I'm pickin' dividends off it now, ain't I?

"And I've gone out to the barn and helped Pa dig up the old horse corn he'd hid in the ground from the Yankees or the hungry neighbors, I can't remember which. Ma made lye hominy out of it. And he made us girls dry blackberries and apples and cherries to sell in the store." Here a shadow, a dark look, would come to her sallow Irish face. A tightening of the mouth and a shake of the double chins. "And from Christmas to Christmas, one pair o' shoes is all we ever got for our pay." Then she'd go on to tell how those shoes were more precious than gold, and how she'd go barefoot to church to keep from muddying them. "But when we got to the Turnipseed House, I'd go in to see Miss Doriah and she'd let me wash my feet in her room and put my shoes and stockings on. She was a sweet kind old woman and had a pet mockingbird in a cage and every spring I'd bring her a mess of creasy salet; and one time I remember Anna Pulaski, the child balloon-jumper, was there for a long time sick in bed and Miss Doriah nursing her."

Then suddenly her jollity would return. "What if I *do* belong to the Piping Rock Country Club, I've not forgot which end of a cow you milk. And I remember how to dry a cow, too. You milk some on the ground and that absorbs the milk . . ."

It was in their brief alightings at their halfway home in Warham, sojourning there for a few days rest before the next take-off, that Hélène and Margaretta had the hardest time keeping Mamma out of mischief. In New York they and Papa could hold her down fairly well (though it was recalled with chagrin—it was still a cruel thorn in the girls' memory—the time they'd caught Mamma telling Emily Vanderbilt about how, when Warham was Minktown, the church bell was rung when a beef was butchered; and everywhere they went, to the girls' great mortification, Mamma continued to hold the world championship for hunting longest for lost golf balls, and she'd pick up other peoples', and shortchange the caddies). But in Warham Mamma seemed to always escape and toss to the winds all their hard work of training her to be civilized. In the locale of her nativity she was always slipping back, a kind of automatic atavism, into her childhood and the deeply rutted influence of a departed skinflint progenitor. . . . In Warham she'd go on a regular orgy of haggling with tradespeople over groceries and such vulgarities. Even though it called for shoving and pushing around among the dirty masses she so despised.

. . . In the twilight, going home in the long slinky Packard threading Warham's main thoroughfare like a dark bright needle and Louis, the chauffeur, honking at the dark stinking tide of the factory workers, Hélène looked through the rain-drizzled glass of the motorcar and shuddered to recall how Mamma in Hodgkins Meat Market had called the tradesman by his first name as though he might have been her long-lost boy friend or something. . . . I really must see about a coat-of-arms, she thought. Like the Du Ponts. It would look forbiddingly baronial on the doors of the cars. Also on stationery and done in mosaic at the front doors. . . .

*   *   *

The womenfolk of Warham's mill villages, however—of its cottonmills and tobacco mills, of the niggertowns, in the "City of Opportunity"—went on, of driven necessity, amusing themselves at the washpot and the cooking pot. Hacking the dull blade of a hoe into their leisure time from the loom or the long hours in the stemmeries. Weeding in the bean vines and collard patch to hold the wolf away a little longer from their scuffed and broken doors. Dropping their clothes to quench their squalid menfolks' lust; having also the tugging pap-lust of their too-fast-arriving excrementitious young to dance attendance upon.

Suffering is a refining fire—so said the Reverend E. Scully Randelle, of the Ruby Mill Presbyterian Mission. And they also received the extra dividends of diphtheria and whooping cough, hookworm, the rickets, and pellagra. And drank, when they could get it, the raw plain hootch for the jolt in it.

Down at the Ruby Mill, the linthead girls on the night shift couldn't half sleep in the daytime. After the ear-splitting racket roar of the machines, their poor ears ached, still registering the roaring, and their nerves were jangled. Ofttimes the foreman would be screaming again with his PD headache-powder bone disease, and they'd give anything for a little rest. Anything at all, bigod, to get away from the stink of that fuckin' Shit Creek and the flies.

Back in the home hills, in the backwoods of Warham and Lemon and those other Carolina counties, the tobacco-farm women, the cotton-farm women, labor everlastingly with their menfolks making the stuff, the "whichum," with which Warham's every-hungry and overprocreant machines are by night and day nourished.

All year long the treadmill wheel of sharecropping, of small farming, must be turned. There is the tobacco. Tobacco is the first thing and the last thing in the country around Warham. First you burn your beds and sow the seed. Then you must put the fertilizer and the sody over them. You cover that bed over with mosquito-cloth till the plants get big enough to set out. You set them out if the wilt or blue mold or root rot doesn't get them. You have to water the young plants when it's dry. But not if it is rainy. You'll give them the wilts if you water then. Then you hoe tobacco twice, you plow it, and when it blooms you top it. The top has to be cut out with a knife. You work and you sucker it. The suckers come out after the topping and you have to keep it suckered.

When tobacco goes to getting ripe it turns spotted. It freckles up with spots the farmers call "frog-eyes." It is then that you cut it and let it lie and wilt. If you cut it, say, this morning you don't haul it in till late in the day. At evening, about cow-milking time. And next you hang it up on sticks in the loft of the curing barn. If you are a Warham farmer making bright, or cigarette, tobacco, you will have a flue in your barn and will sit up with the tobacco day and night to cure it by fire. If you are one of those in the "burly belt," making the old killdaddy stuff for long-cut, for the world's "jimmy joypipes," then you will air-cure it, the way the Indians did. And when tobacco is cured, you'll "hand" it. Then it has to be "classed," leaf by leaf, and tied up in bundles.

"I'll say tobacco's work. From the time we light the brush piles at the new-ground till we pack up the damn stuff in bed quilts under the stars of a frost-kivered December morn and haul it off to market to try and turn it into a little bread-and-meat." This is what they'll tell you back in the tobacco country.

But often enough, after his crop was sold in the fall, the way Tom Warham was forcing the price of raw tobacco down, the farmer would not receive enough money to pay his fertilizer bill, let alone the labor of his family. Coming back on the wagon . . . a tobacco farmer and family man, troubled—Zeke Jones, perhaps, with a headache and muttering to himself: "Goddamn it, a farmer can't pay the floor charge. I've worked all the year and I'm now two dollars and fifty cents in debt for my floor charges . . ."

Yet, in spite of it all, the Warham County farmers did not blame their plight on the masters of the machines, but upon Lady Luck.

The Railroad Bridge

It was starbreak, the blue and coral commencing faintly to suffuse the eastern sky.

John Anders stopped on the railroad bridge to watch the coming dawn. Aloft there was a surge of dark, soft-winged birds. Swallows. Eager as himself to meet the day. The town's nearby roosters were sending up their lusty special prayers for daylight and chicken-feed; and tomcats were yet on the prowl and ardently yowling from roof and alley.

As the few first lines of daybreak streaked the sky, the invisible broom of a sunrise breeze was beginning to push back the thick smoke-sodden cloud flock, and out across the town the air was warming, threads of tobacco smell enlarging with the light.

This town, especially in the early morning, fascinated him. It was all an endless and vast obbligato: heavy and droning with one-ness, complexity, sweetness, and meaning. In the half-light of dawn and under a mist that had enveloped everything, its roofs and fog-wet lawns, shanties and church steeples seemed to have melted and run all together. Fused in this way, it appeared at first glance to be no more than a great shapeless lump of slag.

Up on the Warham Power building the sign lights still winked. The similarity of the clockworked lights to a swarm of fireflies put it into Anders's mind that the sleeping town was a flower. He began to imagine it a great wilted flower in a bowl, at which fire-flies sucked and glimmered. Later on, when the sun rose, it would revive like rock fern after rain. In daylight the rim of hills forming the bowl would recede. Shrink away serpentwise into the dim thicket of distance to become a dusty hyacinth blue. A frontier between things near and familiar, and things and shapes not of earth. Veiling substance and moments once immediate and savored, but vanished now into the past and forevermore untouchable.

There is an old, old, untraced story ingathered in every foot of ground, he realized. Under the dark and secret roots of old houses, old trees, old stones. All the town's ground soaked and sodden in primal, dateless wonder. Underlying the sappy little tobacco burg's boom-time real estate was the old sandstone stratum that had once, in the brief and hectic seven days of earth's creation, coagulated beneath its surface. All its ground watered by a creek of old but living moisture pressed out of the maturity and strangeness of time, and that rose in springs of the past. Since autumn dusks primeval, when the pioneer woods, the Mink or Warham County lines, yet lay beneath the sea and there was no place for winged creatures to roost but on its wet and vasty bosom. Since pre-Columbian days—prior to even Dan Boone or the settlement of Mink's Hollow, or the flowering of the village of Mink Station.

Before the coming of the horse and the iron horse; antedating the advent of the first brass cannon's boom and the Spanish, the French, the British, soldiers—the blue and gray soldiers—millions of migratory wild pigeons: and ofttimes dense clouds and defilings of crows and blackbirds, robins, swallows, plovers, and bullbats, had blackened this sky. Had surveyed from their aerial heights this Warham Town's future nestling place and seat of business. Had come the forest buffalo, the long-time back founders of the Buffalo Trace. And turkey vultures, with their telescopic eyes, spotting and circling about any animal that had grown old and thin and had fallen. Sharp-eyed jays and whiskey-frisky wrens and tomtits had spied and scolded at the first red hunter to come that way: with his stone ax and arrows, his first uprolling smoke of fire. And then some fifteen thousand years later their descendants had done the same identical thing when the first white huntsman passed through with his flintlock. Poked about down there along the streams and around the base of the hills. The mudsnipe and woodhen had noted the first lean-to of boughs, the teepee of skins, the hogan of mud and sticks; the forest road and the first forest clearing and cabin of logs, ax-hewn. The thrush, the lark, the crows, and the redbird had awakened the first settler's family with song.

. . . So much beneath. . . . A story in all ground. The ground under the depot there had been Elijah Morris's slave lot and the Upper Clover Patch. Before that the cabin of Nathe Chisenhall, the deer hunter, had stood there on a rise of ground. But when the tobacco boom came in the spring of '75, the hillock had been torn down by Giles & Broughton—"We Move the Earth." Only put back that dissolved hill for a moment.

. . . Nathe could stand in his doorway then, in the 1820s—a bear's paw was nailed on his door—and see only woods. From the highest part of the hill, up the path by the Big Poplar Spring, mule-head high in goldenrod and cocklebur, he could spy a little clustering of cabins and shanties and a curl of smoke off to the west. The Spratt's Paradise settlement. A riproaring old neighborhood where wild men came down from their diggings of a Saturday to brawl, crack heads, and screw the slatternly daughters of Ketch-Eye, the half-white Indian. A rendezvous for horsethieves. All there was then of the town's roots.

Big Oak you could spy the top of. The broadest tree anywhere. A mile south, near the Wolf Den. Where, when the town sprouted and Sunday school came, people went on picnics.

"I've skins of my own shooting as was kyored by the Injuns," Granpappy Dannigan had said . . . had said that name Wolf Den was but a white man's name, though. The Injuns had called it different. The Pound-up Place Where They Make Acorn Meal. In Sapony talk, *Yap Hintu Himi*. In the deeper and more wordy tongue of the Tuskies, *Ga-sea-no-ra-ga-wa-ta-chrean-ya-taw*. Granpap had done some traveling. His old ears had heard the war horn and the smoke drum, and he remembered the old redskin that had told him all this at Stinking Quarter on the Alamance. Remembered their talk, their rum drinking together, at that deer-skinning place, all the ducks quacking in the rushes. . . .

And there, where the old log courthouse used to stand, had been two very large sugar-maple trees. Just outside the jail. Just when their leaves had turned and they had begun to strew their gold around on the plank sidewalk and over the high board fence into the jail yard, quite a wonderful thing would happen among their branches. Some hot afternoon in late September, thousands upon thousands of a kind of swallow the farmer boys called "bee martin" would assemble in those courthouse trees from all over the surrounding country. Here they set up a big communal roost, and for several days the air would be black with their comings and goings and the entire block noisy with their chatter. Every so often they would quit the trees to mount high in the sky—there to race, dive, wheel, and maneuver in drill formation like soldiers. Then, as if by some prearranged signal or common impulse, they would as suddenly return to their meeting hall in the trees and their clack-fest. And then one morning the canny chatterboxes and sidewalk soilers would all be gone. Gone south in the night.

For as long as anyone could remember, the annual meeting of the bee martins had been one of Minktown's choicest marvels. Even before Muleshoe Mink's progenitor, Elliwell the hunter, came. Which was, of course, before there was any courthouse or any Minktown, which was about the same time as Daniel Boone. The philosophers and local wits each had his own theory as to why the bee birds always returned to the martin trees, year after year. But had they known it—could they have looked back up the bee-martin family tree—millions of hatchings of their forefathers and little grandmotherkin hen-martins had held their annual autumn conventicles in these same trees (and their parent trees) for a hundred and more years back; before there was even one brick or nail of the town. And the bee birds were as loath to change their custom, to cease their flockings to their consecrate places as ordained and taught them by their feathered "old folks," as men are unwilling to scuttle their established sacred habits.

But now, alas, regretted Anders, no warbling bee martins fill the sky. The old maple trees are gone—with the old log courthouse and log jail. And doing duty for them all looms up the pretentious and monstrous modern Warham County Courthouse.

. . . A story unread, untold, in all ground.

The Methodist church was built in the '50s, and here came Will Leake and Enar Spratt to sing thanksgiving to the Lord-God-of-Hosts. For His great sovereign mercy in the fertility of their soil and slaves. For His loving kindness in making Spratt's General Mer-

chandise & Hardware store—and Leake's Ginnery and grogshop—
to prosper, and having given the best land and dominion of the town
into their fat freckled hands. (It was '58 now, and the hamlet called
Mink Station). . . . And for holding up with His strong right arm
the price of cotton; and hoping He would see fit, in the majesty of
His wisdom, to do likewise by tobacco, and niggers, and to confound
all damn-Yankee abolitionists. And under the Methodist church
was the ghost of a Baptist church. Planted under it like a seed.

The Rose of Shalem . . . with its horse-hitching grove. . . .
Horses tossing their heads because of the gadflies. . . . A
Shawnee-wood tree in front. And under that a graveyard long
forgotten. In it Reverend Jesse Judd, whose folks had pioneered
down from Penn's Woods. Tucked away where he'll never be found
by prying genealogist nor steam shovel. Gathered with his fathers
like a tall slim shock of corn. And with him buried the Mink's Hollow people—hunters, witches, and tale-tellers who could not now
ever tell their tales—and buried with him, too, the light of a lost and
green gold afternoon. The soft sifting of maple leaves—scarlet and
yellow—on his pine box Duck Erdmann had knocked up back of the
smithy. And all the grasshopper twitter and chirkings and the drone
of their crankling flight.

They were everywhere that day—on everything and everybody
. . . walking about, like little horses or slow old men, on the coffin,
and Sarah Teazly brushing them off her old brown shawl while
Elam Benson prayed. And in that forgotten graveyard Old Man
Salithius Allarbay. Two teeth and a coffin nail now.

A blue fog of perfumed dust, of words long laid and settled and
soft dusty remembrances, is rising where the old church used to
stand.

. . . I sowed the winter oats thus and so. (Kincher Grindstaff,
that was back from San Jacinto and trying to forget the cannon
smoke, the dust, the heat, the drum-and-fife's crazy shriek above
the rattle of the guns, the cursing Texans' lathered mustangs, the
knife and sword-flash, the shrieking poor caught Mexican camp-
sisters Oh Señor goddamn in the name of God for the life of your
mother, do not kill me! . . .) Plowing barefoot in the cool of an
August morn he yet resaw through rifts in the mist, over the pine
woods, just beyond the robins hopping in the furrow, the falling

white stallion, old Deaf Smith ahead in the blood and blinding heat hacking. . . .

. . . "I fed my old cow on 'taters and she got pore as a snake." (From Malinda Marcum.)

. . . "Lor' child, I kin recomember when thar was *several* painters in this neighborhood. In the evening, right at turn o' dark, they'd be crying p'intzblank like a womern body on yan very hill." (This from Aunt Lennora Mink.)

And then—back beyond the Yankee War—they talked of the struggle of the poor to get some of the good things of life. Of those who stole, and what happened.

. . . "Thar was Hardy Caroll, hanged in Louisburg for stealing a pair of suspenders. And Enoch Tate getting his ears cut off for lifting Aaron Erdmann's pig. And the two women hanged in Walterville for stealing twenty-five-cents'-worth of bacon. (Granpappy Gully had passed *those* horrors down. Chalked them up, as it were, behind the broad tavern door of the Bleeding Past as part of that long uneven score of the ragshags against the rich—a thing for the wretched and the ragged to remember.)

Homely words rising from where the people used to stand and talk.

. . . The sound of feet and of sobbing. They were taking Cuba, Titus Hodgkins's wench, to be hanged. (Down along the edge of the meadow they passed, passed right by the church and the Shawnee-wood tree. It was dark of the moon, the moon giving no light. And afterward three generations of Reden Green's people were to remember it so: it was in a March, whilst Reden was working late in the gray evening dusk, planting his potatoes.)

. . . The creak of a wagon's wheels. It was Jeff Warham, the peddler, going past old Shalem downhill on the long red clay Simmon Tree Hill and putting on his brake. His wagon packed full of tobacco and young'uns. The scrimpit old fool'd go clear to the ocean and wouldn't be seen in those parts again for three or four months, maybe. . . .

. . . The whispers, laughter, the feel of wet wind. A rainy dark night this time . . . "A meetin' house should be better than a barn," a young fellow said—"Oh you ornery boys—you're some shucks!" The woman laughed huskily, her brown eyes humid. (Kate Page, Richard Page's woman. Braving her man's whip, and hellfire, to encourage and teach those youthful admirers, those young goats, her evening class. They were vigorous, ardent, bullocky hunting farming lads; young potential backwoods Belvederes, ladies' men, senators, stud horses: plenty willing though yet a bit scairt. They were uncouraged and novitiate, but in the gloam and sanctuary of the meetin' house she'd learnt many a boy the most genteel biblical ways and all the wicked and Frenchy ways for sowing the springtime wild oats. . . .)

Stories within stories. Boxes nested within boxes: a host of boxes to fall spilling, rattling out at Judgment Day.

The Leakes and Solomon Gare, Enar and Willie Spratt, and the rest worshiped at the Methodist meeting house. On that sacred ground, above the dead, to pray and sing the old hymn tunes. Without instrument music—as the Lord intended. "Hark From the Tomb a Doleful Voice!" "Hosanna to the Lamb of God" . . .

The old church was embalmed in a complex and moldy odor of sanctity. Its sweet unpainted pine wood warmed with sunlight. The scent of leaves and tulip tree and the musky acrimonious dust of oak pollen drifting in the open windows with the piping of larks. The sweet pure breath of young sinners and the brassy, corrupted breathings of age. The composite aura of bodies; virility of men and the urinous foxy smell of mice and small boys; and standing apart in the ethereal pool from these, the elemental nimbus of femininity—Iladine Spratt's Hoyt's German cologne—that brought the soft mood of daydream and carnal longings to all in its mystic reach. The brash smell of wool homespun cutting sharply across this and the other. Blending in a good clean chord with the mellow sunned crispness of soapsuds on gingham frock and homemade lace and Sunday shirt. Sanctified farmers' feet and sweated leather; the tincture of cattle and barn on their hands. The molasses aroma of shoe-blacking and tobacco-chewers' juice hissing out at window and under benches. The strong hot stench of unwashed slaves in the loft.

Up in the loft, old uncle Doddy Morris. Big Sugarfoot Bullock. Dinah Gare—with her string of brats running the whole scale of brown, from bright-tobacco to black. "Blackern a black cat's ass at midnight," Snipe Quackenbush, the auctioneer, classified her the time of her sale as a girl to Jesse Gare: "*Gen*-tle-men: notice this here nigger's so black she's blue. It's a good stock. We call 'em the

San Domingo snowballs." Abner Leake's good-looking mulatto house-wench Savanna. Slaves in the loft. . . .

"Be humble. Humble ye your hearts," Preacher Dillas Hopkins preaches up to them with his voice. His harsh eyes say more. Slaves can't read in reading books, but they can read the harshness and hate in white men's eyes. Mind your p's and q's, niggers. All you Gares, Garrots, and Cozart roustabouts! Preacher Hopkins's hard eyes—cold and ungiving gray stones— shout. You there, young Curly Spratt, and Ishmael Trice. You too, Redbone Leathers . . . because your grandfather was a Cherrykee Injun heathen chief's no why-so for holding your head so high. "Blessed are the meek," his mouth says, out of the Book of God.

"Amen!" sing out brothers Spratt and Gare, chimes of a double-striking clock. And deaf old sister Savrena Snotherly. . . . (The Methodists sitting where the Baptists had sat. Those Methodists now sitting, those Baptists now lying. One manner of God-fear falling, another taking over. On the same ground. The green bark and the old.) "*A*-men."

But no backjaw. (Preacher's eyes rant up to the loft again.) Or Pateroller Puryear'll lash your black backsides, you bastard sonsabitches, and salve the lash cuts with salt brine. And Columbus Puryear, the patroller on church ward, grins knowingly and splatters tobacco juice across the Indian's bare feet in insult and benediction. "In the name of Our Lord and Savior Amen."

Stories beneath stories, lives beneath lives.

Gilchrist College. Ghosts and the seed of ghosts under that, too. And God-fearingness. The campus had been part of Zack Wraxbee's farm. Zack Wraxbee, sojourning on his rump like a vegetable, talking blue ruin. A surviving Stone Age citizen still whittling out tomahawks. An Enoch, a king crab and a gar-fish survival from the Deluge.

"What if some Yankee *has* got a conjectiment to grind hossfeed?—they'll never grannylate smokin' tobacco. . . . All poppycock. This talk about Mink Station land goin' to ten dollars per acre."

And then one day he woke up to find himself hog-rich. "I'm rich, boys. You gotta use your head, as the billy goat said when he butted the city feller into the crick . . . wha-wha! . . . The Almighty's never made better land—as I've always maintained—than Minktown land. *God's* country . . ."

Zack's pig pasture became the choicest business property on Main Street. The Baptists wanted to name a church after him, if he'd donate the lot. And his womenfolk got so stylish they served his chitlings, his creasy salet, and his sweet-potato pie upon an imported chiny salver of state imported all the way from Petersburg, Virginia.

Looking out over Warham in the primordial darkness of early morn, Anders felt a sudden poignant rush of affection. For its acres of night-damp earth; its thoroughfares and alleys—Great and Little Cigarette, the Ruby Mill Bottom, Main Street and Old Uncle Ned Street and McLauchlen's Hill and the Mud and Morning Glory alleys; and the familiar pleasant tobacco pungence hovering over it eternally like a mellow aureole above the features of a hard-faced saint. Or like Cyrus T. Badger's pith-helmet hat—acquired in the 1880s in one of his tropical travels, and which no one had ever seen him without (that is, except in deep winter—when Cyrus affected a special custom-built black derby equipped with earmuffs) and which had long ago become an integral part of the community.

Here—down on Cackleberry Street, next to Susan Tolloch's Grocery and hard by Mangan & Yarbo's Coffin and Furniture Shop—he had drawn his first breath. Over forty years ago now. But his destiny had lain here ever since. Fattened and taken its substance in this particular rutted wrinkle of the Earth Mother's green-haired breast. So that now he knew the land's deeper rhythms . . . as the child, within its mother's womb, sharing the glow of her heartbeat and deep sufficiency, knows her flesh as its own; feels the springs and creeks of her core run as the milk and blood and marrow of its own being. In this strange blind attachment washing over him, Anders knew the pulse and pull in the flesh of steel at the magnet's seductive undertow. The secret tug and grip of the leaf's kinship with the tree.

There was something about the railroad bridge that appealed to John Anders. He frequently stopped here on his way to or from work. It was a good vantage point from which to overlook the town. The rich pass over this bridge, and the poor also take this way. Nearly every one of its thirty-seven thousand citizens comes along here at one time or another. From the sandstone trestle bank jungly tufts of coarse grass leap out, their fronds black and stiff from soot.

Comes a little rustle of morning wind.

Two carriers of the *Morning Bugle* pass. They radiate—with lusty stride, words, laughter—a lot of freshness and crackling vitality.

". . . Sure—I know I know—now don't tell me, Bob!" Talk flinging back on the breeze from the fog-swallowed high-school youths. "We haddim in History One . . . Sir Walter Raleigh! Aw *that* guy. Sure. The guy my old man says was the real daddy of this town. Sir Walter Raleigh the guy that went definitely nuts, dizzy-lirious, and threw his coat—some say also pants—in the mud puddle as a publicity stunt to advertise Queen Elizabeth and smokin'-tobacco. Sure—I know!"

At a certain age a boy sure had a lot of git-up and gusto, John thought, smiling. In the crepuscular gloom they pass on without seeing him.

Some of the students from the college also worked their way through school carrying papers—or on the cars. You could tell them, even behind conductors' greasy leather-bound coats and change belts. A fresh unwilted way of seeing life that the regulars—old men, mostly, or those ironed out flat by care—didn't have.

He spent many hours of the day and of the night thinking odd thoughts. For him there was a deep symphonic mood in the commonplace. Common objects and people assuming uncommon and beautiful shapes. Resolving into their secret inner keys and harmonies. He nearly always rose in darkness to cherish the town's earliest light—lest he miss any part of the morning's mysterious uncoiling, the saneness and freshness of odor and sound.

. . . There were machines down there in the great Warham factories that could do things human hands couldn't begin to. Any damned thing at all . . . a new wizard race of funny iron scarecrows down there in the cottonmills, the cigar and cigarette mills, the mills turning out flour, fertilizer, mule feed, electric power. . . . Tireless gibbetty arms, greased-lightning fingers, all working together . . . rolling, chittering. Enchanted machines. Puppet brains of cams and levers outsmarting the best weavers or the highest-priced brown-skin cheroot-making swifts from Key West,

Florida. Marble switchboards, with governors, pilot lights. Time-clocks. Controls on kilowatt-hours and workingmen's juice. Chibbling, chuckling. Machine parts. A million actors in a miracle play: gibbering, sobbing, crooning, shrieking; rattling off their lines in the split second. Fecund as fruitflies, rabbits. Machine parts. All parts dancing together for the glory of production. A dizzy whirligig dance of cogs, wheels, pinions, levers, couplings, shaftings. Forever begetting and bringing forth. Witch womb and wizard piston.

Monsters of steel and brass . . . with razor-edged hands, steam-shovel beaks. . . . Heaving coal cars, fabricating overalls, silk hosiery, plug tobacco, ice-cream cones, Sunday papers. Scissoring granite and cross-ties like snipping out paper dolls. Automatic weighing, wrapping, cellophaning-and-tinfoiling packing monsters. Nightmare hippogriffs and chimeras patting, thumping, coaxing, softening, extenuating, chocolate-flavoring, adulterating; sacking, baling, bottling, or packaging tobacco, cotton, fertilizer, Coca-Cola, and headache powders. One kind rolling cigarettes fifteen hundred a minute . . . chopchopchop . . . blended, violet-rayed, toasted. A regular Paul Bunyan . . . chopchopchop. . . . Rolling his own. And yours. Rolling out the cigareets and jimmy joysmokes by the millions for millions of discriminating smokers. Chuffing great snapping turtles and dragons, chomping up bales, hogsheads, streams, townfuls, of material and human lives . . . chopchopchop . . . and farting out steam and monoxide.

And yet there is so much beneath it all, he reflected, with his hands on the new iron-pipe railing, aluminum painted, of the railroad bridge.

. . . Beneath the town's layers and rhythms and folds of darkness and light, of night smells and chemical process, the gigantic machine process sweeping the floor of the night with rhythmic din. There on McLauchlen's Hill and the other hills encircling the town were the sleeping white palaces the machines had raised by their magical rub-a-dub, Aladdin-like, for the Hammers, McLauchlens, Warhams, Badgers, Erdmanns, McCubbinses—and a deep dark shadow-stream of stench and curse and hate wound through alley and bottom. . . . He thought of that not-quite-bright Erdmann boy with forty tailor-made suits and the red Stutz "bearcat" and all his father's millhands out-at-the-ass. . . . His mind played over the slums and fetid places like the dull red light of a high-held flare . . . Scroggins, Verbena, Badger's Bottom, Doom's Hill where lived the workers.

From the bridge Anders could hear the throbbing tread of factory workers' feet. It was the night shift coming off at one of the mammoth cigarette plants. Emptying by thousands, as from a great sausage grinder, into silent dark streets. Fresh hordes—men, women, old, young, black, white—of the day shifts going into factory and mill. Being sucked forth from sleep and the fried smell of sowbelly, croaker-fish, onion tops; from the back streets, from Railroad and Mooney, and Bulldog Hollow and the Hog Wallow; from Barbados Avenue and Jigaboo and the North, West, South, and East Warham niggertowns . . . snapped-up and tumbling into the hopper's trembling vortex; swept on into its growling roaring steaming redolent interior, between a marvelous supercunning anatomy of machine parts.

His town, like all towns, was but a creature of stone and metal. A monstrous sphinx-thing with claws and the hard insensitive ways of steel and griffon. Since boyhood, he had imagined it a feeling-and-thinking being. A sort of hybrid goddess regarding him, and all her myriad brood, with sheltering wing and favoring eye. But this he knew now, of a sudden, for a shallow unrooted dream. Men everywhere, he remembered, longing to fix the tentacles of their loyalty to something—anything—to tether unstable existence; (if only by the memory of a lane-turning, a mist on a hill) speak of the land that has held the bright illusional days of their childhood as of a golden chalice, a place and thing heroic, holy, and apart. God's Country. The Garden Spot of the World. Dear Old Dixieland and the Land of the Free. In this folly he was not alone.

In a flash of emotional insight—a liquid moment blazing up from the abysmal tar pit of cosmic darkness making formless thought clear in lightning-bright briefness—he was aware that his love for his home town was as futile as the blind unreasoning attachment of parents for a mindless and degenerate child.

Finale
(1923)

It was the last Sunday-night orchestra practice. Up on the stage back of the curtain. The grand finale. There would never be another Sunday night and no one's heart was in it, for it was the end of their opera-house world.

The Warham Opera House, the people's proud place of drama and dream—along with their mosque of mutton and pantheon of pork—was to be pulled down and demolished.

The city fathers, sitting on their composite rump in their quarters up over the market, had adjudged it passé and unnecessary. Found it guilty of cluttering up the landscape. Of impeding Dame Progress's skirts in her ever-onward march. (That was what they gave out as they condemned it to the sledgehammers and the wrecking ball, but the cunningly covered-up truth was that certain enterprising members of the aldermanic crew had hatched-up a plan to build a hotel there—with promise of big fat pickings for themselves.)

Gazing about him, dreaming, John Anders remembered scenes, stars, singers, that had once brilliantly appeared here. Davy Crockett with the blizzard and the wolves; Lionel Barrymore in *The Copperhead;* all the Hamlets and Macbeths, Mikados and Three Musketeers, all that long stream of gay and beautiful girls and laugh-bringers. As he passed the empty dressing room Joe Jefferson had used, its door standing ajar and now containing only a cracked mirror, a rickety chair, some part of a dusty costume hanging from a hook on the wall, he stood fascinated, remembering that rare glimpse he had had of the famous actor just after a performance of his great Rip Van Winkle. Regarding himself reflectively in the mirror as he was wiping off with a rag all of old Rip's wrinkles, Dutch smiles, heavy eyebrows, and weather-beaten complexion so painstakingly created but a few hours before. For over thirty years Joseph Jefferson had been creating and then demolishing that quaint, appealing face that had become familiar and beloved all up and down the land. Down on his haunches at a low property trunk had been his assistant, packing all the paraphernalia that had traveled with that face for thousands of miles about the world. Old Master Winkle's rusty, fallen-apart fowling-piece; his tattered old deerskin jerkin, sadly discolored during his long sleep, and hanging in such shreds that the wardrobe man was folding it very carefully lest it completely fall apart. There, too, was his peaked and battered hat, the old powder horn, his worse-for-twenty-years'-wear knee-breeches and broad buckled Dutch shoes—and the skeleton of his faithful dog.

On that dark rainy midnight, after Sherm Josephburg's musicmakers had folded up and gone home, all glancing back nostalgically at the old gray stage, at the breeze-trembled back side of the curtain, the stage mice came out again to cavort histrionically about. And up from the drafty scenery loft onto the vacant, brooding, deserted stage came the disembodied auras of the Great Heartthrobs and the Brummels, the great proteans and the hams; up in the galleries the ghosts of peanut-hull slingers and of those special young friends of old Charlie Wilkus, the night watchman, who for certain considerations, had been allowed to sneak up there for love-nest purposes.

And now also on stage were assembled the banshees of the Great Voices, of those capricious double-chinned prima donnas walking like piggies on high French heels. And the wraiths of the Dirty Heavies, the Oh-God-the-Pain-of-It School, the Cacklers and the Cane-and-Spats types. Flocked the ghosts and overtones of big hits and big flops past. Of jazzbos, ingénues and leg-artists. Making their grand entrances as icy gusts of melodramatic air, or curls of thin blue smoke, or falling as light-footed snowflakes.

Flocking out of nowhere-at-all, Lady Isabelle Vane of East Lynne promenades arm-in-arm with the Count of Monte Cristo;

Salvation Nell and Parsifal and Doctor Jekyll and Mr. Hyde wander companionably about together; Falstaff and Little Lord Fauntleroy are watching Will Rogers do his rope tricks, and the great Galli-Curci comes to the footlights to sing an inaudible aria.

Though the stage is being torn up by the roots on the morrow, the show must go on. There is no hope, no hall, no soap, and yet the Stage Driver drives. "All right, you clearers! Over there, board-shovers—let's go, you fanny-shakers! Shake it up, there, you pansy boys! . . . (That nigger heel-beater comes on here, we got to cut to the seagulls here.) . . . All right for the love-interest now. Enter George Spelvin! Well, do your stuff, you sheik-ham, peddle your wares. This is the punch-scene. Kiss-kiss—clinch! . . . Aw hell, don't hold her like a hot potato! *This* way—like this—see? . . . Migod!—kill the baby . . . Kill the hesitation. Step it up! break it up! We'll try it again. Stand-by! . . ."

But now the last heavy thunder-and-lightning act of the Wag-nerian Dusk of the Gods is being rehearsed, and more realistically and noisily than anything that had ever been on the boards. This is no stage wind, no paper snowfall, nothing artificial. Somebody is jolly-well really knocking down the house of music and art . . . for the last time they are "bringing down the house" . . . the rats are leaving with the mice for the barns and the bushes . . . the Joseph-burg Orchestra is playing the last "chaser" (it's the lively military march, "Yankee Girl," with the rich whine of clarinets and the bold birdy whistle of piccolo).

Then the music is over; the lights have gone down for the last time.

The opera house's historic bones of yellow pressed brick were scraped and bartered off at auction. The proceeds were returned to the town treasury; but there was a lot more junk, tons and tons of it—much of which got lost, got swiped, by certain avaricious alder-men. There were the heavy Florentine pilasters—between the which, on pleasant early summer mornings, before the dry-flies had started to shrill, had passed, in crisp, new-laundered frocks, most of Warham's model housekeepers. All the backstage stuff and sacred thespian trappings and accessories, the folding chairs, the special scenes, the drops and the drapes and the Asbestos, Ad, and

Oleo curtains. That oleographic Watteau lady of high degree with the plumed hat and buckled slippers and plump dolly legs and shepherd-boy admirer. The no-smoking sign with the fly lines.

The sacred timbers of the stage—the very core and heart of the denuded and betrayed theater—were hauled off. That sacrosanct flooring whereon Chernevskaya had danced her Dying Swan; from which McIntyre and Heath had rolled them in laughter; where many a romantic actor had, in his days, fluttered the dovecote and struck the classic calf-eyed pose and yammered his honeyed lines.

The timbers of the stage are hauled away.

Away to one of the Negro ghettos to become part of a monstrous and especially profitable double-decker flop joint.

To do long years of hardwood duty yet: enfolding the blasphemous, misery-drowning drunk; concealing from the weather and the eyes of the Law the cocaine-peddler's den; embracing unholy stinking poverty.

The monolithic chunks of that once-brave new concrete sidewalk are bitten up by steam shovel and hauled off to fill suburban building lots bought up cheap and by the acre by honorable city fathers. Whisked away from sight, from remembrance, the last pieces of that holy hardness laid down by those wizards in compact and durable cementation, M. Hoegger & Son, then newly come from Philadelphia. Lying there hodgepodge in bog or ravine, they provide a place where serpents often sun; and in rainy weather mottled salamanders waddle about on their bleak and mossed-over obliquity or stand like small fierce splayfooted dinosaurs astride the corpse of snail or shrew mouse.

"Now what can we do with all them sceneries and rigs?" Alderman Belly asked Alderman Hogg.

"Aw, the cloth 'uns will make good kiver for 'bacco beds and cold frames. Mebbe we could sell one or two to a photographer to use for his backdrop business. And that's a lotta good dry framing that'll make good kindling wood."

Around the big hole that had been steam-shoveled out for Warham's new million-dollar hotel and in which a tremendously busy gang of construction workers swarmed, a crowd of early risers tarried on their way to the "early bird" shifts. Hung around this life-opera—this new landmark being manufactured and born under the powerful yellow artificial light that threw its glare and nervous flickerings over the spectators.

At a plank railing, John Anders stood watching. Up in his little secret office in the Warham Fire Insurance building, he had been working all night on his writing; and had cut through this way while walking homeward to take the kinks out of his mind and muscles. And now with the others he stood there gawking at the bridge stiffs, nut splitters, Stillson-wrench artists, and master maniacs moving briskly about in the garish light. At the big-hook man handling the crane, the dinky punchers at the winch and the mud-chickens. At the efficient and aggressive nigger-pushers and big yes-and-no men of the George A. Fuller Construction Company.

The people loitering to gaze were spellbound by all the clatter and technological din—the peculiar woodpeckery noise made by riveters heading their white-hot bolts against the "dolly," the clang and bang of steel on steel, the shouts and echoes, the winches' racing bump and tugging grind.

"Gee, ain't it wonderful? But dangerous, my God!"

"Wish I had a job like that—I sure could use some of that George A. Fuller kind of jack."

"It's a wonder to behold on God's green footstool," a Negro woman on the way to one of the stemmeries whispered loudly to her man.

Now in the last hours of darkness, the moving factory-bound horde hastened along like animals going to the Ark. Here Oakey France, operator of a cigarette-making machine; there Violet Brown, a worker in the Strip Preparing Department; and Jake Harten, bobbin boy; Mamie Harris, sheet tearer; Tootsie Shelton, skilled operator of a machine that packed Cheltenham Cigarettes. . . . Passing into the bright flood of light, they were pulled down to slow motion like durable slow-fading figures at the edges of a dissipating dream.

Oakey France stepped out of the procession to watch the excitement around the Big Hole for a while. His cheeks were hollow, his skin the hue of pale mud. He was a bearcat for saying wry things. ("When I got money, it goes like snakes a-fleein' from a snowstorm. . . . Now way back yonder, when Christians was frogs. . . . Hit's all right fer a man and wife to have disagreements, jes' so they're little ones, like Who's gonta slop the pig. . . .") John Anders, who on several occasions had heard him thump out a stream of funny throwaways, thought, "He might have been a rich and famous wisecracker of stage and screen if he'd been educated."

"Rubes," reflected a bystander, short and dapper, with plump manicured hands and a loud pink tie—Mr. J. Knolly Munch, representing the Dee Loox Clothing Company of Brooklyn, New York. ("Our Clothes Have Got the Zing/And that Certain Thing/That Puts You Out in Front.")

"These little backside towns down here in the Land of Cotton certainly are something," Mr. Munch is soliloquizing. "Grab a look at these hicks hanging around to giraffe at a bridge-monkey with a rattle-box!"

"Great God!" he sniffs, his hickophobia getting the best of him. "How *do* they stand it? Living in a little Appleknockerton like this? No speed, no style. Nothing exciting ever happens here. Never did, I guess. Poor boobs. No past, no future, no nothin'."

The bookbinder and drummer Boozer Bobbit is on his way to the Anders Printing, Binding, and Engraving plant down on Baltimore Street this morning. He has gotten up in the dark to get an extra early start on a "special rush" job. While his best friend, editor Sherman Josephburg, alias "Tink," is on *his* way home to bed after his night's work in the composing room of the *Morning Bugle*.

Love of excitement and activity is a strong and common denominator in their twain bloods; and neither can ever ignore a dogfight, a fire, any kind of a show, or the poor drunk or lost lady being put in the paddy wagon. There is something of the magnet and the pin's invisible attraction in the croneyhood of these two human landmarks. Rarely does a day pass when they fail to meet, apparently without any premeditation or plan—though their homes lie far apart.

"It seems like no time at all," says Tink, "since they were tearing down the Jumbo to make room for the opera house." (And they both have a vision of that great gargantuan temple of leaf tobacco that was Warham's first tobacco-auction warehouse.)

"Right," agrees Boozer. "And remember when everything around here was nothing but a broomstraw field?"

"Sure do!" And Tink, who chewed tobacco morning, noon, and night, spat his quid into the Big Hole; watching its downward flight with sharp mischievous interest. It spattered on the head of a straw-boss—who swore and looked up; but the quidder was now in earnest conversation with his comrade.

"Seems like just last week that old man Groot Van Kloppen and his boys were painting Mike Pulaski's livery stable that bright barn red."

Tink and Boozer are talking away almost beside John Anders, and he, too, is thinking of the old livery stable. It is as if his thoughts of the old town and of his own past have been excavated from this maw in the ground. . . . What a strange, brave, colorful child Anna had been!

A desperate longing for her sweeps over him. God! To have her in his arms again, to hold the radiant warmth of her creamy body against his bare skin. To know once more the sweet, hot, and secret joy of that first love.

A rough cough tears from the flat chest of Oakey France, shivering in his cheap brown suit, long ago worn shiny. "Gee! I've got to have more than a cup of java and sinker for breakfast after this," he thinks. "Been livin' on the fat of my guts too long, I reckon. . . ." His nervous eyes travel down the layers of sandstone and the striated red and blue clay as if he, too, is having some part of his early life dug out.

"Why the first gal I ever had was in that weed patch back of where the opera house was. . . ."

"Remember how us fellows used to go swimming in the old pond that was down the hill that used to be here? Down at Mangan's sawmill?" Boozer asks his old friend.

"Sure-tootin' I do. We'd start undressing right where we're standing now. The top of the hill was about here. And where Zack Wraxbee's pigs used to wallow was just about where the big revolving door and the fancy entrance of the Jefferson Warham Hotel is going to be. I can smell those pigs yet, can't you? And that

old pond, so cool and nice on a hot day, with the bullfrogs and cattails. . ."

"Yeah, and sometimes there'd be a crane or a wild duck there.
One time I remember, in a storm, a big white pelican came
through."

They both could see quite plainly across the years all the enchanting chiaroscuro of their youthful summer days; could hear
the birds singing in the bright cherry tree halfway down; feel the
good warm red earth on bare feet and the cool mud of the pond between their toes.

"And remember how the First Baptist Church used the pond on
Sundays for its holy baptistery?"

John Anders looked over toward the Warham Power building,
where a hazy swarm of red-white-and-blue lights twinkled at ma-
chine-made intervals. The Chamber of Commerce electric sign.
From a large scaffold of iron piping up on the roof that had been
erected by Elmer Godwin, the electrician, it broadcast nightly to a
breathless universe—in civic pride and fifteen hundred and six
forty-watt Mazda lamps—the legend

WARHAM THE CROWN
OF ALL THE EARTH AROUND

Below in the darkness were the railroad tracks near Big Cigarette
Street—once called Jefferson Davis Street—and across the still-
sleeping town was the fertilizer factory, with the smell of it strong
on the air.

But all eyes were drawn hypnotically to the Big Hole; all ears at-
tuned to the rivet machines' trill. The song of the red-hot rivets,
tossed and caught by invisible workmen high up in the dark and
describing brief meteoric arcs: putting Anders in mind of the
smithy of the Nibelungs, of the dwarf overseer Alberich cracking
his whip and making his dwarfs forge treasure for the quarrelsome
old fat-bellied giants.

Under the din and the witching light, both Tink and Boozer are
dreaming. Of the dead-and-gone opera house. Of the big old
wooden Stoeger's Hall, over on Main Street, further back in history, where they had seen their first shows when they were kids.
Its ten-twenty-and-thirty stock-company dramas come trooping
past. . . .

But the talk and ponderings of most of those people chancily thrown together—hodgepodged about the rim of the Big Hole— were welded into coherency by the shrilling of the riveting machines. By this evangel woodpecker, latest word in unbeatable American ingenuity, that was, with every stuttering pop, executing the past—as by a firing squad—and minute by minute and peck by peck and shiver-shake by shiver-shake, shaping up Progress and Prosperity like nobody's business in this "Foremost City of the New South."